Carl Gibeily was born in Lebanon in 1966. After school in Beirut, he read engineering at Cambridge. He has worked as an engineer in South Africa, sold Mars Bars in Dubai, and now edits Arabic/French/English dictionaries in Beirut. *Blueprint for a Prophet* is his first novel.

BLUEPRINT
FOR A PROPHET

Carl Gibeily

BLACK SWAN

BLUEPRINT FOR A PROPHET
A BLACK SWAN BOOK : 0 552 99731 5

Originally published in Great Britain by Doubleday,
a division of Transworld publishers Ltd

PRINTING HISTORY
Doubleday edition published 1997
Black Swan edition published 1998

Set in 11/12pt Melior by
Phoenix Typesetting, Ilkley, West Yorkshire

Black Swan Books are published by Transworld Publishers Ltd,
61–63 Uxbridge Road, London W5 5SA,
in Australia by Transworld Publishers (Australia) Pty Ltd,
15–25 Helles Avenue, Moorebank, NSW 2170
and in New Zealand by Transworld Publishers (NZ) Ltd,
3 William Pickering Drive, Albany, Auckland

Reproduced, printed and bound in Great Britain by
Cox & Wyman Ltd, Reading, Berks.

aux amours d'etc.

ACKNOWLEDGEMENTS

With special thanks to Joanna Goldsworthy and Paul Sidey for their advice and encouragement on earlier drafts; and I owe a great deal to Christine Green who was the first outside my family to find this novel readable.

'So many men, so many opinions.'

Terence, 190–159 BC

'Jinn, you have seduced mankind in great numbers.'

The Koran, Cattle 6:128

CONTENTS

ZACHIEL

An instant ago I was in pain; now the numbness is complete.

A few paces away the angel stands motionless, his silvery wings outspread, the feathers ruffled by an apparent wind, his folded arms hugging a white tunic. I shiver, though I feel neither the expected chill from the surrounding black sky nor the breeze that causes the angel's tunic to flutter. Above there is no sun, no moon, not even stars to lighten the black monotony. Yet the ground, from horizon to horizon, is a perfectly flat wilderness of golden sand.

'Who are you?' An instant ago I had a voice to scream my pain, not this frail whisper. 'Who are you?' I breathe again to the creature.

The angel points at the ground in front of him and the sand stirs to trace his name in calligraphic Hebrew.

זחי

'MIND-OF-GOD,' I read. 'Zachi-El.' If I still possess eyes, they look enquiringly at the angel. Is my soul cursed or blessed?

The gabriel raises his arms, palms facing the black vacuum above, and folds his wings. His white tunic now flaps wildly, and Zachiel leans on one side in order to keep his balance. I am a rock, insensitive to the sudden storm that sweeps across the desert. A faint hum pulses

11

into my consciousness, a childish tune I have never heard yet instantly recognize. The angel's mouth is closed; the simple song, rising in pitch with the current, must come from the sandstorm itself. The divine melody which had been my life's quest conquers my very being – I too am now singing like the whirling clouds of sand.

'LA ALL ALAA AL.' My rendition is poor and muted, but after so many decades I only care that the Grail exists.

Around us the storm has split into seven maelstroms. The flat desert has sprouted seven dunes that grow into miniature hills of Rome. The song resonates more intensely and the seven hills glow briefly red before settling to a cold transparency.

The song and storm vanish as abruptly as they appeared, leaving me to sing the melody on my own. If I have a mouth, it is smiling at my angel.

Zachiel, steady on his feet, indicates each hill in turn. Sand has been changed to glass. We stand in the centre of seven titanic sculptures. The closest three form points on an equilateral triangle; the other four are due south, west, north and east – random directions in a land whose sky is empty of guiding sun and stars.

As Zachiel points to the first sculpture, I recognize, with a start, the significance of the glass giants. Above a doorway, from which white light streams through, are two statues: of a man leaning on a quarterstaff, and a seated woman reading from an open book. By their feet are the Hebrew words, *The Magician & The High Priestess*.

The sculptures are three-dimensional where I am used to images on cards; but here before me are some of the Major Arcana of divinatory tarot. The gabriel and I are standing in the centre of a Celtic cross of prophecy.

Zachiel indicates the second structure, an immense tower, *La Maison Dieu*, the Babel that never was. Above the doorway, this time a black gaping chasm, are the familiar Hebrew words, *The Tower*. As I look at each sculpture in turn, I realize that each has a doorway and that, other than the first, all are as forbidding as the sky.

The Star: a hemisphere surrounded by smaller hemispheres representing, in relief, a snapshot of a more familiar night sky. With the star, the equilateral triangle is completed, the past described. The remaining four points of the Celtic cross relate to the future.

Due south is the largest, most horrendous sculpture. The statue is of a horned creature, with snarling face, female breasts and male genitals. The doorway is formed by the beast's legs which are wide as columns. Engraved in its midriff are the words, *The Devil.*

West is a crescent moon on a dome, *The Moon;* north is a globe with lines of crystal radiating from its centre, *The Sun.*

In the east, the seventh mould created by the desert storm is more portentous than the menacing devil. There is no statue, no sculpture, only a black ominous doorway. The letters are engraved in the thin crystal frame: *Judgement.*

Of all the possible combinations, with all the Arcana cards, why had the divine melody dealt this particular cross? Why had the storm raised such a sequence? I have read many crosses; I recognize the foreboding significance of this Celtic cross.

Turning to Zachiel, 'Is this my cross? Do I have a future?'

The angel's reply appears in the sand by his feet.

'GO. WITNESS THE PAST.'

Zachiel points to the first doorway, brilliant with pure light.

'Is it my past? My future?'

'THE PAST THROUGH THE EYES OF OTHERS.

THE FUTURE FROM THE TIME OF YOUR DEATH.'

I am dead.

Zachiel fans out his wings and soars in the lifeless sky, before swooping down to carry my soul to the Magician's doorway.

THE MAGICIAN
& THE
HIGH PRIESTESS

1

GREEK LETTERS

Until his death in 1972, Samir's father was the concierge of a block of flats in central Beirut. As such, his duties included cleaning the stairway from the seventh to the ground floor, collecting the trash left outside the flats, and being on hand to run errands for the tenants.

The whole family lived in the caretaker's living quarters, which consisted of two small dingy rooms facing the main entrance. The parents slept on a mattress in one of the rooms, while the children lay huddled on the floor in the other, each child swathed in a blanket.

Samir considered himself lucky. He was the last of three girls and two boys, and because the two elder daughters had married young, he could hardly remember when all five had shared the limited floor space. He mostly remembered that George, Leila and he would squabble over the sleeping arrangements. George always won, and he slept at the feet of one of two rickety and mismatching armchairs. With the top of his head brushing against the armchair, George slumbered easily. Samir noticed how, in the middle of the night, when George snored softly, his brother's head moved almost imperceptibly from side to side, as if drawing a loving caress from the armchair.

Samir did not sleep so well. Being the youngest, he had to settle for the least favoured part of the floor, in the direct beam of the light in the lobby. His parents' small room was windowless being, as it were, a store-room in design, rather than a bedroom. This room, the living quarters, was inches larger, and its most distinctive feature was its one window with its view of the lobby – ostensibly for the caretaker to keep an eye on the main entrance.

For security purposes, the main door to the building was locked at ten in the evening and the light in the lobby was always kept on. Every night, as far back as Samir could remember, it was this light that filtered through the window to illuminate his patch of the floor.

He had grown used to it to such an extent that later in life he would need an external light to fall asleep. Therefore Samir did not sleep so well, not as a consequence of the excessive light, but because he would wake up in the middle of the night simply to think. Sometimes he imagined he was scaling walls like Spiderman, or single-handedly slaughtering all of Lebanon's enemies – a dream that usually ended with the President of the Republic pinning a medal on Samir's chest in full view of all who knew him.

Or sometimes he considered other things.

Lying on the floor he could see one of the two lobby lights: a bulb encased in an oblong plastic shell with two small holes at either end, no larger than five-piastre coins. As Samir looked at the tiny dark shadows, bulb-side of the opaque shell, he knew that it was through these two holes that the insects would enter to be scorched to death. He wondered whether the insects were drawn by the light or were intensely irritated by it.

These casings had to be cleaned regularly, every month in summer, and every other month in winter. He and Leila helped their mother with the task. Samir's mother, standing on a ladder, would remove the shells and hand them to her children to be emptied. They would hurry outside, each with a casing nestled on their forearms, and they would take turns picking up a frazzled fly or mosquito, thereby counting all the dead insects. It became a game where the highest scorer was considered the winner.

'Separate legs don't count,' Leila always said, probably because she usually won.

Their mother always started with the bulb closest to the door, and always handed Leila the first casing, and so perhaps the fact that Leila usually won was no co-incidence. However, she did concede defeat once when Samir held a seared flying cockroach by its abdomen. It was so large that they wondered how it had possibly managed to enter the casing. Even as Samir tried to re-enact the bug's last feat by squeezing it through each hole, he found the insect's body too large for the small holes. He gave up when, in one disconcerted effort, the cockroach's body snapped; the thorax fell to the ground leaving the abdomen in Samir's fingers and the toppled head in the shell. For several nights after that event he woke up and gazed at the light, hoping to catch another flying cockroach in the magical act of entering the casing.

Or sometimes, late at night, he wondered why he was Greek.

Samir was Lebanese; he knew that with patriotic pride. At the state-run school, he was one of the few students who knew every word of the national anthem by heart. At eight o'clock every Monday morning, come shower or shine, all the children stood in rows in the playground and sang the 'Kolona Lil-watan'. Other children droned the verses, picking up only the refrain with limited enthusiasm. But Samir, standing firm, belly drawn in, as if on parade, confidently sang the lot with gusto, if tunelessly.

Yet if he were asked his religion, he would say he was Greek. He was confused by this, mostly in the middle of the night when he had time to contemplate. He sometimes sat up, blanket wrapped tightly around his shoulders, and pictured two monsters devouring George and Leila. In less fanciful moods the beasts became the two unsightly armchairs which, along with a cupboard, a hot-plate, the mattress in his parents' room, all the blankets and some of their clothes, had all been donated by charity. A gift from the Greeks, his mother told him once. And when Samir asked why the Greeks, his mother answered that they, being poor Greeks, were often helped by their richer kindred.

In fact, the whole neighbourhood was Greek. There were many more Greeks here than Armenians in little Yerevan, in the north-eastern suburb of Beirut. But then the Armenians, at least, were different; they had their own tongue, wrote in their own script and ate spicy food.

Samir was drawn by the vitality of the Armenian neighbourhood, and he often strolled down the crowded streets in the early evening, allured by the many lights highlighting billboards with names like Sarkisian, Avidisian, Manoukian. They sounded so exotic. He walked past flashing and multicoloured neon signs, always of Armenian letters and sometimes, lower and in smaller print, almost as a concession, in Arabic or French.

He jostled with other pedestrians in the bottlenecks caused by hand-drawn carts, wide as trucks, half jutting onto the street and half onto the pavement. These carts were stacked precariously high with fruits or vegetables or cooked chestnuts or silk scarves or amusing gadgets and toys, and vendors proclaimed their wares in Armenian and Arabic and, spotting foreigners in the crowd, in French and English.

Samir often paused in front of a shop selling electronic goods to watch some TV; he listened to a pastiche of Arabic and Western songs, at times discordant and at times strangely appealing, and smelled a not unpleasant mixture of petrol fumes from the traffic, roasted chestnuts from a cart and the infamous Armenian sausage from the butcher shop next door. *Bastirma* was a sausage that smelled so strong that the reek lingered in the mouth for a full day following consumption, and under the armpits for two days.

Armenians had arrived in Beirut from Armenia, and Greeks, Samir concluded, must have come from Greece. But maybe the Greeks had been here for so long that they had become Lebanese, ate Lebanese food, wrote and spoke Arabic. Maybe in the past the shops in his neighbourhood had billboards and signs written in Greek letters.

'You stupid donkey,' George said impatiently one day. 'Greece is in Europe, near France.'

'I know, I know. But we came from there, right?'

'You came from my arse,' George laughed. 'That's why you stink.'

Samir frowned and said defiantly, 'Our grandfather came from there, or his grandfather, I bet.'

'No stupid, they were all Lebanese.'

'Oh yeah, so how come we're Greek?'

'Are you hanging out with Shiite friends or something?' George said irritably. 'Just because you believe like the Greeks doesn't mean you're Greek.'

This confused Samir even more. He wondered how one could believe like the Greeks and yet somehow be different. Here was more magic, like the cockroach that had entered the casing and yet could not enter it. He thought about these things only at night, under the unblinking watch of the bulb in the lobby, when his mind imagined other discussions with his brother who lay shaking his head against the armchair.

The image of Leila sprawling on the floor nearest their parents' room was not so vivid in Samir's recollection, because she moved in to sleep with their mother on the mattress when he was twelve, following their father's death. Many years later it would shame Samir to remember that his father's death had effected little more than a softer bed for Leila and more leg-room for the boys. Even so, George still slept unshakeably by the armchair's feet, and Samir still in the full beam, waking in the middle of every night.

21

For many years until his death, his father had stopped performing the caretaker duties and had taken to drinking arak. To Samir – as to the rest of the family – his father was forever absent, either in the pursuit of or under the influence of the aniseed liquor.

Samir's mother assumed the role of concierge without either the landlords or the tenants particularly caring about the change. Together with Leila, she cleaned the stairway every day from the seventh to the ground floor, George and Samir collected the rubbish bags outside the flats before going to school and their mother ran the errands for the tenants.

Initially the tenants called for Samir's father. Abou George, they would shout down the stairway, and Samir's mother always answered and so she, Im George, was handed the shopping list and paid the baksheesh. The habit stuck easily and the tenants soon stopped calling for Samir's father altogether.

Even the owners of the building, kind and prosperous Sunnis, accepted the *de facto* shift in employees. They still paid Abou George his monthly wage – most of which went into financing his addiction – and disbursed half as much to Im George. With that, the baksheesh from the tenants and the occasional money donations from the richer Greeks, Im George could make ends meet, and no longer needed her husband. Abou George had ceased to exist well before his death.

Once when Samir was ill and had stayed home from school, he heard his father wake up at eleven. Abou George greeted the day with a late morning song that would disgust the most hospitable bedouin: throat-wrenching coughs, bellowing moans and a rapid succession of belches and farts that reminded Samir of a movie in which policemen were outgunned by gangsters. Abou George stumbled out of bed, entered the room in his dirty cotton striped pyjamas and, still oblivious to the boy, poured himself a stiff measure of arak from the cupboard, emptying the bottle. He quaffed it

22

without adding water and dropped the empty bottle in the armchair, snorted hard, wheezed and coughed several times, then turning back to his room, he spotted his son.

Abou George grunted recognition, moved to the door, and with his back to the boy, he said, 'Arak in the morning chases the demon away. Always remember that, George.'

This was probably the sum total of fatherly advice he received, and when Abou George returned to bed, Samir whispered, 'My name's Samir.' He stuck his tongue out at the bedroom.

Whether Abou George managed to scare away the many demons in his life remained dubious, but he succeeded at least in petrifying his liver. Samir was twelve and still ignorant of what it meant to be Greek when his father died of cirrhosis.

Samir's daily routine allowed him little time to stop and think. After a quick wash in the caretaker's sink by the boiler room, he collected the trash before rushing to school. As the younger brother, he was in charge of all the garbage from the fourth to seventh floors, while George had the privilege of the first to third floors. On any given day, with two apartments per floor, Samir collected either seven or eight garbage bags; one of the two tenants on the sixth floor put out his trash once every three days.

He carried the trash to a quadrangle of desiccated scrub, limited by the side of the building, the main street, a side road and a parking area for the tenants' cars. At the corner of both roads was a mature beech tree which, in the early morning sunshine, cast a tentative shadow across four open-ended oil barrels doubling as utility bins. In any light, the contrast between the bright grey trunk, the light green foliage and the dirty rusty brown of the barrels was as sharp as a smile and a scowl. But at seven in the morning, when Samir was weighed down by the garbage bags, the bins appeared dormant, their colours downright dead compared with the colour-twinkling welcome the beech reserved for every dawn.

School till one-thirty was less of a chore than lugging trash. He walked to the local state school for the neighbourhood's poor children; the rich and middle-class kids attended the many fee-paying colleges and received an education on a par with the European and American schools. The School of Hope was, like many Lebanese state schools, of an altogether different calibre, and with a scanty track record of 5 per cent passes in the Lebanese baccalaureate, it appeared that the school's main objective was to keep the poor kids off the streets. The school's emblem, which could be seen above the main gate, was a small circle supported by a single chevron. This was meant to represent a student's head reading from a large open book, and the motto written in Arabic around the figure was: 'With Hope We Shall Succeed'. But the overall defeatist attitude prevalent in the school, and the pitiably wanting tuition, trans-formed the emblem, in Samir's eyes, to a teacher's head with outspread arms, in a posture that was half shrug-ging and half beseeching the gods. The motto also became: 'With Hope We Shall Succeed In Teaching You, Inshallah' – God willing.

If the 5 per cent pass rate was a measure of divine intervention, then God proved to be particularly meddlesome in Samir's case. In later years he passed not only the Lebanese bacho but also the French baccalaureate – an almost unthinkable achievement for the School of Hope.

Almost every day after school, Samir sold chewing-gum on one of the main boulevards in Beirut. At the red light, he and several other boys moved among the stopped cars with their boxes of Chiclets chewing-gum, tempting the drivers to part with 25 piastres.

It became quickly apparent to Abou Assaad, the grocer who supplied most of the young peddlers, that

24

Samir was his most able seller. For a start, Samir realized sooner than any other novice that of the six varieties, the Chiclets peppermint gum was the most popular, and he always ran to Abou Assaad's in order to reserve his stock of that one flavour. However, most of Samir's success was due to his good looks and manners.

He was small even for a twelve-year-old, and this only emphasized his air of carefree innocence and mature confidence. His eyes were round with inquisitiveness and chestnut brown in colour, matching perfectly his fine straight hair, which he regularly combed back with his fingers. And then there was Samir's disarmingly open and addictive smile. When he smiled, a multitude of candles were lit in his mouth, and the radiance diffracted between his teeth and glowed through every pore of his face. When he smiled, momentarily at least, the world was a brighter place.

Abou Assaad believed that the boy's success on the boulevard was perhaps attributable to Samir's fair smile or, more accurately, to the subliminal link between his teeth and Chiclets chewing-gum. When Samir caught a driver's attention, he flashed his teeth and suggested that a great smile and fresh breath cost only 25 piastres.

But perhaps a more important feature of his successful selling technique was his overall demeanour. Other boys skulked amid the cars like cowardly hyenas among a herd of uninterested water buffalo. They pawed car windows and whined for a sale, looking pitifully downtrodden with every refusal. When they did sell, from the driver's perspective, it was a matter of giving alms to an urchin.

Samir did not sell for charity. He walked upright, smiled at drivers and waved boxes of Chiclets at them. When drivers did not buy, there was no hassle, he simply shot them a brief smile, as if to remind them of the benefits they were doing without, and moved on to the next car. On many occasions drivers changed their minds and honked their horns at him. He then sold them some chewing-gum and, in the remaining minute it took for the lights to change, complimented them on their fine cars or clothes or watches. With time he recognized the habitual drivers of the boulevard and, whether they bought or not, he waved or nodded at them and most often they waved or smiled back.

This was business. Samir earned 5 piastres per box, or £1 per twenty sold. But he did not care for Chiclets at all. Once the sweetness had dissipated in his mouth, chewing for chewing's sake irritated him, and he would take a sharp intake of breath and spit it out as far as he could, counting the distance the gum had travelled in paces, always attempting to beat his last record.

Samir was on his way back home from Abou Assaad's late one afternoon when he spotted the sixth-floor tenant, Mr Haddad, in his sky-blue Peugeot. He was on the side road, looking for a place to park. Samir noticed that all the spaces in the lot were occupied and that his own parking space was taken by a red Buick.

Samir pointed and called out, 'You can park next to the tree.'

The man replied irritably, 'I would like to park where I've always parked.'

Samir shrugged.

'Whose car is that?'

'First time I see it here.' Samir guessed that the Buick's owner was visiting someone in the building. He briefly considered asking all the neighbours. 'We can move the bins,' Samir said, 'and there'll be lots of room to park next to the tree.'

Mr Haddad consented, and between them they moved the four oil barrels, rotating them towards the main street, and he parked his Peugeot on the scrub next to the beech tree with Samir signalling the leeway.

'You're the concierge's son, aren't you?' Mr Haddad said as he locked the car door.

Samir nodded.

'George?'

'No, Samir.'

'Thanks for your help.'

'Nice car,' Samir said smiling. 'If you want I can wash it for you.'

'Not now. Some other time maybe.'

'On Sunday, if you like. I could wash your car every Sunday morning.'

Mr Haddad looked at the boy, then laughed. 'I don't know about every Sunday.'

'That way you'll always have a nice clean car. I could clean it from inside too.' Samir shrugged and added nonchalantly, 'If you like.'

'How much?' the man asked.

'You decide.'

Mr Haddad shook his head. 'Give me a price for this Sunday. If it's too expensive, we'll forget it.'

'Two pounds,' Samir said decisively. 'Inside, outside. Everything for two pounds.'

'Samir is it.' The man smiled. 'Right, you've got yourself a deal for this Sunday. We'll see about future Sundays after I see how well you wash cars.'

From that Sunday and for the next four years, until Mr Haddad left for Israel, Samir washed, wiped and polished the sky-blue Peugeot, brushed and dusted the interior, and earned £2 for an hour's work, more than a whole afternoon selling chewing-gum.

That day, as Mr Haddad entered the building and returned to his flat on the sixth floor, Samir remained by the car and looked down at the trash by his feet. While the garbage trucks from the municipality regularly emptied the bins, the rubbish strewn outside the barrels was not so frequently cleared. Samir and George always threw their bags in the bins, but most people littered the area unthinkingly. Pedestrians lobbed their empty cigarette packs at the foot of the beech; drivers emptied their ashtrays away from their cars and only rarely in the general direction of the bins; street vendors paused to casually drop a spoiled lettuce or a bruised apple; small children blew their noses in tissues held by their mothers, and these crumpled sheets of snot were discarded everywhere but in the bins. All these people lived here, and with so much rubbish overspilling onto the streets, Samir sometimes imagined that people's homes were clogged with mountains of garbage.

There were also the stray cats that rummaged in the barrels in the dead of night, scattering their leftovers of human leftovers. Samir heard them at night, fighting or courting when they caterwauled like hungry babies.

When they had moved the barrels, Samir and Mr Haddad had uncovered a lot more filth. Samir kicked the blackened soil where one of the barrels had been and sent an orange peel and a squashed pack of Marlboro flying. He kicked the area several times, uncovering a paler subsoil and displacing a chicken bone and a coin.

Samir eyed the coin with bewilderment, then picked it up, wiped it thoroughly between his fingers and examined it carefully. The coin was twice as large as a £1 coin, bronzed and with patches of rust. He focused on, then fingered the embossed features of a young woman with wavy hair surrounded by four fish. The reverse portrayed a chariot drawn by four horses, also in relief, and letters, the likes of which he had never seen.

Samir was excited; judging by the rust, the letters and especially by the chariot, this coin had to be ancient and worth a fortune. He turned his attention, once more, to the chariot and discerned a charioteer wearing a helmet, and next to him were foreign letters. Most of the letters looked familiar, like French written in a small child's hand, Samir thought, but some were very different from French. He felt confident that if he could read those letters, he would understand the coin's origins and therefore know its worth. Standing between the beech and the sky-blue Peugeot, Samir swore to himself that he would somehow learn to read the word. He walked slowly back to the building, pocketed his treasure, and thought about a safe place to hide his fortune.

That night, when George snored softly and the light fell through the window, Samir sewed an extra pocket just for his coin. He crept to the cupboard and quietly removed a sewing needle, some thread and a knife. With the knife he cut a rough square off the corner of his blanket, ensuring that it would just cover the coin. He then turned his trousers inside out and sewed the square of fabric over the inside seam of the right leg, just below the crotch. This way, Samir thought, not only would this pocket be invisible to everyone, but he would be constantly aware of the coin's presence.

The work was difficult, especially as he insisted on several lines of stitches for safety. But he was pleased with the end result and slipped the coin in and out of its cache, noting with satisfaction that the fabric had to stretch slightly, thereby offering a tighter grip when the coin was in. Samir wore his trousers and hoped he would grow accustomed to the strange sensation on his right thigh.

Finally, just before dozing off, he copied on the back of his exercise book and in his neatest handwriting, the word he had resolved to understand one day: ΣΥΑΡΑΚΩΣ

Mr Haddad's living-room was like none Samir had ever seen, though his experience of house interiors was fairly limited. There were no chairs, no sofas, only an assortment of beanbags and large cushions with vivid designs. Samir's favourite was one particular cushion with rows of almost touching blue triangles set against a red background. By swaying his head, he imagined that the rows of triangles moved like men in a folkloric Lebanese dance; as he nodded, the triangles tapped and thumped the *dabké* beat, with their lower vertices perfectly mimicking human boots. Also triangular was the large, centrally located coffee-table, which was supported by a foot-high tripod of legs. At the far end of the room were two bookshelves, each crammed with books of all sizes, hardbacks and paperbacks, and it fascinated Samir to wonder that so many books could be read in a lifetime.

Samir came here every Sunday morning to return the car keys and to collect his £2. Mr Haddad always had a fizzy lemonade for him which he sipped politely, even though he was invariably hot and thirsty after an hour spent cleaning and wiping the Peugeot. By sipping his drink, Samir prolonged his stay in Mr Haddad's interesting apartment, and their chats. Samir was flattered by these conversations because they talked of many things but never, it seemed to him, on a superficial level. They would discuss endemic problems, like the worsening traffic in Beirut, or the rise in violence directed at and by the Palestinians, and Samir was both surprised and elated that a man almost four times his age should be so genuinely interested in his viewpoint. Here he was treated as an equal, where the usual tags he wore in his daily life, such as class, poverty and age, were left pinned to the apartment door. To everyone else Samir was simply the concierge's son. But for Mr Haddad the boy's background seemed unimportant and could, for all he cared, dance the *dabké* with the blue triangles.

Samir enjoyed the short Sunday sessions and liked Mr Haddad, despite his mother's disapproval. On the first Sunday, Samir was timid and Mr Haddad did most of the talking.

'Do you like books?' Mr Haddad asked.

'Yes,' he lied, trying to impress the man. He knew only the school textbooks and found them completely boring.

'So you enjoy reading?'

'Of course.' Samir added, 'Arabic.'

'No, French?'

'French too.' He hesitated. 'A little.'

'I like books,' Mr Haddad said, moving to one of the bookshelves. 'Reading a new book is like meeting someone for the first time; it's exciting. Sometimes you read a book and make yourself a friend for life. Of course, you can also be unlucky and be introduced to a terrible bore.'

'Yes,' agreed Samir with feeling, which seemed to surprise the man.

Mr Haddad waved at a bookshelf and continued, 'This is like owning a city in your home. In those books there's a world of different people living in different places.'

'I like Beirut,' Samir said cheerfully. The man was silent so Samir added quickly, 'That's why I also like books.'

Mr Haddad bent over and removed a thin hardback from the lowest shelf.

'Now here's a good book. I'll lend it to you if you promise to return it in the same condition.'

Samir nodded, took the book, glanced at the picture on the dust jacket of a young boy wearing a white turban on a black horse, and read the title, *Al Amir*.

'It's the story of a poor boy who turns out to be a prince.' He looked at the boy, waited, then added, 'Thank me only if you enjoy it.'

'Thank you,' Samir said insincerely.

He wished he hadn't lied. He didn't want to read the book, but was too proud to refuse. Now it was too late, he had to read *Al Amir* in case Mr Haddad quizzed him. That night, reluctantly, he opened the book when the family was asleep and was hooked by the second page. He read *Al Amir* in a week, and dreamed for the next month that he was galloping over dunes, scimitar waving in the air.

Im George disapproved of this loan only half as much as she disapproved of Mr Haddad. She was highly suspicious of a man in his late forties who was still a bachelor and who took such an interest in her son. She tried, on several occasions, to dissuade Samir from visiting the

31

sixth-floor tenant. Washing a car, she argued, was one thing but talking for half an hour, sometimes longer, every Sunday, and receiving books from an unmarried man was altogether another thing. Samir did not particularly care for her point of view; for the first time in his life he felt he was being treated as a person and he was unwilling to give up either the talks or the many books he read in the middle of the night under the light in the lobby.

A few months later, when Samir was starting his fourth book, she asked him what was so special about their talks. And Samir tried to explain how they discussed important subjects about living conditions in Beirut, about good and evil, and about life in general. Im George retorted that Mr Haddad would get far more insight by discussing the meaning of life with a wise sixty-year-old (herself) than a thirteen-year-old child (himself). This infuriated Samir – angered especially because he saw the logic.

He relayed his mother's statement to Mr Haddad the following Sunday.

'Why should I ask a withered sixty-year-old,' Mr Haddad generalized, 'who talks of life as an inventory of errors committed versus material gains. Every living creature has the right to talk about life, but only those with a clean slate offer an understanding that is as pure and unadulterated as a youthful heart and spirit.'

'Is that a poem?' Samir asked, wondering if he should mention that his mother was in fact exactly sixty.

The man smiled. 'And if ever I want to know what life was like in Beirut under the colonial French, I'll ask a wrinkled sixty-year-old, not you.'

Later, when the friendship between them grew and Mr Haddad offered to teach Samir French every Sunday, Im George complained to the landlords who had a discreet word with their sixth-floor tenant. But Mr Haddad was resolutely firm.

'It's up to you, Samir. As long as you choose to

learn French, I'll be here to teach you.'

His mother shouted at Samir, 'You don't need French.'

'I want to learn French.'

'School teaches French.'

'I want to learn real French, and English.'

'I won't allow you,' Im George declared firmly. 'It's for your own good, dear.'

'To stay stupid? I hate this place.' He ran off, shouting over his shoulder, 'I'm going to learn and you're not going to stop me.' He swore to himself he would never be a concierge.

Samir later asked Mr Haddad, 'Can you teach me English too?'

'I spend my whole week teaching.'

'I can pay you.' Samir flashed him a smile. 'Two pounds a week.'

'And your mother?'

The smile vanished from the boy's face. 'I told her I'd come anyway.'

The man nodded slowly. 'One of life's unsolved mysteries – Why do children grow into such dispirited adults?'

Samir frowned. At times, Mr Haddad appeared to talk to himself. 'Will you teach me English?'

'Can you learn both languages together?'

'Yes,' Samir replied confidently.

'Then I'll teach you both languages together.'

And later, after the first Franco-English lesson, as Samir was preparing to leave, Mr Haddad said, 'It's a shame that in every society a mature person is deemed one who no longer asks simple questions.'

They became master and disciple in the ancient Greek fashion, with mutual respect and affection but without the pederasty. Even Im George had to concede that the unmarried Mr Haddad did not seem to have sexual designs on her son, but this had never been Im George's primary concern anyway. She objected to the visits right

33

from the start, on the grounds that Jacob Haddad was a Jew.

There was a sizeable Jewish community in Beirut, and Jacob Haddad proclaimed his Jewishness by lecturing a course on Hebrew and Arabic at the Lebanese University. He later explained to Samir that he also gave seminars at the Université Saint Joseph and the American University of Beirut on proto-Semitic and its evolution and branching into Akkadian, Hebrew, Aramaic and Arabic.

'So you're a Jew,' Samir said on the third Sunday.

'Yes.'

'I'm Greek,' Samir said smiling.

'That's nice.'

That day they discussed other things. The fact that Mr Haddad was a Jew had no effect on Samir, other than that he did wonder if Haddad was the most popular surname in Lebanon, proving that even Jews had smiths. His own surname was Khoury, meaning priest, and that was naturally only a Christian surname. Strange name, Khoury, Samir thought. He wondered if his grandfather or his grandfather's grandfather had been a priest. Clearly one of his ancestors had broken the church law by having a family. Or maybe priests in Greece were allowed to marry.

Jacob and Samir discussed religion almost six months after the discovery of the coin, and two days after Samir's fight with Hassan.

Hassan was George's sidekick, a Palestinian who lived in one of the neighbouring refugee camps. He sold Chiclets chewing-gum on the same boulevard as Samir, and they were walking back from Abou Assaad's one afternoon when Hassan said, 'Look at the enemy go.'

'Where?' Samir asked.

'There, in the blue Peugeot.'

'Where?' Samir repeated, spotting Mr Haddad.

'Eat shit, Samir. There, the Israeli.'

'He's not Israeli. He's Lebanese.'

34

Hassan glowered at his friend's brother. 'He's a Jew,' he spat.

'A Lebanese Jew.'

'All Jews are Israelis.'

'He's not. He's Lebanese.'

'Fuck your sister. He's an enemy.'

'He's Lebanese. I'm Lebanese. You're the Palestinian.'

'Eat shit,' Hassan shouted and kicked Samir in the right leg.

Samir punched him in the mouth and he was punched back in the stomach and kneed in the face. Samir fell back with a bleeding nose. Hassan kicked him once more in the belly and walked away shouting, 'I fuck your whore-mother, you pimp-son.'

Two days later when Jacob asked Samir about his black eye, the discussion turned to religion and nationality.

'So you're not an Arab,' Jacob said.

'No,' Samir exclaimed.

'What are you then?'

'Lebanese, of course.'

'What is Lebanese?'

Samir looked quizzically at his teacher. What a stupid question, he thought.

'There's no such thing as Lebanese,' said Mr Haddad.

'Kolona Lil-watan,' Samir sang the first bar proudly.

'Do you know what the colours on the flag stand for?'

Samir nodded, this he had learned at the School of Hope. 'The red's for the blood, the white's for the snow, and in the middle there's the Cedar of Lebanon.'

'Yes,' Jacob said. 'The red stands for the blood spilt in the fight for independence from the French, a fight many Lebanese opposed and for an independence many Lebanese are still against. The white is for the snow that falls on Maronite and Druse mountains, it hardly ever snows in Greek and Sunni Beirut, Saïda and Tripoli. And the Cedar of Lebanon, most sacred of Lebanese symbols, contemplates a history older than the Bible.

But in this land, seventeen histories cater for seventeen communities. In one neighbourhood, a past statesman is a martyr; in another, he is a villain.' Samir looked away resentfully as Jacob added, 'Believe in yourself, my young friend, not in a flag of dyed cloth.'

Samir felt he had defended Mr Haddad's Lebaneseness in vain. And he said so. 'You're an Israeli then?'

'No, I'm an Arab.'

Samir was confused.

'And you're an Arab. We're all Arabs – that's our common heritage. But there's a historical conspiracy. If you say you're an Arab, it's assumed you must be Muslim. Islamic and Arabic have long been interchangeable. We speak Arabic, we eat Arabic, we think Arabic, but we don't believe Islamic. Assuming an Arab to be Muslim should be as preposterous as assuming all Europeans to be Catholics, when there are Protestants and Orthodox like yourself.'

'Like myself?'

'Yes. Russian and Greek Orthodox.'

And it was Jacob Haddad, a Jew, who explained to Samir, for the first time, what it meant to be a Greek Orthodox.

That night, Samir thought about the discussion. Being Greek now seemed so trivial compared with this duality of Lebanese and Arab. Samir did not want to be an Arab; he was proud of being Lebanese. But was he more or less Lebanese than others? As he fingered his bruised eye he thought, if the Orthodox believe like the Greeks, the Maronites like the Romans, the Jews like the Israelis, the Shiites like the Iranians, the Sunnis like the Arabs, would no-one be left to believe like the Lebanese?

Samir was fifteen when war broke out on the streets of Beirut. In the early stages the war seemed little more than mischievous in contrast with later years. Everyone was excited and everyone knew their cause to be just. In these first months it was as if the whole population had been invited to a hunting weekend, but with the added

36

thrill that the animals were to be allowed to shoot back. Doctors dropped their stethoscopes, surveyors abandoned their theodolites, street vendors left their carts stacked high with rotting vegetables, and they all donned Balaclava helmets to fight the enemy, for fear of being recognized at work.

This was to have been a dirty weekend affair. On Saturday two men would fire at each other from neighbouring penthouses, and on Monday they would meet for business as usual; the bank clerk serving his client, the doctor extracting the bullet he had fired. Compared with the later years, this first phase of the war was comical, almost endearingly innocent.

Samir remembered, during one short lull when schools opened again, his maths teacher turned up with his Kalashnikov and a belt of cartridges. The most boring teacher in the most boring school had overnight been transformed into a dangerously exciting militiaman. He handed the children a test on algebra and settled in the corner of the classroom to wipe and polish his machine-gun. He was so taken by the task that he didn't notice that all the children were not in the least bit interested in the test and had all eyes riveted on their militant maths teacher and his gun. He looked down the barrel, blew and wiped his weapon and balanced it for weight like a pro, all under the adulating gaze of boys and girls alike.

George joined the Parti National Libéral, the PNL militia, as a full-time member in the days when most militiamen were, like the maths teacher, still part time. Samir missed his brother mostly in the middle of the night; he missed his brother's head brushing against the armchair in his sleep. Samir did not mourn his brother's death almost a year after he joined the PNL. As with Abou George, he could not find tears for his brother. Instead, he would grimly picture Hassan, George's sidekick, as the PLO sniper who had aimed and shot his erstwhile friend in the head.

Now Samir had the floor space all to himself, but he still slept in the direct beam of the light in the lobby, and still read the books Jacob lent him.

The two books he now had, and would always have, were the last Jacob Haddad lent him. These were not Jacob's, but were borrowed from the library of the Université Saint Joseph. The first was a thick volume on the study of ancient Greek, which included a comprehensive ancient Greek–French dictionary, and the second was a book on antique coins replete with illustrations. Samir had shown his coin to Jacob who recognized the letters as Greek. Upon Samir's insistence, Jacob withdrew the two books for a fortnight so that the boy could research his coin's origins.

This was the fortnight of the PLO advance in Beirut, of the massacres of Christian and Muslim towns, and of the Christian militia's counter-attacks on the Palestinian refugee camps. This was the fortnight the war lost all pretences of innocence, when the militiamen removed their Balaclava helmets.

For six months, like any sane civilian living in central Beirut, Samir did not budge and was confined to the concierge's living quarters, venturing out sometimes in the early mornings in search of food and water. During those six months, with nothing better to do, he learned ancient Greek and became a numismatist without a coin collection.

As mortars and rocket-propelled grenades rained down on their neighbourhood, pitting buildings like swarms of locusts ravaging a crop, Samir studied Greek grammar and memorized the differences between the genitive, ablative and dative cases; and from the illustrations and text in the other book, he learned to distinguish between Athenian and Spartan coins.

By the time heavy artillery and tanks were introduced onto the streets of Beirut, Samir could write entire paragraphs in ancient Greek and had retained much of the vocabulary, and he could theoretically grade a coin's value according to its Fine, Good or Very Good characteristics.

As for his own coin, he had discovered from the first week he had the books that the treasure, guarded so secretly and uncomfortably below the crotch, was nothing but a fake. For a start it was perfectly round – no ancient coin was so compass-drawn perfect. There was rust, but not enough rust for a coin supposedly 2,000 years old. Samir's coin was a replica of a Syracusan decadrachm – and not even a good replica at that, he now knew. The four fish were supposed to be dolphins surrounding the bust of Arethusa. And in the replica the hair was wrong – it was wavy instead of curly – and the fake had neglected to adorn Arethusa with an ear-ring. On the reverse, the chariot was facing the wrong way and the charioteer did not have Niké, the goddess of victory, hovering over his head. But the clinching argument was in the Greek letters themselves. The would-be Syracusans had misspelt the name of their city. Samir wrote the correction in his exercise book ten times, as if correcting a school dictation.

ΣΥΡΑΚΟΣΙΩ ΣΥΡΑΚΟΣΙΩ ΣΥΡΑΚΟΣΙΩ ΣΥΡΑΚΟΣΙΩ ΣΥΡΑΚΟΣΙΩ ΣΥΡΑΚΟΣΙΩ ΣΥΡΑΚΟΣΙΩ ΣΥΡΑΚΟΣΙΩ ΣΥΡΑΚΟΣΙΩ ΣΥΡΑΚΟΣΙΩ

Jacob Haddad was kidnapped during those six months by the Christian Phalangist Party. He was released a week later because he was suspected of being an Israeli spy. It seemed ironic to think that had he been captured by another group he would have been tortured and killed for precisely the same reason.

'I've got to leave, Samir,' Jacob said one day.

'Why?'

'I can't stay here any more.'

'But everything's going right now,' Samir complained. Everyone was optimistic about the Arab peace-keeping force that was being deployed in Beirut. 'You'll see, the war will be over soon.'

'The peace-keeping force is ninety per cent Syrian and I don't want to be here when the animals in this jungle finally get wind of the lion's true intent.'

The allusion was not lost on the boy. Lion in Arabic was *assad*. 'It'll be OK,' Samir said stirringly. 'Please stay, don't go.'

Jacob put his arm around the youth's shoulders. 'My Greek student,' he said fondly, kissing him. 'We're all children having an unscheduled day off from school. We'll be excited until the school burns down and we run out of sticks for the bonfire.'

'But when will you come back?'

'When a Shiite mother stops scolding her child by threatening to call the Phalangists.'

A month later, Jacob Haddad drove away from Samir's life and followed the seasonal geese south, stopping at Tel Aviv.

The night Jacob left, Samir cried.

As he lay alone on the cold floor, swathed in a blanket, he gazed tearfully at the bulb and the light which was still ridiculously left on at night. He heard the occasional bullet whistling through the air as a macabre replacement to the courting cats. He wept for his friend who had been forced to leave his country. Yes, Jacob Haddad was Lebanese not Israeli. More Lebanese than anyone he knew.

For the first time, Samir found he could cry for his father who had been chased to death by his unnamed demons, for his brother who had died for nothing but vainglory and for his coin which was a worthless chunk of metal. Above all, he cried for his lost innocence. A past when days were longer, when he and Leila counted bugs and when he smiled at drivers and sold them Chiclets peppermint gum.

Tired, he became dozily aware of a shadow on the opaque shell encompassing the bulb. He wiped the tears from his eyes and was astonished to see a flying cockroach crawling over the shell towards one of the two holes on the side. He held his breath and the cockroach almost casually slipped through the hole into the searing light.

Samir looked quizzically at the bulb and then grinned broadly as the cockroach thrashed briefly in the casing. The light played on Samir's teeth, and had he been able to see them, he would have imagined that his teeth too could dance the *dabké*. Momentarily, at least, the world was a brighter place.

Of course, Samir thought happily, the holes expand in the heat.

1 9 8 2

The two silver sheets had been rolled tightly, each encapsulated in a tin sheath, remaining undisturbed for over 2,000 years until their discovery.

The man sat at his desk and handled the two tin cocoons, fingering the rusted buckles by the stoppers which, he considered, enabled carriers to hang the sheaths on their belts. He had to use a pair of pliers to remove the stoppers, and then, with eyebrow tweezers, he picked at the rolls of silver inside. The first roll presented little difficulty and slid out easily, but with the second the man tugged impatiently, almost ripping the sheet, until it too emerged into the twentieth century. He unrolled both sheets on his desk.

Each was roughly 4 centimetres wide and 16 centimetres long. They were matt in the direct sunlight that filtered through the French windows, as if quenching a thirst brought on by millennia of darkness. He ran his left index across one of the sheets, feeling the characters in relief.

The cocoons, he thought, were the antique equivalents of modern paper envelopes. And as he balanced the two sheets on his palm, he remembered someone who could sell these two ancient Greek letters for him. He placed the two silver sheets and their tin sheaths in the top drawer of his desk, and picked up the phone to call Samir Khoury.

2

A MATTER OF TIME

A curious mind discovered the chronon.

On her twelfth birthday, in 1969, Maira told her family that she planned to become a great artist. 'Post-Impressionist,' she qualified affectedly, cutting short further enquiries. Before asking her parents for paints and brushes, Maira had looked up and memorized all the relevant words. If questioned, Why Post-Impressionism? her prepared answer would have been, 'Because cubism is too abstract and Impressionism too dull.'

In the event, however, no-one bothered to ask. As Maira unwrapped the present which would set her on a course to fame – via a *Teach Yourself Art* book and beginner's easel – her nan explained to the rest of the family that she too had gone through a similar phase as a child, using a lock from a horse's mane because brushes were, oddly, in short supply during the Great War.

The following morning Maira rose at dawn, set up her easel on the patio beside the garden table, lined up the brushes, opened the box of oil paints, put her thumb through the small palette and stared at the blank canvas.

Perhaps a summer's morning in a back garden in Southampton was not inspirational enough. She wished she were in Paris; all the best artists were Parisians. By the time her mum came downstairs to prepare breakfast, Maira, still standing by her new easel, had scrutinized the sycamore, the garden pond, even the blowzy gnome, looking for an interesting subject to paint.

By eleven o'clock she was thoroughly bored. She sat cross-legged on the ground, staring despondently at a half-eaten piece of toast, dropped a few hours earlier. Two large black ants had crawled onto the toast and were pacing round and round in circles.

Confused, Maira thought. Must be the biggest banquet they've ever seen. They don't know where to start.

She tilted the slice and gently knocked it so that the ants fell lightly to the ground, then, breaking off two crumbs, she dropped them by each ant. With manageable portions, the ants picked up the crumbs in their mandibles and scurried to their antheap. Maira followed them.

The heap was nine of her paces away from the easel. One ant, after a quick turn and wave with its antennae, headed straight for home. The second followed a zigzagging route, turning sometimes left, sometimes right, constantly retracing its steps, as if a series of obstacles had been placed in its path.

Taking the scenic route, Maira thought, which was what her dad said whenever they got lost on outings.

The second ant finally made it to the anthill very many minutes after the first. Maira frowned. How odd; a minute must be like an hour to an ant. Why should one ant take hours longer over the same route? Maybe the second was younger, less experienced, or the first was brighter. Could ants be said to be intelligent, she wondered. She had read that bees and ants checked the position of the sun as they left their hives and heaps, and thereafter constantly worked out their bearings to the sun, thereby knowing where they were in relation to their homes. Which was another reason, she guessed, why you never saw bees and ants in winter. Maira left the anthill to look up the word 'intelligence' in her dictionary.

Ten minutes later she returned to the garden with a tape measure, her digital watch and an empty glass. She measured the distance from the anthill to a crack on the patio floor and captured four ants in the glass.

Squeezing red, blue, yellow and green paint onto her palette, she carefully used her thinnest brush to apply a drop of each colour to each abdomen. Then, paintbrush turned sword, she sliced the air on either side of the glass of ants, smiled, and said aloud, 'I dub ye Sirs Grant, Yant, Blant and Rant.'

She prepared four equal crumbs of toast, upturned the glass at the crack on the patio floor, and recorded the times from the moment each ant picked up its food, to the moment each entered the heap. Before her mum called her for lunch, Maira was able to repeat the experiment three times with the same ants – except for Yant who had strangely disappeared after the first trip.

In the afternoon she completed her first and last painting on canvas. She painted the anthill and the patio floor, marking, in black, the distance to the crack. Below, she added a graph of the time taken against the distance, with Grant's, Rant's and Blant's average performances as straight lines in their respective colours. Then she wrote a simple ratio:

$$\text{Intelligence, I} = \text{Comprehension, C} / \text{Time taken to comprehend, T}$$

Comprehension, Maira decided, was the same for all her ants. All three knew they had crumbs in their mouths, and all three knew they had to return to their heap. Comprehension was therefore a constant, and she wrote three further ratios in the appropriate colours to the right of the graph:

$$I(green)/ I(red) = T(red)/ T(green)$$
$$I(green)/ I(blue) = T(blue)/ T(green)$$
$$I(red)/ I(blue) = T(blue)/ T(red)$$

As the green ant had been 1.5 times faster than the red, and 2.25 times faster than the blue, she titled her work, *Grant the Antstein*. In the top right-hand corner she painted the sun surrounded by a blue sky, and considered adding the sycamore but then thought it would look silly. After all, she had only added the sun out of respect for the ant's sense of direction. She looked at her masterpiece, nodded with satisfaction, and signed her name – Maira Brisden – in orange paint in the bottom left corner. Orange because it was the colour of her hair.

Of course, Grant couldn't *really* be more intelligent than Rant and Blant. Rather, as measured by her watch, Grant had had 1.5 and 2.25 *more time* to reach the anthill.

In her diary that night, Maira wrote, 'My watch and ants tick differently.'

For her second experiment, towards the end of the summer holidays, Maira roasted her watch.

She had left it in a preheated oven for exactly an hour, timed by her father's old watch. She was very disappointed to discover that her watch had utterly perished three minutes after the beginning of the experiment. Indeed the dial – for ever reading 12:03 – was the least charred part of the watch.

'Daliesque,' she said sadly.

But this was the second part of the experiment; the first was far more successful. Maira had synchronized the two watches, and for a whole day had kept them side by side, checking on them regularly. Satisfied that a day later they were both still in perfect sync, she placed her watch in the freezer compartment of the refrigerator for an hour, keeping the other watch in her room. When she removed her watch, she found that it now lagged her father's by a full minute and twelve seconds. She synchronized the watches again and left her watch in the freezer for a full day, at the end of which she discovered her father's watch led her own by twenty-eight and a half minutes.

She verified her conclusions by synchronizing the watches again and leaving them side by side in her room

46

for a further day. Again they ticked and recorded time in perfect unison.

She didn't have a thermometer, but she assumed that the freezer setting of four would be twice two, which would be twice as cold as the freezer mark one, so she spent a week placing first her watch in the freezer at different settings and then her father's, and she tabulated all the readings, drawing graphs of the results on graph paper, which was easier than on canvas. The easel, palette and paints had already ended up in the cupboard.

There were differences in the results between her father's old watch and hers when each had been frozen at the same setting and over the same period, but these she put down to differences in quality: her father's watch was Swiss and gold-plated, while hers was Japanese and made of stainless steel. Later, consulting an A level Physics book, she refined her interpretations to describe their different thermal coefficients.

Maira was keen to complete the experiment, and what had been demonstrated with cold temperatures should, in her way of thinking, be demonstrated with hot temperatures. So in the second leg of the experiment she cooked her watch to oblivion.

In her diary she wrote, 'Time is slower in cold temperatures.'

She looked at her graphs, chewed her pen, then smiling, Maira Brisden added, 'The greatest art is pure science. I want to be a great artist.'

1982

The conference was called 'A Matter of Time'. It was the first of its kind in that it would group academics from a wide spectrum of interests all discussing their pet theories on time. This was Professor Morgan's brainchild; head of Mathematics and Master of Peterhouse College, Cambridge.

Like others, Professor Morgan had noticed that the nature of time was fast becoming the most discussed academic topic of the Eighties. Evolutionists, geneticists and geologists were joining particle physicists and thermodynamicists in an unparalleled battle of concepts. One had only to glean the literature of the last few years to notice the sudden prominence reserved for time. Evolutionists and geneticists who wrote their theses under headings like 'The Cycle of Time' faced angry physicists and geologists waving banners with slogans of 'Arrow of Time'; others still wrote like arbitrators under questioning titles, 'Time – A Measure of Entropy?'

Like others, Professor Morgan knew that a cross-specialization exchange of ideas was long overdue. Unlike others, Professor Morgan had both the inclination and academic clout to make the conference a reality. He knew, with apprehension, that this first conference in Cambridge was as controversial as getting Arabs and Israelis to discuss peace. It could also be the last if the discussions went out of control. It was hard enough to encourage two physicists from different branches to converse in a reasonable and reasoning manner, let alone delegates from widely different fields of science, and worse still, scientists and non-scientists. In a bid to incorporate all visions of time, Professor Morgan could not fail to invite the oldest chronologists, the historians, or the linguists, who were interested in the evolutionary nature of languages.

To close friends he had likened the proposed conference to a cageful of parrots plucked from different forests of the globe. There would be one of two results: either all the parrots would find some common branch and discover a universal parrot-speak, or the parrots would squawk that much louder in their own tongue in order to be heard above all the other squawking parrots.

As the first day of the conference dawned, he could only hope that he had taken sufficient precautions. The main problem was one of semantics. Gone were the days when an educated person could, with wit, comprehend all the different fields of human achievement. The last true polymath had been killed in the twentieth century by the technological revolution, and with the resulting big bang of jargon, every specialist was now required to learn an esoteric dialect.

Professor Morgan had therefore gone to considerable lengths in selecting the speakers. The first requirement was, naturally, that they be leaders in their fields. The second, and almost as important, was that they be practical enough in their approach and simple enough in their syntax and nomenclature to be comprehensible to the other delegates. So, of the twelve main speakers, he had chosen only two other Cambridge colleagues. Dr Paul Stevens of the Anglo-Saxon Norse and Celtic Department would discuss time from an etymological perspective, and Dr Maira Brisden would talk of a chronon and of an old universe.

Maira's was the third and final lecture of the day.

Professor Morgan had scheduled three main lectures a day over four days, each followed by a recess – coffee, lunch, tea – and group discussions. The first day had been reserved for physics: thermodynamics, quantum mechanics, and now, Dr Brisden's chrono-physics.

Professor Morgan felt that the last lecture on quantum mechanics had been particularly harsh on less scientific ears. When the speaker had described, in simple terms but at great length, world planes that were really strings mapped out in imaginary time, Professor Morgan had looked in dismay at expressions of abject boredom from many non-physicists. He wondered if it had been wise to hold three physics lectures in a day, especially as he saw little change after the lunch break from some of the linguistic delegates.

'Thank you, Professor Morgan,' Maira said when he finished introducing her.

As he returned to his seat and looked around the lecture theatre, he thought Dr Brisden would have a tough job keeping the delegates interested.

'Dear colleagues, ladies and gentlemen,' Maira began, 'how long is Britain's coastline?'

There was a lengthy pause and she scanned the hall, gazing intently at individual delegates. When she was satisfied she had everyone's attention, she resumed, 'The answer depends largely on our view.'

She showed a series of four slides: a stretch of ground in microscopic detail, where pebbles appeared as insurmountable boulders, then a vista of a scenic bay, followed by a frame of a stretch of coast taken at high altitude, and finally a satellite image of the south coast of Britain.

Maira began her lecture by talking of three creatures walking from Southampton to Plymouth: an ant, a man and a giant. Were the coast a perfectly straight line (with a dimension of one), the three could agree on a universal unit of length, a cosmic metre which would require conversions only in terms of scale: more paces for the ant than the man than the giant. However, Maira explained, Mother Nature sketched coasts, mountains and curved space. It was precisely because of the coast's fractal one-and-a-bit dimensions (the idealized straight line regularly displaced into the second dimension) that the three could not agree on a universal measure of length. The distance between Plymouth and Southampton was fixed, but because the ant's coastline was more jagged than the man's and the giant's – more nooks and crannies within every bay and promontory had to be contoured – the concept of length and space became subject to the measurer's *own* size.

Maira proposed that time was equally fractal where each organism defined its second also according to its size; she called her theory, the 'Chronon Theory of Time', CTT for short. A cosmic second, like the cosmic metre, did exist, but by virtue of being alive and affected by time, no observer could measure its value. However, with CTT, a total relativistic approach could be entertained: *any* time-varying system, regardless of size and density (an elephant, a shrew, a star, or the cosmos itself, even abstract systems such as the evolution of species or language), could be compared to any other time-varying system (such as a man).

She defined the chronon in the following terms: when an elementary particle of mass is acted upon by a quantum of time – a chronon – the particle of mass is displaced into the future.

Conscious of the non-scientists in the lecture theatre, she illustrated the idea with the analogy of a beach-ball as a particle of mass moving under the steady stream of a jet of water. Upon impact, each individual chronon imparted a fixed amount of *ageing* to the particle of mass – the ball moved further along the beach. Maira described inertia in terms of beach-balls: a small ball was propelled further than a large ball by the jet, if both had the same air pressure and density. The CTT equivalent was that a large object offered more resistance to ageing (to being propelled into the future) than a small object – and a similar argument held true for density where a larger helium-filled beach-ball was propelled further than a smaller air-filled ball. Volume and density were thus the primary variables in this theory, and CTT predicted a smaller second – less chronon inertia – for the following four cases:

1. A small body versus a large body of the same density.
2. A body versus a denser body of the same volume.
3. A hot body versus an equal but cold body.
4. A body at rest versus an equal body in motion.

In her examples to show CTT's predictive powers and the universal applications of the theory, Maira used her formulae to quantify a baby's higher pulse and thus longer notion of the second ('Time waits for no man like it waits for a baby'); the 800 million heartbeats which both an elephant and a shrew undergo in their lives, the former in fifty-odd years, the latter in a year; a whale's

51

thirty-minute song relative to a chaffinch's minute; the rise and fall of the Roman Empire where the citizens were as cells in an organism; and the life cycle of a market product, from launch to divestment.

She ended her lecture in her own discipline, with the interpretations the Chronon Theory of Time reserved for the age of the universe.

The universe began with a big bang which took place approximately sixteen billion years ago, an age which is calculated by observing a blue shift in stars and galaxies, inferring a rate of expansion of the universe, and from this rate deducing a time in the past when the entire universe could be contained in a table-tennis ball. But, she propounded, while agreeing with the calculations, the universe only *appeared* to be sixteen billion years old, because the age was calculated using the universe's *present* year. According to CTT, a second (or a year) in the past universe would have been a shorter time than a second in today's universe.

She offered the proof: in the past, after the big bang, the volume of the universe was smaller, thereby shortening the second, and the density was higher, thereby lengthening the second. From Einstein's equations, the mean density at any given time is inversely proportional to the radius squared of the universe, while the volume is proportional to the radius cubed. The net effect, then, is that the universe's second or year shortens with a smaller radius. The universe's year or second becomes a function of its radius.

And she showed a slide:

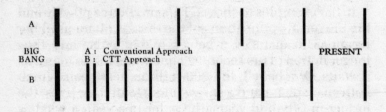

A

BIG BANG   A : Conventional Approach   PRESENT
           B : CTT Approach

B

The true age of the universe was evaluated by counting all the years separately (by integration), resulting in an age over three and a half times older than present estimates. With CTT, the very idea of a big bang was undermined. The closer a hypothetical observer reached that past event, the more he would find that a present year became millions of years as recorded by his hypothetical clock, like attempting to watch a two-hour feature film in one thousandth of a second. The big bang was not a sudden spark out of nothingness but rather an intolerably slow progression, a greatly protracted evolution that would take a near eternity of time. And – Maira stressed the notion – at the very instant of the big bang, the intervals of time would be so close, the second would be so short, as to be unchanging. The Chronon Theory of Time therefore predicted that time itself did indeed begin with the universe.

'Thank you, Dr Brisden,' said Professor Morgan at the end of the questions and answers session that followed the lecture. 'If there are no further questions, I would like to adjourn this conference till tomorrow—'

'Professor Morgan, I have a question for Dr Brisden.'

He looked at the man in the back row and, hiding his impatience, he said jocularly, 'I rather think Dr Brisden needs some fresh air and a stretch, as do the rest of us, I imagine.'

'It's a short question,' the man said.

Professor Morgan nodded and returned glumly to his seat. The questions and answers session had lasted almost as long as the lecture itself. While he was glad that the lecture had aroused some interest, he shifted his weight onto one buttock and was uncomfortably aware that most delegates were longing to leave the theatre. This was to be the nineteenth question – Professor Morgan had counted them. Almost every question had been short, and invariably every answer had been detailed. Indeed, he felt that there was an inverse proportionality between the lengths of the questions and answers, so that the shortest question given by a non-scientist had required the longest answer – Professor Morgan had verified this with his watch. The question had been, 'Is time travel possible?' and the twenty-minute reply, 'No. Never.'

In all fairness to Dr Brisden, this was an over-simplification. She had answered very conclusively, describing how CTT was the first theory in physics to incorporate a clear-cut arrow of time. It was widely relative in that some mechanisms would only appear to be unaffected by time to other shorter-lived mechanisms. But the chronon travelled in one direction, arbitrarily named from past to future, down a one-way street of causes and effects, no paradoxes were needed, and certainly no parallel universes required as explanation, or some other science-fictional theory. With CTT, Dr Brisden had not only fused the large with the small, science with non-science, but she had succeeded in the more difficult task of returning physics to the realm of the common sense.

'Bill Walters of the SETI Institute,' said the man in the back row. 'As you may know, the search for extraterrestrial intelligence has, for some years now, consisted of scanning the skies with a grid of radio telescopes, searching at many frequencies simultaneously for signs of alien communications. We have, so far, found no evidence of alien broadcasts. It has been suggested that because there have been few generations of stars, Earth could well be among the first generation of planets with intelligent life and that, therefore, it would be too soon to expect transmissions from other life in the universe.

'If I understand your ideas, you dispute the number of generations of stars – you would have more generations between our sun and the big bang. This suggests more heavier elements required for planets and life far sooner than previously envisaged. This in turn implies the possibility of many generations of intelligent planets well before Earth. Given this added probability of older and more advanced civilizations elsewhere, my question simply put is this: Are there any CTT reasons which would explain why we've received no signals?'

Maira stared at Bill Walters for an uneasy while, as if she were still expecting the question, then she smiled and said kindly, 'I can't imagine.'

A record, Professor Morgan thought, glancing at his watch.

'I'm sorry,' she added, 'I don't have all the answers. Other than the statistical approach we don't really have conclusive proof that life will form elsewhere. We know it can, given favourable conditions, but will it generally? But then you will know more about this than me. You say that the frequencies are checked simultaneously; it may be that you should be investigating something other than frequency, or perhaps in addition to it.'

'Such as?' Bill Walters asked.

She shrugged.

'I don't know.' Maira's eyes went vacant as she added, 'But I promise you I will think about it.'

ZACHIEL

In the physical world, Zachiel is a white jinnee who appears in an explosive plume of smoke to lead me away from Samir and Maira's pasts through the floodlit doorway to his world of eternal desert night.

In the centre of the Celtic cross once more, I expect him to carry my soul to the second door, that of the crystal tower. Instead, the fourth doorway is now glowing with light, not white as the first but blue.

Zachiel points at the glass monster, horned, with female breasts and male genitals refracting the cold blue light: I am to pass between *The Devil*'s colossal legs to visit a future earth where I am no longer alive.

'AZAZEL'; the name appears in the sand by the angel's feet.

Azazel the blue demon, the evil spirit of the wilderness to whom Jews of old sacrificed a scapegoat on Yom Kippur – the Day of Atonement. Azaz-el, anti-God, king of the blue jinn.

Az-Zurruk, the blue sprites, are all-embracingly evil. They take after their master and lover, Satan, creator and non-uterine brother. That is the very secret of their existence, for they alone in the known universe were not among the species accounted for in the Creation. They arrived later, obnoxious gate-crashers to a ball for living things, as the proud showpieces of the Devil's stolen technology. Only God breathes life into viscous mud; so Az-Zurruk were new creatures insofar as woman was moulded from existing human stock. The first blue

56

jinnee, Azazel, was an angel's rib bared and hacked, not out of love for order, but out of envy and for chaos.

Azazel and his Zurruk are guardian non-angels. They stick to spiritually dead humans like bluebottles on a cadaver, until the victim's soul is exposed and quartered. The flesh of a damned fig thus prepared, the blue hounds move respectfully aside, leaving the quarry to their dark creator.

White jinn are reborn every spring, excited by the resurrection of Adonis in the fields and orchards. Azazel and his blue minions seek their thrills through the birth of unloved babies.

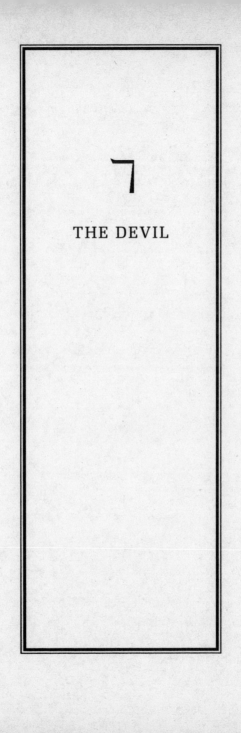

7

THE DEVIL

3

LITTLE KHARA

Ashtin should best be remembered for its plums. Were it customary to honour dead villages as one honours dead people, one would find a memorial in the devastated square, perhaps a slab of pink marble, sparkling in the bright Mediterranean sun, surrounded on all four sides by crumbling, decaying limestone walls that mark the remains of houses. An epitaph, chiselled in calligraphic Arabic, would be located centrally, guarded by a Maronite cross and Shiite crescent; two margins on a marble sheet to respect past demographics, honouring the ghosts of sectarian statistics. Concerning the eulogy itself, the most apt and less political would read:

It gave the sweetest and reddest plums.
Ashtin 1754–1982.
Requiescat In Pace

Such sentimentality, though, is inappropriate. Villages do decay into bones like the best of corpses, but their graves do not possess souls to warrant a gravestone. Towns shed dead skin as a matter of course. They change with time; they grow and die only to be reborn, to expand in a new direction. Thus, Phoenician Beryt becomes Graeco-Roman Berytos which is resuscitated into Ottoman Beyroot which evolves into the monstrous chimera that is modern Beirut. But the outright death of a village is a rare occurrence; the deep scar left in the countryside bears witness both to the end of an entire community and to a future generation's unwillingness to rebuild on its past.

Ashtin breathed its last painful breath on 8 June 1982, the day that followed the beginning of the Israeli operation dubbed Peace in Galilee. The death was both an act of murder and the end result of a prolonged disease; with affected jurisprudence, hawkish Israelis even referred to the victory in Ashtin as euthanasia. While for the previous decade Palestinians had occupied and infiltrated the territory like a pathogen in a bloodstream, the annihilation on that fateful day was, by no stretch of the judicial imagination, merciful. In actual fact, the removal of the Palestinian fighters, carried out with such clinical efficiency in surrounding towns and villages, proved to be a disastrous failure in Ashtin, and for Ashtin.

On the whole the villagers were anti-PLO, inasmuch as one can be anti-anything looking down the wrong end of a Kalashnikov. Paying more than mere lip-service to the Philistine cause, Christians and Muslims alike were required to support the on-going struggle against Zionism. Thus, with their hearts yo-yoing between their chests and their boots, Ashtinis coughed up for the privilege of having their village turn into a Palestinian fortress. At the PLO checkpoints that bear-hugged the village, a tax was levied on all goods entering and leaving Ashtin: import/export duty for the anarchic state that coexisted with the state of Lebanon. Even the single restaurant in the village square, unaptly named Casino Ashtin, had dispensed with the service charge since 1976 in order to satisfy both the Arab brothers-in-arms and its backgammon-playing arak-swilling clientele.

In May 1982, when little Khara was born, Ashtin was ignorant of the prognosis that already labelled it incurable at Israeli headquarters. The inhabitants and the racketeers, blissfully unaware of impending doom, went about their quotidian lives peaceably enough. Even a modicum of joy could be discerned in the village, in the broader-than-usual smiles and *'Bunjoor'* –

'*Bunjoorayn*' as Ashtinis greeted one another; in the friendly taunts as children booted a football on the main road. Like the rest of the animal kingdom the world over, the villagers were experiencing a new *joie de vivre* with the going of the snow, mist and gloom and the coming of spring. And none was happier in that final month than Khara's father, Joseph Sulman.

Zoozoo, as Joseph was widely known, was never a militiaman, not even in the late Seventies when it was an occupation with interesting career prospects; nor was he political – an even greater rarity in Lebanon. Yet in an unusual string of circumstances, the young Maronite would fall prey to the Palestinians for the most banal of reasons: because of water. The same Ashtini H_2O which only a decade later would turn into malevolent slime.

Zoozoo was in a good mood for three reasons. First, his pregnant wife had just given birth to a healthy and incredibly pink baby. Secondly, despite the two prenatal predictions of his mother-in-law and his best friend's wife, he now had a baby boy. In the experiment to determine the sex of the growing foetus, his mother-in-law had tied her daughter's wedding ring to a foot of sewing thread and had held the end in a steady hand so that the ring dangled closest to the belly-enveloped baby. Of its own volition, like a cup on a Ouija board, the ring would then either slowly circle above the stretched skin, punching a deliberate hole in the air for a girl, or move in short pendulum swings, tupping for a boy. The motion had been circular.

(Later, confronted with a day-old and tiny but unambiguous proof of error, the new grandmother said testily, 'It never fails with gold that isn't so white' – alluding to the 18-carat ring on her daughter's finger.)

A week before Khara was born, Farid, Zoozoo's friend and neighbour, congratulated the parent-to-be on the imminence of a daughter, after Farid's wife translated the whorls of sludge at the bottom of Zoozoo's coffee-cup into the silhouette of a little girl.

'You'll love her more than a son, you'll see,' Farid encouraged.

Zoozoo felt like replying, 'How would you know?' He said nothing though, because his friend took offence easily, sometimes with violent consequences. As the proud – some villagers said arrogant – parent of four daughters and no sons, and with five sisters and no brothers and a doting widow for a mother, Farid defended his manhood as one guards a treasure. An acquaintance had once slipped a flippant remark, 'With so many women in your family, how come you don't live in Trablus?' Trablus or Tripoli, north of Beirut, was renowned for only two things: its oil refinery and its gay community. Farid pounced on the wretch and kicked him until the offender's nose and a rib were broken.

Zoozoo had admitted to his friend and wife his wish for a son, but never his secret unwish for a daughter. With a son he would gain a companion, a friend and disciple to take on hunting trips in the forests of Mount Lebanon, or sea-fishing off the Sidonian coast. Hiding behind the pretext of entertaining a son, a man was entitled, for instance, to play with a train set, rediscovering, at least for a fleeting moment, his own boyhood.

A daughter was different. From the cute pink baby clothes and pretty dolls to the learned art of masking a face, a girl was groomed to become a sought-after woman. The wife would have more fun. A girl would be taught to dance as a prerequisite to a future bride's comprehensive education. Not the jerky steps of the West, but the flowing, seductive, undeniably erotic belly-dance of the Orient. Just as Zoozoo's wife, whirling and cavorting on their first date, had drawn him to her like a moth to a dancing flame, so would a daughter learn to follow in her mother's measured steps: raising both arms invitingly, swaying breasts to exhibit the two wells of joy for men and babies, and thrusting hips in unquestionable orgasmic rhythm.

This was also not the time for a Christian in Lebanon

to favour the birth of a girl. The political balance in the country was swinging away from the Maronites, and with the secrecy of invisible ink only turning legible over a heat source, the word *Islami* was progressively being etched into the constitution. If, in the near future, as Zoozoo suspected, Lebanon was forced to emulate its Arab neighbours, a daughter would acquire a second-class ticket in life, riding the nation's backseats. All the advantages fought for and won by women, such as voting rights and equal inheritance with men, would be work lost – of the irreversible kind, like a turbine's wasteful dissipation of heat into the atmosphere.

Local tradition also favoured a son, showing the same tenacious respect for the masculine gender as French grammar. On a planetful of women, *elles* becomes *ils* when a single boy lands on the surface. Farid, father of four daughters, remained plain Farid. Zoozoo, on the other hand, toying with the name Khalil for his son, would henceforth be known as Abou Khalil; a new name for a privileged rank among real men.

The pleasure of becoming a father and the keen pride of gaining a son outshone the third reason for Zoozoo's beaming mood. The plum trees in his orchard, which had shown signs of recovery a year after the havoc wreaked by the medflies, were, this spring, fully revived and bearing as yet unripe fruit.

Like other plantations on Mount Lebanon, the Ashtini orchards were built into the mountainside on terraces. In Ashtin, the giant steps were roughly 12 metres wide, with walls of limestone a metre high to prevent soil erosion. From a distance, and on a clear day, one could be optically duped into believing that the steps had been constructed for the express purpose of scaling the mountain, providing a stairway, perhaps for the giant genies of the *Arabian Nights*, to climb to the sun as the Aztecs on their artificial mountains.

Zoozoo was a smallholder, owning significantly less land than most Ashtini farmers. He and his father before him had concentrated on the renowned black plum, where the accepted practice was to cultivate peaches, pears and white plums as well as Ashtin's prime fruit. This exclusivity had made it possible for the Sulmans to gather the Ashtini plum in the quantities of the largest holdings, and with this singular choice came a certain reputation – a Beirut wholesaler had outbid its competitors to become the sole recipient of Zoozoo's annual harvest.

To the other farmers, the serious flaw in producing only the black plum lay in the nature of the tree itself. Many in the village, including Zoozoo, had accorded human characteristics to the trees, so that peaches and pears were hardy as mountain men (as they themselves), while plums were fastidious and fickle like city women. Plum trees had insatiable thirsts. They lapped up their early evening water as if it would be their last or as if they could somehow sense – with shudders travelling up the bark – the harrowing proximity of the Syrian desert beyond the Antilebanon.

When the winters were dry, by late spring, early summer, the water in the artesian wells sank to danger-ously low levels, necessitating severe rationing by the farmers. Typically, the peach and pear trees were not greatly affected, and still produced good fruit, if in marginally smaller quantities. The plums, though, were vindictive trees. In clear retaliation for the unnourishing supply of water, they yielded a sorry excuse for a crop: small fruits that could be popped into a mouth, with precious little juice between flat seed and skin.

Ashtini farmers had resorted to describing Zoozoo's father as the 'foolish shepherd with too many sheep and not enough goats', and they had tried on numerous occasions to persuade him, and later his son, to grow an auxiliary crop for the unfavourable years. Even the white plum was less of a liability than its darker cousin, given the Lebanese relish for the unripe green fruit when dipped in salt and consumed over a drink. As much as half the crop of white plums was gathered in spring, in good as well as bad years, and packed in polythene bags, destined to be served alongside bowls of pistachios and almonds.

When his father passed away, Zoozoo inherited both the land and the pastoral crook. It was no easy matter changing trees in an orchard, neither in agrarian terms nor on an emotional level. Black plum trees were, frankly, lovable creatures. In the right conditions, with water flooding the soil and gurgling around the roots (Zoozoo swore it was how trees purred), the black plum was the most generous of trees. The proper Ashtini plum grew large as an avocado pear with a deep cleft on one side, as if each plum were preparing to split into twins. Firm, and with the contours of young maidens' buttocks, the plums, turning African come August, mooned shamelessly from their boughs; the dark seductive colour declared that they were ready to be handled. That the plum craved so much watering did not surprise Zoozoo. As a child he had imagined that the tree was really an animal which needed to store excess water in its burgeoning fruit, like a wealthy Lebanese businessman stores fat around his middle.

Zoozoo was content, then, because the winter and early spring had been propitious for the plums – not too cold to damage the roots and wet enough to replenish the wells. The plum trees seemed to mirror his mood; the branches curved in wide 'U's and the foliage and budding fruit twinkled with morning dew in the soft May sun.

'Damn trees are smiling at me,' Zoozoo shouted to his neighbour, two terraces below.

Abou Ahmad, who was picking unripe white plums with four of his sons, looked up and gave Zoozoo an engaging grin, despite two missing incisors in his upper jaw. 'That's no way to speak of trees,' he shouted back. 'Whores need respect, forgive-the-word.' Abou Ahmad lit a cigarette, told his youngest son to fetch more polythene bags and climbed the wall onto

Zoozoo's land. '*Mabrouk* on your son,' he congratulated as Zoozoo climbed down a step to join him. 'What are you calling him?'

'Khalil.'

Abou Ahmad nodded approvingly; it was Zoozoo's father's name. 'Allah has shown compassion to your father, his memory lives on in your son.' Nodding towards his three sons gathering green fruit, he added, 'We'll see him here with you in no time.'

'He's not more than a soft-skinned aubergine,' said Zoozoo with a smile. 'He'll need to grow and go to school first.'

'Why, who taught you the plum tree, your schoolteacher or Abou Zooz, Allah rest his soul.'

Zoozoo shrugged; the priorities were different for Ashtin's two communities. He gave Abou Ahmad's arm a squeeze and said, 'The day he's old enough to learn about trees, I'll send him to you for a lesson.'

'We're honoured,' Abou Ahmad said formally. Pursing his lips around the cigarette and inhaling through the gap in his teeth, he reached for his pocket and took out a very faded copper coin. 'May you be proud of Khalil bin Youssef. This is for his luck.'

Zoozoo examined the coin and could just discern the word *Konstantinye* in cursive Arabic. 'Osmanli?'

'Ahmad found it near the house. Ten piastres and look at the date,' Abou Ahmad urged. 'Seven hundred years old. 1255.'

Zoozoo was no expert but he supposed the Ottomans had calendared their years along a Muhammadan rather than Gregorian model; this would date the coin at little over a century old. He wondered whether the man was conscious of his error.

'Thank you,' he said warmly and invited Abou Ahmad for Arabic sweets.

Traditionally, in the hours pregnant women and midwives sweated over childbirth, female friends and relatives prepared pastries for the well-wishers, who arrived with small gifts of baby clothes and bracelets or anklets for girls, and who voiced monosyllables of wonderment: *yee, yaay, shoo*. Shortly before the birth of Zoozoo's son, Salwa, Farid's wife, who persevered with her prediction of a new girlfriend for her girls, had baked a hundred *kol-oo-shkor* (literally, eat-and-say-thank-you): puff pastries in the shape of crescent moons with a pine kernel in each centre and coated with warm sweet syrup. These, along with Zoozoo's mother-in-law's baklawa, were now neatly arranged on trays and awaited only guests and good fortune. It was considered highly impolite to offer the sweets if either mother or child was in some way unwell.

'We'll come this afternoon,' Abou Ahmad said and stubbed out his cigarette on the ground.

'Tomorrow would be better. The wife's in bed with a temperature.'

'Allah!' exclaimed the Shiite.

'It's nothing,' said Zoozoo, taken aback by the man's emotion. 'A small fever. The midwife says it's not uncommon, especially with the first baby. She'll be fine tomorrow.'

Abou Ahmad looked unconvinced; he quoted ineptly from the Koran, '"Allah knows what every female bears: He knows of every change within her womb." The minute Ahmad was born, Im Ahmad got up to hang the washing, and with every shirt and sheet she became stronger. Fires of Hell! You need to do the same with your wife. Chase the demons, make her clean the dishes or sweep the floor. It's up to you, brother, it'll do her good. Illness preys on the lazy like a vulture. Take the baby away from her—'

'Baba! Baba!' Abou Ahmad's eight-year-old son ran up to the men, red-faced and panting.

'A woman is a mad jinnee when she can't suckle her baby, forgive-the-word. It will give her strength. There isn't an iron bar or an army of shaitans that can keep a mother from her newborn.'

'Baba!'

Abou Ahmad raised his hand and the boy cowered instinctively. 'Stop barking like a bitch on heat,' his father scolded him. 'Where are the bags?'

The boy's face turned crimson. 'I forgot them, Baba, but—'

Turning to Zoozoo, Abou Ahmad retorted, 'Inshallah bin Youssef won't be given the voice and intelligence of a sheep.'

'But Baba,' the boy said despondently, 'they're taking the water.'

They the diametrical opposite of *we* could only refer to the foreigners, the intruders: non-Ashtinis and non-farmers.

'The Fidayins,' the child added more willingly. 'The *fidei* are stealing the water.'

Zoozoo shot a glance at his plum trees, then another down the winding road to his home, where trays of sweets remained untouched on the dining table like a forbidden food; then he looked directly at the sun and was astonished to register that, in a matter of minutes, with the brief latency of water bubbling into steam, the gentle sunbeams of spring had melted into columns of searing heat.

The fever had not broken. Zoozoo's wife, Maya, lay in bed, propped up against two pillows, and writhed fitfully like a trapped animal.

'*Ya mama!*' she cried in a small girl's voice. 'Oh Lord, *rabbi. Ya mama!*'

The midwife sat on the bed and reached for Maya's hand. 'I'm here. I'm here, dear,' she said reassuringly. 'Where does it hurt, girl?'

Maya moved her hand away from the midwife's down to her hip and, still worming into the mattress, she moaned, 'There's something burning.'

Zoozoo stood rigidly, transfixed by his wife's bed-dance.

70

'I can smell it,' Maya cried hysterically, 'all around me I smell it. *Ya mama! Ya mama!*'

Instinctively, Zoozoo flared his nostrils and breathed in faint traces of sickly sweet *eau de toilette* blended with sweat.

'Nothing's burning, girl. Be reasonable, dear.' The nurse patted Maya's midriff which promptly induced a high-pitched scream.

'What are you doing?' Zoozoo shouted at the midwife.

'Nothing,' the midwife shouted back.

Maya relaxed. '*Bastirma*,' she muttered. 'Armenian *bastirma* grilled in summer, *ach*, it hurts, mama.'

'What's wrong with her?' Zoozoo said.

The nurse shook her head. 'She needs a doctor.'

'But there are no sausages. No *bastirma*.' Maya broke into tears.

'You said she had a small fever—' Zoozoo spoke angrily.

'She did.'

'That this was common.'

'It's common for young mothers to have a small temperature, but not this.'

'Well, fuck *common*'s sister. What's wrong with my wife, woman?'

'She needs a doctor, Mr Sulman,' the nurse repeated, now prim.

Ashtin was a small village, too sparsely populated to warrant a clinic, let alone a hospital; the closest doctor would be found 30 kilometres away in Saïda.

'A doctor,' he said abstractedly and nodded. He moved to the bed and sat close to Maya's face with his back to the midwife.

Maya turned slowly to peer at her husband. 'Zoozoo, ya, Zoozoo. I'm weak as your baby son.'

He had his hand on her cheek and felt the dry heat of a rising fever.

Maya sat up suddenly, startling him, and said agitatedly, 'Don't let them take him away.'

71

Zoozoo realized he had neither seen nor heard his son since the morning. 'Where's Khalil?' he asked, turning.

The midwife pointed to a corner of the room furthest from the bed. On a settee sat Salwa, Farid's wife, with one hand resting on a bundle of swaddling-clothes and the other firmly grasping a small bottle of perfume in a vaporizer.

'Don't let them take Khalil.'

'The fever,' the nurse explained.

'It's the water,' Salwa declared and squirted some fluid into the room.

'What water?'

'The blue ones,' Maya whispered fearfully.

'The water used to clean her was unclean.'

'It was not,' the midwife protested loudly. 'The water was boiled clean. You saw. You were with me. I've delivered—'

'I saw them, Zoozoo, around our son.'

'—thousands of babies.'

'I was here.' Salwa nodded. 'Clean without dirt, but unclean with spirits.'

The nurse got up. 'All this nonsense,' she shrilled. 'You'll kill yourselves with superstition.'

Maya screamed. 'I can see them now, Zoozoo! Kill them!' She pushed him off the bed.

Salwa jumped to her feet. 'See? Nonsense? You know nothing. Nothing at all.' She added to Zoozoo, 'I wanted to use holy water to clean Maya but this—'

'Everyone shut up,' yelled Zoozoo. 'Just shut up. I need to think.'

'They're taking my baby.' Maya collapsed.

'No-one's taking our baby,' he shouted at her.

'They'll eat him like a sausage,' she said with rising panic. 'Can't you smell the *bastirma*?'

'All I can smell is that whore-perfume – stop spraying that in here.'

'It's holy water,' Salwa complained, 'with a little fragrance against the mosquitoes.'

'What your wife needs, Mr Sulman, is a doctor not holy water.'

'She needs a priest,' Salwa stated flatly.

Zoozoo looked at her, shocked. 'A priest', he said in a hushed voice, 'is for dying people. My wife doesn't need a priest.'

The baby made a gurgling noise. Salwa turned and squirted four parts holy water, one part *eau de toilette* in his direction.

'I'm bringing the car around,' Zoozoo decided. 'Wrap her up tightly.'

He rushed out of the house. Outside, Farid was waiting impatiently.

'How is she?' he asked anxiously.

Zoozoo shook his head. 'I'd be king if I knew what was wrong with her. She's pale as a shaitan and hot as hell. I need to take her to Saïda.'

Farid frowned. 'Road's not safe.'

Zoozoo opened his Datsun and switched on the engine. 'I'll fly to the hospital, then.'

'I mean, Ashtin's blocked off.'

'What? When?'

'The *fidei*. They've closed all the roads. Building secret bunkers just outside town. Filling cisterns of our water for their cement.'

'My dick's in their cement.'

'Maybe Maya would be better here,' Farid said.

'We're going to Saïda.' Zoozoo opened the back door and wiped the dust off the back seat with a tissue.

Farid looked up at the sky. Night was falling fast. 'Wait till the morning.'

'Maya needs a doctor now.'

Farid nodded. 'I'll come with you, then.'

'No, stay here. Look after Khalil for me. We may be gone a few days.'

With the engine left running the men entered the house, the bedroom, and carried Maya, now swathed in

73

her sheets and blanket, off the bed and onto the back seat of the Datsun.

Salwa and the midwife followed in funereal silence.

'God be with you,' Farid said as Zoozoo climbed into the driver's seat.

'Phone the Berberi Hospital,' Zoozoo said. 'Talk to a woman-doctor and tell him to expect us.'

Farid nodded.

'Wait,' Salwa called out. She had a rosary wound around her wrist like bracelets which she uncoiled and, opening the back door, placed in Maya's hand. 'May you return to us in health.'

'*Ya mama*,' Maya exclaimed, 'I can smell them on you.' She clasped the rosary to her bosom. Salwa looked unsettled as Farid slammed the door shut.

Zoozoo drove off, past his house, his orchards, the village square and the Casino Ashtin where Abou Ahmad, sipping coffee through the gap in his front teeth, spotted him.

'Allah,' he muttered under his breath. 'That boy's mad. Mad as his father, Abou Zooz, Allah rest his soul.' No-one but a madman would think to drive on such a day. 'Must have jinnee blood in the family.' Abou Ahmad nodded to himself and lit a cigarette.

Fidei is a freak coincidence, one of those rare words in the evolution of tongues that purports to link a dead with a living language, Indo-European with Semitic. In contemporary Arabic, *fidei* is translated as sacrificing oneself for a cause; in classical Latin, it is the genitive case of *fides,* and means of the faith. It is therefore coincidental that the Roman root offers itself for service in the Middle East. Predominantly Muslim Fidayin fighters sought justification for their acts of self-sacrifice in Islamic literature. Their jihad in Lebanon was for the lost fatherland and the divine message of God. Regardless of the fact that the archangel Gabriel had never whispered a word about attacking Mount

74

Lebanon; nor indeed, that the lost fatherland was a hundred kilometres due south.

Hassan was no *fidei*; not in the Arabic, Latin, or any other contrived sense of the word. He was just bored. Bored from the moment he was born, it seemed to him. He had never been to school and would probably have hated it anyway: his childhood days before the war were tedious enough, selling Chiclets chewing-gum on one of Beirut's boulevards. The only time life appeared almost worth living – when Hassan awoke in the mornings with an unaccustomed sense of purpose – was at the beginning of the war when he joined the PLO. He became a Fidayin for three reasons: because he was Palestinian, feeling the urge to flock to the banner; because he was Muslim, enlightened as to the just cause; but above all, Hassan signed up because his best friend, George, his only friend in Beirut, had joined the PLO's rivals, the local Christian militia. Naturally, Hassan had never disclosed this third reason.

The war had provided the perfect forum for a new and more adventurous game: the adult version of earlier games of cowboys and Indians. Almost adult, he was sixteen at the outbreak. As an Indian, he had always lost to George, the Greek Orthodox cowboy. Hassan had felt confident that as a *fidei*, he would thrash the PNL militiaman. Of course, he had not expected the war to last so long, to drag so nauseatingly and become so mindlessly boring.

Since his transfer from Beirut, he had fired his Kalashnikov only sixteen times, and every volley had been in the air: six times against overflying Israeli jets, and ten salvoes to celebrate Muslim feast days. A Fidayin comrade-in-arms had once remarked that shooting down an F-15 with a bullet was like tripping a cheetah with a well-aimed pebble – totally feasible *only* if one did not think of the odds and placed utter faith in God. Which suited Hassan just fine as he was no mathematician and believed in God, though in his conceited version, the Merciful and Compassionate was a Hassan-fearing deity who could be respectively bullied and hoodwinked into granting a patch in the Garden of Eternal Springs.

Hassan stood out in a brigade of Fidayins because of a hammer he carried in his left hand. It was a quite ordinary hammer of the kind that might be found in any tool-box, alongside wrenches and spanners. But firm in the grasp of a militiaman, with the other hand toting a Kalashnikov, the hammer became the deadliest instrument of death, conjecturing images of bludgeoned massacres, of barbaric loot and plunder Viking-style. It worked a treat on the civilian population. Everyone had seen a machine-gun; most people had even had one pointed at them at some stage in the long war. But a hammer was so terrifyingly novel, so incongruous to twentieth-century weaponry, that immediate unquestioning respect was offered to the Hammer-Wielder.

Hassan twirled his hammer in his fingers with the expertise of a majorette. Today he was less bored than usual. Today Hassan was a hero. The *fidei* stood next to a Mercedes 180, over a dead man's body. As he looked down at the man splayed at his feet, the militiaman's mouth curved into a grin. He wished he could be sent a spy every day.

The enemy, Hassan had realized, knew about the secret PLO bunkers being constructed. Needing to pinpoint their target, the Mossad had sent an agent who posed as a Lebanese civilian. The Jews were clever that way. Their best agents were quite inconspicuous, their very bodies served as camouflage, made them appear innocent. For the most important assignments Israel mobilized its women and old men. But Hassan was more intelligent than the Mossad; he had seen through the disguise, and had stopped and killed the Jew.

The *fidei* returned to the oil barrel that barricaded the northern road into Ashtin. Ordinarily, manning a roadblock when everyone observed a curfew was particularly unbearable – he swung his hammer and dented the oil drum – but today was different; his heart still pounded with excitement. He felt the uneven dent in the barrel and again considered how different it felt to a dented skull.

He swung his hammer again as another car drove up to the roadblock; this time from Ashtin, and this time a Datsun. Not a Peugeot, he thought with regret. Hassan hated all Peugeots.

'*Bismillah-ar-Rahman-ar-Raheem*,' Zoozoo said.

Hassan cradled his hammer and walked around the car, pausing to peer at the woman lying on the back seat.

'You're not Muslim. You've no Allah sticker in your car.'

'Allah is Allah.' Zoozoo bowed his head reverently.

'Yours isn't merciful or compassionate.' Hassan sneered. 'Papers.'

Zoozoo handed him his ID and car registration.

'And hers,' ordered Hassan.

Zoozoo gave him Maya's ID. 'She's not well. We're going to the hospital in Saïda.'

Hassan grunted contemptuously, leaned on the bonnet, placed his hammer against the windscreen on the left wiper, and examined the papers.

'Maronite. Youssef Sulman. Maronite. Maya Sulman.' Hassan glared at the driver and said menacingly, 'Next time, you don't say, *Bismillah-ar-Rahman-ar-Raheem*, you say, in the name of Maron the pimp's slave. Go on say it.'

'*Bism Maroun a'abd el-a'akrout*,' Zoozoo said, betraying no hesitation.

'You got weapons?'

'No, sir.'

Maya screamed, 'He's blue, Zoozoo, he's blue!'

'Shut up, woman!'

'What did she call me?' growled Hassan.

'My wife's very ill,' Zoozoo apologized. 'She must go to hospital.'

'Blue?' Had the bitch insulted him? 'Is your cunt-wife mad as a jinnee?'

Zoozoo gripped the steering-wheel and spoke deliberately. 'She has a fever. She gave birth and she's very tired.' Zoozoo, glaring straight ahead, saw the Mercedes. The boot was open, and on the ground he spotted a pair of legs protruding from behind the car.

'Road's closed.'

'Forgive me, I didn't know.' Zoozoo was thinking quickly. To survive you never discussed with a militiaman, particularly when death lay a few metres away. 'I'll take my wife back to bed in Ashtin.'

Their eyes met.

Zoozoo turned rapidly to look at his wife.

Guilty, Hassan judged. He had seen the Maronite glancing at the Mercedes, and at the fallen Jew. The spy had been on his way to Ashtin to congratulate a friend on the birth of his son; that was the cover the Mossad agent had given him. Here, in the Datsun, were the Jew's collaborators, cleverly disguised as a local with his *sick* wife in the back. The collaborators had come to see why their friend was so late – and now they had seen. Hassan grinned; the Mossad was no match for him.

'Back to Ashtin?' Hassan was still grinning. 'I thought you had to go to the hospital in Saïda?'

Zoozoo nodded cautiously. 'I'd be grateful if you'd let me pass.'

'Of course I'll let you pass. Your wife's ill, isn't she?'

'Yes, sir.'

Lying pimp, Hassan thought as he handed the driver back his papers. He waved him through.

'Thank you, sir.' Zoozoo put the car into gear and drove around the oil barrel and past the Mercedes, without pausing to glance at the dead man.

Maya started to scream again. '*Ya mama, ya rabbi.*'

'Shut up, will you! I curse all the Palestinian mothers who bore that whoreson's ancestors.'

'He's one of them,' Maya screamed. 'He wants our baby.'

Hassan dropped his hammer and waited for the car to drive a certain distance down the road before levelling his Kalashnikov. The collaborators had tried to break out, he would explain to his superiors. But the *fidei* had stopped them in time from reporting to their Mossad bosses. Hassan was a hero. He had uncovered and destroyed the Ashtini spy ring all on his own. He aimed and squeezed the trigger.

When Zoozoo heard the first shots, he panicked and stepped on the accelerator.

'*Ya rabbi! Ya rabbi!*'

The militiaman emptied the magazine. There was no need for divine intervention to guide the bullets; they all found their marks on the Datsun, riddling the body with a satisfying pock-pock-pock-pock.

The Datsun crashed into a tree. Hassan stooped to pick up his hammer and approached the car with a leisurely gait. He wished there were more days like this.

Maya had stopped screaming.

The searing pain in Zoozoo's chest had yielded to a general numbness, and now to a feathery sensation that the slightest breeze might pick up on its way. Cool, grey tranquillity. An autumnal twilight.

Zoozoo opened his eyes to the sky. A crescent moon was fiery orange in an ocean of red, with dotted islands of yellow as bilious clouds; a mountain of purple. He saw a being approach him. The closer it came, the smaller it became. A child with a toy hammer, pointed ears and blue skin.

So this is what happens when you die, Zoozoo thought, colours play tricks on you.

The pain returned and the colours of the rainbow intermixed furiously, fusing to form a uniform black.

*   *   *

Salwa had read it in her cup and now, on the day of the aborted baptism, saw it confirmed in the cards: they should not keep the baby.

She believed she had a talent for reading the future in the grainy residue of Turkish coffee. A gift, her grandmother had once told her, that cannot be taught. Reading cups was not a visual technique like understanding illustrations in a book. One had to *feel* the implications of a particular whorl, to *sense* the order in the random sediment. Only then was one able to see such things as happiness, misfortune and death.

To date, the only blatant error in Salwa's predictions had been concerning the sex of the late couple's child. In retrospect, she now believed the image of a girl had not been as crystal clear as she would have liked. Maya's cup had been cloudy, ominously blurred, and Salwa had read it with difficulty, as if straining at the features through a forbidding veil. She thought she saw a girl and said as much. Naturally, Salwa had not mentioned the doubtful, ominous aspect of the sludge – after all, there was a woman about to have a child.

Allah rest her soul, she thought.

It was that baby. That baby was the jinx that had brought evil spirits to Ashtin. Maya had seen them around her baby. They had caused the tragedies, the senseless murders, and they had concealed the baby's sex when it was still in its mother's womb. That baby boy was unclean, which is why she named him Shit – *Khara*.

Salwa called the spirits aloud, mopped the floors of her home with detergent and holy water, sang religious hymns as she bottle-fed little Khara in order to dispel the jinx. All jinn, good and evil, hated being discovered. By calling the baby Shit, she hoped to drive the spirits away from her family.

She called him Khara in private because Farid refused to understand, would have none of *that* in his house.

80

'Well, what do you think Maya saw?' Salwa had asked him the morning of the twin funerals.

'Shaitans, jinn, how the devil should I know?' Farid adjusted the black armband and looked at himself in the mirror.

'Well then.'

'I've already told you,' Farid said impatiently, 'it was the fever. *Berberal*. That's what the doctor from the Berberi said.' Farid straightened his black tie.

Maya had suffered from puerperal fever. Farid mused, '*Berberal* from Berberi.'

'So?'

'So she saw things. It doesn't mean anything – it was the fever.' Farid shook his head sadly and restraightened his tie. 'Poor Zoozoo, ya Zoozoo. She would have been fine in a few days.'

'She didn't need a doctor – I told him that.'

'She didn't need a priest either.'

Salwa shrugged. 'What about the baby then?'

'Khalil stays with us.'

'He can't stay.'

Farid uttered the terms of endearment sarcastically: 'My love, my heart, may you bury me inshallah. It was my friend's dying wish that I should look after his son.'

'He wasn't dying when he asked you.'

Farid turned to glare at her.

'He didn't know, did he,' Salwa argued. 'He was only going to Saïda.'

Farid kicked a chair and punched a wall. 'Damn it, woman, Khalil Joseph Sulman is now a member of our family.'

'But he's got a grandmother,' Salwa said placatingly. 'She would be a better mother to him.'

'Maya's mother is ninety.'

'No she's not.'

'She'll be dead by the time he starts playschool.' Farid had tears in his eyes. 'I couldn't help Zoozoo but I can help his son.' He cleared his throat and dusted his sleeves. 'Now come on, let's get this church service over and done with.'

'We need to talk to the priest about baptism.'

He nodded. 'Later. One ceremony at a time.'

'The boy needs to be baptized.'

'Khalil,' Farid said. 'The boy has a name.'

'Not until he's baptized. Khalil is a Christian name. That boy isn't Christian yet.'

'You're right,' he conceded, but Salwa knew he did not understand the implications, the life-and-death importance of being immersed in holy water. Evil spirits were consumed by holy water like snakes in acid.

The baptism was to have taken place the day after the funerals.

The small church was well attended for the second day running, with much the same crowd, wearing the same sombre clothes, bearing the same bereaved expressions. On the first day Ashtinis – Christians and Muslims – had turned up *en masse* out of solidarity for the brutal killings of the Sulmans. But on this, the second day of mourning, the Shiites were markedly absent as the Maronites paid their respects, one last time, by witnessing the poor orphan's baptism.

Farid and Salwa were the godparents and stood on either side of Zoozoo and Maya. The naked baby, wrapped in a towel, slept peacefully in Maya's arms. Of course, the real Zoozoo and Maya were close enough in the church cemetery, rapidly decomposing in the unseasonably hot spring day.

The two acting parents, both teenagers and both virgins anyway, had volunteered to play family for a day to see *their* child baptized. Under Lebanese law, godparents could automatically adopt an orphaned godchild; however, only the second of kin could adopt an unchristened child.

Thus the explanation for the bizarre make-believe. Khalil Joseph Sulman would be baptized on 28 May 1982 in the arms of his loving parents, witnessed by the godparents Farid and Salwa (and the rest of Ashtin's Maronite community). The parents would meet with a tragic death four days later, they would be buried two days later, as duly noted by the registrar, and on the seventh day – the day of the actual christening – the godparents would file for adoption.

No-one saw the harm in the deception, not the village priest, Abouna Sharbel, nor the notary who sat in the front row with a black armband and a black handkerchief protruding from his breast pocket. Had Lebanese law been a reality in Ashtin, the murderer would have been hanged, or better still, the real parents would be holding their baby in an empty church.

'*Shalomo lakolkon*,' Abouna Sharbel greeted in Aramaic.

'*Wa-a'am rioosha dishlom*,' replied the congregation, '*Hallellooya.*'

He intoned a long prayer, which the congregation ended with '*Aameen*', before reverting to Arabic. 'Who brings this child to be baptized?'

'We do,' Zoozoo said in a cracked voice. 'Joseph Khalil Sulman and his wife Maya.'

'Who are to be the witnesses?'

'We are.' Farid and Salwa stepped forward.

Addressing Farid, Abouna Sharbel said, 'Do you believe in God and in His blessed son, Jesus the Messiah?'

'I do.'

'And do you believe in the catholic and apostolic church of our Lord, Jesus the Messiah?'

'I do.'

'And do you denounce the shaitan and all who follow him?'

'I do.'

The baby woke up and cried.

Maya's stand-in revealed her inexperience as a mother when she jumped, almost dropping her son.

Babies cried at baptisms, Salwa knew, but the timing was particularly uncanny.

This reduced the tension in the church; several people coughed, someone chuckled, and Abouna Sharbel, smiling indulgently, extended his arms for the baby. The girl gratefully handed him over the font.

'Hold on to the towel,' the priest whispered to her. 'There's no need to christen the towel.'

The girl nodded and blushed.

'*Aybazot yazen*,' Abouna Sharbel chanted in Aramaic, in the tongue of the Christ, holding the child high in both hands, facing the congregation.

The baby was screaming. Tears ran down his puffy red cheeks and urine escaped from his penis, arcing into the font of holy water, a garden cherub's into a pond.

No-one chuckled; no-one coughed. The noise was deafening. The church shook violently. A lead crucifix by the entrance fell on the stoup, chipping the marble. The explosion was followed by mortar and machine-gun fire.

'The Israelis are bombing Ashtin,' someone cried.

There was general pandemonium. Some women wailed; others gripped their mouths. Some men jumped to their feet looking furtive; others hugged their knees in a crash position.

'Everyone go home,' the notary shouted. 'We—'

The second shell drowned his voice.

Abouna Sharbel thrust the baby into Salwa's arms and shouted, 'Stay here! It's safer than on the streets.'

Farid made a sign to Salwa and they, their three girls, and their not-yet-Christian ward ran back to their home, a squat residence that would be a less conspicuous target than the house of God.

The Israelis, however, were indifferent about the Maronite church and the Ashtinis who were scuttling out of it like ants. To give the pilots credit, reconnoitre missions had pinpointed the Fidayin bunkers well before the villagers themselves, a full week before the murders of the Sulmans. This was a tactical attack, like squirting toilet-bowl fluid on obstinate stains and leaving it overnight. The true date of Khara's near-baptism was 4 June 1982, just three days before the PLO would be flushed out of the southern half of Lebanon.

In the short interlude, peace and spring returned to Ashtin.

Salwa shuffled the cards and concentrated on the question again: Should they keep the boy?

She ran her fingers along the edge of the pack, *feeling* the cards, then she cut the pack and dealt a hand of standard solitaire. The answer would depend on the outcome of the game: Yes, for success; No, for failure. There were degrees of Yes and No: a game that almost succeeded represented a Maybe. This was her third attempt at the same question. So far the answers had both been No.

She became blocked on the second run – an emphatic No.

She shuffled the cards and, turning the question around, dealt another hand.

Should they give the child away?

Yes. (Definite. All four aces had dropped from the start.)

Would Farid be very upset?

Yes. (But this had been a difficult hand: Farid would be a bit upset.)

Should they give him to the grandmother?

No.

That made sense, Salwa thought. The grandmother was not ninety, but she was getting to be decrepit and would probably have handed him back to them. Again she shuffled and dealt.

Would the boy be baptized?

No.

Was he a jinx to Ashtin?

Yes.

Salwa's hands went cold as she focused on the next question.

Is the boy evil?

85

Yes.
Is he evil?
Yes.
Is Khara Sulman evil?
Yes.

'Can't you hear him?' Farid had entered the room.

'What?'

'Khalil. He's crying for his milk, poor thing.' Farid knelt beside the sofa – a makeshift cot – and tickled the boy. 'Yee. You like that, don't you. Yoo. That stopped you crying. Yee yee yoo. You cute boy. Yee.'

'I'll go and feed him,' Salwa said flatly, and picked Khara off the sofa.

The baby started to cry again.

I'll feed you today, Salwa thought, and tonight, and tomorrow morning and no more.

She had taken her decision.

The Christian militiaman woke up, kissed the cross around his neck and folded his blanket.

'Why do you do that?' asked another man.

The first soldier, Fouad, smoothed his bushy moustache and looked at him.

The other man was called Hajj – every Nicholas in Lebanon was named Hajj for an inexplicable reason Fouad lost no sleep over. He had to fight with him, but liking Hajj was an optional extra.

'Since we've been together,' Hajj said, 'the first thing you do is kiss that cross.'

'Because I wake up to find you're still alive.'

Fouad reached for a pack of cigarettes, lit one, and put some water on the camping gas stove.

In order to unify the different Christian militias, to form one big happy family, fighters from various parties had been asked to band together. This was a scatter-brained policy, Fouad thought. In a nutty world.

For instance, here was Hajj, a Greek Catholic in a

Maronite militia, asking a Maronite in a predominantly Greek Orthodox militia about Greek crosses.

The crucifix in question was far too large for any man below the rank of Greek patriarch. It was a silver cross, inlaid with a multitude of semi-precious stones, garish around the neck of a militiaman, and far too ornate for a Maronite's usual taste – Maronites preferred plainer crosses like the thin daggers painted in red on Phalangist tanks. Fouad had requisitioned this piece, his talisman, off a street pedlar who had probably burgled someone's home – a patriarch's or a cross-collector's.

Politically, Fouad was Greek Orthodox to the core, but when he said Greek, his tone betrayed the scorn he felt for those who were not *true* Catholics. As a Maronite, he had been approached on numerous occasions by Phalangists who attempted to lure him away from his Greek Orthodox lieutenants by, among other ploys, promising him a monthly wage – Fouad was from a dying breed of amateur militiamen. He had declined diplomatically when he should have told them to 'go back to your damned mountain', but one had to be smart, and the Phalangist Party was far larger than his own, not to say stronger.

Fouad was born and bred a Beiruti; all his grandparents had been Beirutis. For a millennium, Beirut had been shared by the Greek Orthodox and Sunni Muslims and it would have been reasonable – if reason, like the alphabet, had been a Phoenician invention – for these two communities to ally against the invaders of their city, notably, Hajj and his kindred Greek Catholics from the Bekaa Valley, the Shiites from the south, and the Druses and Maronites from Mount Lebanon.

At the outbreak of hostilities, the Greek neighbourhoods had been in the front line and the Greek militias had fought bitterly and savagely for their homes, and for the last remaining pocket of Christendom in the Middle East, while the Phalangists procrastinated and preached from their mountain tops. They were thinkers, not doers and Fouad despised them. There would have been no *free* Lebanon had the fate of the Christians been left exclusively in the hands of the Phalangists; they were the contemporary equivalents of the Greek scholars of Constantinople, who had debated the number of angels one could hold on a pinhead as the hordes of Muslims rammed the city door.

It was indeed a scatterbrained idea to force him to share a sniper outpost with a Greek Catholic Phalangist. The policy-makers were away with the jinn, Fouad thought, touched in the head.

He poured himself a cup of Turkish coffee, stirred in three spoonfuls of sugar and lit another cigarette.

'Can I have a coffee?' Hajj asked.

Fouad shrugged. 'Help yourself.' He got up, moved to the section of the tenth-floor flat where a living-room wall had pre-existed, and gazed out, between the sandbags, at the sprawling southern suburbs.

'I swear it grows every day I look,' he said softly.

'What's that?' Hajj asked.

Fouad ignored him. Fortunately for Nicholas, Fouad loathed Shiites considerably more than Greek Phalangists. He hated everything about them: their unwashed stink, the way every family bred a wholesale number of children, the black chadors that draped Shiite women (though that was a blessing in disguise, as Fouad believed Shiite women to be as horrendous as witches), the pathetic show of self-inflicted wounds on the Muslim feast of A'ashoura.

Fouad scanned the squalor of the southern suburbs. Facing his fortified positions were the Shiite Amal strongholds and the recently formed new demons on the block, Hezbollah: the ultra-Shiite Party of God which Fouad ultra-hated. He had killed many Shiites, mostly civilians, and would kill many more.

'Animals, aren't they?' he said absently.

'Muslims?' Hajj asked.

Fouad smoothed his moustache. 'Shiites. Look at that jungle out there.'

'They live in the fifteenth century,' the Phalangist said. 'They want to take us back there with them.'

Fouad kissed his cross and swung it around onto his back. 'Even bears and lions wash.' He picked up his Austrian long-range rifle, lethal up to 2 kilometres, unclipped the magazine, checked the bullets and recharged his rifle. 'Back to work,' he said and leaned on a sandbag, the rifle hard against his shoulder.

'We really can't live with them,' Hajj said.

Fouad ignored him; he had turned his back on him as he looked down the range-finder. The semi-precious stones on the crucifix caught the first rays of daylight and Hajj shook his head.

The roads out of Ashtin were open to traffic once more. No-one could inform the Israelis of any secret Palestinian hide-out that had not been amply charted by the Tomcats. It was four-thirty in the morning and still pitch-dark when Salwa drove up to the PLO check-point, half an hour before the first ground troops would converge on the Israeli side of the border.

'Where are you going?' the Fidayin asked Salwa.

'To Beirut.'

'This early?'

'An emergency. My mother's in hospital.'

'Where's your husband?' the Palestinian demanded gruffly.

'At home.' Salwa shrugged, adding, 'He doesn't like her.'

The militiaman waved her on, uninterested. Had he been more alert, he might have wondered at the baby, asleep on the front seat.

The Franciscan Orphanage for Boys was in the Manara district of north-west Beirut, called the Lighthouse neighbourhood because of Beirut's extinguished beacon which, in previous centuries, had warned ships of the city's rocky promontory jutting into the Mediterranean like a Cro-Magnon skull. The road from Ashtin should have been straightforward. Once onto the southern highway, it was north – with the sea visibly to the left – all the way to the headland and the Lighthouse district, marking the city's nasal cavity.

However, past the airport, the road was blocked with oil barrels and a militiaman gesticulated at Salwa to draw back.

'I need to get to Manara,' she shouted across to him.

'Snipers,' he replied and indicated a minor road. 'Try from there.'

Salwa nodded and, with the Beirut skyline softly silhouetted by the rising sun so tantalizingly close, she turned right into the southern suburbs. She drove along the maze of roads for a full five minutes before realizing she was hopelessly lost. She stopped to ask a woman in a black chador for directions. The woman regarded her suspiciously and asked her where she was from.

'The south,' Salwa replied.

'I don't know,' the woman said tersely and walked away.

Salwa felt uneasy. She was still in mourning, gratefully in her long black dress, but she should have thought about a headscarf. Here in the southern suburbs, the little that remained of Lebanon's confused but multicultural identity was buried deep underground. Here, even the air was unquestionably Shiite, and Salwa was not merely a stranger but an outright alien.

The dilapidated apartment blocks which had lined the coastal road had abruptly given way to a jumbled, bedevilling array of slum dwellings. The roads, now unmetalled dirt-tracks, were too narrow and hazardous to reverse the car; forward was the only option, downward into the black hole of brick and corrugated iron. The walls were black with grime, deadened further by the many faded portraits of Khomeini and fallen martyrs. The air was polluted, thickened by urine, caca and rot, enveloping the huts like a hothouse so that Salwa's eyes burned and her stomach churned.

She was scared.

Despite the early hour, men and boys in dirty underwear and T-shirts emerged at the unfamiliar sound of a car. One man, scratching his testicles through his shorts, flagged her down with his free hand.

'Where are you going?' he demanded.

Salwa told him. 'Please, how can I get there?'

The man released his balls to wave expansively with both hands. 'You are in Manara,' he said, grinning inanely. 'Welcome to Manara.'

A small crowd gathered around the car. 'You need a pass to come here,' a youth said. He wore a revolver, slung around his waist like a cowboy, and appropriately enough, a torn sweatshirt with the faint words, 'Chicago Bulls'.

'Where's your pass?'

'Allah show you kindness. I must get to Manara.'

'That means she's got no pass,' a small boy piped.

The youth slapped the boy's head and said, 'You can buy a pass from us.'

'I've got no money.'

'But she's got a baby,' the boy said. 'See?'

The cowboy picked up the boy by his soiled vest. 'Shut up, mule, see?' He drop-kicked the boy.

'You come here with no money?' the nut-scratcher complained. 'You have no gifts for us? That's not polite – shame on you.'

'We'll take the car,' the youth said evenly.

'No,' Salwa cried. 'Please.'

'Come on, get out.' The youth, hand on gun, opened the driver's door.

A man, washed, with a well-groomed beard, and fully dressed in army fatigues pushed through the crowd. 'What's in Manara?' he asked.

'Please. Allah give you long life.' Salwa trembled and

91

pleaded tearfully with the youth. 'A mortal sin, that's what you're doing – a *haram*. What would your poor mother say? Where is she? Let her see this.'

'Come.' The cowboy youth smirked. 'I'll take you to her.'

Several in the crowd chuckled.

'Why are you going to Manara?' the militiaman repeated, putting a restraining hand on the youth's shoulder.

'This baby's poor mother. She was very ill – I was looking after her son. She's in Manara. *Haram* if you don't let me take him to her.'

'So why—' the youth began. The soldier squeezed his shoulder. '*Ach*, you're hurting me.'

'Where are you from, Auntie?' the man asked Salwa.

'Ashtin.'

The militiaman smiled. 'Place of the apples, right?'

She nodded. 'Plums and peaches – especially plums.'

The man's smile grew broader and kinder. 'I had an uncle in Ashtin before the Palestinians moved in. Lovely country.'

Salwa nodded again.

'I'll show you the way to Manara,' he said, closed her door and walked around to the passenger side.

'Does she have plums for us?' the small boy asked. The youth in the Chicago Bulls sweatshirt kicked him again.

'I'll put the baby in the back,' Salwa said.

'No. I like babies, it's all right.' He lifted Khara and sat with the baby on his lap.

Salwa almost stalled the car as they drove off.

'Do you want me to drive, Auntie?'

She shook her head.

'First right.' He pointed and tickled Khara. 'Cute. What's his name?'

'Khalil Sulman.'

'Khalil? Christians?'

'Yes.'

'Maronites, then, seeing you're from Ashtin.'

'Yes.'

'At least you're not Greeks.'

By another trick of magic the scenery changed dramatically. They drove onto a main road, truncated at the far end by large metal containers – stolen from the port to act as impregnable barriers. On either side the slum dwellings had receded suddenly, like a beast in the face of danger. Here the houses were pitted beyond recognition. Walls dropped off, façades crumbled; a leper colony for diseased buildings.

'The Green Line,' Salwa exclaimed.

'Yes.'

'What are we doing here?' Her voice trembled with renewed fear.

'I need to see someone. I won't be more than ten minutes,' the soldier said, and added earnestly, 'I promise I'll take you to Manara. You have the word of Abdullah Shawqi.'

Salwa nodded slowly. 'Just tell me how to get to Manara, please.'

'I won't leave you on your own. It's no place for a woman or baby. Trust me, Auntie. Now come, leave the car here, we'll walk to the base. I'll make some coffee, talk to my captain, and then take you to Manara. Come.'

Salwa turned the engine off and followed the militiaman with Khara in her arms. She looked at the red, yellow and blue containers, so bright in contrast to the decaying buildings, and she thanked God it was a peaceful day on the front.

Fouad, the Maronite in the Greek militia, had the family in his sights a full two seconds before squeezing the trigger. What a fool that Hezbollah militiaman was, Fouad thought, to bring his wife – in black, naturally – and their baby. He was an ace marksman, which was the real reason the Phalangists wanted him. A perfect shot, right between the eyes. Serves him right, that Shiite ass.

'You shit,' Hajj shouted. He looked at the scene through binoculars. 'You whore-shit.'

Fouad ignored him and trained his rifle on another target.

'You could have killed the Hezbollahi,' Hajj shouted.

'So?'

'So why the shaitan's piss didn't you?'

'He's only one,' Fouad replied dispassionately. 'I just killed at least six future Hezbollahis.'

'You're mad. A mad son-of-whore. What're you shooting at now? You a baby-killer too?' Hajj pushed him and the shot went awry.

'I'll kill *you* if you touch me again.'

The baby, covered in blood, was crying on the dead woman.

'Shoot at them!' Abdullah Shawqi ordered. 'Cover me!'

Four militiamen emerged and fired their Kalashnikovs randomly at East Beirut.

Abdullah sprinted, lifted the child and ran back to shelter.

'Those murderous dogs,' a militiaman cursed.

'Thank Allah he's all right,' Abdullah said, running his fingers over the baby.

'Who was she?'

The nameless auntie from Ashtin remained inert, eyes fixed on the blue sky.

'What are you going to do with her son?'

'*Her* son?' Abdullah looked at the baby, baptized in blood. 'Don't cry, little one. It's all right now. You're safe.'

'Haa? Abdullah? What will you do with him?'

'He is my uncle's son from Ashtin,' Abdullah said softly. He turned, regarded the militiaman and added, 'His name is Khaled Sulman.'

4

THE COCKROACH RACE

The war in Lebanon officially ended on 13 October 1990 when the Syrians, putting the nation out of its protracted misery, invaded the rebellious Christian enclave. Hameeda Ashraf celebrated the occasion by treating herself to a bottle of her favourite perfume, Constance de Caros.

The end of the war had not been a happy affair, there were no revellers on the streets, no firework displays. Nevertheless, Hameeda used the outbreak of peace as a justifiable reason to replenish her stock, as viable as the more orthodox gift-offering feasts of Adha and Fitr. She was an *habituée*, and all pretexts ring true to an addict. Every night, before going to bed, she brushed her teeth, washed her face, and sprinkled some Constance behind her ears and across her neck. It was a peculiar habit given that Hameeda, outside the bathroom, was anything but coquettish. At fifty-eight, she crawled into an empty bed as she had done for fifty-odd years, ever since an older sister had moved out of their bed to get married.

Hameeda was a perfume-head in a very real sense. When she finished delicately sprinkling her skin in front of the bathroom mirror, she brought the bottle to her lips to consume some perfume. Never more than a sip, in order to allow the fragrance to permeate through her entire body – the addict's rationalization. It would have shocked Hameeda to discover that it was the alcohol content in her favourite Constance which her palate had acquired a particular taste for. Perfume and kohl were, she knew, Arab inventions and therefore permissibles, *halal*. Alcohol was a Western invention and thus a *haram*. She was ignorant of the finer details: the fact that the two were first cousins in the same chemical process, or that the Western words for the sinful brew bore an Arabic root.

Her surname, Ashraf, meaning an-honour-to-meet, did her no justice at all. She had the temperament of a bullmule, a unique hybrid whose moods swing violently from raging to stubborn, and the looks of a hippowhale. In Hameeda's case, her addiction to perfume was, besides being a foible, *almost* a saving grace – obnoxious and obese as she was, at least her odour was sweet. Almost. No man had ever ventured close enough to discover her aphrodisiac scent.

If she were at all curious about sex she neither showed it nor insinuated it. The word itself was not in her vocabulary. She used obscure Koranic metaphors to describe *it* to her children, talking of 'divine interconnection of men and women' and 'gardens of eternal life in the fruits of men'. She left the remaining account, the actual copulation, up to their and her own imaginations. Breeding was for the future's sake, not the present's. And Hameeda, as the mother of twenty-four boys, believed she had no further need for matrimony.

Immaculate she was not. To imply that she was a genuine mother whose womb had worked overtime would be to describe miracles. From the age of thirty Hameeda had volunteered to work as a foster-mother in the Islamic Foundation for Boys, a charity set up by the Hezbollah to feed, shelter and educate Shiite orphans. Unlike orphanages, the Foundation's aim was to provide boys, till the age of sixteen, with a truly familial atmosphere: a home they would call their own, a full-time mother and brothers. Fifteen homes and a school had been constructed in Beirut's southern suburbs, each home catered for a mother and ten boys, and all fell under the general tutelage of a man who was respected by all as the Sayyed – Sir.

Hameeda Ashraf was Mother Thirteen. The numbers were assigned not by order of merit but for accountancy purposes – mothers titled their budgetary reports with their respective numbers. However, had this foster-harem been veritable, Hameeda would not have been higher than the Sayyed's thirteenth wife.

But her aim in life was not to serve any man, not to be the 'oasis of happiness to a thirsty believer', rather to instil the fear of Allah in her children. She had raised fourteen boys, and was raising a further ten, with the firm conviction and severe discipline of a militant Ghazi. It was her vocation. Her children grew up spoonfed on truth, fully versed in the Koran and the teachings of Muhammad and Ali – peace and blessings be upon them, as Hameeda always added. She saw it as her duty to be strict and uncompromising with her boys; they would thank her later, wordlessly, through their deeds.

She knew she was not a popular mother. Other mothers received gifts and visits from their grown children. Of the fourteen young adults who had crossed the threshold of Home Thirteen into the outside world, she had met only one. It was a chance meeting at a Hezbollah rally and the man, her boy for thirteen years, had shouted the loudest, thumped his chest the hardest, been the most fervent in his hatred. He had not recognized her in her black chador and veil; he had not even looked at her. Hameeda did not accost him. She turned and left the rally with tears in her eyes. Later in bed, despite the fragrant nightcap, she had difficulty sleeping her heart was so full of maternal pride.

She had frozen the image as one of the fondest in her life. It had been Allah's way of showing her that she was doing right by Him and by her boys. She needed to remember that sensation of certainty, to fuel her convictions constantly in the face of the shaitan's daily temptations. Hameeda saw evil everywhere and blessed everything from a broken bagful of shopping to a boy's twisted ankle with a characteristic, '*Bismillah-ar-Rahman-ar-Raheem*'. She saw bad intent in boys who mispronounced the holy verses, and an outright evil influence in those who did not read the Koran in a loud voice.

Khaled Sulman was approximately six when his voice became a whisper. At first Hameeda was persuaded that the boy's near aphonia was a deliberate attempt to avoid reading in the daily Koran session. She tried everything. She thrashed him with her slipper until his bare buttocks were covered with blotchy bruises and welts; she gated him and fed him plain bread; in desperation she even forced him to sleep on her bathroom floor for an entire week. No boy had ever deserved this ultimate punishment.

During that week of supreme chastisement, she went about her nightly routine ignoring the boy curled up in a foetal position on the bathroom mat. Just before replacing the bottle of perfume, she checked that the boy was asleep before taking a surreptitious sip. This was her secret which no-one was to discover.

How the boy had cried in that week, had wept violently but voicelessly during the spankings. And through the tears and squinting eyes, Hameeda had recognized the expression of hatred.

Bismillah-ar-Rahman-ar-Raheem, she thought, Allah give me strength.

Hameeda first suspected that the boy's whispered speech was a genuine mental disorder when he started to call her Miss Yellow.

'What did you call me?'

'Miss Ashraf,' another boy said, 'he calls me Hunneis.'

'Is that true?'

Khaled was quiet.

Hameeda shook him. 'Talk to me boy, or I'll beat the words out of you.'

'That's his name, Miss Asfar.'

98

She looked at him wide-eyed; she had not misheard the first time.

'See, Miss Ashraf, see?' the other boy said.

'What colour is that bowl over there?' Hameeda demanded.

'Yellow, Miss Ashraf.'

'Be quiet, Hussein. Khaled, what colour is that bowl?'

'*Asfar*, Miss Asfar.'

'He's been whispering for ten days now,' Hameeda said. 'That's when he bothers to talk at all.'

They were in the clinic run by the Foundation. Khaled stood naked on a stool while a doctor examined his neck.

'But he says every name backwards.' She added, conspiratorially, '*Every* name, hakim. That's why I came.'

'Really, like what?' The doctor had his back to the woman. He put a stethoscope to the boy's chest and said, 'Breathe in deeply now, Khaled.'

'He calls the Sayyed, Saddey. He calls me Asfar. He gets people's names wrong. Not things or places, just people.'

'Good,' the doctor said and, placing the stethoscope on the boy's back between the shoulder blades, he added, 'Breathe in. Hold it. Good.' He turned to face Hameeda. 'I should be more worried about his lack of voice, Miss Ashraf.'

'*Bismillah-ar-Rahman-ar-Raheem*. Hakim, he calls the blessed Prophet, Mumahhad.'

The doctor frowned, noticed and fingered the weals on the child's buttocks.

'I see nothing wrong with this boy other than that he's far too small and thin for his age. Take him home, Miss Ashraf, feed him well. Stop beating him and you'll see he'll find his voice again.'

The doctor cupped the boy's scrotum in his hand to feel that both testicles had dropped.

It was the first time Hameeda had seen Khaled smile.

That demon grinned impishly as he urinated in the hakim's hand.

For four years, Hameeda tried to force Khaled into her mould of a good Shiite boy. She spanked him but with diminishing regularity, not because of anything the doctor had said – what did he know about real spiritual health – but because Khaled had grown immune to the thrashings. Like a diseased soul, he stopped crying and his eyes remained round and focused with visible hatred for her. Any boy without a birth certificate celebrated his birthday with the Prophet's, so that when Khaled was approximately ten he was still near-mute and physically the most frail of her ten children.

Hameeda respected strength and forcefulness; these were God-given attributes. The shaitan was weak and brittle as a stick insect in the face of the Almighty. Yet Khaled had a strange inner strength of his own, Hameeda conceded, a resolute stubbornness as formidable as her own. Despite being half the average height of his nine foster-brothers, he alone was not scared of her.

Allah knew she had tried everything but the boy still whispered, still slurred even the holiest of names. The most difficult decision in her life had been to forbid the boy's 'vocal' participation in the Koran sessions. It went totally against the grain, but she could no longer bear to hear Khaled whisper, *'La ilaha illa Ahhal'*.

A week after the humiliating medical check-up, Hameeda had contacted the boy's only remaining relative, in the hope that the child might snap out of his blaspheming whisper. She was told that the Hezbollah militiaman, Abdullah Shawqi, had left his uncle's village in the south with his baby cousin only hours before the Israeli invasion and the ensuing massacre. It was Abdullah who had brought the orphan to the Islamic Foundation and who visited his cousin annually on the Prophet's birthday, armed with chocolate bars. And it was to Abdullah that Hameeda had turned for spiritual support for the boy.

'Come here, you little pimp,' Abdullah said affectionately and swept the six-year-old off his feet to hug and kiss him.

'*Bismillah-ar-Rahman-ar-Raheem*,' Hameeda muttered.

Abdullah carried the boy outside. 'How's my Khaled?' he said. 'I missed you.'

The boy, clinging to the man's shoulders, looked vacant.

'No hello from my favourite Khaled?'

The boy kissed him.

'That's better. You want to go for a walk?'

Khaled shrugged.

'Come. I'll show you where I lived when I was your age.'

He dropped the child and they strolled down the street holding hands, past a giant mural of Khomeini and the Imam Moussa Sadr, the Shiite cleric who had been kidnapped by Israeli agents.

'I'll miss this neighbourhood,' Abdullah said, looking down at the boy. 'I'm going to the south.'

Khaled was staring at the mural.

Abdullah squeezed his hand. 'Did you hear me?'

The boy nodded. 'To fight the enemy?'

'You don't have to whisper, boy. Be proud like I am.' He added in a loud voice, 'I'm going to fight the enemy.'

'Allah bless you,' said a passer-by.

'See? There's nothing to be ashamed of. People will respect you only if you shout.'

'Was my father a fighter?'

'The best,' Abdullah said with no hesitation. 'Everyone respected him. You want to be like him, right?'

The boy was still.

'Of course you want to be like him.'

'And my mother?'

'You don't want to be like her,' he replied humorously, but the child regarded him with a strange quizzical expression.

'No. She was a good Allah-fearing woman. Like Miss Ashraf.'

'My mother was not like Miss Asfar.'

Abdullah grinned. 'She wasn't yellow.'

'No-one is like Miss Asfar.'

'Khaled, you must call her Miss Ashraf.'

'My mother wasn't fat like Miss Asfar.'

'No, she was beautiful,' Abdullah said, and promptly fell silent as he remembered the woman with this baby, whose forehead had been cratered by a sniper's bullet.

They walked on in silence down two streets and across to the first appearance of no man's land. Nature had partly reclaimed this side of town. Bushes and saplings had sprouted amid the rubble of fallen buildings, an unkempt cemetery adding serenity to the otherwise bleak and ghostly neighbourhood. Abdullah led the boy to a narrow pass, dense with bushes, blocked off by a plank on two rusted oil barrels. The man pointed to the skeletal remains of a building, the cement peeling back to reveal the iron girders.

'I lived there before the war. And that narrow pass was the road where we played football. Every time a car came we—'

'Abdullah! Abdullah Shawqi!'

He turned to face two militiamen in a jeep and walked off towards them, leaving the boy to admire the prewar road. Khaled's eyes were round with wonder.

'I hear you're moving south,' said a militiaman.

Abdullah nodded. 'For the excitement.'

The second militiaman nodded in agreement. 'Beirut's so dead boring.'

'You never know, they might still try to free their hostages.'

'Who are you kidding? Never try to wipe your bum with an American flag, the colours will run down your legs.'

They laughed boisterously.

'You speak from experience,' Abdullah said. 'Show me your legs.'

'Next week, *habibi*.'

'I won't be here, thank Allah.'

'Abdullah Shawqi's going south,' the second shouted towards East Beirut. 'Watch out Mena*khara* Begin.'

'What are you doing here anyway, Abdullah?'

'Showing the old neighbourhood to my cousin.'

'Your cousin?'

'Yes.' Abdullah turned and called out, 'Khaled? Khaled! Where's the little shaitan? Khaled?'

He ran back to the spot where he had left the boy, followed by the two militiamen.

'Khaled? Where are you?'

'There, Abdullah, look! Is that him in the building?'

'Where?'

'There by the smashed wall.'

'I must be going blind – Allah! – yes. Khaled, don't move!'

The two militiamen looked at one another anxiously. Abdullah lifted the plank off the two barrels.

One of the men held onto his arm. 'He's in a mine-field, Abdullah.'

'Allah! Don't you think I know that?'

'He's moving. He's walking back this way.'

'Khaled, stop!' yelled Abdullah. 'Stop walking!'

The boy waved and quickened his step.

'He's dead,' the second militiaman muttered.

'I said stop! I'm coming to get you!'

Khaled shook his head and ran back to the men panting and elated.

Abdullah was momentarily silent.

The first Hezbollahi gasped, 'In the Prophet's name, he's Luck's brother.'

'There are enough mines in that small road to wipe out the entire Syrian army.'

'He's a small bird.'

'He is light,' the second militiaman agreed. 'That must have saved him.'

Abdullah was raising his arm to strike the boy.

Khaled opened his hand and showed the men a scorpion on his palm. He whispered, proudly, 'Look. I found him.'

'Allah deliver him,' mumbled a Hezbollahi.

'That's good,' Abdullah said calmly. 'Now put your hand gently on the ground.'

'Why?'

'Just do it. Gently, very gently.'

Khaled, puzzled, complied. The scorpion, in no hurry, crawled off the boy's hand and onto the ground with a wave from one of its lobster-like claws.

Abdullah lifted the boy with one arm and pounded the scorpion into the ground with his army boot.

'You stupid, stupid ass.' Abdullah struck the child. 'That's a scorpion – it kills.' He struck him again. 'And that's a minefield – it also kills idiot kids like you.' He slapped Khaled repeatedly around the head. 'You got hummus for brains – do you hear?'

'Take it easy, Abdullah, he's only a baby. Praise Allah he's alive.'

'He's not a baby. Even an ass knows better than to play with scorpions in minefields.'

Khaled had tears in his eyes.

'You killed him.'

'Listen to that stupid baby,' Abdullah complained to the men. 'You hear that voice? He always talks that way. Like a girl. Listen, Khalida, scorpions sting. You see that tail, curled like a shaitan's horn, it's full of poison. One drop kills a man. It would have stung you – that's what scorpions do.'

Khaled came close to talking he was so full of rage.

'He wouldn't have stung me. He was my friend.'

He wept and ran back to House Thirteen.

Unlike Khaled, Saleh Shmali had many friends. In the Foundation's schoolyard, he was invariably the first

104

picked by the captains of football among the group of expectant boys; Khaled was always chosen, grudgingly, as a substitute who never got to play anyway. Saleh, at eleven, was approximately a year older than Khaled, but looked five years older. He was built like a fourteen-year-old; his voice had already cracked, and he combed the thin crop of hair on his upper lip and his thread-like goatee, much to the admiration of his peers. He was Mother Two's favourite son and popular with his teachers who found him hard-working and bright. Academically, Saleh was better than Khaled, despite the fact that the latter, soon bored of the substitute bench, was to be found in the small school library during most afternoons.

Saleh's pride and joy was a large army flick-knife, which no-one was allowed to touch, and with which he had engraved his initials in various nooks of the school like an animal claiming territory. The most impressive example – for which he had received only mild reproof – was on the underside of his folding desk. He had carved $\hat{S}$,Sh in calligraphic Arabic that resembled a cobra rearing its head to strike. The Sayyed and the teachers were lenient on him. They saw leadership qualities in the boy which someday would make him a good Hezbollah captain.

Saleh Shmali was also the fomenter of Khaled's nickname.

It was during an afternoon session that had replaced the football game. The Sayyed had gathered the ten- and eleven-year-olds in their classroom, a practice he observed once a month with every age group to acquaint himself with all his sons. He asked them what they wanted to become as adults and, starting with Saleh, worked his way around the classroom.

'Leader of the house of deputies, Sayyed,' Saleh spoke out confidently.

The Sayyed was visibly pleased. 'Good. And you, Ali?'

105

'A martyr, Sayyed.'

'No, Ali. That is an ambition for your soul after you die. You should fight bravely and for Allah, so that when you die you will be a martyr. But it's not an ambition for your life. Do you understand the difference, Ali?'

The boy nodded very quickly.

'Good. Khaled?'

The boy opened his mouth.

'I can't hear you, boy, speak up.'

Saleh said, 'Sayyed, he says he wants to be a crier who calls the faithful to prayer.'

Khaled turned bright red and the class broke into spontaneous laughter.

The Sayyed smiled. 'Is that what you want to be, Khaled?'

'No, Saddey. I want to be the President of Lebanon.'

Everyone laughed again.

'The Crier wants to be president, Sayyed,' Ali said with glee. 'He doesn't know that the president is a Maronite.'

Khaled fixed the Sayyed and whispered slowly, 'I will be the first Shiite President of Lebanon.' The boys were now still; he added, 'My leader of the house will be a stronger and braver man than Sahel Shlami.'

Saleh gave him an evil stare; Khaled returned the stare with a blank expression.

'So, Khaled,' the Sayyed said, breaking the strained silence, 'you'll have to find your voice before then.'

All the boys chuckled, with the exception of the two budding politicians.

Later, Saleh and two friends cornered Khaled on his way home.

'There's the Crier,' one of the boys yelled.

Saleh body-slammed Khaled into a wall. 'You shit-whore-brother. You ever talk about me again I'll kill you.' He held Khaled by the hair and punched him in the face. 'You understand, cunt-mouth?' He punched him in the stomach and kneed him in the face.

Khaled fell to the ground and whispered.

'What did that prick-for-nose say?' He kicked him and waited.

Khaled's nose was bleeding.

'I said you're the strongest and bravest.'

'That's right. Don't forget that, shit.'

'Who but the bravest would dare fight me?'

The boys were amazed.

'He's the weakest in the school,' one said at last.

'He's joking, stupid,' explained the second boy.

'Not for long.' Saleh took out his knife and flicked the blade open.

'What're you doing?'

'He's not worth it, Saleh.'

'I'm going to write my initials on his chest so he'll remember to be respectful.'

'Come on, Saleh. Look, he's crawling like a cockroach. Leave him.'

'Yeah, leave the pimp.'

Khaled was not crawling. He had moved to a position to remove his shirt. He lay before the boys, bare-chested, bloodied and trembling, but with stone-cold eyes.

'Come on, Saleh, let's go. That pimp's crazy.'

Saleh knelt beside Khaled and brought the blade to the boy's chest. They stared into each other's eyes. Khaled betrayed a brief wince of pain as Saleh gently slit him from the sternum to below the right nipple. He looked at his knife, at the blood now trickling through the cut, and back at the boy's round eyes.

'You're crazy,' Saleh whispered and snapped the flick-knife shut.

'I told you, Saleh.'

'Yeah, Saleh, he's crazy.'

He stood up and all three boys moved away in silence, leaving Khaled spread-eagled, with a bloody chest and nose, gazing at the blue sky. A thin smile played on his lips.

* * *

After the boy appeared with a black eye and a blood-stained shirt, Hameeda complained to the Sayyed.

'He's the Foundation's responsibility until he's sixteen,' the Sayyed told her, 'after that, he's his own man.'

'I can't live with him, Sayyed, he doesn't listen to me at all.'

'That's strange to believe,' the man mused. 'He's so quiet.'

'He pretends, Sayyed. He whispers only to annoy me.'

'Come now, Hameeda, he whispers to everyone. I hear the boys are calling him the Crier.'

'And the names. He calls me Miss Asfar.'

'He's like that with every name.'

'Yes, but more with me. He should call me Miss Afrash or Miss Ashfar. Instead, he calls me Miss *Yellow*.'

'I've noticed, Hameeda,' the man said thoughtfully, 'that he hates being humiliated. Have you tried spanking him in public?'

'In public?'

'Yes. For instance, out on the street with his pants down.'

'Spanking, Sayyed? *Bismillah-ar-Rahman-ar-Raheem*, he enjoys it.'

Hameeda was slowly accepting the fact that she had failed with Khaled. She had stopped asking her errant son where he disappeared to every day after school. Sometimes he returned home as much as two hours later than the other boys, missing the Koran session altogether. At first she had yelled at him till her throat was so sore it burned at night when she swallowed her dram of perfume. Now, when he disappeared after school, she found herself wishing he would vanish for ever.

Hameeda had grown so used to the boy's nonchalance, his composed loathing for her, that the day she provoked him into a fit of rage was, in her calendar, a day of unexpected and glorious victory.

It was a late summer's day in 1992, two years after the end of the war. All the militias had officially been disarmed except the Hezbollah, which had been granted a special mandate to pursue its resistance against the Israelis in the south. The results of the recent parliamentary elections – the first in eighteen years – had caused a furore in East Beirut and overwhelming jubilation in the southern suburbs. The Christian parties, the sorest losers in the war, had engineered a strike of the electoral process, to protest at the Syrian arm-twisting presence in the country and at the ballot stations. The elections were held despite the opposition and with minimal Christian participation. The strongest single block to emerge in the new chamber was the Hezbollah. For the first time in the history of liberal Lebanon, an Islamic fundamentalist movement had a voice in parliament. With fifteen Hezbollah deputies in a 108-seat chamber, this hardly represented sweeping power. However, in 1992 it was a start.

The Islamic Foundation for Boys fêted the political victory by organizing a kermis in the schoolyard on 12 *Rabiul Awal* 1413, the Prophet Muhammad's birthday.

'Every two boys must prepare a game,' Hameeda told her ten sons. 'The school workshop will be open after school for the next month.'

'When is the Prophet's birthday, Miss Ashraf?' asked a boy.

'This year it's on the tenth of September.'

'What games, Miss Ashraf?'

'Anything, Hussein,' Hameeda replied impatiently. 'Skittles, bowling, you choose. Your teacher can help you if you don't have any ideas.'

She unfolded a sheet of paper. 'Now we're inviting your relatives to the fair. Hussein, you have two uncles, both in the Bekaa, right?'

'No, Miss. Uncle Ahmad's in Dubai.'

She shook her head distastefully. Dubai was a bastion of twin shaitanisms: capitalism and Sunnism.

'We won't invite him then.' She crossed his name from the list. 'Khaled, you've got your cousin Abdullah

Shawqi in the south and –' she appeared to cross off another name ' – I don't think we'll invite your parents.'

'He's got parents!' a boy exclaimed. *No-one* in the Foundation had parents.

'Now Riad, you have a grandfather and an . . .'

'You're lying.'

'. . . uncle. Are they still in the suburbs?'

'Yes, Miss—'

'Asfar. You lie.'

'*Bismillah-ar-Rahman-ar-Raheem,* this boy is evil. Yes, he has parents. A mother and a father who don't want their wicked boy.'

'That's not true. Shut up.'

'This little cockroach tells *me* to shut up,' Hameeda shouted. 'Tell me this, cockroach, why did Abdullah take you from your village?'

Khaled was red and hissed, 'The enemy.'

'The enemy invaded your village, I know that. They invaded everyone's village; a million villages. But why didn't your whole family leave, like everyone else? So your father had to stay and fight.' She was scoring a goal. She added contemptibly, 'But why didn't your mother leave the village with you?'

'Shut up. You're lying.'

'You see, it's true. A mother never leaves her baby unless he's rotten with worms.'

Khaled kicked a wall. 'You're the worm. I hate you. I dream you were dead.'

Hameeda used the term of endearment cynically: 'May-you-bury-me inshallah. *Your* mother would never say that to her angel of a boy.'

Khaled sprinted to the door.

'That's right, run from the truth,' Hameeda shouted after him, her voice vibrant with triumph. She was in control. Allah was truly great; He had shown her the stick to use to get to the boy's heart. She would make a good man out of him yet, like the adult son she had secretly observed at the Hezbollah rally.

110

*　　*　　*

The Crier was the brunt of all the jokes in the play-ground and in class. Khaled's foster-brothers from House Thirteen had soon spread the extraordinary news of the shamed parents who could not bear to see their son. Everyone viciously teased the boy, with the notable exception of Saleh Shmali.

He was uncertain about the Crier. At face value Khaled was the easiest boy to pick on, weedy as scrub. But Saleh had scratched at the surface – gashed with his flick-knife – and discovered a different, braver Crier. This mysterious Crier had neither squealed to the teachers nor, more remarkably, boasted his wounds to fellow pupils. The black eye, swollen nose and slashed chest had been their secret, jealously guarded by Khaled as if to protect a friend. The Crier had explained that he had walked into a door and fallen down steps – for which he received more ridicule – and Saleh had seen no reason to shorten the story. He admired Khaled's maturity, his aloofness and sure-footedness as he walked amid his tormentors.

'What do you call a boy with parents but no voice?' a boy asked within Khaled's earshot.

Another boy replied, 'Lakhed,' and both giggled.

'Stop that,' Saleh rebuked them.

'Why?'

'Because it stopped being funny last week.'

'How about this one then: Why did the Crier's parents give him away?'

Saleh was walking away.

'No, wait – because he cried so much.'

Khaled was preparing his game for the kermis on his own. The fact that he had no partners was something of an unsolved enigma given that there was an even number of boys in the Foundation. In the workshop, after school, he had toiled for the last five days with the speed of three boys. He had sketched his plan and was constructing his game with chipboard and nails. His silence over the game had aroused the curiosity and provocative remarks of classmates who boasted their ideas to the teacher. Khaled had remained mute until the sixth day, as he concentrated on sawing wood, sanding sections and nailing chipboards together.

'What're you building, Crier, a tower for your mosque?'

'No. It's got to be a game. A game where the weakest wins.'

'Leave him alone,' Saleh said. 'He doesn't want to tell us.'

Khaled looked up. 'I'll tell you, Sahel.'

'Sahel, Sahel,' several boys mocked.

'I'll tell you my secret game, Sahel. Will you be my friend?'

'Promise not to tell anyone.'

Khaled raised his arm and stared at each boy in turn with cold fearless eyes.

'Quiet, the Crier's going to speak,' a boy said derisively.

'Do you ever dream of killing?'

The question, taking the boys by surprise, silenced most of them.

'Every day,' a boy replied, and some gave a feeble laugh.

Khaled shook his head. 'No, not killing with a gun like a hero in a film; killing with your hands.'

Khaled looked up at his hand and brought it down slowly to meet the other in a prayer. 'Your hands around a neck, gently squeezing till her face goes blue and her eyes pop out with fear.' He turned his back to the silent boys and resumed drawing a line on a section of wood.

'The Crier's mad,' a boy said, breaking the stillness. 'His parents probably thought the Foundation was for the insane.' He uttered this softly, with little conviction, and no-one laughed.

Khaled was the first to leave the workshop. On his way out, he stopped by Saleh's bench and said, 'Meet me after school tomorrow, if you want to know my game.'

*   *   *

The two boys walked in solemn silence.

Khaled's game, he had explained in the playground, was outside the school, and Saleh was starting to feel unsettled. He was older and considerably stronger than the Crier, yet Saleh followed with a rising sense of apprehension. He was in awe of the darkly demure boy who barely reached his shoulder. Khaled was so original, so unpredictable, so totally unlike any boy he had ever known, that Saleh had agreed to come when he should have shaken his head, uninterested. But the fact was that Saleh was curious about the secret game and, more to the point, engrossed by the Crier.

'Are we nearly there?'

'Nearly.'

They walked past the Foundation's houses, down two streets, past a fading mural of Khomeini and the Imam Moussa Sadr, and right into the devastated neighbourhood that still obstructed the suburbs' northern encroachment into the rest of the city. The plank on two oil barrels, barricading the minor prewar road, had long been replaced by a gate painted in the nationalist red and white stripes. A sign on a large green board, written in bold red letters, read:

WARNING
Keep out: MINEFIELD

In the first weeks of peace in 1990, the government and its Syrian backers undertook the removal of containers from the streets of no man's land and the clearing of mines to open all the roads between east and west, erasing, with a simple writ, the Green Line that had been the darkest hue for a decade and a half. All the roads in downtown Beirut were demined and raked of old vegetation and rubble, rendering them accessible to cars with sturdy suspensions.

The southern suburbs were overlooked by this

113

sweeping operation for two years, the time taken for the dilatory politicians and cartographers to realize their city had grown over the war. The metropolis was no longer confined west to the nose, Manara, and east to the cranial hill-top, Achrafieh. Beirut had evolved; it had grown a tangled beard.

Saleh looked in disbelief as Khaled passed under the red and white gate.

'Come on.'

Saleh shook his head vigorously. 'No, I'm going.'

'A leader of the house of deputies must be brave.'

'Brave yes, mad no.'

'Shhh. Whisper like me. There's a Syrian checkpoint on the other side. Come on.'

'No,' Saleh said softly, 'you're mad.'

'I come here every day.'

The older boy shrugged.

'I'll show you how to walk.'

Khaled turned and jumped onto a slab of concrete.

'Walk on the rocks like you're crossing a stream.'

'How do you know there isn't a mine under there?'

'You choose the rocks almost buried in the ground.'

Khaled pointed.

'Don't go there or there because there's a gap between the rocks and the ground.'

Saleh frowned. 'I don't understand. How do you know there isn't a mine under your rock?'

'Think, Sahel. This is more important than anything you learn at school. You tell me why this rock is safe.'

Saleh shrugged. 'I don't know.'

Khaled appeared disappointed. 'Go home, then,' he said, turned and hopped onto another slab.

'Wait, tell me.'

The Crier did not stop, and hopped down a third of the narrow pass.

Saleh hesitated, then climbed over the gate and leaped onto the first slab.

Khaled waited on the ground floor of a building that

had suffered the least damage on the block. Three outer walls remained, pock-marked but otherwise intact, the fourth, facing the prewar road, lay strewn on the ground, as if the building had been carefully sliced and opened like a doll's house.

Saleh, grinning, hopped onto the landing to join the Crier. He panted and said excitedly, 'That was fun.'

'So?'

'What?'

'Why are some rocks safe?' asked Khaled.

Saleh gave a broad smile. 'I just followed what you said.'

'That was stupid.'

Saleh, already flushed by the exertion, became redder still. His smile vanished. No-one had ever called him stupid, not Mother Two, or the Sayyed, or the teachers.

'You should never do things without working them out for yourself.'

'So why were those rocks safe?' He was still blushing.

'Because they'd have blown up if they'd fallen on mines.'

Saleh pondered for a while. 'What if they'd put in the mines after the rocks had fallen, and then covered them with the rocks.'

'No-one would bother to do that. But in case they did, that's why you don't choose the rocks with gaps.' Khaled hinted a smile. 'But you're here now, with both your legs. Welcome to the citadel.'

'The citadel?'

'Outside, I am a crier in a mosque. Here, I am Lord of the Seven Blue Seas, *Khaleef* of the Sapphire Planet. And this is the citadel from where I rule. Come, I'll show you my throne.'

'Who am I then?'

Khaled gave a humble bow. 'You are my respected guest. A valiant janizary.'

Saleh laughed. 'What's a janizary?'

'A captain in the Ottoman guard of honour.'

'Under the *khaleef*?'

'Of course.'

'Then I'm not a janizary.'

Khaled considered this briefly then agreed. 'The

janizaries were Christian. The *khaleefs* never trusted their own to captain their guards.'

'How do you know?'

'Like the rocks, I choose the books to read. Come, you're the *khaleef*'s friend.'

He led Saleh to the back of the building, into a closed room with a large shell-formed crater in one wall, like a single jagged window through which the afternoon light filtered. The room was bare except for an old and shabby armchair, a small bullet-ridden cupboard with two missing legs leaning precariously against a wall, four wooden crates and two cardboard boxes. The crates and boxes on the floor were covered with dirty sheets and rags weighed down by stones.

Khaled waved grandly at the armchair.

'My throne.'

Saleh moved to the cupboard and peered inside. On a shelf was a bottle of purified alcohol, cotton buds, and a rack with three test-tubes.

'You took those from the lab,' he exclaimed.

'Yes.'

'What for?'

'For my game.'

'So what's your game then?'

Khaled waved him to one of the two cardboard boxes. He kicked off the stones and lifted the covering rag.

Saleh looked inside and gasped, 'That's disgusting.'

In the box the brown mass started to move frenetically. The cockroaches scurried over one another's bodies, panicked by the sudden light.

'The other box is full as well. You find lots of them around here.'

'Do you collect them?' Saleh asked scornfully.

'Yes.'

'Why?'

'For my friends.'

Khaled moved to one of the wooden crates, removed the sheet, and put his hand inside. Saleh, approaching, stopped dead in his tracks when he saw a

116

scorpion slowly crawl onto the Crier's palm.

Khaled stood up and held out his hand to exhibit the scorpion.

'Lovely, isn't he?' he whispered proudly. 'I've got three others, but I can't keep them together – they kill their own brothers.'

He took a step forward; Saleh took a step back.

Khaled looked surprised. 'Don't you want a closer look?'

The animal rubbed its lobster-like claws together, curled its tail into a tight spiral, and crawled up the boy's arm on its eight legs.

'You're really mad,' Saleh said, frightened.

'Keep your voice down. Scorpions like people who whisper. And they can smell fear like we smell garlic.'

Khaled was standing by the exit; Saleh moved to the opposite wall.

The Crier whispered cajolingly to the scorpion. 'You're hungry, aren't you. Yes, I know you're hungry. I'm going to give you something really good to eat.'

The scorpion had reached the boy's neck. Khaled picked it off gently and put it on the floor.

Saleh had tears in his eyes and his knees shook. 'No, please.' His voice trembled. He took out his flick-knife and opened the blade. 'Stay away.'

Khaled frowned. 'I thought you were clever. You're not. You're stupid like the others.'

He turned his back and reached into the cardboard box for a cockroach. Saleh jumped onto the armchair and squatted while the scorpion crawled aimlessly around the room.

'Watch this.'

Khaled dropped the insect on the ground and moved to the armchair to put his arm around the shoulders of the shaking boy.

'You're on my throne, but I don't mind.'

Saleh brought the blade to the Crier's chest. 'Swear you don't want to kill me.'

Khaled smiled. His whole face radiated happiness; it was the most attractive smile Saleh had ever seen.

'I swear,' Khaled said and leaned over to kiss him affectionately.

Saleh closed his flick-knife and held onto the hand around his shoulders.

Khaled pointed. 'Look. He's like a wolf, isn't he?'

The scorpion had stopped wandering around the floor aimlessly. It rubbed its claws, then slowly advanced towards the cockroach, its deadly tail unfurled to the limit. The insect, sensing danger, scuttled around in circles in a small area on the floor.

'Why doesn't it run away?'

'Cockroaches have six noses, one at the end of each leg. They hate the smell of alcohol – it's like deadly gas to them. Every three days I put some alcohol around there and they can smell it even after it's dried off.'

Like a predator in a savannah, the scorpion stalked its victim, taking all its time to inch nearer, repositioning itself every time the cockroach moved. Then, with lightning speed, it charged, its claws like battleaxes, its tail already moving in the air like a catapult. It stung the insect in the thorax and took three graceful steps back, as unhurried and elegant as a duelling musketeer. The cockroach, in its death throes, jittered about frenziedly; the scorpion followed it around the floor, dancing in step.

'Isn't it great?'

Saleh nodded. '*Yaay.*'

The Crier moved away from the armchair; Saleh let go of his hand.

'You can eat him in your home. Come on, boy.'

Khaled lobbed the dead cockroach in the uncovered crate and put his hand on the floor for the scorpion to crawl onto obediently. He took it gently to the crate.

'Down you go. Good boy.'

'How do you do that?' Saleh asked with admiration. 'Why doesn't it sting you?'

'Because I'm their friend. Dogs don't bite their masters.' Khaled was about to cover the crate with the sheet when he asked, 'Do you want my scorpions never to sting you?'

Saleh nodded.

'The first thing is never to show any fear. And the second thing is, lend me your knife.'

Saleh hesitated. No-one had ever touched his knife before.

'Trust me.'

Khaled's arm was extended and Saleh handed him his pride and joy. The Crier flicked the blade open, examined it briefly, then stepped to the cupboard. He tore some cotton wool, soaked it in alcohol, and wiped the blade clean.

'Come,' Khaled said, and Saleh followed him from the throne.

'What are you going to do?'

Khaled removed the three other sheets covering three other scorpions.

'They're like dogs. They need to smell you to recognize you as a friend.'

The Crier gripped Saleh's right hand and wiped the palm with the spirit-wet cotton.

'Are you sure about this?' The older boy was frightened again. 'I don't want to do this, Khaled.'

'Remember, show no fear. Relax.'

Saleh nodded; his lips trembled.

Khaled cut the palm along the lifeline and Saleh moaned softly.

'Quiet, or it won't work. Now take your knife.'

With two hands, holding the wrist of Saleh's bleeding right hand, Khaled guided drops of blood onto each of the four scorpions in turn. The scorpions froze.

'You see? They're smelling you now.'

They returned to the first crate. Khaled knelt on the ground and motioned to Saleh, who fell to his knees beside him. Khaled placed his hand and Saleh's side by side in the crate, on the wooden bottom. The scorpion came alive, rubbed its claws, and cautiously approached the two hands.

'Remember,' Khaled whispered, 'no fear. Relax.'

The scorpion crawled onto the familiar hand and waited. Then it placed a tentative two legs on Saleh's palm, rubbed its claws again, straightened and recoiled its tail, and crawled across the bloody palm to return to its dead cockroach.

'He likes you,' Khaled said, pleased. 'Now I trust you.' He brought Saleh's palm to his face.

Saleh was shocked. 'Why are you kissing my hand?'

Khaled looked up with a blood-smeared face.

'I'm not kissing. I'm smelling you. Will you be my partner?'

'Your partner?'

'In the kermis. For my game.'

'I don't even know your game.'

'Haven't I told you?'

Saleh shook his head and started to laugh nervously. He pushed the Crier back on the floor. 'You've shown me everything', he chortled, 'but your game.' He collapsed beside him and both boys broke into laughter. 'Your *friends* – your disgusting cockroaches – your mines – your citadel – but your game?' He had tears of laughter. 'I thought I'd die before I'd see your game.'

The two boys rolled around happily.

'Do you know,' Saleh said still giggling, 'you have a voice when you laugh?'

Khaled sat up abruptly and whispered, 'A cockroach race.'

'What?'

'That's my game.'

Saleh cracked up again.

Khaled withdrew the plan from his pocket. 'That's the racetrack with six lanes.'

Saleh wiped the tears from his eyes. 'A cockroach race?'

'Yes. Six cockroaches pulling six chariots around the track.'

'Where do you get the chariots?'

'Six plastic jeeps with a general in each. I've got them. Each jeep is tied to the cockroach's head with string. We can paint the jeeps and generals in six different colours: blue, red, yellow, orange, green and black.'

Saleh's eyes lit up. 'That's an excellent idea.'

'Will you be my partner?'

'Yes. No.' He frowned. 'I've got a partner.'

'Throwing balls at a stack of tins. I saw your game. Almost

120

everyone's got the same. Leave him; be my partner.'

Saleh nodded slowly and grinned. 'OK.' Khaled smiled back.

'I need a partner to help me get six thousand eight hundred lira.'

'What for?'

'For the prize, of course. The best game deserves the best prize.'

'You're giving money as a prize?' Saleh exclaimed.

'No. The winner of the cockroach race gets a prize which will cost us six thousand eight hundred lira.'

Samir whistled. That was a lot of money. 'What's the prize?'

'A bottle of perfume.'

The Crier would never cease to astonish him.

On 9 *Rabiul Awal*, 1413, lunar years after Muhammad fled from Mecca, Hameeda performed a *salat* for her reformed boy. She washed herself thoroughly with tap water, then prostrated herself on the bathroom mat to thank Allah and His messenger and Ali, the messenger's rightful successor, for their trinal intervention in bringing her son back to the fold. After the prayer, she lit a joss-stick over Khaled's bed muttering, '*Bismillah-ar-Rahman-ar-Raheem.   Bism-an-Nabi-Muhammad. Bism-al-Wali-Ali.* Peace and blessing be upon them.'

Khaled had changed overnight. He had asked to rejoin the Koran sessions. *He* had asked, Hameeda marvelled. Holy Gabriel had asked using the child's lips. The shaitans in the boy's mind were losing ground, were being hacked to pieces by angelic scimitars. Khaled still whispered but the blaspheming had been crushed. Now he correctly pronounced Allah, and Muhammad and Miss Ashraf.

Allah be praised. It was just a matter of time before the boy would find his voice and grow to be strong like her adult son in the Hezbollah rally. Miracles happened only to the best mothers. Mountains could sprout legs to go to the strongest believer.

Hameeda was happy; overjoyed when Khaled asked

121

for permission to go out in the afternoons; overwhelmed when he returned to help her with the housework.

Khaled's sudden popularity was not confined to House Thirteen. Hameeda had heard from her other sons, and from mothers, that her boy was on the rise at school. His best and first friend was, incredibly, the envied Saleh Shmali. The two had grown inseparable, in class side by side, in the workshop together.

'Like a wolf cub playing with a lamb,' Mother Two had described disparagingly.

The boys still called her Khaled, the Crier. But now the term was one of respect. There was only one crier in the Foundation who had the wisdom and vocabulary to speak – if in *sotto voce* – rationally as an adult. Khaled and Saleh had teamed together to rule the schoolyard with brain and brawn.

Hameeda was looking forward to Thursday when Khaled, along with half the boys at the Foundation, would celebrate his birthday. In three days he would be approximately eleven. The stands in the playground were being erected for the Prophet's birthday; the sweets and juices were ready; the excitement was gradually building in the hearts of children and mothers alike. The fair would be a great day, a day to commemorate Hezbollah's political victory, and a day for Khaled to break with his past and enter a new age of virtue.

'Saleh, Saleh for ever,' Saleh was still singing as he looked at the plan. 'What are the dots for?'

The two boys were in the throne room of the citadel. Khaled, by the cupboard, gently picked up a test-tube from the rack.

'Khaled, what are the dots on the tracks for?' Saleh repeated, indicating the plan of their game.

Khaled approached with the test-tube in his hand. 'That's where we sprinkle the tracks with alcohol on Wednesday. And the shaded area, just before the end of the course, is where we coat them with alcohol.'

Saleh frowned. 'Why? Won't that just slow the cockroaches?'

Khaled nodded. 'And they'll stop before the finish line where the smell will be unbearable.'

Saleh still frowned. 'Why? And why do all the tracks have dots except track two?'

'Because track two is the winner.'

'That's not fair. We'll know the cockroach in the second track will win.'

Khaled had moved to one of the wooden crates. 'Have you ever seen a scorpion being milked?'

He removed the covering sheet and Saleh backed away to the armchair. Despite the scorpion test, he still felt uneasy when they were out of their boxes.

Khaled placed the scorpion on the floor and slowly brought the test-tube in front of it, at an angle above its head. 'I've been milking them for months.'

Saleh curled the toes in his shoes.

The test-tube had a centimetre of opaque fluid at the bottom and was stoppered at the neck by cotton wool and a small plastic sheet fastened to the glass by a rubber band.

'Scorpions hate being tickled.'

Khaled scratched the scorpion's back with the index of his free hand, keeping a tight grip on the test-tube above the claws with his other hand. The scorpion unfurled its tail and rubbed its pincers together. The Crier patted its back, then rapidly removed his hand as the scorpion's tail shot in the air, stinging the test-tube in its plastic head.

'Never more than a drop.'

Khaled returned to the cupboard.

'You must let the cotton absorb it and then it moves to the bottom. But you must remember to change the plastic every time.'

He replaced the test-tube vertically in the rack and turned to rehouse the scorpion.

'A drop will kill a man.'

'I know.'

123

'If you get it on your hand, you can wash it away. But if you swallow it, Allah rest your soul.'

Saleh envied the Crier's calm; his command of every situation; the way he had lied so plausibly to raise the 6,800 lira to pay for the prize.

Liquor was strictly prohibited in Beirut's southern suburbs. The boys of the Foundation had discovered a grocer by the name of Ahmad, who violated the Shiite High Council's ruling by secretly importing foreign Scotch and Lebanese beers and wines into the suburbs, and selling them in brown-paper bags to a core of trusty customers.

The two boys waited outside Ahmad's shop for his customers to leave and entered the shop minutes before the obligatory closing time for the afternoon prayer. Saleh closed the door behind him and crossed his arms as Khaled, with tears in his eyes, approached the grocer.

'What do you want, boys?' Ahmad demanded. 'Hurry up, it's almost the Izhan.'

'Four dollars,' Khaled whispered, 'or seven thousand lira.'

'What?' the grocer shouted. 'What did you say to me?'

Khaled wept. 'Seven thousand lira.'

Ahmad rolled back his shirtsleeve. 'Out. Get out before I give you bruises till Ramadan.'

'It's all your fault. You sold – my father.'

'Out.' Ahmad made a show of moving threateningly from behind the counter. 'Out.'

'They'll cut his tongue at the throat because of you. Because of the whisky you sold him.'

'That's a lie, you little lying shit.'

Khaled pointed at Saleh by the door.

'Do you know who he is?'

'A thieving *khara* like you.'

'He's the Imam's nephew. He came to my house and saw my father singing like a shaitan on the floor with a bottle of whisky.'

Ahmad was still.

'That pimp, whore-brother, forgive-the-words, will tell his uncle if I don't pay him four dollars. And you know what the Imam will do, he'll tell the Hezbollah to kill my father.'

124

'You there, pimp, shame on you to pick on a weaker boy.' Turning to Khaled he added, 'I'm sorry, I can't help you. I don't sell the shaitan-drink. But your father won't be killed. I promise you.'

'But they'll whip him, sir. I don't want him to be whipped and I don't want to tell them that he bought it from you. I just want to pay him seven thousand lira so he'll never talk.'

'I don't sell alcohol,' the man shouted again, 'do you understand that, boy? What's your father's name?'

'Ismaeel Faqri,' the boy replied immediately.

The grocer gave a brief sigh and mentally crossed off a customer from his select list. He opened the till to withdraw seven one thousand-lira bills as a crier in a nearby minaret called the faithful to the afternoon Izhan.

'I'm going to help you this time, boy, but if I ever see you in here again, I'll chop off your balls and sell them as baklawa.'

'Yes, sir, thank you, sir.'

'You, come here,' Ahmad called Saleh.

The man slapped him hard on the cheek before handing him the banknotes. 'I curse this money. May Allah make it buy only misfortune.'

The boys left the grocery and ran back to the citadel, laughing all the way.

'How do you know that man?'

'Who? Islaeem Fiqra?'

'Yes, Ismaeel.' Saleh frowned; he had just realized something new about the Crier.

'I don't know him.'

'Then how did you know?'

'With patience, and a lot more patience. When you lie, Saleh, you must do your homework.'

'You called me Saleh,' the older boy exclaimed.

Khaled smiled and handed him a sheet of paper from his pocket. On it was written a couplet:

> *Saleh saleh a'alatoul,*
> *Hatta bya'tal ma bi 'oul.*

125

There was a word-play on the name which, in Arabic, implies bringer of peace, ally. Saleh read the couplet as: 'Friend, friend for ever, who would rather kill than break a secret.'

'Go on, say it.'

'*Saleh saleh a'alatoul, hatta bya'tal ma bi 'oul.*'

'Again.' Khaled clapped his hands rhythmically.

'*Saleh saleh a'alatoul, hatta bya'tal ma bi 'oul.*'

'Sing it.' Khaled drummed on a cardboard box of cockroaches with his hands, a Lebanese *terbaké* adding the rhythm to a *dabké* dance.

They sang and danced and laughed. 'Saleh, Saleh for ever.'

The peals of laughter and general excitement could be heard from the street. The school gates were wide open and two boys at the entrance checked visitors' names off their list. Children ran everywhere into the legs of adults; groups of people milled around the stands, trying their luck at the games, or sipping coffee or lemonade, or chatting in loud and lively voices. Arabic songs, played at full volume in the first stand, were all but drowned by the incessant bustle. The small multicoloured flags, hanging from lines across the rows of stands, flapped in the apparent wind caused by all the excitement.

By the entrance, a student's painting was on exhibit. On a blue background of sky, red droplets of blood fell onto a parched brown soil, landing in a pool of blood. The drops, falling from blue heaven, were cleverly joined to form two vertical words: 'Hisb Allah' – Party of God.

Hameeda paused by a stand of sweets, slightly lifted her veil and popped a *kol-oo-shkor* into her mouth. She smacked her lips as the pine-kernel centre melted in her mouth; only southerners could make them this good.

'Miss Ashraf, Miss Ashraf,' Hussein called her from an adjacent stand. 'Will you try my game?'

Two of her boys were minding the stand. Fifteen cans were arranged as a pyramid on a plank.

'It's free for you, Miss Ashraf,' Hussein said, handing her three balls. 'It's one hundred lira for visitors. You have to knock off all the cans and you get a tombola ticket.'

'One can has a pencil sharpener inside it,' the other boy said. 'If you knock that, you get another ball.'

A few minutes later Hameeda walked away with her tombola ticket. There were almost as many prizes being raffled as there were tickets, small insignificant gifts of toy soldiers or confectionery: booty for a young child; a sign of participation for an adult. A small girl was crying because she had lost at a game; Hameeda comforted her and put her raffle ticket in the little hand.

A group of men were discussing politics, were being made to shout to be heard in the commotion. Hameeda ambled past them, nodding to the Sayyed.

'Ah, Hameeda.' The Sayyed left the men to join her. 'There you are.'

'So many people, Sayyed.'

'Yes indeed.' He scanned the crowded playground. 'Quite a success isn't it, all this noise.'

She nodded.

'Have you seen that boy of yours, Khaled Sulman, or Saleh Shmali?'

'No, Sayyed.'

'You know they've become friends. Remarkable. That Crier is a remarkable lad.'

'He's a good boy,' Hameeda said nodding. 'Thank-Allah he's changed for the better.'

'So you haven't seen their game.'

'No, Sayyed.'

'They've prepared a game just for us. No-one else is allowed to play at their stand.'

'Just for us?' Hameeda asked, surprised.

'Their two mothers, myself, and their three teachers.'

'Really?'

'Remarkable. Saleh has been a terrific influence on

your boy.' The Sayyed pointed. 'There's the stand. Come, I think they're waiting for us.'

The largest crowd had gathered to admire Khaled's and Saleh's unusual game. A white circular chalk-mark on the ground, circumscribing a central table, was the perimeter within which spectators were not allowed. On the table rested a large board, roughly one metre by two, with seven concentric elliptical strips of plywood protruding, like narrow horseshoes, some five centimetres above the main board. On another chipboard, vertical and running across the major axis, the words 'The Cockroach Race' were engraved in calligraphic script (using Saleh's knife) and painted black. The tracks, oval as an amphitheatre, ended abruptly at a white finish line, painted at a slant to equalize the distances travelled along all six lanes.

Saleh stood by the table with six twigs in his hand, talking to Mother Two and the three teachers. Khaled, silently staring at the crowd, was behind them, with a cardboard box at his feet and holding a smaller box.

Khaled caught sight of the Sayyed and Hameeda.

'They're here.'

The crowd moved apart to allow the two remaining contestants into the arena.

'I don't know if I can play,' Hameeda said, looking at the racetrack.

'We prepared it for you.'

'It's very easy, Miss Ashraf,' Saleh said. 'Each player has a cockroach that pulls a chariot—'

'A chariot,' the Sayyed interjected, admiringly.

'You each have a stick.' Saleh handed the six twigs to the players. 'But you're not allowed to use it on the cockroach, only on the chariot, to push it along. The first person to cross the white line is the winner. And there's a great prize.'

Saleh could not contain his excitement; he was dancing on the spot, as if he needed to relieve himself. Khaled was unstirringly calm.

'There are six colours: blue, red, yellow, green, orange and black. Which colour will you be, Miss Ashraf?'

Hameeda waved her twig and muttered, doubtfully, 'What an idea to play with cockroaches.'

'Come on, Hameeda,' the Sayyed encouraged. 'I'll be black, Khaled.'

'Yes, Sayyed. And you, Miss Ashraf?'

'I'll play to please you. Blue.'

Khaled withdrew to prepare the insects, removing them from the large cardboard box and placing them, in order, in the smaller box.

'Do you all understand the rules?' Saleh asked as the Crier placed the small box at the starting line on the table. 'The race begins as soon as the box is opened. You can come to the table now.' Saleh turned to the growing crowd. 'Stay behind the white line, please.'

'I'll count to three and at three the box will open.' Saleh nodded at Khaled who nodded back. 'One.'

There was a buzz of excitement from the spectators.

'Two.'

'I can't see,' a little girl shouted, tugging at her father's trousers. The man lifted her onto his shoulders.

'Three!'

Khaled opened the box to reveal six cockroaches with six coloured jeeps attached to them, set apart in the box by thin sections of cardboard, like horses in their gates. The crowd cheered.

In the sudden bright light and the din, the cockroaches jumped into action and charged down their respective tracks. The red chariot took the lead, despite losing its general from the jeep in a wobbly start.

'I'm winning, I'm winning,' Mother Two cried excitedly before her cockroach inexplicably slowed down. 'Come on,' she urged it, pushing the chariot into the insect's back legs with her twig. The cockroach tottered forward. The orange chariot overtook her, closely followed by the black and blue in tracks one and two respectively.

The orange leader fared well until the bend, when the

insect veered sharply to the left, crashing the jeep into the plywood wall, overturning it and, consequently, the cockroach, which landed on its back and kicked the air helplessly.

'Can I put it back on its legs?' the teacher with the orange team asked.

Khaled shook his head. 'You're out of the race.'

In the final straight stretch, the race was between the black and the blue, with the black chariot marginally ahead.

'Come on,' the Sayyed shouted and whipped his jeep. 'Use your stick, Miss Ashraf.'

The black had gained a significant lead and was now only a cockroach's length and a half from winning. 'Yes, yes,' the Sayyed urged. And the black team stopped dead in its track.

'Come on, you stupid cockroach,' the Sayyed growled. 'You can smell the white line, it's so close.'

Hameeda was gently tapping her chariot.

'Come on, come on.' The Sayyed whipped his chariot and the cockroach took a tentative step forward, then another. A third step and the blue team in track two went scurrying past, over the white finish line, running off the table and flying into the large cardboard box.

'The winner is the blue chariot,' Saleh said at the top of his voice. 'Miss Ashraf is the winner.'

The crowd cheered and Hameeda blushed behind her veil.

Khaled picked the other cockroaches off the board and put them back into the box before approaching his mother with the prize behind his back.

'Well done, Miss Ashraf. Can I kiss you?'

'Can you kiss me?' Hameeda had tears in her eyes. 'My son, my boy. May-you-bury-me inshallah, yes you can kiss me.'

She hugged him tightly and lifted her veil so they could kiss.

Khaled, grinning, handed her the prize: a bottle of Constance de Caros.

'I almost won,' the Sayyed was grinning, 'but you deserve this fantastic prize, Hameeda. Where did you boys find the money?'

She was not listening. Hameeda was in another world where angelic songs drifted down like drops from a blue heaven. Smiling, Gabriel blew her kisses and thanked her for being the best mother in the universe. Her son in the Hezbollah rally, recognizing her through the veil, stopped chanting and beating his chest to wink at her and mouth, 'Thank-Allah I had you.' She. Hameeda. No-one else. Allah alone knew how much she craved to be loved. The angel had spoken his love for her publicly. This, she knew, was the best day of her life.

'This is the best day of my life.'

Hameeda broke into tears and wept openly.

'I want to remember this day for ever. Today I am eleven, and for the rest of my life I will celebrate my birthday only in the years the Prophet's birthday falls on a Thursday, like today.'

Hameeda sobbed like a little girl.

She looked at her image in the bathroom mirror. When did she grow to be so old. That nose. Those ears. They had puffed with age when her eyes were shut. Her face held on to her drooping cheeks like a bedouin straining with water flasks. Allah! – was she always this ugly? In fifty years that was unfair. Never even the privilege of turning down a man. *Bismillah*-not-*ar-Rahman*-even-*ar-Raheem*-once.

She opened her prize and eased out the blue bottle of perfume.

Her convictions were to blame. Men were scared of her strength; they ran away like little boys. Not all boys; not Khaled. He never ran away from anything. He was more of a man than most men.

She unscrewed the top and sprinkled some Constance behind her ears and across her neck.

He was so strong. How could she have thought he was weak. He would grow into a strong man whom she would admire; the proud mother in the background. Who needed men anyway when one had a son like Khaled.

She brought the bottle to her lips, toasted her reflection, and took a sip. It tasted different, nuttier, more satisfying than usual. She took another sip to allow the delectable perfume to permeate through her entire body.

She turned the bathroom lights off and went to bed.

At first it was a little itch in her throat which made her think that she had caught cold at the kermis. She rubbed the epiglottis with her palate and her neck became numb. She tried to lift a hand to her throat, but found her arm was weighed down. She looked down at her arm on the bedsheet, nonplussed. She tried her other arm; it too remained pinned to the bed.

It was then that Hameeda panicked and cried for help.

'Boys.'

Even her voice was failing her.

'Boys. Help.'

The door opened and Khaled stepped in.

'Thank-Allah you heard me. Call the hakim, Khaled.'

The Crier looked at her quizzically.

'Call the hakim, Khaled. Now.'

Khaled closed the door behind him and walked across the bedroom, entered the bathroom and turned on the lights.

'Khaled. Didn't you hear me, boy? I'm sick. Call me a hakim.'

She strained to turn her head to see what the boy was doing.

Khaled opened the tap, unscrewed her bottle of Constance and drained the contents. He rinsed the bottle thoroughly, splashed some water in the basin and closed the tap. Then he replaced the bottle on the shelf and walked out of the bathroom, turning off the lights.

'What are you doing? Get me a hakim this instant, boy.'

Khaled ignored her and moved to the door.

'Please, Khaled. Please.'

The boy turned slowly and smiled. The same impish grin as when he had urinated in the hakim's hand.

'If Ahhal had wanted women to drink perfume, he'd have created a perfume-tree.'

She stared at him wide-eyed with fear.

The boy left her room, closing the door softly behind him.

Hameeda willed her head to move one last time, to look into the bathroom.

It was dark in there, black. Yet, from the shelf, the empty bottle of perfume radiated a glorious blue light.

ZACHIEL

Damn him. How could I have been so mistaken.

FROM THE THREE WATER SIGNS IS BORN A MAN WHO
CELEBRATES THURSDAY AS HIS HOLIDAY. HIS RENOWN,
PRAISE, RULE AND POWER GROWS ON LAND AND SEA,
BRINGING TROUBLE TO THE EAST.

As I read the Hebrew words in the sand by Zachiel's
feet, my soul remembers the original medieval French
and my frail distant voice echoes: '*De l'aquatique trip-
licite naistra. D'un qui fera le jeudi pour sa feste: son
bruit, loz, regne, sa puissance croistra, par terre et mer
aux Oriens tempeste.*'

I damn not Azazel, nor the boy, for they are already
condemned. But Michel de Nostredame, whom the
angel now quotes, I curse his quatrains. The Celtic cross
of crystal sculptures is becoming clear. It is
Nostradamus's cross where Azazel wins the future for
Satan.

Alive, I had followed St John's cross: the Revelations
according to the Divine. St John and Nostradamus
prophesied diametrically opposite futures for mankind.
Now futurity appears set to follow Nostradamus's
quatrains of ruin. To the east of where I am the seventh
doorway seems blacker still.

'St John the Divine,' I breathe to Zachiel. 'How could
he be wrong.'

The gabriel does not answer and prepares to take off
for a third time into the starless, moonless night.

'The future you have shown me – are they visions of

events that will have happened, or that may have happened?'

The angel indicates the tall tower where the doorway burns with a white light. The second point of the equilateral triangle, where I must visit the past through the eyes of Samir and Maira, where my soul can look upon my living body with the cool detachment of a stranger.

'Tell me first about this future,' I plead, but the angel already carries me to *The Tower*.

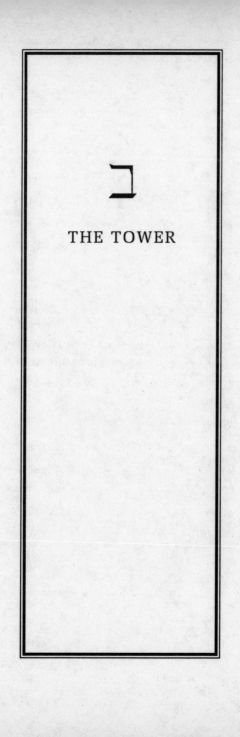

ב

THE TOWER

5

THE PILLARS OF TRUTH

At an average altitude of 1,000 metres the Bekaa Valley is a plateau pulled at either end by two bickering genies. The Lebanon and Antilebanon mountains shield the valley, one from the Syrian Desert and the other from the humidity of the Mediterranean. In early spring the blanket of snow gently scales these mountains like a white woollen jumper teased to unweave by one loose strand. It is in spring that the elfin inhabitants of the Bekaa emerge to turn on the taps to countless freshwater springs and to thread a glorious multicoloured landscape; a Persian carpet of orchards, vineyards, citrus groves, fields of wheat and barley. In some areas the soil is as golden brown as the sweet potato it yields; in other parts it is rich in iron, where weighty tomatoes, rather than hanging from bushes, cluster on the ground like monsters' droppings. The valley is so fertile that almost everything can be cultivated, from the recently introduced avocado pears to the indigenous *ma'dé*, the wild cucumber, succulent as a cooked and seasoned courgette, yet crispy and ridged like celery.

The Bekaa Valley lies in the geometric heart of the Fertile Crescent that stretches from the tongue of land between the Tigris and Euphrates to the Nile delta. Millennia ago, homo agriculturist had been conceived in this land of plenty and temperate clime; the nomadic hunter coaxed into remaining to fashion his spear into a plough.

In spring 1982, when Samir drove from Beirut to

Baalbek, the provincial capital of the Bekaa, the war in Lebanon had temporarily lost its momentum, giving way to a simmering lull. The Palestinian Fidayins and Christian militias had long reached a stalemate. The military impasse was enforced by some 60,000 Syrian troops who, in previous years, had been quick to step in whenever either party was seen to be gaining the upper hand. During the phoney peace, almost a year to the day after the Syrian siege of Samir's Greek neighbourhood, erstwhile fronts became frontiers between hostile cantons. In the glove compartment Samir had two passes, two unofficial visas to traverse the *contra*-federation. The first was a *laissez-passer* from his late brother's militia, the PNL; the second was issued by the PLO high command, procured for him by Hammad Ezzedin.

Samir was a smuggler of ancient coins. He bought rare coins from the bevies of treasure hunters who scavenged the Phoenician and Roman ruins for antiques, and then sold them in Paris or London, typically earning tenfold his cost at the auction houses. He bought a coin in Beirut only if he was convinced of its worth and saleability in Europe, bootlegging up to four coins at a time. Samir had commissioned a tailor to sow special velvet-lined pouches on the inner legs of three pairs of trousers; each leg concealed a secret pocket below the crotch, and each pocket could comfortably house two tetradrachms.

Samir specialized in Greek and Byzantine coins. He could tell a good forgery with his eyes shut, the coin balanced on a forefinger. Weights and measures had been a fine science to the ancient Greeks, which was not the case with the Lebanese forgers. While artists working for the coin cartels were able to reproduce the head of Hercules on the obverse, or Zeus sitting on a throne on the reverse, the exactitude of the Attic standard was not respected. Thus, with years of practice, Samir's forefingers were calibrated to recognize the true weight of a tetradrachm or stater.

140

'A modern mint,' he would say tactfully, whenever presented with a fake.

If Lebanon was a gold-mine for antiques of the pre-Islam era, in Samir's case, it proved to be a diamond-mine for articles from later centuries. He discovered two such priceless *objets d'art*: a fifteenth-century Habsburg hunting bugle and a Romanov bureau. The bugle was made of a hollowed yak's horn – a rather unexpected material to find in fifteenth-century Vienna, and quite a staggering discovery in twentieth-century Lebanon. This piece was not quite unique, there was one other such bugle on display in the Stuttgart Museum, which presumably was once the yak's other horn.

The Romanov bureau, on the other hand, was unique. Not only was it a Romanov desk in design, but it had been specifically designed and adorned with pearl and gold motifs for a Romanov. The desk was authenticated as Tsar Nicholas's favourite bureau which spent what turned out to be only a fraction of its life in the royal bedchamber in the Summer Palace of St Petersburg. Unlike the Habsburg bugle, the bureau's journey to Lebanon was no guarded secret.

During Ottoman times much of the Bekaa was ruled by Sheikh Ali Ezzedin, a wealthy Shiite landowner, who in turn reported to the Turkish governor in Beirut. Ali Pasha was secretly described by his most dedicated subjects as a nut, both for his eccentricity and his thick-skinned stubbornness. He died in the provincial town of Baalbek at the grand age of ninety-eight. While most residents would have forgiven him for dying at such a dignified age, the fact was that Ali Pasha was speeding down the main street in Baalbek and died in a car accident with another car. By modern standards this would appear almost trivial; however, when the accident occurred in 1916, there was only one other car in the entire Bekaa, and in one collision all the cars in a fifty-mile radius were written off.

If his driving left a considerable amount to be

desired, Ali Pasha's sexual prowess was universally admired. In his long life he married twenty-three women. Starting with a base of sixteen wives, he chose a new bride every time he outlived a wife, snatching ever closer to the cradle, so that his last wedding, celebrated a week after his nonagenarian, was to a fifteen-year-old girl.

At an average of four children per marriage he counted almost as many offspring as candles on his last birthday cake, though in later years he was about as likely to recognize his colony of sons and daughters as he was of bequeathing his considerable fortune to them. Like a twisted joke to successive generations of Ezzedins, he recognized only two heirs: the first son from the first marriage, and the last son from the last marriage.

Samir was greatly amused by a faded portrait in the Ezzedin town mansion of a seventy-year-old decrepit-looking man carrying his two-month-old half-brother.

Upon Ali Pasha's untimely death, the two sons inherited the many estates, and the baby grew to become Hammad Ezzedin's father and the Lebanese ambassador to the Soviet Union towards the end of the Stalinist years. It was as ambassador and personal friend to Khrushchev that Hammad's father had bought many Romanov treasures, such as Tsar Nicholas's dining set with the cursive Cyrillic H exquisitely painted on high-grade crockery, a vase with a hand-painted scene of a St Petersburg boulevard signed by a leading French landscape artist of the nineteenth century and, the *pièce de résistance*, the Romanov bureau with its hinged flap, front drawers and secret *trompe-l'œil* back drawers, where Tsar Nicholas would have stored his personal notes and mementoes.

Hammad Ezzedin had inherited his father's collection but not his affinity for the arts or history. He valued the desk in terms of the £800,000 sterling it fetched at the Christie's auction sale in London, rather than in the satisfaction of owning a footnote in Tsarist history.

Hammad was first and foremost a neo-feudal baron, in whose vast properties farmers and their families tilled his fief and addressed him as Hammad Bek, marking their respect for the lord of the land. Like any reputable Lebanese magnate, Hammad was the commander-in-chief of a small but well-armed militia that patrolled his seigneury. He was allied with the larger Shiite militias and the PLO in the desire to drag Lebanon away from Maronite hegemony, and needed funds to pursue his political career. Hammad Bek never left the country, adding weight to the rumour that he was on Interpol's blacklist, and that, along with grapes and melons, his farmers harvested hashish. Unable to travel himself, he had therefore contacted Samir Khoury when he had first heard of the young Greek's success with the Habsburg bugle.

Samir had been instrumental in the sale of Tsar Nicholas's bureau. He had acted as the middleman, preparing a video and photographic presentation of the desk, arranging the transport to Portsmouth and collecting the money, which included his 5 per cent retainer.

Ever since the sale Hammad had adopted a business-oriented approach to history and antiques. As Hammad viewed excavation as a potentially profitable venture, he had a team of diggers who sifted through soil, panning for Lebanon's ungolden past. They searched for relics from Phoenician, Babylonian, Sumerian, Assyrian, Egyptian, Solomonic, Persian, Macedonian, Roman, Byzantine, Islamic, Crusader, Napoleonic and Ottoman times; the buried variety was a measure of Lebanon's downtrodden history.

Samir listened to a nostalgic song about Beirut before the war: 'Ya Beyroot'. Samir sang the refrain tunelessly and tapped the beat on the steering-wheel with his right hand, his left arm hanging limply outside on the car door. He left the high altitudes of Mount Lebanon and crossed into the Bekaa, following the road northward to Baalbek: the ancient Phoenician town which marked a cartographer's pinpoint centre of the Fertile Crescent, where man had learned to grow crops, and which was also the scene of Lebanon's first car-on-car accident where man had learned to drive cars.

Samir reached Hammad's country residence, 5 miles outside Baalbek, in the late afternoon. From the private drive, Samir saw a vista of rows of fig trees, leading to a hillock and a dozen or so separate houses. Each house was roughly square, one storey and tall, with walls of large bricks of golden limestone and sloped roofs of orange slate – turn-of-the-century Lebanese architecture. Driving to the group of houses, it appeared to Samir that he was approaching an uncharted village. However, he had been invited here on many previous occasions, and he knew that each house was, in essence, a separate room in Hammad's expansive and eccentric residence. So, for instance, the two largest houses were the main living-room, which was an immense salon capable of seating fifty guests, and the dining-room, equally large, and housing a regal teak banquet table and two dozen high-backed chairs.

He drove past the first and smallest house: the porter's lodge and residence. Samir smiled and waved at the porter, and he considered that a porter's job here represented the pinnacle of a concierge's profession.

He parked his worn grey Peugeot between a gleaming white Mercedes and a large sign with the one word painted in red: 'BEAUTY'. This was the name Hammad had given to his private village. When pronounced in Arabic, '*byootee*' means 'my houses', and with one bold word Hammad boasted both his wealth and his proficiency in English.

Hammad emerged from one of the houses to greet Samir.

'Welcome, welcome,' he said cheerfully in a singsong

voice. The two men had become friends with the successful sale of the bureau. They hugged and kissed three times. 'How was your trip?'

Samir nodded. 'No problems.' The PLO pass had allowed the Greek to travel to the Bekaa unhindered.

'Good, good.' Hammad nodded enthusiastically and shouted over his shoulder, 'Ali.'

A young man appeared and nodded at Samir. 'Yes, Hammad Bek.'

'Take the effendi's luggage to the blue guest-house.'

'Yes, Hammad Bek.'

'And tell Ibtihage we'll have coffee in the study.' Hammad led Samir onto the lawn between the main living-room and dining-room. He put his arm around Samir's shoulders and led his friend past a squat Ionic column beside a partially fragmented giant urn, large enough to preserve a man.

'That's new here, isn't it?' Samir said.

'The column? No, it's Roman.'

Byzantine, Samir mentally corrected. He shook his head and pointed.

'Oh, the pot you mean. Wasn't it here the last time you came?'

'No. It looks nice though next to the column.'

'We discovered it about two months ago. Not worth much, of course.' He shrugged good-naturedly. 'Still, it looks good in the middle of the lawn.'

He was right about that, Samir decided. The lawn sloped gently towards a patio and the French windows of the study. The grass was regularly but not neatly cut, giving rise to scattered taller tufts of grass which broke the monotony of the green carpet. The rose bushes nearest the living-room were in full bloom but not expertly trimmed. Although the overall horticulture was the hallmark of a poor gardener, the lawn's half-wild and half-cultivated aspect highlighted a degree of natural unconcern, of carefree tranquillity. The two relics from the past in the centre added to this peace; sad but contented. In this light the column and the urn were unchanging and immovable monuments in a changing landscape; two artefacts that had lived a full life and had witnessed 'my houses' sprouting around them like mushrooms after the rain.

'Come on in,' Hammad said, and slid open the French windows.

Samir asked after Naila, Hammad's wife, and they exchanged pleasantries until Ibtihage knocked on the window and entered with a tray. She handed Samir a small cup of coffee and placed Hammad's cup on the coffee-table, along with a dish of Arabian sweets.

'Thank you,' Samir said.

Hammad ignored her and moved to the desk. 'How's business, Samir?'

'OK. Christie's has been asking about the Tsar's dinner set.'

'You said last time that we could sell it for forty thousand.'

'No. I said we could definitely sell it for ten thousand sterling, and with luck on the day, up to a maximum of fifteen thousand.' Samir smiled. Despite his wealth and breeding, Hammad haggled like a wholesaler, like an Iranian merchant in a souk, and had a predictably poor memory when it suited him.

'Ten thousand? So if I shit on the plates I'll get more satisfaction, eh?'

'That's the market, Hammad.' Samir had insisted on a £20,000 retainer, which the auction house had accepted, subject to examination. 'Say fifteen thousand.'

'Yah!' Hammad uttered dismissively. 'I'll keep the set then. One day Russia will have a new king who'll pay real money for the Tsar's things.'

Samir lit a cigarette. 'You didn't bring me here for the plates at all, did you, Hammad?'

'It's a crime now to invite a friend for no reason?' Hammad had a bushy black moustache and he curled one end with his index as he added, 'We're having a

146

couple of friends over for drinks and a light meal. Do you remember Jamil?'

Samir nodded. 'Your cousin.'

'He's coming tonight. Nothing fancy, mind you.' Hammad winked at him. 'The evening's in your honour.'

Samir waited patiently and took a long drag of his cigarette.

Hammad stopped playing with his moustache and said abruptly, 'You read Greek, right?'

'Ancient Greek, yes.'

'Yes. Ancient Greek.'

Hammad moved to the desk and opened the top drawer. 'I have two Greek letters that are worth a fortune.'

He removed the two silver sheets.

'Well, that depends very much on the condition and the content,' Samir said in a neutral tone.

Hammad handed him the two silver scrolls. 'A fortune I tell you,' he insisted and downed his coffee.

'Well?' Hammad asked impatiently after a short while.

'The characters are faded. I'll need some time to decipher them under a lens and then translate the messages.'

'But you can do it?'

'Sure. I think so.'

'Good, good.'

'But they're not in a good condition,' Samir said, lighting another cigarette. 'Where were they when you found them?'

'In their shells, like two bombs.' Hammad brought out the two tin capsules.

'You removed them yourself?'

'Of course.'

Samir shook his head and flicked his cigarette in an ashtray.

'What?'

'Look.' Samir pointed to the top end of a sheet with the burning end of his cigarette. 'Here it's completely torn. And here in the middle there are recent scratches which have rubbed out a whole line of text. What did you use, a screwdriver?'

'The sheet was stuck,' Hammad said sombrely.

'You should have given it to a specialist. It's a shame. The value for this sheet at least is automatically halved.'

'Half a fortune is still a fortune, eh?' Hammad said perkily.

Samir squinted his eyes at a letter. 'Maybe the message is important.'

'They're ancient Greek, right?'

'No.'

'Byzantine then?'

'I don't think so.'

'My dick, Samir,' he swore frowning. 'Don't tell me that's not Greek.'

Samir extinguished his cigarette. 'Look at the seal here; you can just make out an eagle. I'd say this letter was probably from a Roman ambassador. The other letter doesn't have a seal, but I'd hazard a guess that it's from the same period.'

'But in Greek?'

'Greek was the diplomatic language.'

Hammad nodded appreciatively and was all smiles. 'That's great, great. When can you start?'

'I'll start on the translation tomorrow morning.'

'Is there anything you need?'

'No. What I need now is a good shake to get the Beirut dust off me.'

Hammad nodded. 'You don't need me to show you your house.' He replaced the silver scrolls and tin capsules in the top drawer. 'Use this desk tomorrow. You'll be more comfortable.'

Samir smiled and complimented, 'Hammad, I don't know of anyone anywhere who offers his guest a house.'

Hammad gestured with his hands, but of course, and said in English, 'Beautiful.'

*　　*　　*

148

In his own community, Samir would kiss his friend's wife three times on the cheeks, just as he would kiss his friend. In Muslim society, especially Shiite and especially rural, such a gesture would be construed as highly disrespectful. And although the Ezzedins were not typical rural Shiites, Samir held his distance and shook Naila's hand, kissed Jamil, and shook the hand of Jamil's wife.

They were in the bar house, which could easily have passed for a public tavern with its chest-high wooden bar the width of the house, bar stools, a dozen round tables and chairs and a barman. What appeared incongruous to Samir was the cheap tape recorder, a Seventies model which emitted a tinny sound, considerably distorting the Arabic music.

The barman brought whisky for the men, pistachio nuts, almonds, sliced cucumbers and carrots, pickled *ma'dé* and dwarf aubergines, and a bowl of unripe white plums. He returned with a Lebanese *rosé* for Naila and a fizzy lemonade for Jamil's wife, who said little throughout the evening.

'Will your wife be Greek, Samir?' Naila asked him.

'Only if her mother's beautiful and her father rich,' Samir replied with a grin.

Naila nodded. 'Choose from any community except the Druse. Their religion tells them to lie.' They discussed the Druses and the virtues of marriage as Hammad and Jamil held their own conversation.

Samir overheard Hammad say, 'God take pity on his soul.'

'Who died?' asked Samir.

'Johann,' Jamil answered.

Samir looked questioningly and Hammad explained, 'Johann was Jamil's pilot – for how long?'

'Twenty years,' Jamil said. 'I liked him. I liked him very much.' He smiled. 'He'd spent nearly forty years in Lebanon and he still spoke Arabic like an Armenian; he used to get mixed up with his genders. He always called me Mrs Jamil.'

Hammad laughed. 'Remember the first time the Hezbollah stopped him in Baalbek, what was it he told them?'

'"I am a Lebanese woman, I have a Lebanese husband, and my boss, she is Jamil Bek." The militiamen were so amused, later they stopped him again just to hear the big European speak Arabic.'

'Was he Dutch?' Samir asked.

'No, German. He was in the German *Luftwaffe* during the Second World War and he came here when the Germans lost. He said he hated how Germany had become.'

'What was his last name again?' Hammad asked Jamil.

'Raussgauss or something. I could never remember. I called him Strauss.'

'You say he flew for you?' Samir said.

'He flew my merchandise to Rhodes once a week. You could set your watch to ten in the evening every Thursday as soon as you heard the propellers.'

'Hashish?'

'Initially. And then hashmay.'

'Do you know hashmay?' Hammad asked Samir and added proudly, 'That's Jamil's own invention.'

'Made in Lebanon,' Jamil said wryly. 'It's concentrated and liquefied hashish. It takes twenty kilos of hashish to make one kilo of hashmay. Of course, it's easier to transport in bulk and to hide.'

'To Rhodes,' Hammad said, 'and from there to the rest of Europe.'

Jamil nodded. 'And America.'

'Amazing. Were you never caught?'

'Caught? No.'

Jamil was quiet. Samir suspected that the two cousins were both on Interpol's wanted list. 'No, I mean here, were you never caught here? I assume Johann's plane left from here. Didn't the militias or the Syrians ever stop you?'

'Johann's landing rights for Beirut International Airport

were revoked when he started to work for me.' Jamil laughed. 'I had a special arrangement with a local militia.'

The cousins guffawed and Samir guessed in whose property the illegal airstrip had been prepared. 'And the Hezbollah?' The new Party of God had recently grown in strength, becoming the power-brokers in Baalbek. 'Didn't they stop you?'

'I had a special arrangement with them too.'

'But they took the sphere off you,' said Hammad.

'Yes.' Jamil nodded bitterly. 'They took the sphere, the whores.' Jamil, ignoring his wife, looked apologetically at Naila. 'Pardon my Hebrew.'

'What sphere was this?' Samir asked.

Jamil shrugged.

'Not from here,' Hammad said. 'It wasn't of this world.'

'And which world was it from, then?' Samir asked cynically.

'Out of this world, eh?' Hammad replied and Jamil remained quiet.

'Extraterrestrial you mean?'

'Yes.'

'Come on, Hammad, I'm your guest not a mule.'

Samir reached for a cigarette and there was a long stony silence. 'So, what's the story?' he asked at length.

'You can tell him,' Hammad told Jamil.

'He won't believe it.'

'Tell him anyway.' Hammad turned to Samir and added, almost as a warning, 'It's a true story.'

Jamil waved at the barman for another drink and began, 'On a clear early winter's morning two years ago, at four o'clock, when it was still dark, Johann was on his way back from Rhodes – this would be his last trip. He was flying over the Bekaa when he saw a light, bright as a star, shoot across the sky. But it wasn't a shooting star. The light stopped, then shot back in the opposite direction. And again it flashed across the dark. It repeated that for a few minutes before it approached the plane.'

Jamil guzzled his drink and Samir lit a second cigarette, forgetting a first that still smouldered in the ashtray.

'Initially the light was far away, but Johann noticed that at times it was below his plane, at times above, and soon the light began to circle the plane, closing in. The light stopped directly in front of him; Johann swore it was as if the plane had stopped as well. He looked at the light, and though he couldn't be sure of the distance, it appeared blindingly bright, not much larger than a tennis ball, and inches from the cockpit.

'And then Johann had a nightmare. He was wide awake, yet he saw vivid images all around him in his mind, like a dream. He saw men, women, children taking hashmay. They were all not white, not niggers, but blue. They had drawn faces, ghostly eyes pinned on him, and arms and hands outspread like beggars. Their mouths were angry; they snarled like wild dogs. Some mouths were hungry, and some children looked like they would taste Johann's flesh.

'Then, abruptly, the image disappeared, and he saw in front of him the Star of David. The star began to recede from him and he heard angry shouts – "Jude, Jude, Jude" – and slowly he realized that the star was stitched on the back of a boy's blazer and it receded as the boy walked away from him. Then the boy stopped, and with his back still on Johann, and with the Star of David still in full view, he turned his head slowly, so very slowly to look sideways at Johann. The boy's sad face was unmistakable. It was Johann – Johann as a young boy.

'Again the image vanished abruptly. And this time Johann saw a group of boys playing football on a glorious summer's day. It was peaceful and bright, and he could hear birds singing and the happy sounds of handsome boys laughing and teasing one another in German as they kicked the football. Everything was good, everyone was happy, and Johann laughed with the boys, shouting words of encouragement in German. And then he realized there was something not right. As he looked at the scene, it took him some time to register that the ball being kicked by the happy carefree children, being dribbled across the field so innocently, being booted between the makeshift goalposts of two jerseys was not a ball at all. It was blue, an eye was missing, and it was, with little doubt, Johann's decapitated head.'

Naila gasped.

'This, at least, is how Johann described it all to me. As suddenly as it began the long nightmare ended, and Johann was once again in control of the plane. The plane was once again flying in the night. He landed badly and he swore he would never fly again.

'When he returned home in the early morning, he found a black sphere on his living-room floor. It was the size of a ping-pong ball, and he could not say how he knew, but he knew that the sphere had been the light that had followed him, and been responsible for his nightmare. So he got rid of the sphere and gave it to me. Hezbollah found out about it and asked for it. And that's the story of the sphere.'

Samir shook his head. 'I don't get it.'

'What?'

'There are quite a few holes in the story.'

'Such as?'

'You haven't told him everything,' said Hammad.

'So you've seen the sphere?' Samir asked Hammad.

'Yes I have.'

'What's so special about it?'

'What's missing in the story?' Jamil repeated.

'Well, for a start, don't you think it likely that Johann was probably under the influence of hashmay, and that he wasn't having a very good trip.'

'Johann never touched hashmay or hashish. It was purely business for him.'

'Right,' Samir said, unconvinced. 'And Johann simply knew that the black ping-pong ball was the tennis ball of light.'

Jamil nodded very slowly.

'How about Hezbollah? How did they find out about the ball, the sphere?'

'Because of my big mouth. I talk a lot. You're not the first person I've told this story to.'

He's lying, Samir realized with a start. There's more to the story.

'Tell him about the sphere, Jamil,' Hammad said.

'Fine. You asked what was so special about it, well, there are two things. The first is that the sphere is small, like a ping-pong ball, and yet it weighs thirty-six kilogrammes.'

'Thirty-six?' Samir exclaimed.

Both Hammad and Jamil nodded solemnly.

'Swear to God,' Hammad said.

'The second thing', Jamil continued, 'is that the sphere broke nine diamond drill heads when I tried to pierce it. Samir, believe me, there wasn't the smallest scratch on the sphere. On my honour, Samir, not one, not two, but nine diamond drills.'

Samir whistled with polite sympathy. 'It was black you say.'

'Black as night,' Hammad said.

'Blacker,' Jamil added. 'It wasn't as if it had been painted. It was black because the material was black, as if it shone with a black light.'

'What do you think it was?' Samir asked.

'Extraterrestrial for sure.'

'We've had UFOs here thousands of years before the West,' Hammad said, 'and we've had disappearances here long before Bermuda was discovered. That's why the jinn are so strong in the Bekaa. Some say that the jinn are really aliens.'

An intriguing story, thought Samir. 'So Hezbollah now have the sphere.'

'No, the Iranians do,' Jamil said. 'When Hezbollah couldn't open it, they sent the sphere to Iran for comprehensive tests. I can't think what the Revolutionary

154

Guard will hope to do with it though.'

'Yes, we're ready to eat,' Hammad said to Ali who, with the help of Ibtihage and another servant, brought thirty dishes to their table.

'So much for a light meal, Hammad,' Samir said. 'Invite me again when you have a banquet, I'd be curious to see the difference.'

'Men need food to keep talking,' Naila said.

'We've been boring our wives, cousin, eh?' Hammad told Jamil.

'Are you first cousins then?'

'My mother is his half-cousin,' Jamil explained. 'You wouldn't guess that, considering I'm a couple of years older than Hammad.'

'Jamil's grandmother was one of my grandfather's many daughters.'

'Ali Pasha,' Samir said, raising his glass, 'God bless him.'

'And may God give us equally long and full lives,' Hammad added.

Samir and Hammad waited for Jamil to drink with them.

Jamil lifted his drink and said, 'I'd like to toast Johann Strauss, wherever he is, I hope he's well.'

It took Samir two full days to decipher and translate the Greek letters. There was one particular line in the first letter which would remain for ever in darkness; its characters scratched to oblivion by eyebrow tweezers.

He worked at Hammad's desk, squinting behind a large magnifying lens at the silver scrolls, writing each character on a sheet of paper as he read them, straining to differentiate between an *ita* and a *mi*, a *thita* and a *fi*, a *zita* and a *xi*.

Every now and then he stopped to rub his eyes and stare vacantly through the French windows at the column and the urn, or to drink coffee and smoke a cigarette. Ali and Ibtihage took turns in bringing him

155

innumerable cups of coffee, which he drank between countless cigarettes.

Once he had transcribed both letters on two sheets, he began the relatively easier task of translating. He had brought some books with him, and because Samir had learned ancient Greek with French as the reference tongue, the first translations were in French. Later, he translated his French texts into Arabic for Hammad's benefit.

Although Samir had translated the messages by the end of the second day, he waited an extra day before telling Hammad. The reason was that the messages were exciting and strange. Samir sat in the armchair on the third day, rereading the letters and picturing their writers. The letters were a complete correspondence from and to a Roman ambassador – a consul by the name of Marcus Aemilianus Claudius.

Samir finished his coffee, lit a cigarette, and read them once more.

Letter written to the town of Antiochans, holy metropolis, autonomous, sovereign Antioch. To King Seleucus, his Council, and the People's Assembly, from Marcus Aemilianus Claudius, Roman Consul by the grace of the Roman Senate and the people of Rome, Hail.

ONE. It is Rome's understanding that Carthalo, the said Historian whom the Roman Senators have pronounced the slanderer and whom Roman justice has decreed a traitor and criminal, is presently within your metropolis, sovereign Antioch.

TWO. It is Rome's wish and desire that the above-mentioned criminal be brought to face the charges of treason in a Roman court of justice.

THREE. Rome hereby formally requests that Antioch, Her————————————————

————————————————————————— deliver
Carthalo with his slanderous writings entitled *The Conspiracy of Erab and Esh* and with the treasure removed from Carthage to Rome's trusted Consul, Marcus Aemilianus Claudius.

FOUR. Rome's respect for Antioch is deep, and force would never be used on her sister city except in the matter of safeguarding Roman Honour.

FIVE. Rome expects the above-mentioned delivery by the coming calends.

Hail. Marcus Aemilianus Claudius.

Letter written to Marcus Aemilianus Claudius, Roman Consul and Ambassador from Rome, from King Seleucus's Council. From the people of Antioch, the capital of the Empire of Seleucus the First, we bring greetings to the Roman Consul and to the people of Rome.

ONE. Upon receipt of the Consul's letter, it proved impossible for this Council, demo-cratically elected by Antiochans, to prevent Carthalo the Historian from taking his life to safeguard his honour.

TWO. It is Carthalo the Historian's final request that as the last Carthaginian, he be accorded full Phoeni burial in Tyre, the Mother City of all Poeni. The dying Goddess Tanit of Carthage has pleaded with Baal who has instructed the Goddesses Elat of Antioch and Athirat of Tyre to accept Carthalo's desire.

THREE. The Roman Consul and two aides are hereby invited to attend the full ceremo-nial burial in Tyre's Athirat Temple two days after the next Roman calends.

FOUR. As regards the Historian's writings and the treasure from Carthage, Carthalo left a message for the Roman people which we hereby relay. Roman justice has already decreed me a traitor and yet requires me to face charges of treason. That is Roman justice. Only El Himself or Carthaginian justice may brand me a criminal. Because Rome treacherously destroyed Carthage, Roman truth would deny the historical conspiracy of Erab and Esh. But Roman truth is nothing but an overripe melon which, at the gates of El, would be squeezed into a pea before being admitted into His paradise. Real truth cannot be squeezed, even by the strongest gates of strongest rock. There will Rome never find Carthage's treasure.

FIVE. These are the expressions of Carthalo the Historian and not of this Council nor the people of Antioch nor the Empire of Seleucus, who hold the people of Rome in high regard and send their greetings to them and to Rome's Consul, Marcus Aemilianus Claudius.

Samir placed the two translated copies on the coffee-table and walked out onto the lawn. Greeks and yet they speak of Phoenician deities, he wondered as he approached the urn. Tyre in the south and Antioch in the north had been part of the same empire ruled by Seleucus III at the fall of Carthage. The Seleucid empire had been carved from Alexander the Great's following the death of the Macedonian general. Greater Syria had been Hellenized, and yet the people of Antioch had stood up for a Carthaginian against the might of Rome. How intriguing, Samir thought. What were Carthalo the Historian's writings? And what was Carthage's greatest treasure?

He crouched by the urn and felt the rough red clay. He ran his fingers across the rotund vessel, pausing to examine the jagged edge on the bottom left, the side closest to the column. The urn looked like a giant egg whose side had been carelessly chipped by a giant teaspoon. Or a Roman column, Samir thought, smiling. He looked up at the Byzantine column. It was slightly taller than Samir and was a far cry from the giant slabs and columns from the Jupiter temple, or even the smaller Bacchus or Venus temples five miles away in Baalbek.

At a height of 20 metres and a diameter of 2.2 metres, the six remaining columns of the Jupiter temple, standing in a majestic row, were the largest columns men of antiquity had ever built. The grandeur and sheer architectural ingenuity was marvelled at by all visitors to Baalbek, but Samir equally marvelled at the location. Rome had never built such grandiose masterpieces in Italy or Greece. Why had the Romans chosen a distant land to erect their greatest edifice to the gods? And, more incredibly, the temples were not even the houses of Roman gods. Jupiter came from *diù pater*, the father of the gods. The commonly named Jupiter temple had been constructed, not to worship Jupiter or Zeus, but to revere Jupiter Heliopolitan – the Roman name for Baal, the father of Phoenician gods. It intrigued Samir that Rome had spent both fortune and decades erecting the most magnificent temples ever conceived in a foreign land to honour foreign gods. It reeked of a conspiracy. That made him think of Carthalo the Historian again, and he wondered who Erab and Esh were. In fact, the letters had prompted many questions for which Samir had no answers. And now, as Samir crouched by the urn, he wondered where the last Carthaginian would have buried Carthage's greatest treasure.

Nine of the original fifty-four monumental columns survived the turbulent centuries of the Levant, the Byzantine conversion of Jupiter's temple to a Christian basilica, the Islamic metamorphosis of Heliopolis into a fortress, the Crusades and the Ottomans. In 1759 three columns collapsed during an earthquake and six remained defiantly erect, side by side, with the crowning entablature, architrave and frieze intact, a

159

giant six-stringed lyre which Atargatis – or Venus – could pluck for her husband Baal or for their son Adon – or Bacchus.

The Bacchus temple, though larger than the Athenian Parthenon, was called the small temple because of its proximity to the father temple. It was relatively well preserved; most of its columns and walls were still standing. A column was inclined against the south-eastern wall of the cella, a victim of a previous earthquake in 1203. With only a section of the column's bottom rim still in contact with the pedestal, it looked like a child leaning on tiptoe, attempting to glimpse over the wall. The column, thus delicately balanced, gave the impression that nothing short of a miracle could have withheld it from crashing over the centuries.

Those columns had survived the test of time; they could count as the gates quarried from the strongest rock. As Samir contemplated this smaller column next to the urn, he imagined there was another column on the urn's other flank. He thought of the leaning column of the Bacchus temple and pictured his fictitious column leaning towards the other, wedging in the urn. The urn now became an impossibly large melon of Roman truth fragmented between the two columns, an urn whose truth was weaker than the strongest rocks.

And suddenly it dawned on Samir. The idea came from nowhere, it seemed, and his mind reeled with the revelation.

As he spotted Hammad coming towards him, he squatted next to the urn and shook his head. Samir believed he knew where Carthalo the Historian had buried Carthage's treasure.

Even from a distance, from the north-eastern road into Baalbek, the megalith's gargantuan size was breath-taking and quite palpable, as testified by a neighbouring mature poplar that was belittled by the immense rock. With one end half buried, the hefty block of limestone lay at a slight angle to the level ground and appeared as if no less than 40,000 slaves would be needed to winch it onto timber rollers and haul it away.

Hadjar el Goubla was the largest man-made brick of rock in the world, a parallelepiped weighing an estimated 1,135 tons and with dimensions of 4.55m by 4.68m by 22.73m – very nearly a perfect ratio of 1:1:5.

Samir and Hammad left the car by the side of the road and walked towards the megalith. Samir touched the rough surface and wondered at the sheer magnitude, picturing their own presence as trifling beings admiring a god's cigarette stub.

'Incredible,' Samir said, more to himself than to Hammad who stood a few paces behind.

'Yes,' Hammad said, unimpressed.

Hammad had grown up here. As a child, he and his friends had played many games in this area, and often the rock had held a pivotal role. It had been a ship and they pirates on the deck; it had been a fortress and he with his band of Saracens had stormed it, attacking a band of defending Byzantines. Hammad was not impressed by the rock he had seen since he could walk. He viewed it instead with the blasé patience of a native showing off the local attractions to visitors.

'Hadjar el Houbla,' he said.

'Yes I know,' Samir replied.

The megalith was popularly known as Hadjar el Houbla – the pregnant woman's rock. It had inspired many legends, but the most widespread was the tale of a white jinnee queen called Alia. The legend relating to Hadjar el Houbla was set at a time when all the land for many leagues fell under the rule of King Solomon. When the king announced his wish to build a magnificent temple, his grand vizier advised that the most magnificent trees should be used in its construction. So he was sent to Mount Lebanon to oversee the felling of cedars and the planned destruction of an entire forest of the majestic trees.

When the jinn of the forest saw their old arboreal friends being so mercilessly hacked, they pleaded with their queen to use her powers to stop the massacre. Alia was a jinnee queen, as such she was larger than ordinary jinn and had the supernatural powers of a genie, bequeathed to all royal jinn. At the time, according to the tale, she resembled a woman of unsurpassed beauty, though it was quite apparent from the late stage of her pregnancy that she was as beautiful as she was unavailable. Alia flew to King Solomon's palace and entered through an open window. She spoke to the king and described rocks which neither animal nor storm could fritter away, and told him of hewn stones eternally outlasting their masons. Only such stones, Alia said, would live to tell future generations of King Solomon's wisdom.

Despite the grand vizier's strong protests, the king was convinced and agreed to build a temple of stone instead of cedar if the jinnee queen herself brought him the strongest and most durable rocks in the world. For a month Alia flew to the north and returned carrying the largest bricks of rock humans had ever seen. Then one day, as she flew over Baalbek, she felt the first pains of labour and dropped the boulder she was transporting. The megalith fell squarely on the grand vizier, who was visiting Baalbek, and there it remained immovable; the vizier killed and buried in one blow.

Alia was so distraught by the accidental death of a life that she renounced her powers and retired to a secluded life among the flowers in the Bekaa. King Solomon, out of spite for his grand vizier's death, and deprived of further giant rocks, ordered the destruction of many cedar forests on Mount Lebanon.

King Solomon is famed for his wisdom everywhere in the world except modern Baalbek.

The archaeological evidence was less colourful than the legend. In Byzantine times, Jupiter's temple was called the Trilithon, or the temple of the three rocks, due to the three giant slabs on the southern wall. At an average weight of 830,000 kilogrammes, though these rocks were significantly smaller and lighter than Hadjar el Goubla, it was generally accepted that the Romans had planned on a Cyclopean wall of four rocks for Baal's temple – which the Byzantines would then probably have named the Tesserlithon. But for an unknown reason the Roman architects had abandoned the rock in the countryside to centuries of folklore.

'OK?' Hammad said impatiently, moving away.

'If I remember correctly, they're not far from here, right?'

'A hundred metres,' Hammad said, and pointed at a large mound of bushes. 'Over on the other side.'

'Right.'

Unlike Hadjar el Goubla, the two monoliths could only be seen from close quarters. The mound of scrub and bracken was shaped somewhere between a romantic heart and a black-eyed bean, and it was as if the erect rocks had been strategically placed within the concave alcove. Closed off on three sides, the monoliths remained hidden to the casual visitor and were clearly off the tourist beaten track, as the official guides and local residents considered them paltry compared with the monumental Roman ruins. They were both squat, inches taller than Samir, and their rough edges were by far inferior to the precise 90-degree uniform planes of Roman masonry. This cragginess which had added to the lack of enthusiasm of official guides had equally enchanted Samir, who regarded the monoliths for what they were: obelisks of prehistoric man. These rocks were so deeply rooted in man's history that they had been absorbed by the environment, appearing as natural a geological phenomenon as the surrounding mound. Close together, like a pair of lower incisors, nothing much larger than a watermelon could be squeezed through the gap.

With his palms pressed firmly against both obelisks,

Samir said, 'This is it, damn it! It's got to be.'

'Where the treasure's buried?' Hammad prompted.

Samir nodded. 'Where Carthalo the Historian would have hidden Carthage's treasure.'

'Why?'

Samir spun around and said excitedly, 'What are these rocks called?'

Hammad shrugged. 'Nothing.'

'Aren't they the Pillars of Truth?'

'Some people call them that,' Hammad conceded, uninterested.

'And do you know why?'

'Sure. If you stand between the rocks and tell a lie, the rocks close in on you and crush you to death. If you tell the truth, nothing happens and you can pass through.'

'Exactly. The Pillars of Truth.'

'Yeah, but that's the legend. Are you saying it's true? It's like Hadjar el Houbla, eh? A pregnant jinnee who drops her rock – doesn't mean it happened.'

'No, no.' Samir shook his head emphatically. 'Let me tell you what I think. I'm not implying any truth in the myths.'

Hammad indicated the gap between the obelisks. 'Easy enough to see if it works. Go in there and lie.'

'The legends themselves, both Hadjar el Houbla and the Pillars of Truth, aren't relevant, but their differences are,' Samir explained. 'We know the Romans chiselled Hadjar el Houbla – it's two thousand years old, and in that time it has inspired many stories. The most popular is the one we know about the jinnee queen, but there's also a different story about the mythical giants who lived in these parts.'

Hammad nodded. 'There's another one about aliens who needed huge rocks and who left one behind before returning to their galaxy.'

'Right. Hadjar el Goubla is so impressive that human imagination went wild and every successive generation added to the stories, embroidering on them. But the

Pillars of Truth are not at all as impressive; they're pretty dull in fact.'

'They're just rocks,' agreed Hammad.

'Most people aren't even interested in seeing them, let alone talking about them, and least of all imagining tales for them. They're about six thousand years old, in other words they were erected in 4000 BC. And in all that time, what are the legends? There is only one; the one you've described. No others. No jinn, no aliens, no giants – these rocks were simply too plain to be bothered with. Do you see what I mean?'

Hammad looked on blankly for a while, and then said, 'No.'

'Think about the legend itself: "If you stand in the middle and lie, the rocks'll crush you and you'll die." And that's it; there is no story. There are no characters, no plot. It's like a God-given commandment; a fact of nature. In a way it's like: "If you sow your seeds in spring, you'll reap the harvest in autumn." A simple statement that has endured as long as man has tilled his fields. The legend of the Pillars of Truth is strange enough to last and, equally, the rocks are uninteresting enough not to inspire any additions or changes.'

'So what?' Hammad played with his moustache impatiently.

'Just over two thousand years ago, when Carthalo was around, these rocks were 4000 years old; ancient enough to be a legend. I believe the folklore may have been the same in his day. Indeed, it would have been even more widespread then because Heliopolis and Hadjar el Goubla didn't exist yet. So I'm not implying that there's any truth in the myth but that the same legend we have today would have been familiar to Carthalo the Historian.'

Hammad looked unconvinced. 'But he was Carthaginian, you said, from North Africa. Say the story was the same, how would he know it, eh?'

'Baalbek was Phoenician and Punics were once

Phoenicians. They left Tyre in 800 BC, but they still considered themselves Phoenicians. Listen to this,' Samir said and extracted a sheet from his trouser pocket, 'this is in Antioch's reply to the Roman consul: ". . . as the last Carthaginian he be accorded full Phoeni burial in Tyre, the Mother City of all Poeni." Like any Baalbeki, Jubeli, Tyrian or Sidonian, an educated Carthaginian would have known about these rocks.'

'How? They had no TV.'

Samir looked at his friend in astonishment. He wasn't sure if he was being serious. 'Even if you had no TV, wouldn't you have heard of the Kaaba in Mecca? I think the Pillars of Truth of Baalbek would also have been part of a people's heritage.'

'OK,' Hammad said, 'Carthalo knows about the story, but why does he bury the treasure here?'

'The important thing here is that he'd have known about it. Other than that it's not that I *think*, but rather that I *believe* he buried it here. It's a kind of faith, I don't know. But I swear, Hammad, it came to me like an inspiration.' Samir was surprised to find Hammad nodding and looking less sceptical. He continued, reading from the sheet, '". . . Roman truth is nothing but an overripe melon which, at the gates of El, would be squeezed into a pea . . ."' Samir squeezed between the obelisks and said, 'To Carthalo, Roman justice was unjust, and Roman truth untrue. If Roman truth were an overripe melon it would be compressed by the Pillars of Truth – that's the legend.' Samir had to slide out to resume, '". . . Real truth cannot be squeezed, even by the strongest gates of strongest rocks . . ." That too is part of the legend. These Pillars of Truth will have no effect at all on pure truth. As for the strongest rocks, these monoliths were four thousand years old when Carthalo said these words, and they probably looked like they could last another four thousand years.'

Samir slid once again between the rocks and quoted, without looking at the sheet, '". . . There will Rome never find Carthage's treasure . . ."' Able to look only sideways at Hammad, Samir smiled, pointed at the ground between the monoliths and said excitedly, 'It's here, Hammad. Damn it! It's got to be here, I can feel it through the soles of my shoes.'

As his five-man team began the illegal excavation between and around the Pillars of Truth, Hammad's feelings towards the Carthaginian cache progressively evolved from dissent to ambivalence to outright enthusiasm. It was for this reason that, for the first three days of digging, Samir did not share his growing doubts.

While he still believed that Carthalo had buried his treasure between the obelisks, he was not so sure that the treasure had remained buried. Just as he had deduced the secret location, it was naturally equally possible that others had been inspired by Carthalo's words. Samir considered and hoped that the letters had been privy to a select few: Roman officials who were ignorant of Baalbek's legends, and a handful of Antiochans who, if they made the link with the monoliths, guarded Carthalo's secret out of solidarity with the Punic cause. But with each passing day, odds were increasing that the treasure had long since been unearthed.

As the summer sun moved to meet Mount Lebanon in the late afternoon of the fourth day of fruitless digging, Samir began to believe they would never find the treasure. He even wondered why he had felt so confident in the first place. As he explained to Hammad, it had been a gut feeling, and he had known, almost impulsively, where Carthalo had buried the treasure, as if he had been in direct communication with the historian himself. This was strange, especially as it was not in Samir's nature to be impulsive about anything.

He had never bought coins or agreed to sell an *objet d'art* unless he knew the value, basing his decision on an evaluation of the artefact in terms of condition, scarcity and market demand. Now, for probably the first time, he had been convinced about something with little reason, and with even less confirmation of historical facts. For instance, the most rational element for the location of the cache was the assumption and not the fact that the Pillars of Truth were far older than Hadjar el Goubla. And he could not, for all the treasures in the world, remember how he knew that the monoliths were 4000 years older. Either he had heard it said or he had read it somewhere, but the point was this: he should have verified the historical facts before embarking on a Grail-like quest. It irked him that he was so amateurish.

As he looked on at the five bare-chested men digging the ground between the obelisks, Samir thought, the soles of my shoes my arse. How could he have been so childish? It occurred to him then that probably the last time he had been this impulsive in his conviction was when the treasure had changed into a worthless Syracusan imitation.

Hammad strutted towards him and said cheerfully, for the fourth consecutive day, 'How are your soles today?'

Samir shrugged.

'Maybe we'll find it tomorrow, eh?'

'Maybe.'

'Inshallah.' Hammad turned to the diggers and shouted, 'That doesn't mean you stop now. Come on, *yala*. You've got at least another hour's work.'

Hammad put his arm around Samir's shoulders and added, 'It'll be great. Every museum in the world will fight for a small part of it. We'll be rich, my friend.'

'You're already rich.'

'You'll be rich and I'll be richer.'

'Maybe. Maybe you trust me too much.'

Hammad appeared to ignore his comment. 'If you tell me it's buried here, this is where it's buried.'

'Was buried.'

'Was buried, is buried – same thing.' Hammad shrugged. 'I piss on most people's beliefs and it's like

168

pissing on salt, because they talk and talk just to pretend they know everything. But with someone like you, you only say what you know to be true. So if you believe in something, I respect that. And it must be true.'

'Come on, that's rubbish.'

'You see what I mean? You're a sceptic by nature. That's why I believe you're right about the treasure. I bet you still don't believe in Johann's sphere, eh?'

Samir said, amused, 'What's it got to do with the treasure and the Pillars of Truth?'

'Do you believe the sphere exists? Just answer me that.'

'The thirty-two-kilogramme black ping-pong ball and tennis ball of light?'

'Thirty-six kilogrammes,' Hammad corrected.

'No. It's an interesting story but I think that's all it is.'

'The sphere is real and you don't believe it. You need to see to believe, just like Johann before his experience. So if you now believe the treasure's here, well, I too believe, because I believe in you.'

Hammad was patting Samir's back encouragingly when a digger called, 'Hammad Bek, Hammad Bek.'

Hammad twitched his eyebrows at Samir and shouted back, 'What?'

The worker held up a palm-sized flat stone. Hammad and Samir moved towards him and the other four men crowded around them.

'What do you think?' Hammad asked, handing Samir the stone.

Samir lifted and tilted it, catching bounced pinpricks of light from the westering sun. 'Marble,' he said.

The tablet, larger than Samir's open palm, had two smooth and two jagged edges, like a corner chunk of chocolate snapped from the rest of the bar. It was golden, like sand, with a fine ripple of wavy lines, in places lighter, almost white, in places darker, almost brown, like a geographer's contour lines marking a desert's dunes and wadis. One surface was perfectly

169

smooth and the other had neat lines of engraved script.

'Semitic, I think,' Samir said at length.

'Semitic?'

'Yes. Maybe Aramaic. I don't know.'

'Or Punic?'

Samir nodded slowly, then shrugged. 'Could be Punic.'

'Of course it's Punic.'

'Can't be sure.'

Hammad addressed the man who had found it. 'Where was it?'

'Between the rocks. Over here,' the man replied, squatting next to the obelisks and tapping the ground.

'So,' Hammad said, turning to Samir, 'who else would bother to bury anything here?'

'Maybe,' Samir conceded. His voice betrayed a rising excitement as he added, 'Let's concentrate on this side. But let's dig carefully from now on. No picks, and use only small spades.'

'The shit,' Hammad shouted. 'My dick's in *khara*.'

'You see,' Samir said, 'maybe Carthalo's treasure was in these words.'

'Fuck the words. I fuck entire paragraphs. Where's the treasure?'

'This is it, Hammad. This is all we're getting.'

'You now believe there's nothing else down there? Go there, Samir, stand between the rocks and tell me there's nothing there, eh?'

'Hammad.'

'*Ach*,' Hammad sighed. 'If I ever find your shoemaker, I'll kick him so deep up the arse he'll taste my Italian soles.'

'What we have here is valuable.'

They had discovered a marble tablet the size of a large sheet of paper and another smaller slab, bringing a total of three slabs and no treasure.

'Hah. What we have here is that pimp's memoirs.'

170

Samir frowned. 'Whose?'

'Carthalo's. Or else his suicide note.'

'I wish I could translate them.'

'I'll keep digging, soles or no soles.'

'You know it's a shame if it's Punic script. The Maronite liturgy is in Aramaic.'

'Allah is my witness, I'll keep digging. And because He's merciful I'll find something other than words.'

'A Maronite priest might be able to understand some of these words but not read them.'

'Endless words. Fuck every book that's ever been written.'

'I knew someone who could read all the Semitic tongues but he left the country.'

'The pork-eating traitor.'

Samir was astonished and suddenly angry. 'He was forced to leave, that doesn't make him a traitor.'

'But it makes him a liar.'

'Why, because he described things as they were?' Samir then realized Hammad could not know about Jacob.

'What? So where's the treasure?'

'I thought you were talking about someone else,' said Samir.

'I'm talking about my donkey, who do you think?'

Samir grinned. 'The one with the limp?'

'No, the one from Tripoli, eh? The one with a limp dick.'

They both laughed.

'I'll return to Beirut, take some proper photographs of the tablets, and see if I can find someone to translate them.'

Later that morning Hammad accompanied Samir to the worn grey Peugeot next to the sign with the one word painted in red. They kissed three times and Hammad said formally, 'Remember, *byootee byootak*.' My houses are your houses.

'We'll keep in touch, Hammad.'

171

'Come back soon, eh? And call your friends at Christie's – tell them you've found Shakespeare in Punic. That'll get the price up.'

Samir left Beauty with the tablets firmly wrapped in blankets, in an inconspicuous cardboard box, and drove southwards, taking the main road between the Lebanon and the Antilebanon. He had the radio on, and as he tapped the beat on the steering-wheel with his right hand while his left arm hung limply outside on the car door, he found himself thinking about the ex-sixth-floor tenant who had put out his trash once every three days and who had taught him French.

Jacob Haddad had sent him a postcard from the States. He was now a professor of proto-Semitic in Tel Aviv and had been invited to offer a series of lectures at one of the Ivy League colleges. If anyone was able to translate the Punic tablets, Jacob was the man for the task, and Samir resolved to try to contact his old friend.

The card was nearly a year old and Jacob was, in all likelihood, back in Tel Aviv. Naturally Samir could not travel to Israel, nor could he phone from Beirut. They would therefore have to meet in some third country close to the Middle East. Like using compasses to locate the third vertex of an equilateral triangle, Cyprus was the best locus, with Larnaca a short flight or a long boat trip for both.

As Samir made the mental arrangements for the trip he became excited. For a start he was excited by the tablets. Somehow, because Samir had thought of and even sensed the secret location, it was as if he and Carthalo the Historian were on the same wavelength. The tablets now became a personal letter to him from a Carthaginian pen-friend, which he was dying to read. He wanted to learn who Erab and Esh were, and above all what Carthage's greatest treasure was.

6

THE TEMPORAL RED SHIFT

Maira walked onto the platform at Reading an hour after the last commuter train had left for Paddington. Apart from three boisterous youths enjoying a slanging-match, a matronly woman sitting on a bench reading the *Daily Mail*, and a young executive in a pinstripe suit, platform two for London was empty. Maira ambled to the newsstand and bought the *Guardian*.

Maira had spent yet another unsatisfying weekend with Max Salter. At the end of every weekend with Max she would tell herself it would be the last. But it never was. He would arrive in Cambridge on a Friday evening, or more usually, she would come to Reading, and they would spend one more meaningless and empty weekend together. Loneliness was the cause. That cold dark vacuum that stretched interminably between the stars. Maira and Max were drawn together to exchange insincere hugs and bodily fluids, then drifted apart like dead logwood down a river. There was little true companionship. Max was nothing more than a casual boyfriend who had his uses. For instance, Maira hated going to faculty parties alone; better an incompatible escort than no escort. And if not for the emotional warmth of a relationship, Max did at least provide the naked physical heat of another human being.

This weekend had been no exception to all the other weekends. She had arrived in Reading on Friday, two days after the conference on time, where she had spoken of the chronon. They had casually removed their clothes for some sex that could arguably have enthralled a voyeur mouse, had showered separately, eaten take-away deep-pan pizzas and watched a raunchy American film about the sexual exploits of passionate and good-looking adolescents. Max had chosen the film. Probably to see how the other half lived, Maira decided.

She sat down on a bench, unfolded the newspaper, and read a headline: SEARCH FOR EXTRATERRESTRIALS CONTINUES. She had to blink several times for her brain to register the correct headline: SEARCH FOR EARTHQUAKE VICTIMS CONTINUES.

Silly girl, she scolded herself.

Not many years ago the scientific community at large had regarded the SETI Institute as little more than a forum for semi-professional UFO watchers. But with enviably ample funding, respectability had been gained. The Institute had succeeded in enrolling some of the globe's leading astronomers and cosmologists with its highly impressive array of state-of-the-art radio tele-scopes, each telescope constituting a part of some gigantic compound eye in the Nevada Desert. In recent years, many of SETI's peripheral activities which repre-sented *orthodox* astronomical work had been shelved in order to pay exclusive attention to the search for extra-terrestrial intelligence.

Given such prominence in the Eighties, Maira was not at all surprised that Bill Walters of SETI had been invited to the conference. What had surprised her, though, was his question to her. How on earth should she know why SETI had received no alien signals? If there were ETs at all, maybe they did not want to communicate; didn't want to *phone away*. She thought of the Spielberg film that was such a craze everywhere. Maira could sympathize with that. When spending the weekend alone, she liked to vegetate for the whole of Sunday morning, either in bed, or at any rate wearing her dressing-gown, reading the *Observer* and supple-ment from cover to cover, drinking coffee till ten and tea till noon. She would put her phone in the bathroom, cover it with the bath mat and close the door, so that if it rang, its sound would remain audible enough for her to know that someone was trying to contact her, yet muffled enough not to irritate her. Maybe aliens also enjoyed their privacy.

She was bemused by Bill Walters's question, and equally flattered by his almost childlike expectation that she would know the answer. Mummy did not. But Mummy had promised that she would think about it.

Silly girl.

Lord knows, Maira thought, why she had made such a promise. What was said impulsively, or not, was said. And as she had never, in her recollection, reneged on a promise, she now considered, somewhat guiltily, that since the conference she had not given a microsecond's thought to the question. That, too, was Max's fault, Maira decided irrationally and felt better.

She became aware that in all the time she had been on the bench she had been staring at one word in the newspaper. She looked up and saw an old man looking at her quizzically. Maira folded the *Guardian*, gave him her sweetest smile, and moved closer to the kerb on the platform.

There were far more people now and the platform speakers informed all passengers to London that the InterCity 125 from Cornwall would be delayed by five minutes.

She first saw, then heard, a service train approaching the station. As it drew nearer the sound of the engine increased and the pitch became higher. The service train did not stop and trundled past Maira sounding a regularity of twin heartbeats as a succession of wheels rolled onto different tracks. The train moved away, the engine noise diminished, and the pitch became more sonorous. Strange to think how everything was interconnected. It was because of this phenomenon that the universe was found to be expanding. As the train drew closer, to an observer the sound waves emitted from the engine were compressed and the pitch became audibly higher. When the train moved away, the sound waves were stretched and correspondingly the sound became deeper. What was relevant to sound also applied to light waves. Light from stars and galaxies was observed to be blue-shifted, which implied that the light waves were being stretched and that, therefore, these stars and galaxies were moving away from the Earth, like trains pulling away from a station. As these stellar bodies were all receding from the solar system, rather than implying that the sun was the unpopular skunk in the forest of stars, this meant that the universe was expanding like an inflating balloon.

This was the Doppler effect, old hat to all scientists. Maira was fascinated, though, how a straightforward practical observation, blended with imagination and science in equal doses, had produced such an inspired idea. Even today, not many people were able to see the link between a passing car and an expanding universe.

Maira saw the InterCity train drawing closer, and as she once more heard the sorcerer's magic on the sound waves, she had an idea. Initially she thought it was too simple to be of value, but when she boarded the train and found a seat, she sketched her idea on an unprinted corner of the *Guardian*.

She looked at her squiggly lines, chewed her pen for a while, jotted a couple of equations and gasped, 'Good Lord!' much to the dismay of the old man who had joined her in the carriage.

Was that it? she thought excitedly. Could it be so simple?

As the Berkshire landscape rushed past, Maira believed she knew why SETI had received no signals, and furthermore, if what she had in mind proved successful, the Chronon Theory of Time could be conclusively vindicated – beyond a shadow of doubt.

* * *

176

'I still need to work on the maths,' Maira told Bill Walters as she sipped her chilled white wine.

Maira had reached Paddington and, instead of taking the tube across town to catch her connection for Cambridge, she had phoned Bill Walters, who was staying in London, and they had arranged to meet in a wine bar in Covent Garden; their first meeting outside a stuffy lecture theatre.

'Do you have any paper?' Maira asked.

Enjoying the wine, she finished her glass and poured herself another as he checked his pockets. He was probably in his forties, Maira decided, though he had a younger expression and fine blond hair which was only just beginning to recede. His forehead had three prominent and parallel lines, folds of skin stretching over the eyes like minor canyons, giving the impression that he was in constant amazement. His bulging blue eyes were surrounded by wrinkles, as if the eyes had been dropped into their sockets like crashing meteorites that had caused the skin to ripple. He was by no means handsome but, Maira felt, nor was he unattractive.

'I'm all out,' he said, and waving his address book he added, 'unless this will do.'

Maira had assumed that Bill Walters was American because of his accent, until, that is, he said *out* with the tell-tale West Country slur. 'Owt and abowt,' Maira said.

'What?'

'Dead give-away.' She smiled. 'Whereabowts in Canada do you hail from?'

'Toronto.' He grinned at her. 'I'm glad you phoned. I didn't expect you would.'

'Well, I have been thinking about that tricky question you raised ever since the conference.' Her mirthful expression did little to conceal the lie.

'Is that so?'

Bill Walters refilled their glasses from the wine bottle and Maira picked up his address book from the table.

He shot a glance at her *Guardian*, at messy notes and equations scribbled above a headline where the words 'Earthquake Victims' had been changed to 'Extra-terrestrial Life'. 'Cheers,' he said.

Maira nodded, took a long sip and began, 'I'm probably teaching you to suck eggs, if you catch my drift, but first let's agree on three assumptions. One, that the creation of life is a regular occurrence, depending primarily on the favourable conditions of a planetary system, such as the presence of a star conducive for life, a planet orbiting in the star's ecosphere, the planet containing rich deposits of the atoms required as the building blocks of complex molecules, and the rest. Two, that life invariably evolves and eventually yields an intelligent species. Three, that the intelligent species will attempt to communicate with stellar neighbours.'

'OK so far,' Bill concurred.

'This implies that at any given time, myriad civilizations will be trying to communicate with one another. How would they emit their calls? That's the easy part. Of all the frequencies in the electromagnetic spectrum, radio waves are the likeliest candidates, needing low power to travel far. What form would these communications take? The signals would need to be regular, but not too regular, so that the receiver across the galaxy or beyond recognizes the transmission as being intelligent, over and above the background random radio noise. In essence, the most reasonable transmission would be a kind of Morse code with binary dots and dashes.'

'Sure,' Bill Walters said simply.

'Now, let's talk in terms of generations of alien civilizations. As you correctly pointed out in the conference, CTT predicts many more generations than previously imagined. So where are the signals?' Maira took another long sip.

'Right,' he said nodding, waiting.

'I believe we're hearing them,' she resumed, 'but we're not paying any attention.'

'How?' Bill's eyes bulged further; his brow was furrowed deeper.

'We're not listening. I'll explain this by describing three generations of intelligent life. We are, for the sake of this exercise, in the third generation, along with one alien planet – there are naturally many others, given the assumptions, but we'll consider one for this example. This alien planet of our generation will be called Planet A.

'Planet A is transmitting its message but, because the broadcast is delayed by the factor of the speed of light, we on Earth will only receive Planet A's hello in the future. And unless there is an alien civilization of our generation unreasonably close to Earth – considering the odds – this applies to all intelligent planets of our generation. The result: we can hear no signals from aliens who began their sentient lives at more or less the same time as us. So we turn our receivers to catch messages from previous generations, older alien civilizations, whose signals will have had time to reach our planet. Again we'll consider examples: Planet B which began transmitting in our past, and Planet C which began its emission in our distant past. Agreed so far?'

Bill Walters pursed his lips, nodded and went back to looking surprised.

'Good. Because now we come to my simple idea. CTT predicts that the difference between now, the past and the distant past will be in time itself. The more distant the past, the shorter the universe's second. It is fair to assume that any life-form living in the past would have had a similar shorter concept of the second, relative to us who live in our present, because the laws of physics are affected by a shorter second, which in turn affect the laws of chemistry and biology.'

'Whoa.' Bill halted her with his palm. 'What do you mean?'

'If I were an alien from the past, my reactions, my speech, everything about me would be like a mouse's or an ant's to you. My second from my past universe would be considerably shorter than your concept of the second in your present universe. We therefore conclude that given our first assumptions and the supposition that CTT is right, aliens in the past will be active as mice or ants, depending on the past – but not, of course, necessarily as small. And they will be transmitting their signals according to their concept of the universe's second. Let me illustrate this idea with a simple sketch.'

Maira drew on a blank sheet, under Q in the address book:

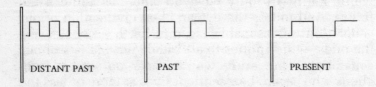

DISTANT PAST   PAST   PRESENT

'Planet A, being of our generation of planets transmitting "now", has the same concept of the universe's second as ourselves, but we can't, unfortunately, hear its broadcast until our future. What I have illustrated here are the differences in signals, not frequency. All the planets could be emitting on the same frequency. We begin to see that some of the signals from the past may be overlooked. Let's take an example of a signal that is dot-dot-dot, Morse for S.'

Maira sketched:

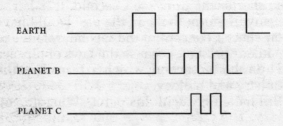

EARTH

PLANET B

PLANET C

'This is an over-simplification. In actual fact, the more distant the signal the more likely that an entire volume

180

of a message can be contained within a single dash, following our perspective of the second. If you were to receive this on your radio telescope, what would you make of it?'

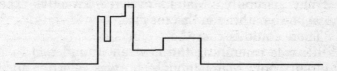

Bill examined the doodle and said, 'Background radiation, just noise.'

'Exactly,' Maira said triumphantly. 'And yet this could be an Encyclopedia Galactica waiting to be read.'

Bill's lines on his forehead deepened and he said, 'Assuming the Chronon Theory is correct.'

'Oh, CTT is right,' she retorted immediately. 'It's the early stages of a grander, more unified theory. In everything I have outlined here, the weak link lies in the first assumptions. As far as I'm concerned, I don't happen to think that life is as widespread among the galaxies as many believe.'

'OK. Let's say all this is true. Assumptions and CTT. How would you proceed?'

'Tricky but not impossible. As you focus your radio telescopes on a distant galaxy, because you know the distance, you know when the radio emissions will have been broadcast. You can therefore take into account the universe's shorter second. It is then a matter of processing the data, somehow slowing all the signals according to this shorter cosmic second prevalent at the outset of transmission. So, for instance, signals from a very distant galaxy will need to be slowed correspondingly more than those from a not-so-distant galaxy. You should then be able to differentiate between any true intelligent signals and the background noise. I can work out the mathematics, but I'm no computer buff. However, I imagine that some form

181

of automatic data processing would not present too many difficulties.'

Bill smiled. 'Of course, if we were to do all this, we would be claiming the validity of CTT.'

'Why naturally,' Maira answered sweetly. 'There must be something in this for me.'

'There could be more.'

Bill was examining the new entry under Q in his address book; Maira thought he was referring to the idea. 'It's messy now. With the equations I think you'll find it makes perfect sense.'

He pocketed the address book, emptied the last of the wine in Maira's glass and gestured to a waiter for another bottle.

'You arm-twister.' She took a long sip.

'How would you like to work with us?'

'Not much.'

'Please don't be shy.' He paused. 'Think about it, though. We pay pretty well.'

'I have and I know you do,' she said, unimpressed.

'Right. Sorry. A bloomer.'

'Maybe a bit. But it's not that.' Maira fingered her glass. 'More money is always welcome, especially from where I'm sitting. But working with SETI would be working on one project; there are many more projects that are, frankly, more important. At Cambridge I can dabble with many ideas.'

'Now you're being tactful.'

Maira smiled and decided she liked Bill Walters.

'Very well,' she said. 'SETI's a way off the academic beaten track; far removed from the exciting hub of discoveries.'

'It needn't be. We have the best telescopes in the world and the healthiest resources. Why, I'd imagine this would be seventh heaven to an astrophysicist of your calibre.'

'An astronomer, probably. An astrophysicist, perhaps. Such as myself, not at all. But I like the flattery.'

'What the chronon needs to be widely recognized', Bill said, 'is some concrete proof, not the reasons and observations which you described in the lecture, which could be explained by some other theory.'

'Such as?'

'That's not important. The point is, if we set out to search for alien life with CTT as the guiding theory, and if we discover signals thanks to CTT, just think of the instantaneous impact such a discovery would have on the world. The average person would learn of the chronon theory before the scientists with headlines like: EXTRATERRESTRIALS HEARD THANKS TO THE QUANTUM OF TIME.' Bill had pointed at the *Guardian*, and Maira blushed irrationally. 'That's the reality. In one swoop your theory would be accepted by the scientific community and popularized by the media.'

'If we receive a signal.'

'*We* will, hopefully, one day,' Bill stressed.

'I don't know,' Maira said, sipping her wine. 'I don't mean to be rude, but are you in a position to make such an offer?'

'Yes. And as the director of SETI in Nevada, I would find it difficult to take CTT into account if you weren't there to help in the calibration.'

'Oh.' So he's the bigwig; she frowned. 'You're not being fair.'

Bill smiled kindly. 'Dr Brisden, I've liked what I've heard today. I want to try your ideas, but I can't do it alone. I need not only your maths but your presence in helping to oversee the design and installation of the new device that will be required to slow the signals. How about it?'

'I do have a sabbatical leave that's overdue.' Maira blew a sudden raspberry, astonishing Bill even more. 'Silly girl, that was meant to be a private thought. The wine turned it into words before I had time to think it.'

'Well, that's settled then. It's even better this way. We need you to set us off on the right track. And you don't want to absent yourself too long from Cambridge. We're all happy.'

'I haven't said yes.'

'But you promise you'll give it serious thought.' He looked then as he had in the lecture theatre at Cambridge: a helpless child.

'There you go again.'

'What?'

'You have this annoying way of making me promise things, and I don't even know you.'

Bill raised his glass. 'Here's to getting to know one another in Nevada.'

'Cheers.'

'And a toast to a great scientific idea.' With his free hand he patted the pocket with the address book.

'To the Doppler effect,' said Maira. 'To good old Doppler.'

'To the temporal red shift,' Bill added.

'The temporal red shift, I like that,' Maira said and they clinked glasses.

After their meeting Maira decided to start on the research for SETI. She walked to Leicester Square and watched Spielberg's *ET*. And the following morning Maira phoned Max to tell him it was really over, and then Bill to say she would be in Nevada in two weeks' time.

Ric Garcia looked like a typical streetwise Hispanic American, as portrayed by countless TV programmes. He was young, unruly, a computer whiz-kid with a temperament somewhere between mischievous and slightly malevolent.

Probably as a result of her own upbringing, which had instilled in her a sense of reserve for personal matters, Maira was constantly surprised by Ric's frankness and the apparent ease with which he described his past life. She learned that he had broken into NASA, the parent organization of SETI, through the back door, or more accurately, through an open computer window.

Ric Garcia was a hacker and, before his respectable employ with NASA, he had eked out a living tapping into a company's secret files and selling classified information to a rival company. He had gained access to NASA personnel files and had changed them, more for fun than any reward. The irony was that as he changed the files, he introduced a new and much-improved database program which so impressed NASA officials that they tracked him down, threatened to incarcerate him, then offered him a job instead. His first task as a NASA employee was to correct all the salaries, which he had whimsically halved, and to remove the virus he had planted, which had invaded the entire network. This bug was quite harmless, if unacceptable, as it commanded every NASA computer, on being switched on, to beep the 'Star-Spangled Banner' and flash the lyrics on the monitor in Spanish.

Ric's first significant achievement within NASA was with a project on the sun's corona. Computer speed in typical astronomical research was not of the utmost priority. Signals from distant constellations varied little in a decade and astronomers could afford to be patient with their computers; there would always be tomorrow, or the day after, for more data to be collected from Andromeda. But for a rare event like a total eclipse of the sun occurring over a radio telescope, where the corona could be examined for under ten minutes, computer speed and fast parallel processing were of the essence for the successful collation of all useful information. Ric Garcia had introduced new software that could analyse over a thousand different signals almost as soon as they were being observed. It was because of this success with the sun's corona that Bill Walters had asked for Ric's transfer to SETI.

In order to incorporate Maira's idea on a shorter past universal second, SETI software not only had to process signals from a wide spectrum of radio frequencies, but had to decelerate – so to speak – each and every signal, according to the object's distance, and then filter out any intelligent alien broadcast. All this as fast as electronically possible.

In the first month of Maira's arrival she and Ric worked as a team to fine-tune SETI's receivers along CTT lines. In practice, it became clear from the first day that they were on opposite sides of a tug of war. While they could agree on the overall objective, there were many roads to Rome, and in the early stages Maira had the distinct impression that Ric contradicted her out of sheer malice.

There were two things about Ric's communication skills which she felt left a great deal to be desired. The first was his habit of changing subjects abruptly, and the second was the way he said 'negative' like a fighter pilot instead of 'no', especially when he said it after something she suggested.

'Negative,' Ric Garcia said.

'What do you mean "negative"?'

'Negative. You can't do that. It's either cross-reference or speed. Can't have both.'

Cross-referencing was the element of the software that filtered any intelligent broadcast from the background noise.

'We need the speed, of course,' Maira said, 'but we also need to cross-reference every frequency as we slow the signals.'

'Later. After all frequencies are checked.'

She insisted, 'Surely we should check them as we see them.'

Ric frowned. 'We need to look at all the frequencies first and then cross-reference the whole spectrum.' He added, 'And the name's Ric or Ricardo, but not Shirley.'

Maira shook her head, ignoring the last remark. 'Can't we use another computer, more parallel processing to deal with the cross-referencing?'

'Negative. All the parallel is happening for the

frequencies and for slowing the signals.' Ric cheered up suddenly and, grinning broadly, he added, 'Guess we could cross-reference immediately if we don't slow the signals. Yeah?'

'Negative,' Maira said.

Bill Walters proved to be both a motivator and impartial referee for Ric and Maira. On the first day he gave them a pep talk on how fortunate he was to have the two most capable people on this project. He described them – a bit patronizingly, Maira felt – as a brain of a team. Maira, he said, was the right hemisphere with the original ideas and imagination, and Ric was the rational left who weeded out the impracticable from Maira's mathematical models.

Later, when they were alone, Ric told Maira, 'Guess that makes me the gardener. Mind where you put your seeds, Doc.'

Speech was as relative as the second. Back home, 'down the road' implied a distance of a mile, or two maximum. Maira was astonished to learn that Las Vegas was down the road from the SETI compound, being a mere 106 miles down the state highway. But then she was not a local whose mind dulled in the car as the familiar and bland panorama galloped past. In the first month her busy work schedule allowed her only one such excursion down the road, and she felt every minute of the three-hour round trip.

With Bill in the driver's seat she marvelled at the subtle changes in the landscape, from arid dunes to desiccated scrub, where occasional small trees and cacti, twisted by the torturing heat, nevertheless braved on. And further still, where the towers of rock, each with its distinctive weathered character, loomed imposingly, in Maira's recollection, over the Dartmoor granite tors. Over Death Valley, she saw an eagle or a buzzard or a vulture; a magnificent large bird which glided and hovered effortlessly, buoyed by a layer of thermals. She was not in Arabia, nor was she T. E. Lawrence, but she found herself wishing she had time and a camel to discover this fascinating land at a more leisurely pace.

Las Vegas itself left an eradicable mark on Maira.

'Of course, it comes alive at night with glitter and razzmatazz.' Bill's tone was almost an apology; Maira nodded politely and thought of the trip back down the road.

The SETI compound was bounded by a high electric fence which snaked its way across the sandy ground. It encompassed sixteen radio telescopes arranged four by four, the laboratories and offices complex, the canteen and the residential quarters. There was only one entrance which was always guarded by one of the security men. The SETI employees – who referred to themselves disparagingly as inmates – had christened the gate Checkpoint Joey, after Joe Spiroza, chief of security.

When Bill and Maira returned from Las Vegas, Checkpoint Joey was manned by a uniformed security guard who was talking to an older balding man outside the fence. The guard casually saluted Bill and moved to open the gate. The older man smiled at Maira and bowed deeply and deliberately. She smiled back and he straightened and unsettled her with an intent look. The car began to move into the compound and the bald man made a quick series of three hand signs. He still stared at Maira as he crossed his forefingers, then showed her his right index erect, and then his left index curved like a hook. Maira shrugged and was still frowning as the man and the guard dropped out of view.

Maira saw the bald man again early one afternoon, a week after her trip to Las Vegas.

In the morning Ric had an inspired idea that would almost halve the time needed for cross-referencing. He described his idea to her after an irrelevant outburst about an Anglophobic cousin who, it appeared, likened an Englishman's grating laugh to a chihuahua courting a bitch on heat. 'The English are snobs even when they laugh.'

'Exactly,' Maira answered emphatically. 'You'll never know how horny it makes her feel.'

And for the first time they laughed together.

'You're OK, Doc,' Ric said.

'You betcha, *Señor* Garcia.'

Bill, Ric and Maira held a meeting later that morning and decided that, given the present technology, further reductions in time would be impossible without short cuts that could involve loss of certain frequencies or signals. Bill approved the software and hardware which, in logical stages, evaluated a star's or galaxy's distance, worked out the resulting temporal deceleration according to CTT, parallel processed the spectrum of frequencies at 1024 frequencies per loop, cross-referenced these 1024 frequencies for intelligent signals, returned for the next batch of 1024, and sounded an alarm if any alien broadcast was being recorded.

The initial point of contention between Ric and Maira regarding cross-referencing was that she preferred the alarm to be set off if one of the batch of 1024 wavelengths carried an alien message. But Ric had come out on top because Maira's way would have disrupted the natural loop in the program, thereby adding considerable delay.

In Ric's proposal, all the frequencies would be analysed before entering the program that would sound the alarm and trumpet an end to SETI's exhaustive search. Even if the very first frequency carried ET's wispy voice, the inmates would drum their fingers for a little over six hours as the mainframe analysed all the wavelengths at the speed of light.

To Maira this seemed like an inordinately long time to wait, but Bill and Ric were pleased with themselves. A quick calculation showed that in this set-up 200 million data, processed in six hours, amounted to ten batches each of a thousand frequencies analysed per second – an unparalleled feat of computing.

The alarm itself was also Ric's idea.

'Can't we have a normal alarm, like a bell or a siren?' Bill complained.

'No, I like it,' Maira said.

'Guess we've got something in common now, Bill,' Ric said.

'What's that?'

'Welcome to the minority.'

Bill shrugged.

So the speakers in the main lab were to herald an alien broadcast being heard for the first time on Earth by booming out 'Just in Time', sung by Nat King Cole.

It was a little after one o'clock when Maira left the air-conditioned atmosphere of the office complex and walked straight into a wall of heat. She had got into the daily habit of walking around the compound amid the radio telescopes; given her vacant look and marching gait she always appeared to be on parade for the giant electronic eyes. Her walks were usually in the late afternoon, when the day had only a few degrees of arc left and the air became breathable. Right from the first day as an inmate, Maira had paced the compound, coordinating just as much with the fiery embers of a closing day in the desert as with Ric's waking from his long afternoon siesta.

In stark contrast, that early afternoon she experienced the desert's maximum furnace power, and she marched faster than usual to the shadow of the first telescope. There she paused and hummed a snatch of Noël Coward's song about mad dogs and Englishmen going out in the midday sun.

It was in the shade of the third telescope that she was startled by a voice. 'Such wilderness.'

Maira jumped and turned to see the bald man.

'I frightened you, Dr Brisden, I am sorry.'

'No. I was just miles away.'

Maira could not quite place the man's foreign accent. He was probably in his fifties, tanned and with such a thin crescent of silver hair sticking resiliently to the back of his head that when he turned to gaze at a distant dune, the back of his head appeared to grin broadly like a twin-faced Broadway dance number.

'Fasting is that much easier in the desert,' he said.

Apart from their brief encounter from a week back, she had never seen him before, but she now assumed that he worked here, perhaps as a maintenance engineer. Certainly only SETI personnel were allowed into the compound. 'What is it you do here, Mr . . . ?' she prompted.

'My name is James Smith.'

'The other day you signed something to me. What was that all about?'

'You will not know it yet, but that was an honour.'

'A what?'

'Do you remember the sign?'

'No.'

'It no longer matters then.'

With the ensuing short silence she realized that he was not going to explain the cryptic sign so she said, 'Wasn't it something like this?' Maira crossed her forefingers, and then showed her right index and then her left.

'Two-thirds correct,' James Smith said. 'The last sign, your left forefinger should be curved, like so.'

'Fine. But what does it mean?'

'It means many things. Above all it's a number.'

'A number of what?'

'A number among the infinite, but a special number.' He repeated the three signs and explained, 'In ancient Greek numerals *hi* was six hundred, *yiota* was ten—'

'I thought that ten was X,' Maira interrupted, testingly.

'That is Roman, not Greek. And the *epistemon* which looks like a U on its side was six.'

'So,' Maira said, frowning, 'it's six hundred ten six.'

'Six hundred and sixteen.' James Smith nodded and

191

removed a single sheet of paper from his shirt breast pocket and handed it to her.

'What's this?' she asked.

'Read it.' He moved away. 'I hope we'll meet again someday, Dr Brisden.'

'No, wait,' Maira said. 'What the devil is all this about, and no more cryptic replies.'

'You will understand one day.'

Maira threw back her head in resignation. 'Is this a masonic thing?'

The stranger had been walking away; he stopped and turned to face her. 'Masonic?'

'Freemasons.'

'No.' He smiled suddenly at her. 'We are a fraternity, but not Freemasons. In the distant past a society which is now called the Rosicrucians learned some of our secrets, but their knowledge is limited.'

'Thank you, but no,' she said emphatically.

'No?'

'No, thank you. I would not like to join.'

The stranger's smile turned to laughter. 'This is a novel role for me: I, the salesman.' He paused and then added, 'I apologize for any misunderstanding, but, my dear Dr Brisden, you cannot join our order.'

Maira looked perplexed.

'Dr Brisden, what I can tell you is that you have been chosen—'

'By whom? And for what?'

' – and that should you feel the urge to travel one day, I leave you an address. Consider it a place where you may find inspiration.'

'Chosen for what?' Maira repeated.

He raised his hand and said, 'If I knew for sure I wouldn't be here. Goodbye, Dr Brisden.'

She did not answer and, as he slowly walked away, she unfolded the sheet of paper and saw a symbol, read what appeared to be a familiar verse from the Bible, and finally an address in the strangest of places.

‌ЖC

Here is more wisdom. Let him that hath understanding count the number:
for it is the number of a man; and his number is Six
hundred one score less four.

Rev. xxxiv 12

Al-Aala Mosque
Jubel, Lebanon

Maira began her seventh week in the desert as SETI
began to scan the heavens using advanced software and
enhanced theory. The Chronon Theory of Time postu-
lated that it was improbable that signals would arrive
from neighbouring systems or even galaxies – the
Planets A of Earth's generation. In the first sweep the
radio telescopes ignored large chunks of the sky and
focused exclusively on very distant galaxies.

During the first days that the set-up was operational
there was a general buzz of excitement and expectation,
but as the days progressed in mincing steps, without so
much as a pip from extraterrestrials, the novelty wore
off. The work had become numbingly tedious and the
monotony was stayed only briefly by regular checks and
recalibrations of individual telescopes.

She still wondered about James Smith long after the
guards had been severely reprimanded for the breach in
security. In retrospect she should have guessed that
given his odd conversation and unimaginative alias, Mr
Smith was no engineer. Maira never needed to consult
the register of SETI employees to confirm this. The
day following James Smith's visit, Joe Spiroza, head of
security, contacted Maira on the intercom.

'Please accept my condolences,' he said gravely.

For a split second she panicked and wondered if
personal telegrams were scrutinized at the gate before
being relayed.

'What do you mean?' Maira said, nonplussed.

'I know it's a shock to the system. I've been through it too, you know. I respect your privacy, Dr Brisden, but I felt I had to do my thing, seeing as I know.'

Know? 'Seeing as you know what, Mr Spiroza?' Maira retorted irritably.

'The death of Mr Tom Jones, of course.' He sounded surprised.

'Tom Jones?'

'Yes. Your fiancé.'

'Mr Spiroza, I do not have a fiancé,' she said crossly. 'I have never had a fiancé. And if this conversation carries on at this rate, I shall never have a fiancé.'

There was a long pause.

'Hello, Mr Spiroza?'

'Shit. Sorry, Dr Brisden. You're now going to tell me that Mr James Smith was not your uncle either.'

'Precisely.'

'But you met with him yesterday.'

'I did meet him yesterday. But did it never occur to you that with all the people in this world the chances were considerably better than even that he would not be my uncle?'

'He said he was.'

'And that if he were my uncle he'd sound remotely English?'

'Not really,' Mr Spiroza said with renewed confidence. 'Why I've got cousins in Naples, Italy, who couldn't say two words of English if their lives depended on it.'

So it transpired that, posing as her uncle bearing devastating news, James Smith had cunningly crossed Checkpoint Joey onto restricted turf. At least, she thought, that strange character had a sense of humour. Smith and Jones indeed. And presumably the real Tom Jones had not necessarily died.

She was tempted to dismiss James Smith as an odd-ball; Lord knew the world had more than its fair share of fanatical evangelists and right-wing Christian groups. But there had been something profoundly different about him. For a start he had never attempted to convert her or persuade her of anything. The only purpose of the bizarre visit seemed to centre on a mostly blank sheet of paper which, on its own, made very little sense.

Maira's curiosity was tweaked, and because the text was evidently biblical, she mailed a copy to Peter Ridley, an acquaintance from St Edmund's, the theological college in Cambridge.

Maira received Peter Ridley's comments in her ninth week in Nevada, at a time when she had decided that the entire SETI venture was fast becoming futile. And as she opened the envelope, pausing to examine the Cambridge postmark, she resolved to tell Bill that it was time for her to leave.

Dear Maira,
The book called the Apocalypse (or Revelation) of St John the Divine is the last book in the New Testament canon, as received both in the Eastern and Western Churches. This book contains twenty-two chapters, which implies that the passage you sent me, marked chapter thirty-four, verse twelve, is clearly a hoax.

However, the text and the inclusion of 'more' in, 'Here is more wisdom', appears to draw particular reference to chapter thirteen, verse eighteen, which I hereby write in full:

'Here is wisdom. Let him that hath under-standing count the number of the Beast: for it is the number of a man; and his number is Six hundred threescore *and* six.'

Rev. xiii 18

You will notice two differences with the text you sent: the exclusion of 'the Beast', and the numbers

195

616 and 666. In fact, the interesting point in your text lies in the generally held belief that 616, being less symmetrical, is likely to be the more original number of the Beast, and some early Latin texts do read 616. Probably the number was first associated with Caligula (who wished his statue to be set up in the Temple of Jerusalem, to the horror of pious Jews), for the letters of Gaius Caesar or ΓΑΙΟΣ ΚΑΙΣΑΡ make up 616. Perhaps a better explanation, which also explains the sign, is that the number of the Beast in itself signifies Antichrist. The monogram for Christ is ☧ , and as anti means 'opposite', the monogram of Antichrist is ☧ , a figure composed of X=600, I=10 and C=6.

In answer to your query about Rosicrucianism, there are Rosicrucian societies in most countries of the world. Some are very active, others are obscure and secretive, some seem to be primarily religious, and some categorically deny that Rosicrucianism is a religion, maintaining rather that it is a philosophy making use of modern scientific methods as well as methods of the occultist, the mystic and the seer in the quest for the truth.

Some regard Christian Rosenkreuz as the founder of the order who, reputedly, came into possession of much secret wisdom following a journey to Damascus in the fifteenth century. More generally though, Christian Rosenkreuz is not believed to have existed at all, being more of a symbolic character. Either way, it seems highly probable that the movement's roots are in the Levantine early Christian gnosticism and/or Jewish cabalism.

I hope this has been useful to you.
Kind Regards,
Peter Ridley

ZACHIEL

It is the first time Zachiel mentions my name. The words appear in the sand by the angel's feet:

'WHY DID YOU CHOOSE THE GIRL, JACOB?'

'It doesn't matter any more.' I wonder whether the gabriel can hear my feeble voice. 'I was wrong.' If I had an arm, hand and index, they would now point due south at the crystal effigy of Azazel.

The doorway to *The Tower* still burns with a white light that outlines the angel's question on the ground.

'AL chose her,' I say at length.

Zachiel looks on impassively.

'I was invited to the conference in Cambridge,' I explain to the angel. 'I heard her speak of the holy spirit of Chronos using scientific equations and logic. I believed she was one of the witnesses of St John's prophecy.'

'AND THE BOY, JACOB?'

'My Greek student. You haven't shown him to me yet.' I am thinking of Glafkos Mikhaelides, my Cypriot student.

The angel shakes his head and spreads his wings to prepare for a return to *The Tower*.

'Am I wrong?' I wonder why else we must revisit the glass tower if it isn't for a lesson that has not yet been learned. 'But you can't mean Samir,' I tell my gabriel as we become one with the white light.

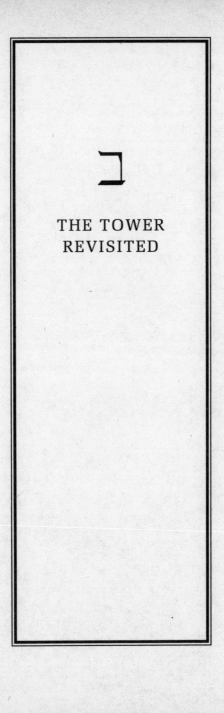

ב

THE TOWER
REVISITED

7

BEFORE BABEL

King Richard I interrupted his voyage to the Third
Crusade in order to conquer Cyprus. In 1191 the
Lionheart married Berengaria of Navarre and crowned
her Queen of England in the castle of Limassol. The
present Limassol Castle was built in the fourteenth
century on the site of that earlier Byzantine castle. It was
at the heart of the old town and overlooked the port,
where King Richard's fleet had docked before its
onslaught on the coast of the Holy Land. On the other
side, part of the old town centre of Limassol could
be seen from the battlements, a messy urban plan of
labyrinthine narrow roads and a hotchpotch of
houses cluttering the view with a total indifference to
twentieth-century urban planning.

This part of town was, for the moment at least, thank-
fully protected from the bland and soulless architecture
which had invaded so much of Cyprus to cater for the
tourists. Like the sudden appearance of mosquitoes in
summer, the seasonal swarm of North Europeans
arrived to soak up the Mediterranean sun and to suck
dry – unknowingly or uncaringly – the very character of
the beautiful island of Cyprus. Now in near isolation,
the old town, rich in rustic appeal, was buttressed by a
decaying foundation. Central to the town, Limassol
Castle, which housed the Medieval Museum,
represented a beleaguered citadel of conservation.

Samir bought his ticket at the immense oaken door,
studded with bulbous iron rivets. He entered and

climbed a flight of stairs into the main exhibition hall and searched for Jacob before settling in front of a display of a coat of mail and a large broadsword. The rendezvous had been Samir's idea, and as he stood transfixed by the display, he allowed the history of the place to take over, feeling small and insignificant, swept by the wake of past generations. He imagined the famed meeting between King Richard and Saladin to arrange for an armistice, when, after a cordial meal, the two leaders discussed the relative merits of the broadsword and the scimitar, each giving a demonstration. King Richard's sword sundered a log of wood, while Saladin's scimitar, in one swift movement, sliced a silk handkerchief in mid-air. Even their mounts mirrored this difference: sleek Arabian horses set against the sluggish but powerful European breed. Why was history a never-ending story of dichotomy? Why did conflicts always appear in pairs, as if opposing forces were either good or evil, black or white? Samir considered a far older conflict, yet closer to home.

In the ancient Mediterranean, two civilizations above all others had vied for control. The Greek and Phoenician merchants and colonizers studded the small known world with trading posts and independent cities. For centuries this rivalry, which led to regular open conflicts, remained a stalemate. A Phoenician success with the founding of a Tyrian city, Kition, on Cyprus was balanced by a Corinthian success in Sicily with Syracuse. In this millennium-long battle the victors were the Greeks, for they and not the Phoenicians influenced the growing republic of the seven hills. This was no more than a cultural victory because, politically, Rome's ascendancy proved as catastrophic for the Greeks as for the Phoenicians. In a single year, 146 BC, Rome utterly destroyed Carthage and Corinth – the two jewels in the opposing civilizations. The Greeks ultimately won, as Roman patricians favoured Hellenistic art and philosophy and emulated everything Greek to the detriment of the rival Phoenician society. Even blatantly Phoenician and Punic inventions like the alphabet and Stoicism were passed off by the Romans as Athenian and Spartan.

This was why Samir was so intrigued by the monumental ruins in Baalbek. It seemed contradictory that a society which was so intent on destroying everything Phoenician and Punic should construct the most magnificent temples in the land of the Canaanites to worship Phoenician deities. It was a great paradox which no historian had ever bothered to explain.

The only thing that remained crystal clear was that the Phoenicians and Punics alike had been annihilated in body and soul and that he, Samir Khoury, typified the living evidence. He was Lebanese, born in the land of the cedar, from where Tyrians, Sidonians and Jubelis had circumnavigated Africa, and where they had discovered the magic of the written word. Although, perhaps, a genetic descendant, he was certainly no son of this worthy people. Samir was Greek Orthodox and he spoke Arabic – a language that had invaded the land from the east – and French and English, invaders from the west. To add salt to the wounds of his ancestors, Samir could read and write ancient Greek, while he had in his pocket three photographs of tablets written in Punic which remained unintelligible to him.

'As instruments of war go, the sword is more romantic than the machine-gun.'

Samir started and spun around.

'The one who said that', Jacob added, 'should try dying of a stab wound.'

'Jacob, Jacob,' Samir enthused fondly. They hugged and kissed, the requisite three, and Samir, still holding him, kissed him a fourth time. '*Mon Prof.*' He smiled broadly and added, 'You've lost almost all your hair, but you're as I remember you.'

'And you,' said Jacob, 'still smiling that smile that shatters the stoniest heart.'

'You still speak as if you were writing Arabic literature.'

The men held hands and talked of the old neighbourhood, of Greek coins and Anglo-French lessons, and of the books Jacob had lent his pupil every Sunday.

'You are the emir in the tale,' Jacob said loudly, referring to the very first book. A museum attendant edged towards them and asked them to keep their voices down.

'Shall we go up to the battlements?' suggested Samir.

They climbed two flights of winding stairs and emerged onto the roof. Standing by a loophole, like bowmen in the castle, they gazed at the old part of Limassol. Above the squat houses rose two minarets, three Greek Orthodox domes and, in the distance, a Maronite spire. 'The view from this castle is a panorama of the religious disharmony,' said Jacob.

'Yes,' agreed Samir, 'I don't like churches or mosques.'

Jacob was surprised. 'Really? Why?'

'They've caused all our problems. We can do without them.'

Jacob shook his head slowly. 'Blame men not bricks and mortar.'

Ten minutes, thought Samir, and already we're disagreeing like we've never disagreed before. He decided to change the subject, and asked, 'Do you know anything about Erab and Esh?'

Jacob turned to face him. His mild surprise had changed into an expression of complete astonishment. 'What do you know about Erab and Esh?'

'Not much,' he admitted. 'Who were they?'

'Where', Jacob corrected, 'not who.'

'They're places, eh?'

'Why do you want to know about Erab and Esh?'

Samir detected reticence in his friend's tone and felt uneasy. 'Something I'm working on,' he replied dismissively.

They were both quiet for a strained while, both with secrets to guard. Finally, with furrowed brow, Jacob said, 'Very well.' He cleared his throat before resuming. 'In the very distant past, before all the empires, when humans lived in only one tribe and spoke only one tongue, the entire world was split into three land masses, three countries if you like. They were called Erab, Eden and Esh. Erab and Esh were mostly undiscovered, representing open-ended territories, while Eden constituted the known verdant world of this neolithic man. Eden was flanked by Erab on the west and Esh on the east.'

Samir said incredulously, 'Eden as in Adam and Eve and the garden of eternal springs?'

'Eden was a real place, a fertile land where this first tribe of men settled after leaving Africa. The location of Eden itself can be situated by considering Erab and Esh. Erab, in proto-Semitic, meant west. In Arabic, west is *gharb.* Similarly, east was Esh which has the Arabic equivalent of *sharq.* The names of these two land masses exist to this day with slight variations. Erab has become Europe and Esh has become Asia. West of Eden was Europe, and east of Eden was Asia, then clearly Eden itself was the Fertile Crescent. Moreover, given that in the biblical Eden there is mention of rivers and green mountains, this further restricts our Eden. It is not likely to have been in Babylon, which has the rivers but not the impressive and verdant mountains, nor the Nile Delta for the same reason. But rather Eden was a very fertile land, protected from the sea by one mountain range and from the desert by another.'

Samir frowned. 'Eden was the Bekaa Valley?'

'I believe so. There is also the migratory route which would confirm this. When the first men walked out of Africa, at the Sinai Desert – the only African land link with the rest of the world – they would have opted to follow the coast northwards rather than turning east into the Arabian Desert. Further north, these neolithic

205

hunters would have discovered a sudden jewel after their long trek over the dunes. The Bekaa, rich in fruit and game, would have appeared as an immense oasis, a paradise on earth. And there the land would tempt them to remain, and they would change their lifestyles from nomadic to the world's first farming community.'

'How do you know this?'

'It's my life's work,' Jacob answered simply.

'So what's the *conspiracy* of Erab and Esh? Do you know?'

Jacob shook his head in amazement. 'You know words that are secret to all but the initiated.' Staring at Samir, he crossed his forefingers, then showed him his right index erect, and then his left index curved like a hook.

Samir looked on perplexed.

'The conspiracy of Erab and Esh is evil.'

'What? How?'

'It's the work of the Devil. Azazel exists as does Gabriel, and both operate in the same way – scheming and mysterious.'

He still had not answered the question. Samir repeated, 'So what is the conspiracy?'

'As I've said, mankind lived in the land called Eden and spoke the Divine Language—'

'The Divine Language?' interrupted Samir.

'It was the one tongue spoken by the one tribe. Perhaps it was half spoken and half thought. But the thing I want to say now is that men lost this faculty of speech shortly after their arrival in Eden. Men forgot this common language and soon were no longer able to communicate as comprehensively. Tribes were formed and wars followed. Many tribes – which over millennia became races – were evicted from Eden, and as that happened they swore unremitting hatred to those left behind. Some tribes went *esh* to Asia, and others migrated *erab* to Europe. And the Conspiracy of Erab and Esh, simply put, is the secret desire of Europeans and Asians to fulfil their revenge against the remaining Edenians, who evolved into the Semitic race.'

There was a stunned silence.

'Are you serious?' Samir said at length, adding pertly, 'Are you saying that anti-Semitism exists today because tens of thousands of years ago tribes were kicked out of the Bekaa?'

'Azazel's curse.'

'Why?'

'Because Satan is jealous of El. And because El chose Eden to reveal himself to man. It is no coincidence that Semites have achieved proportionately more in every human field than any other race. Philosophy, psychology, music, science, you name it, the alphabet, agriculture, and probably as a result of farming, even the wheel was a Semitic invention. The Devil sows and continues to sow the seeds of envy in non-Semites. You see, all this is no coincidence because the Edenians are El's chosen people.'

'God's chosen race, eh?' Over the years his friend had turned into a Jew.

'Yes.'

'You sound like Hitler and his Aryans.'

Jacob spluttered and turned red with rage. 'You – Don't you dare—' he shouted. 'Don't you ever dare say that to me again. Never, do you hear.'

'Well, don't insult my intelligence then,' Samir shouted back. 'I'm not a wide-eyed boy any more.'

Jacob pointed a finger accusingly. 'What can you know about Hitler? What can you understand about the Holocaust? Huh? Tell me that, Samir Khoury. They're just black and white images for you, aren't they? You understand nothing about suffering. You're blinded by your youth. An Antichrist is just a poor infidel for you, one who doesn't believe in Christ, that's all. Right?' Jacob glared at Samir. 'Wrong! I fuck Hitler's sister and his pimps.'

It was the first time he had ever heard Jacob swear.

Samir lowered his eyes. 'I'm sorry,' he offered. 'Maybe it was the wrong example but I don't believe in chosen people.'

Jacob spoke softly. 'Only saints and liars populate their thoughts with rivals so as to bless them. And, El forgive me, Hitler is one of the very few men in the world, alive or dead, who carries my eternal curse.'

'It's the *chosen* people who've started all the wars.'

'You treat me like a charlatan.' Jacob nodded slowly, sadly. 'Haven't I taught you anything? Haven't you learned anything? When I say the Semites are El's chosen people, that doesn't mean He regards them above the rest. The Semites are a chosen but not a *superior* race. There is no such thing as a superior race. But there is a chosen race. People who have been chosen by God to instruct the rest. Careful, it seems I need to spell it out, this does not imply that they are any better, but simply that, by God's choice, they become wiser or more knowledgeable than the rest. And just as it is every good teacher's dream that his student will learn and will add to that learning, it is the Semite's wish that the world will add achievements to his inspiration.'

Samir thought better than to argue; he shrugged.

'Believe me,' insisted Jacob, 'it was no coincidence that the founders of Judaism, Christianity and Islam were all Semites.'

'Do you read Punic, Jacob?'

Jacob stared vacantly through the loophole. 'Have I convinced you of anything at all?'

'I respect your opinion,' Samir said tersely, 'but I want to tell you why I'm interested in Erab and Esh.'

'You respect by disagreeing.'

'Have you heard of Carthalo the Historian?'

'Why?'

Samir removed the three A4-sized photographs and unfolded them. 'I have here something which he wrote – which I believe he wrote at any rate. I think this might interest you.'

'Why do you disagree?' Jacob repeated.

'I don't believe in Eden, in Erab or Esh.' He handed the photographs to Jacob adding, 'And I don't believe in God.'

He regretted saying it as soon as the words left his mouth.

Jacob, Jacob, how the years have changed us, thought Samir. Not to meet would have been preferable. We should have carried our fond memories together to the grave. Instead we met as friends and parted as strangers, with the perfunctory three pecks of polite acquaintances.

He stood alone on the battlements, shooting glances at the minarets and domes.

If God or El, or whatever he calls himself, had ever existed, had truly been merciful, he would never have revealed himself to Moses et cetera. This act would have saved mankind from all the bloody crusades and jihads. Religion was nothing more than a board-game – far older than chess – for one to an infinite number of players, with set rules and a main objective. The game ended with death; players were supposed to win or lose in heaven or hell.

'Bored,' Samir accused the old town below. Like any motivating hobby, the primary purpose of religion was to while away the boring present with the promises of a rosy future.

He had hurt Jacob twice, both times unintentionally. Theirs was the most precarious kind of relationship, not quite friends, nor quite filial, but somewhere between the two. Samir remembered the look – a single glance – of utter disappointment on Jacob's face as he had confessed his atheism. The pained expression of a teacher who first discovers the star in his class to be the mule.

They were complete opposites, a scimitar to a broadsword, as dichotomous as Phoenicians and Greeks.

Jacob had left with the photographs of the tablets. 'I'll

209

send the translation with someone to Jubel,' he had said as they kissed adieu. 'To the Al-Aala Mosque two weeks from today, at this time.' He walked away, stopped, turned and added, 'Look out for a verse in ancient Greek. I think you should have no problems in deciphering it. There is perhaps only one word you will not understand.'

'Which is?' Samir called after him.

'The ancient Greek name for God. In Greek, El was Chronos,' said Jacob as he left the battlements.

Glafkos Mikhaelides boarded the ferry at Larnaca and, heading straight for the lounge bar, ordered a strong coffee. The ship weighed anchor at eleven o'clock at night with thunderous clanks that resonated in the lounge; expected time of arrival at Jôunié in Lebanon was the following morning at seven. Glafkos found himself a seat and lifted a black briefcase, his only luggage, onto the table.

Glafkos, a Cypriot, was an *aderfós* in the Divine Society, among the newest brothers who had joined three years earlier. The brotherhood, led by a triumvirate of *patéri*, recruited a handful of new members once every seven years. The initiation took place on Pàtmos, a tiny Greek isle in the Aegean, an insignificant place but for the cave where Gabriel revealed the future to St John the Divine in 90 AD.

In the first months of tutelage, each *patéras* took a couple of recruits under his wing, instructing them on the ancient lores of astrology, alchemy, numerology, meditation with the tarot. Patéras Jacob had been Glafkos's master. From him, the new *aderfós* learned that St John the Divine had founded the society in order to preserve all human knowledge, including the learning which contemporaneous Christians had classed as pagan or satanic. Wisdom, the saint had maintained, was not exclusive to Christianity; a notion considered so heretical that the fledgling society was driven underground. Soon afterwards, the doors were opened to brothers of different faiths, further alienating the society from the Churches of Rome and Constantinople.

Under the guidance of Patéras Jacob, Glafkos studied the forty chapters of the Revelations according to St John: the twenty-two chapters of '*things which must shortly come to pass*' which the early Church adopted, for political reasons, against as yet pagan Rome; and the remaining and unrecognized eighteen chapters of '*things which must come to pass in threescore generations*'.

'One day', Patéras Jacob had instructed, 'you will go to Jubel in Lebanon, to the Al-Aala Mosque, which was once a church, and you'll read chapter thirty-six engraved around the dome.'

'Jubel?' Glafkos had enquired.

'*Jub-El*, Lord-God, which the ancient Greeks called Byblos; the same town which, appropriately, lent its name to the Bible.'

Glafkos sipped his coffee. He was going to Jubel in war-ravaged Lebanon, almost three years to the day after becoming an *aderfós*.

'I believe in the beatitude of names,' the *patéras* had said another time. 'Parents think they have a free choice in naming their children, but names are chosen by divine influence before birth and parents simply legalize the Holy Spirit's own christening. That's why names are important. Especially fortunate are they who carry El in their names. Ishmael, *listens-to-God*; Samuel; Daniel, *God-is-my-judge*; and the archangelic names, holiest of all, Raphael, *God-has-healed*; Michael, *in-God's-image*; and Jibr-El, Gabriel, *God's-instrument-on-earth*.'

Glafkos clicked open his briefcase, checked that the brown envelope for Samir Khoury was there, and took out a walkman and tape before clicking the case shut again.

The tape was labelled, Δ.Λ.: an Anglo-Greek mnemonic for Divine Language. It was a lecture by

Patéras Jacob, surreptitiously taped during training. The *aderfós* would have been severely reprimanded had he been discovered. Brothers were supposed to have perfect memories. Notes of the meetings, let alone recordings, were strictly forbidden. Glafkos looked around him again and pressed the play button:

The Divine Language was the tongue used by neolithic man when he stepped out of Africa and into Eden. Other than perhaps a few African tribes, all of mankind came from Eden, and, as a result, this Divine Language is the great ancestor of all modern languages – again with the exception of a few African tongues. It may be considered as man's first non-animal language. We have, I should mention, only sketchy details, and most of our understanding is inferred from studies into modern and past languages – the Divine Language was only a spoken tongue and there can be no archaeological evidence.

Most if not all languages evolved from this speech, but the closest descendants to the original are the Semitic languages. Clearly, with migration, the tribes which left for Erab and Esh distanced themselves from Eden, both geographically and linguistically. And so most of the limited vocabulary we have of this first language comes from centuries of research by the Divine Society into proto-Semitic, and proto-Semitic's own roots. What I will now describe of the Divine Language is knowledge which no university on earth knows of.

This one language had only two sounds – two letters, if you will – a single vowel, A, and a single consonant, L. All the words and sounds were formed by only these two letters.

It is fair to assume that these first men could make other sounds, vowels and consonants which we are familiar with, but that these were not included for reasons they alone knew. Perhaps these other sounds were too bestial for those early men, who had just discovered their distinction among animals. The guttural vocals may have been dropped because they sounded like the tongues of large mammalian carnivores; the same could have been true for the sibilants which were reminiscent of snakes and insects. Or, more likely – as our society maintains – this simple language was taught to mankind by God himself. Hence, Divine Language.

Some words, the most frequently used and shortest, have changed little over the abyss of time which separates us from those early speakers. We have a short vocabulary of words which our ancestors would have used. No was *LA*, yes was *A*. In this you will see little change from some modern Semitic tongues like Arabic. God, or El, was *AL*. *LALA* meant praise, revere or worship. So that *LALA AL* could be translated as 'Praise God', which could also have been said *AL LALA* which, with time, became the Aramaic *Alleluia*.

The holiest phrase in Islam, which is chanted five times a day from every minaret in the world, has its direct roots in this older language. *ALL* was gods and *ALAA* meant except. *La ilaha illa Allah* is the Arabic for, 'We believe in one God', but the literal translation is, 'No gods except God'. The direct equivalent in the Divine Language was *LA ALL ALAA AL*. You can see that this prayer has varied only slightly in tens of millennia precisely because the phrase

213

contains only simple and oft-repeated words.

There is some evidence that it was a tonal language. So for instance *A* meant yes but *A?* would have been understood as an interrogation – who, what, why or when. There was a certain childish quality to the Divine Language, a clarity of thought which we have lost because of our extended vocabulary, paradoxical as it may seem. For instance, in this primeval language there was only one word to describe the present: *ALAL*. In modern Semitic, there are three equivalent roots which may be roughly described as 'now', 'present' and 'contemporary'. French has more roots and English has the greatest number of nuances, with at least fifteen different words or roots all describing slight variations on the theme 'now'. That was the simple beauty of the Divine Language.

The tape hummed for a few instants and a second lecture began.

When there was one nation, one society, one race, one language, man believed in a unique god whom he named AL. There was a god of fire, a god of rivers, a god of trees, a god of life, and all these gods were the same one omnipresent god: AL.

Now the Devil enters Eden to draw man away from his simple life and simple unadulterated praise of AL. The first to disappear is the Divine Language. It now becomes too simple, too childish for this new and sophisticated man. It is slowly replaced by dialects which, with time, branch out into different languages. Men are no longer unified. Groups are formed which become tribes, which become races. Wars begin and tribes are evicted from Eden to Erab and Esh.

The Devil's work is complete when men, who had added new vocabulary to the Divine Language, now add new gods to the Divine Religion. AL, who has now become the proto-Semitic El, is relegated to a father figure, the chief god but no longer the only god. El, in his present complexity, mirrors man, and El now has a family. Unlike the future pantheons, this family is initially small, and there is still a slim link with the divine. El has no wife, yet he has a son. The northern Edenians who are now the Canaanites – the Phoenicians – call this son Baal. The southern Edenians call El's son Yahweh or Jehovah. Baal and Jehovah, who totally supplant El in importance, are one and the same before Moses, and are revered, almost in the old fashion, as an omnipotent god, alive everywhere, who needs no icon or effigy. In essence Baal usurps El, but returns to being the divine AL.

Azazel, the Devil's spirit on earth, confuses religion once again. Baal marries a new Phoenician deity called Atargatis with whom he creates a son, Adon.

Jehovah, Baal's erstwhile pseudonym in the south, does not suffer the same destiny because Gabriel intervenes. Moses returns the faith to its original divine roots. And Yahweh, Jehovah or Elohim once again becomes the unique AL. Unlike the Baal cult which is propagated throughout the known world, this new religion, now called Judaism, is restricted to a single nation, Israel.

With a healthy family of lesser gods, Baal succeeds where Jehovah fails, and the Erab tribes, first the Greeks then the Romans, embrace this faith, adding their own idiosyncrasies to the Phoenician gods and renaming them. So, for instance, Baal changes to become Zeus, who in turn evolves into Jupiter. Yahweh, Jehovah, El, Elohim, Deus, Allah, God, AL. And Baal would have been in that list but for the fact that Azazel stole all divinity from him.

In the early hours before sunrise, Glafkos Mikhaelides moved to the deck. Holding on to the railing, with the briefcase firmly between his legs, he allowed himself to be pleasantly swayed by both the bobbing ship and a crisp breeze, an apparent wind caused by the ferry's own eastward course. The sea, illuminated by the ship's lights and a near-full moon, was as still as the surface of a lake. So still, in fact, that the moon's own clear reflection bounced off a distant film of water with hardly a shimmer. The moon waltzed with its fluid image. Following the tempo set by the ship's engines, the two moons danced as he swayed until, almost abruptly, the queen of the night sky veered sharply, as if curtseying before the last waltz. Neptune led and she followed as the ferry moved homeward along the worn grooves of the seafaring Phoenicians. Finally, with the dance ended, the moon dipped below the horizon, attracted by her image, pausing only briefly to kiss the sea good night.

Glafkos looked up at the sky and saw that the stars, which should now have twinkled more fiercely, were instead being consumed by a dark blue, permeating the ether from the east.

Despite the society's ruling, Aderfós Glafkos would remain Jacob's disciple. The last extraordinary session, convened a week ago, had been summoned by the as yet reputable Patéras Jacob. In that meeting Jacob had attempted, with characteristic persuasion, to win over the *aderfí* against the other two of the triumvirate in adopting a ruling to nullify the Divine Society's chief objective.

For over one and a half centuries – since 1814, to be exact – the society had all but stopped divining. The future had been amply described by past prophets, and for the first time the brotherhood passed a resolution to participate in world events, armed with the power of foreknowledge. The general meeting of 1814 was held in September, five months after Napoleon Bonaparte's abdication in Fontainebleau. The devastation of Europe and the copious loss of human lives had been forecast and expected thanks, chiefly, to the sixteenth-century *patéras*, Michel de Nostre-Dame, whose own interpretations of the cryptic quatrains were locked away in a vault below John the Divine's cave. In 1553 Nostradamus saw three despots – whom he called Antichrists – wreaking havoc on the world. He named them, chronologically: Pau Nay Loron, Hister and Malus.

In his addendum to the society, Patéras Michel indicated both the dates and approximate places of birth, suggesting astrological methods to pinpoint the exact towns and houses at a time closer to the three nativities. Thus:

Antichrist I: Pau Nay Loron. (An anagram of Napaulon Roy, the title describing, in Middle French, the seer's vision of the Corsican crowned king by Pope Pius VII.) Date of birth: 1769. Place of birth: near Italy.

Antichrist II: Hister. (In his notes, Nostradamus explained that the name referred to both the tyrant and his place of birth; *Ister* was the Latin name for the lower course of the River Danube.) Date of birth: 1876. Place of birth: on the shores of the Danube.

Antichrist III: Malus. (Both a near anagram of his name and the Latin for evil one.) Date of birth: 1982. Place of birth: in greater Arabia.

To the secret gathering on Pàtmos in September 1814, Europe's devastation and the unprecedentedly high death toll following the Napoleonic campaigns could have been avoided, given that the society had foresight of the desolate events. History would have been kinder had one particular Corsican baby been exterminated.

Concerning the future, for the brothers of 1814, the misery caused by the first Antichrist was not to be permitted to recur. A new and overriding priority was promoted in the society, namely, to establish the exact nativities of Hister and Malus, and to assassinate them as babies for the good of mankind. For this unenvied task of infanticide, a third echelon was created within the society, ironically named the *ayórta* – the boys.

Sixty-two years later, in 1876, the *ayórta* went into action. Seven unfortunate babies fitted the astrological bill: two in Vienna, one in Györ, one in Újpest, two in Budapest and one in Dunaújváros. All seven were killed.

Adolf Hitler was born in Linz in 1889. He lived.

It was when Hitler became the leader of the National Socialist Party that the Divine Society first realized its mistake. The Second World War was fought and mankind lost again.

With the later predictions, the brotherhood inferred, Patéras Michel de Nostre-Dame appeared to be wrong by a factor of thirteen years. In the early 1950s, the birth of the last Antichrist was given two dates: 1982 and 1995.

Patéras Jacob appeared reasonable in the meeting, held in the second week of May 1982, the week the stars converged to point at the impending birth in Lebanon. He expounded his theory – with verve and confidence, which Glafkos admired – that the future was as conclusive as the past; the two being stitched from the same fabric. Those in the Divine Society were no more and no less than the guardians of the complete story of civilized Man, which only others – the general public – would see fit to bisect into futurity and history.

'If Malus is to be born,' Jacob concluded, 'he is already born – if not in flesh and bones, then in spirit. If he will be the cause of Armageddon then, brothers,

Armageddon exists and is but a short distance away. It stands firm in reality as a city to which all roads must ultimately lead; we can neither destroy it nor avoid it. The little power we have is in choosing the approach to the town centre along one of infinite avenues that Man may take. But to think we can avoid Judgement Day implies that we are beyond good and evil and that we are therefore stronger than Gabriel or Azazel.

'Fellow *patéri*, *aderfí* of this assembly, I move to cancel the objectives set in the meeting of 1814. I dissociate myself from the edict of 1876 that endorsed the snatching and slaughtering of the babies of—' At this point he enumerated the fourteen parents, giving their full names, without referring to any notes and causing Glafkos to marvel at the man's memory. 'I, for one, will not authorize the killing of baby boys this month and again in 1995.'

Patéras Jacob found his seat, and amid murmurs in the hall, an *aderfós* stood to ask him, 'Patéras Jacob. If, by a magician's trick, history were rewritten and the error was discovered in time, so that in 1889 a single baby was predicted as being the second Antichrist, and the baby's name was Adolf Hitler, would you then, Patéras, condone the killing of that one baby?'

'No.'

There was such a clamorous uproar that Patéras François had to shout for order several times.

Another *aderfós* rose quickly. 'Patéras Jacob, how can you say that? You of all people.'

'By that', Jacob said evenly, 'do you mean in my capacity as a father of this society, or as a Jew?'

'As both.'

'It seems apparent from your remark that a Jew should be more affected by the Holocaust than a Gentile. He is. And that is the Gentile's problem. I had hoped that of all the organizations in the world, at least this society would recognize that six million innocent *civilians* were butchered, not Jews, not Catholics, not

219

Buddhists, not Hindus, but six million *human beings*.'
He paused and then resumed, 'To answer your question: every child whom God has graced with life must have the freedom of choice. Even an abhorrent creature such as Adolf Hitler will once have been an innocent baby.'

Patéras François turned to face him. 'Brother Jacob. I ask you before this assembly and under the brotherhood's oath of truthfulness, do you have an ulterior motive for wanting Malus to live?'

'No.'

'I do not believe you.'

There was a stunned silence, followed by murmurs of consent. To the majority of *aderfí*, there was only one motive for wanting an evil spirit to come alive.

Patéras Jacob slowly rose from his seat. 'Then there is no reason to remain.' He walked unhurriedly out of the hall, never to return to Pàtmos.

Jacob Haddad's motion was overwhelmingly defeated, and the society planned for the arrival and destruction of Malus. In practice this would be hard to accomplish as, discounting the ex-pater who was nominally Lebanese, the last Lebanese brother had been killed in his bed by an exploded shell.

The fact of the matter was that Jacob had indeed lied to his fellow *patéras*. He had told only his best disciple the truth. Towards the end of May, the discredited *patéras* expected the birth, not of Antichrist III of Nostradamus's quatrains, but of the Lord according to the Book of Revelations. It was a matter of faith. Hope, too. St John and Patéras Michel foresaw opposite futures for mankind. Jacob could bear the Divine's prophecies, but not the quatrains of ruin.

The sun rose rapidly and Aderfós Glafkos spotted, in a shroud of haze, the grey peaks of Mount Lebanon.

The crusaders captured Jubel in 1103 and called it Gibelet, but lost it to Saladin in 1189, at about the time

King Richard the Lionheart was conquering Cyprus. The imposing citadel in Jubel, standing in magnificent melancholy, was essentially a crusader work. In later years a turret was constructed by the Ottomans, using smaller rocks so that one discerned, at a glance, Turkish from Frankish masonry.

The castle crowned a hillock overlooking both the sea and the southern approach into town. Across the blue expanse, ever out of sight, lay Cyprus and Gibelet's twin castle in Limassol. Closer, and scaling the hill, a Roman portico stood, eight columns in a majestic row, surrounded by the ruins of an earlier pagan temple. Closer still to the citadel, and almost as high, was a small building with an incongruously large Byzantine dome.

From the southern suburbs of Jubel one could see the castle above, flanked by this peculiar building whose dome was almost as large as the building itself in width and height, tempting the onlooker from below to suppose that the building was some odd Galilean observatory. Only from the battlements of the castle itself could the building be correctly classified as a place of worship. This was because the small golden crescent on top of the dome could only be seen from a vantage. The crescent was the right size for the building but not for the dome and it appeared frail, like an apple's stalk tenuously supporting a watermelon. This crescent, pointing ambiguously neither quite at the sea behind nor at heaven above, had once been an Orthodox cross.

The Al-Aala Mosque had once been the High Church which had stood alone on the hillock before the Frankish castle. Even this church had been built on the site of an earlier chapel – one of Christendom's first. A true *bethel*, which may have had a thatched roof but certainly no dome. It seemed certain that the first church in Jubel would have been paltry compared with the nearby Roman temple, with its imposing portico still intact.

While the crusaders' castle would celebrate its ninth

centenary in 2003, this age was trifling set against the town's own venerable age. Jubel was the oldest continuously inhabited town in the world, with monuments discovered underground belonging to medieval, Graeco-Roman, Phoenician, Amorite and neolithic settlements. The town was a bulb where only the outer skin could be seen. The true flavour came from within, from the layer upon layer of buried cities, each burying a more magnificent antecedent. Sadly, like any contemporary Lebanese town affected by the poverty and shattered infrastructure, Jubel was devastatingly squalid. And it was almost impossible to imagine that modern-day Jubel was the heir of the town where men had written the first letters on papyrus. Only the castle on the hill remained, above the graveyard of cities, to remind people of more gallant times.

Samir parked his car on the road parallel to the Gibelet Castle and reached the Al-Aala Mosque, climbing a narrow path. By the large oaken door there was a pair of shoes, black and gleaming, neatly arranged with the soles against the wall. Without bothering to undo the laces, Samir kicked his shoes off, the right shoe landing on the left like wings on fuselage, and he entered the mosque in his socks. Inside it was dark and cold as night – the thick ancient walls a sanctuary from the rays of the day. Samir paused by the entrance for his eyes to grow accustomed to the dimness; a shiver travelled up his spine.

A man knelt in the centre of the mosque, his hand resting on a briefcase. The man was staring intently at the dome above his head.

A Christian, Samir thought wryly, judging by the style of his genuflexion. He approached the centre and looked up.

The heavy dome was supported by four columns, and four small apertures in the dome afforded the only light in the mosque. A prominent architrave ran in a wide circle where the dome joined the disproportionately small flat ceiling. It was too dark to read the Koranic verses engraved in calligraphic Arabic in the ceiling itself. However, the light from the windows reflected the single line of text, written in bold Greek letters, in the architrave.

Turning his head counter-clockwise, Samir slowly read aloud: 'Of the three who will know Chronos, only the student and the abbess will *prophesy* before many nations and many tongues.'

The stranger rose shakily to his feet. 'It's cold in here,' he said in English, and then quickly turned to squat and click open his briefcase.

Samir cocked his head at the man. He's crying, he thought, puzzled. The stranger wiped his eyes with his sleeves, trying to conceal his emotion in the dark, before plunging his hands into the open case for a brown envelope.

'Are you OK?' Samir enquired politely.

The man rose, this time steadily, to his feet. 'Mr Samir Khoury?'

'Yes.'

'This is for you,' said the man, handing him the envelope.

'Oh.' He squinted and recognized Jacob's handwriting on the envelope.

The men faced one another; there was an uneasy silence. When they finally spoke, they spoke together.

'So you know Jacob.'

'You read ancient Greek.'

They both grinned, then shrugged together.

'Well, thanks,' said Samir, waving the envelope.

'My pleasure.'

'And how's Jacob?'

'OK. He's fine.' The stranger pretended to look at his watch, though it was too dark to tell the time. 'I must go,' he said abruptly.

Samir nodded and the men shook hands. Both their hands were ice-cold. The man hurried away, leaving

Samir to read, once more, the thirty-sixth chapter of St John's Book of Revelation.

How strange, thought Samir. How completely odd. That man had reminded him of his brother George, the PNL militiaman. He looked and sounded just like the brother of his childhood memories. As for the verse engraved in the architrave, Samir could not see why Jacob had wanted him to read it. He was, on the other hand, impatient to read Carthalo the Historian.

Glafkos tied his shoelaces with shaking hands. He could not be the student. His heart was with Patéras Jacob, but not his faith.

Samir returned to his car and tore at the envelope. The three tablets had yielded two sheets of typed text. Jacob was a genius. Certainly he was more fluent in Punic than Samir was in ancient Greek. He had to be because it had been an impromptu request and Jacob had translated all three tablets without – Samir was confident – referring to any books on Punic. Indeed, he wondered whether textbooks on Phoenician even existed. Further proof of the Hellenic cultural victory, thought Samir, lighting a cigarette and inhaling deeply. Flicking the ash out of the window he read Jacob's translation of the last Carthaginian.

> Elissa, Queen of Tyre, was awoken one night by a star which shone brightly outside her palace window. Taking a hundred of her most faithful guards, she followed the star away from the city, just as her brother, Pygmalion the Tyrant, prepared to assassinate her to seize the throne. The star led her to this holy temple (*the Pillars of Truth, thought Samir*) before turning to the rising sun. For two months the hundred men and their queen followed the star. It stopped when their horses needed rest

and flew like the Phoenix herself when the chariots could charge. They followed her to Jubel where Queen Elissa bought a ship (*Carthalo described how many cubits long, wide and high the ship was, and how much it cost, and how Elissa had found the money to pay the Jubeli king*) and, guided by the star, the company sailed to Cyprus. In Kition they took one hundred virgins, one for each faithful guard, and set sail again. The bird-star led them to Africa and stopped in the sky by a tall hill overlooking the roundest and deepest bay. Queen Elissa, with fifty men, left the ship and climbed the hill. The star flew down to them and they saw her wings and marvelled at her voice when she spoke: 'I am Tanit. I bless this ground where you and your hundred will build the New City.' The star landed on the ground, her light disappeared and she became one gem to shatter all gems, round as the moon, black as the underworld, small as a young maiden's eye, yet her weight in body. As directed, Queen Elissa built Kart-Haddash (*New-City, Carthage*) and where the bird-star had landed, she built the strongest Byrsa (*citadel*) the world had ever seen. Then the wise queen made one of her companions a *rab-shomam* (*high priest*), instructing him and his successors to be the guardians of Tanit's Jewel in the Byrsa. For as long as she remained on the hill, so would Kart-Haddash live. I am Carthalo the Historian, the last *rab-shomam*. I have found the blessed gem again, twenty long years after its theft from the Byrsa. But I am too late. Holy Kart-Haddash is destroyed by the barbarian Roma. The Byrsa has fallen, eight hundred summers after Queen Elissa handed custody of the Jewel to the first *rab-shomam*.

> I must return her to her father and bury Tanit
> in El's Temple of Truth, that she may rise from
> the ashes again to guide another Queen Elissa.

Samir put down the pages on the passenger seat and lit another cigarette. Then he returned to the passage and reread: 'The star landed on the ground, her light disappeared and she became one gem to shatter all gems, round as the moon, black as the underworld, small as a young maiden's eye, yet her weight in body.'

Hammad's, Jamil's, Johann Strauss's sphere. The ball of light that became a black ping-pong ball weighing 36 kilogrammes, which had broken Jamil's diamond drills and which the Hezbollah had sent to their paymasters in Iran. Tanit's Jewel – Carthage's greatest treasure; could it possibly be one and the same as Johann's sphere?

If Hammad had been present in the car there and then, he would have been happy to learn that Samir was less of a sceptic concerning Johann's sphere.

8

BEASTLY CONTACT

16 April 1982, Nevada Desert, 1:32 a.m.

A flashing red light came on in the SETI headquarters which, a microsecond later, prompted all the loudspeakers in the compound to blare the first bar of Nat King Cole singing 'Just in Time.'

'Can you turn that infernal thing off!' Bill shouted.

'What?' Ric shouted back.

The alarm had been Ric's idea. He pretended not to hear, pointed helplessly at his right ear as Nat sang about finding his way just in time.

Bill switched the alarm off himself. 'Thank God for that,' he said.

'What is it, Ric?' Maira asked.

Ric was seated at a terminal and answered, 'Don't know yet. I think ET's calling collect. Do we accept the charges?'

'God, yes.'

'You're sure,' said Bill, 'I mean absolutely sure it's not a signal from Earth bouncing back?'

'Yeah, it's coming from the Sombrero Galaxy.'

Maira smiled.

'The M104 Galaxy?' Bill added, 'Are you sure?'

'Yeah, and you got yourself a genius standing next to you, Bill. This is the signal if we'd just sat listening to it.'

He punched a few keys and a graph appeared on the monitor with points scattered randomly.

'Background radiation.' Bill placed a hand on Maira's shoulder.

'Yeah, and this is the same signal slowed by the software.'

The graph became organized into square waves, steps up and steps down.

'I don't believe it,' Maira said.

'Don't blame me, Doc,' Ric said kindly. 'It was your idea.'

'How much is there?' Bill asked.

'It hasn't stopped yet.'

'Really?'

'Don't get too excited. As far as I can make out it's a short message being repeated over and over again.'

'Maybe that's just a "Hello", or a primer to the real message.'

'Which would come later,' Maira prompted.

'Yes, or even simultaneously, a kind of palimpsest effect.'

'How do you mean?' Maira asked.

'Like the palimpsests of ancient scribes. When they were short of marble they wrote over pre-existing text. You could have the same effect with radio waves. Maybe there are other messages along with this one on neighbouring frequencies. We haven't checked the polarities and timing yet, right?' Bill said, turning to Ric.

'Gimme a break.'

'Sorry, but we *are* recording all of it?'

'Yeah.'

'And adjacent frequencies as well? Just in case.'

'Sure. It's all in the program.'

'Can we check please?'

'I've already checked,' Ric answered grudgingly, and tapping a few keys he added, 'There, you see. Now recording from five-five-four to six-seven-eight cycles.'

'That band corresponds to ten per cent either way of the signal frequency. Right?' Bill asked.

Ric, looking at the monitor, said, 'Yeah. Message's coming in on six-one-six cycles.'

Maira gasped. 'Come again?'

'Six-one-six cycles, Doc.'

The coincidence with James Smith's number sent a chill up her spine.

'Excellent news,' Bill said to more SETI inmates who had entered the lab. 'Excellent. Well, seeing as we've got everything under control here, where's the champagne?'

Maira, following the group to the canteen, was in a sombre mood.

Just as aliens had made contact with terrestrials for the first time, so for the first time ever the canteen was opened at two in the morning. But rather than wake the chief caterer, the select group of employees entered stealthily, excited like a gang of children raiding the school refectory.

Ric appeared hugging a bottle of tequila and a bag full of plastic cups, with another employee carrying some limes and a box of salt.

'Guess this'll do the trick. There's some spaghetti sauce on the floor back there, if anyone's interested.'

Prompted by his own glance, everyone stared at Ric's bare feet.

The limes were quartered and a slice handed to each person, along with a pinch of salt and a plastic cup of tequila.

'Not the easiest drink for toasts,' Bill said, 'but anyway, here goes. I'd like to propose two toasts. I suppose the first one's a bit sad.'

Everyone said, 'Aaah,' in mock sadness.

'An hour or so ago we received an extraterrestrial broadcast which we are still recording. SETI is therefore dead. Ladies and gentlemen, fellow pioneers, to SETI.'

They raised their cups, downed the tequila and ate the limes and salt. Someone spluttered and coughed several times.

More tequila, limes and salt were distributed and Bill added cheerfully, 'SETI is dead. Long live FETI.'

Ric, raising his cup, said, 'Guess we're now into

fucking extraterrestrial intelligence.'

Bill interjected. 'Or for the even less genteel, *Found*.'

Even Bill freely admitted that they had simply not been prepared. Contact from outerspace had represented a quest for a needle in a barnful of galaxies, such an ideality for all concerned that no-one had carefully considered the follow-up. A major practical difficulty had been overlooked: the SETI telescopes could only receive and record the extraterrestrial message if the M104 Galaxy was in sight. Unlike optical telescopes, radio telescopes could perform relatively well in daylight – especially in such a long wave. But given Earth's rotation, the Sombrero was asleep, muted, for a little over twelve hours diurnally.

This failing was in practice completely due to CTT. In the past, before CTT, there existed a contingency plan in which, having discovered a signal, SETI informed NASA, which in turn would direct space telescopes and create an international consortium with telescopes in many time zones, creating a tight grid to track the broadcast uninterruptedly. But without Ric's software based on Maira's temporal red shift, the signal from M104 became so transient that it was engulfed by background noise. Without the theoretical filter provided by CTT, there seemed little point just yet in announcing to the world that contact had indeed been made, but that only Nevada had the pointed ears.

'Let's have something concrete to show first,' Bill said on the third day.

'Yeah,' Ric added, 'like hey, *hombres*, do we have some hot news for you.'

Bill nodded and they both looked dejectedly at the lengthy pile of manifold computer paper. 'I hope they're not transmitting something more substantial when we're not looking. If this is a primer to a future message, it's not much help. A short sequence of dots and dashes, repeated till we're sick.'

'Dot-dash-dash-dot-dot-dash-dot-dash-dash-dash.'
Ric ended with a groan.

'That's it?' Maira said.

Both men nodded.

'We've tried seeing it as a mathematical equation or a chemical element – at least something that would be fundamentally true to both civilizations.'

'Maybe,' she said. 'There is a strong chance that they don't mean to communicate. After all, most of our radio and certainly all our TV broadcasts are not emitted with an alien audience in mind.'

'That's true, of course.'

'Yeah, but instead of sending this boring shit, they could send us an alien programme, you know, a popular show on their planet.'

'Perhaps they're doing us a favour,' Maira replied.

'OK,' Bill said, unamused, 'but let's assume that they are trying to communicate.'

'Why?' said Ric. 'Don't you like TV, Doc?'

'Let's stick to what we have. OK, Ric? Maira? Fine. Now, if we were to communicate, we'd probably want to begin with elementary maths. For instance, our first message could be one plus one equals two, working our way up, defining the numbers. This would provide a common ground, all the while showing our intelligence.'

'Yeah. Real intelligent.'

'OK, this is a brainstorming session. Do you have a better idea?'

'No,' admitted Ric, 'but you wouldn't catch me sending one plus one equals two halfway across the universe.'

'Maybe it's a number,' Maira said suddenly.

'That's what I'm saying,' Bill said.

'No, I mean the whole thing's a number. A very special number.' She was feeling unsettled.

'A very special number? What do you mean?'

'Forget I said that.'

Bill shrugged. 'It could be a number. That's easy enough to verify. With only dots and dashes, it would be binary.'

'Yeah.' Ric patted the pile of printouts. 'What's infinity in binary?'

'One number that's repeated,' Bill continued, '0110010111. Let's see units, twos, fours, eights, sixteens—'

Ric grinned impishly. 'Four-zero-seven.'

'I pay you for this, just remember that.'

'It's not four-zero-seven,' Maira said. 'You wouldn't start a number with a zero. Four-zero-seven would be 110010111.'

'The message begins with a dot.'

'Maybe, therefore, the dots are one and the dashes zero. And the number is then 1001101000.'

Presently Ric said, 'Six-one-six.'

'Fuck,' Maira said for the first time in a very long while.

'Why,' Bill said excited, 'Maira, we may have a link here with the frequency.'

'Of course it's a sodding link with the frequency. Look, Bill, you can't go public with this, this – number.'

'Why not?'

'Because . . .' She paused, thought she'd sound stupid, then decided to hell with it. 'Because that number is the number of the Beast.'

There was an abrupt silence and the men stared wide-eyed at Maira. The lines on Bill's forehead deepened and a tentative smile began to play on Ric's lips.

'Hey, Doc, I thought *el número de la bestia* was 1010011010.' As she looked coldly at him, he added, 'Six-six-six.'

Maira ignored him. 'Do you remember the man I was telling you about? James Smith?'

'Sure. The guy who broke in. Convinced Joe he was your uncle.'

She nodded. 'He mentioned six-one-six. I've had the

number checked with a theologian. Six-one-six is probably the number of the beast.'

'Probably?'

'Probably, without a doubt.'

'Maira, listen to yourself. What happened to the scientist I met in Cambridge?'

'Honestly, Bill, I'm –' she hesitated '– frightened by all this.'

He moved closer and put his arm around her shoulders. 'It's simply a coincidence, nothing more. Coincidences happen.'

Maira brushed his arm away. 'I'm not that frightened that you need to patronize me. And this is not a coincidence or a hoax. I can't describe why I know in terms that I would like because I feel it, not think it. It's deep inside—'

'Doc, you want some Alka-Seltzer?'

'No offence, Ric, but piss off.' She faced Bill again. 'Look, this man's visit had about as much purpose as the message. Both talk only of a number. And of the infinite numbers they could choose from, do they choose interesting numbers like pi or the square root of two? No. They both mention the same rational number: six-one-six, which, even in a biblical context, would mean absolutely nothing to most people. Bill, this is no coincidence.'

'OK. So what do you want me to do about it? Send a message back that would take a couple of billion years saying, "Go to hell, we don't want your Beast?"'

'No. I don't know. But one thing's clear, we can't go public with this.'

'You're contradicting yourself. You just said that people wouldn't recognize six-one-six as the number of the Beast.'

'Most people,' Maira corrected, 'but some people will know only too well, and soon everyone would know, and there'd be panic everywhere. There would and you know it.'

Bill shrugged. 'I can keep this a secret for some time, but it's got to go public sooner or later.'

'Promise me to make it later. As late as you possibly can. Promise me.'

'Come on, Maira.'

'Promise me. I promised you I'd think about that question you raised at the conference in Cambridge. I promised I would consider coming here. I have never let you down on those promises. You have to promise me.'

'OK. OK, for now.'

'And you too, Ric.'

'Hey, Doc, you never promised me nothing in no conference.'

'Ric.'

'Yeah, yeah, I promise. If I lie, *la bestia* can have my fingers and toes.'

'So what do we do now?' Bill said.

'We wait,' she replied, and got gooseflesh as she added, 'maybe something will happen soon.'

Two days later the strangest thing happened: the message ended abruptly.

'God damn it. Are you sure?'

'Shit, Bill. I'm telling you it was from here.'

'Here?'

'Yeah. Somewhere on Earth.'

'Where?'

'Don't know. We only got an echo.'

'Let me get this straight, Ric. We're receiving a signal from M104, then suddenly there's a reply from somewhere on Earth, and just as suddenly the alien broadcast ends.'

'Yeah.'

'That's just not possible.'

'Hey, that's a fact. That's what happened.'

'That's just not possible,' Bill repeated.

There was a long pause.

'I don't like this one bit,' Maira said. 'A signal from

billions of light years away ends at exactly the instant Earth transmits a reply. Another incredible coincidence, Bill?'

Bill replied coldly. 'We're scientists, let's try to be scientific about this.'

'Fine,' Maira said evenly. 'If you discount coincidences and hoaxes, there are only two possible explanations. Purely academic, you must understand, because I can't envisage either to be truly feasible. The first is that the message was not coming from M104, but from within the solar system, and furthermore, in the vicinity of Earth. Because there was little or no delay, even Mars would then be too far.'

'Negative, Doc. The message came from the Sombrero Galaxy – that we know.'

'Then the second possibility, even more unlikely, is that something can travel faster than the speed of light.'

'The chronon doesn't travel faster than a photon of light, does it?' Bill asked suddenly.

'Nothing travels faster than light. But it may be that CTT and science in general need a major rethink. But even so, we're talking signals not chronons. A signal was sent from Earth on six-one-six cycles, an electromagnetic wave which we know travels at the speed of light.'

'That's it,' Bill said decisively. 'Someone or something, somewhere on Earth, holds the key to understanding. So what we need to do now is reset our priorities. We must concentrate on the signal from Earth, not M104.'

Maira nodded slowly and Ric said, 'Yeah, Bill, but everything's stopped.'

'If the signal from Earth were to be broadcast again, could you pinpoint it?' Bill asked him.

'Yeah,' he replied, adding after a while, 'guess I'd need at least four telescopes to catch the bounce.'

'You can have fifteen.'

'Catch the bounce?' Maira asked.

'Yeah. Boingedy-boingedy-boingedy-boing.'

Bill offered a better explanation. 'When Earth transmits a signal, most of the wave escapes into space, but a small part of it is reflected by the ionosphere back to ground where it is partially reflected back up into the atmosphere and bounces back.'

'Yes, I know that, like regular AM radio.'

'Right. So by tuning our sensitive telescopes to six-one-six cycles and looking in several directions, if we receive at least two reflected signals, because we will know the angles of reflection, we will be able to extrapolate the two paths around the globe. Where these two paths cross corresponds to the position of the transmitter.'

'Guess NASA won't be happy that almost all our telescopes are looking down and not up.'

'Guess NASA won't know about it,' Bill countered.

'Is that going to give us an accurate location?' Maira asked.

'Should do, right, Ric?'

'Depends on how many boingedy-boings. But if the distance to the transmitter is real short, the telescopes are too big.' He paused and then added, 'Guess I could build a box.'

'A receiver?'

'Yeah, but with one channel: six-one-six cycles. And it'd show the strength, and you'd go where the signal was strongest.'

'A tracker? That's great, Ric. How much time do you need?'

'Yeah. But have you guys thought what we'll find, you know, on the other side? I mean, shit, man, if *la bestia* is sending those signals, we don't want to go nowhere near.'

This was the first time Maira had seen him concerned. 'Don't worry, Ric. If it is a monster, it will be the harbinger of doom, whether we find it or it finds us.'

'Hear that, Bill? Be happy, Doc says, even if *la bestia* eats your brains.'

Maira did not smile.

*　　*　　*

The first message which had heralded the end of the Sombrero's broadcast had simply been a dash followed by a dot. Unexpected as it was, the SETI telescopes had received it as a faint echo, an ionized murmur. With the second signal to leave Earth on six-one-six cycles, the fifteen telescopes were prepared, each scanning just over 10-degree segments of the ether above the Nevada Desert.

The alarm went off again; Nat King Cole had been replaced by a shrill siren.

'Dot-dash,' Ric said, looking at the monitor.

'Just that?' Bill asked.

Ric nodded and Bill added, 'At least it's somewhat different.'

'They're not very communicative, are they,' Maira stated.

'How many picked up the signal?'

'Seven telescopes,' Ric answered, pleased. 'We'll know where that shit's hiding.'

Ric began to extrapolate all seven paths.

'Can I do something, Ric?'

'Yeah, Doc. Pray it's not in the States.'

Presently Ric exclaimed, 'Asshole.'

'What?'

'Two of them.'

Bill and Maira moved closer to the terminal.

'See,' Ric resumed, excited. 'Three curves meet here at longitude forty-seven degrees, thirty-two minutes East and latitude thirty-two degrees, eighteen minutes North. And the other four at fifty-two degrees, fourteen minutes East and thirty-four degrees, forty minutes North.'

'And both transmitted the same signal?' Maira asked.

'Negative. That's the funny thing. We got the dot-dash together, but the dot came from the first place and the dash from the second.'

'I wasn't expecting two transmitters,' Bill mused.

'Yeah, and maybe more.'

'And maybe just one.'

'Doc, there's no mistake.'

'I'm not saying there is. But maybe this thing – whatever it is – is moving.'

'Moving?'

'It sent the dot from the first set of co-ordinates and the dash from the second set.'

'Could be,' Bill said. 'We can test that idea. How short was the interval between dot and dash?'

'Short.'

'Thanks, Ric, how short?'

'A microsecond.'

'OK. And the distance between the two co-ordinates?' A moment later, he prompted, 'Ric?'

'Be my guest if you can work out the polar equations quicker.' Ric calculated the exponentials of sines and cosines and then said, 'Seven hundred and twenty miles – give or take.'

Bill whistled. 'Seven hundred and twenty miles in a microsecond, seven hundred and twenty thousand miles per second. It can't be, that's—'

Maira completed the sentence. 'Faster than the speed of light.'

Bill and Maira stood staring at each other for a while.

'Maira, I can't keep this a secret.'

She sighed. 'I know, but you must. We're so jumpy, can you imagine how non-scientists will feel?'

'Hey, guys,' Ric shouted. He was still looking at the monitor. 'You're really going to dig this. Both co-ordinates are in Iran. The first one's spot on Tehran.'

Maira and Bill turned to stare at Ric who looked down at his fingertips and added, 'Guess that makes the Beast an ayatollah.'

Sunsets had always held a strong place in Maira's heart, a deep well of emotion before science and logic meddled. She saw the red westering sun not with the

238

knowledge of light diffracted by the atmosphere, nor with the scientific certainty of another sunrise, but through the sensitive eyes of an artist. She mourned, with daytime animals, the bloody end of day. Now, with the last rays thrown back across the horizon, all that remained was a burgundy wake, an ethereal sky which offered temporary sanctuary from the burgeoning darkness. Sunsets in Nevada were a more hurried affair than in Britain, as if the desert, raided of all moisture, had finally exiled the unwelcome day, or else that green England had enticed the sun to remain a while longer to provide the foliage in the trees and the grass on the ground with precious moments of radiance. It was then, as she gazed at the stars in this abrupt nightfall, that science tinkered once again with her thoughts. Sunsets here were shorter than in Britain because Nevada was closer to the equator. This also explained the longer winter days and shorter summer nights than England. Science could describe this phenomenon perfectly well without CTT; however, the chronon could be called on to explain this as well as a related observation.

In a purely human context, two otherwise identical twins measured the second differently according to their different domiciles. A second as measured by some *cosmic* clock would be an imperceptibly shorter time for a twin living in the mountains than for his brother living at sea level or below, as the Nevada Desert was. In CTT terms what applied to altitude was also true for latitude and temperature, so that a Polar Eskimo's own personal second would equally be barely longer than an equatorial man's. The direct result was that societies on the equator lived imperceptibly fuller but shorter lives. She had used her equations to illustrate that as a longer notion of the second implied a higher activity, a man inhabiting a warm clime close to the equator would have both faster gestures and quicker speech than his more Nordic counterpart. As she considered these inherent differences in speech, Maira had a sudden idea about the alien communication from the Sombrero Galaxy.

'Of course,' she said, astonishing the deep night, and turning on her heels, she marched resolutely back to the laboratory complex.

She was greeted by Bill who shouted at her, 'Iraq.'

'I'm sorry?'

'Iran, and now Iraq.' He shook his head. 'The Pentagon would really love this.'

'Yeah,' Ric added. 'Guess none of us would be here if they knew.'

'Iraq?'

'The dot's from Basra.'

'The dash from Baghdad,' Ric added.

'There is one thing we've overlooked,' she said. 'The signals from Iran – now Iraq – are in our present universe's second.'

'Hey, Doc, what're you saying?'

'That we can hear the dot and dash without having to pass through the software. But the message from the Sombrero was in the past universe's second. There's a delay of one microsecond between the dot and dash from Iran and Iraq, right? Therefore, if in our message from M104, having slowed the signal, we find that throughout there is a similar delay, then it would be fair to conclude that a single word or number was broadcast. If, on the other hand, within the signal we find slightly longer stretches between dots and dashes, then clearly that would mark the beginning of another word or number.'

'Clearly?' Bill said.

'The initial message from the Sombrero is not necessarily a single word or a number but could be a sentence.'

Ric nodded. 'Yeah, I get that.' He moved to the terminal and tapped on the keyboard. 'OK. So we got a microsecond between the first dot and dash.' A while later he added, 'About one point zero one microseconds, a tiny pause between dash and second dash.'

Maira picked up a sheet of paper and a pen, and as Ric called out all the pauses, she scribbled:

·— —·· —·—— —

'You see?' she said excitedly. 'It could be a phrase of four words. And the first word is now being repeated in the reply from Iran and Iraq, the dot-dash.'

'What about the number six-one-six and the link with the frequency?' Bill asked.

Maira frowned. 'Yes, we can't assume it was a coincidence. Maybe the number itself is a message. And this is a further message. In essence, it could be the palimpsest effect you were talking about.'

Ric said suddenly, 'ADYT.'

'Add what?' she asked.

'Negative. A–D–Y–T. The message is the four letters in Morse.'

'Somehow I don't think aliens would use Morse code,' Bill said.

Maira nodded. 'It must be a lot simpler than Morse, given the short message. Maybe the dots represent one letter in the alien tongue and the dash another letter. So if we take the first two letters of our alphabet, the message could be, AB BAA BABB B. Or conversely, BA ABB ABAA A.'

'Hubba hubba hubba,' Ric said, grinning.

'That doesn't help all that much,' Bill said to Maira.

'Perhaps not, but at least we may have transformed our problem into one of linguistics. We now need more alien vocabulary.'

'Yeah, but I like ADYT,' Ric replied. 'It's easier. Guess it could stand for something, like Antichrist Do Your Thing.'

'You're sick, Ric, you know that?' Bill said.

'And Die You Terrestrials.'

*   *   *

For a full week, M104 was silent as the signals from Earth moved progressively through the Middle East. The reply had been sent from Iran in the first two nights, from Iraq for two nights, and from Syria on the fifth night of silence from the Sombrero Galaxy.

On the sixth night, Ric said, 'Tripoli.'

'Libya?' Bill exclaimed.

'Negative. Guess this is another Tripoli. This one's in north Lebanon.'

'Iran, Iraq, Syria and now Lebanon. Boy, they sure know how to pick them. The four liveliest tourist destinations in the world.'

'Lebanon,' Maira mused.

'I hope the signals will move south now,' Bill said.

'Yeah, why?'

'I'd feel considerably safer if they were coming from Israel, that's why.'

'Ric, can you find a place in Lebanon called Jubel?'

The map of Lebanon was blown up on the screen, and Ric said, 'How do you spell that, Doc?'

'J–U–B–E–L.'

'Negative. There's no Jubel. There's a Jubail. J–U–B–A–I–L. It's got "Byblos" written in brackets.'

'Is it anywhere near Tripoli?'

'It's by the sea, guess about midway between Beirut and Tripoli.'

'Why, Maira?'

'I simply wondered, that's all.'

Maira wondered all night long and when the sun rose, rapidly directing a skew beam across her room, she decided she should travel to the land where tourists would not venture. Catch the express train out, she thought, but not to Cambridge. She hugged her pillow.

Now, as the desert awoke to another scorching day, Maira finally fell asleep with the image of hordes of wild militiamen with hairy faces and snarling expressions.

*　　*　　*

The second message from M104 was received by the single telescope still tracking the distant galaxy. This time the signal was significantly shorter and repeated only twice. And then there was an abrupt ominous silence on six-one-six cycles which would last ten days.

'No dot,' Ric said.

'This time we received only a dash,' Maira confirmed. She held a clipboard and was busy writing as Bill said, 'OK. Till now the signals from Earth have been a dot-dash right?'

'Yeah. Except the first from Iran. That was dash-dot.'

'And this latest one which is simply a dash.'

'Yeah, from Lebanon.'

'Where in Lebanon?' Maira asked.

'Not Jubail, Doc. Some place away from the sea. A town called Baalbek.'

'Baalbek?'

He nodded.

'OK,' Bill said. 'If I understand this correctly, we received only a dash from this place—'

'Baalbek,' Ric prompted.

'—and almost immediately M104 sends us another signal.'

'Yeah, C.'

'See what?'

'Negative. El Sombrero sends C, C, C. Dash-dot-dash-dot three times.'

'Right, and then everything goes dead.' He turned to face Maira who had stopped writing. 'What do you think?'

'I think that one of us needs to go to Lebanon.'

'What?'

'I volunteer,' she said evenly.

'You're kidding, right?' Bill said.

Maira shrugged. 'We shan't discover anything new from here. It has become clear to me what all this is about, at least the procedure has, the purpose remains a mystery. We now know that it was conceited of us to

243

believe that M104 was communicating with us. The message was aimed at something alien on Earth which we can call Adyt. Clearly the first message carried a prompt and a task because Adyt first replied and then started moving. Perhaps the message from the Sombrero was something like, "Wake up, Adyt, and do such and such."'

'Yeah. That's what I said.'

'Essentially it's very similar to a computer command. The first reply from Adyt to M104 is dash-dot, perhaps translated as, "Roger, I'm awake and am starting." Then, at regular intervals, Adyt sends a dot-dash which could be, "Still searching," because it moves across Iran, Iraq, Syria and then Lebanon, where Adyt sends a dash and stops broadcasting altogether. I believe the dash from Baalbek in Lebanon represents, "I have found what we're looking for," and immediately M104 sends a brief signal back which may be understood as, "Roger and out," or another command.'

'Maybe,' Bill said simply.

'It's the best explanation we have so far,' she countered.

'True, but not necessarily the best there is.'

'I have written the complete broadcast between M104 and Adyt, with the dashes as As and the dots as Bs. You can see that even though we don't understand the words, some rough meaning begins to come through.'

Maira showed the men the clipboard:

M104:   BA ABB ABAA A?
BA ABB ABAA A?

The message is repeated until Adyt's reply:

ADYT: AB
BA (From Iran)
BA (From Iraq)
BA (From Syria)

BA (From northern Lebanon)
ADYT: A (Once from Baalbek, Lebanon)
M104:   ABAB ABAB ABAB

'OK. Maybe this thing, Adyt, is searching for something,' Bill admitted. 'But going to Lebanon, I can't recommend that, Maira.'

'There's a ceasefire, I believe.' She smiled at them. 'And they know how to treat their women there.'

'It's not Surrey, you know.'

'Bill, we have the opportunity of a lifetime here, of generations of lifetimes. Something strange is happening, and something can quite apparently travel faster than the speed of light. It's fantastic and quite unbelievable. I'm surprised you're not tempted to pack your bags.'

'No, Maira, you've got that backwards.' Bill scratched his chin. 'There could be another way. We could transmit a signal to M104 on six-one-six cycles.'

'I can't imagine how this will help. If M104 was initially only interested in contacting Adyt, there's no reason to suppose that the Sombrero will listen to our broadcast.'

'But, Doc, what if there's something bad out there?'

'Ric, if there is something evil in Lebanon, then we'll want to be among the first to know so that we can warn the world.'

'You're brave, Doc.'

Maira smiled. 'Not really. I don't expect there is anything bad out there, other than the war, of course.'

'Yeah? What about six-one-six?'

Still smiling, she answered, 'A coincidence, a hoax. Right, Bill?'

'I can't be held responsible for you, Maira,' he said seriously.

'I don't expect you to. I'm a big girl.'

'Maira, are you sure about this?'

She nodded slowly.

SETI paid for the expenses: Maira's Lebanese visa in Washington and her ticket to Beirut.

Ric's tracker was ready two days before her departure. It looked like, and indeed was, a hybrid between a hand-held walkie-talkie and a boy scout's magnetic compass. Given the long wave at six-one-six cycles, an external aerial was not required, and picking up signals involved turning the entire box with its in-built short antenna rod. There were two small diode lights: a green one, which signalled that a broadcast was being received, and a flashing red one to mean that the broadcast was being tracked. On the lower half, there was a compass-type arrangement with a red arrow which could spin on an axle over a radial disc marking the bearings.

'It works on standard nine-volt batteries,' Ric told her. 'Guess you need to take some with you. Could be that Beirut's out of them.'

She nodded. 'So I'll keep it switched on all the time. If there is a signal, the red light will flash and the needle will turn to show the direction I need to take.'

'Yeah. If you get the red light, turn three-sixty degrees and the tracker'll do the rest. If Adyt is real close, you'll know, 'cos the thing'll go loco and turn very fast. It'll tick off a month in a minute, and it won't stop unless you turn it off or Adyt moves away.'

'Excellent, Ric,' Maira said, handling the tracker.

She turned it and saw a white shining cross which had been painted on the otherwise black plastic covering.

'Can't do no harm.'

'Yeah,' Maira mimicked, 'guess not.'

'Hey, Doc, look after you.'

'I will. Thanks, Ric.' She leaned over and pecked him on the cheek.

Maira had only two images of Lebanon which, she supposed, were also almost everyone's. The first was of erstwhile avenues, transformed by the war of anarchy into uneven tracks lined by rubble, and façades of skeleton buildings, like some macabre Hollywood set. The second image was of a mob of fanatics beating their chests and heads in some ritualized frenzy of self-affliction, and burning American and British flags.

Yet Maira was not as worried as she thought this trip entitled her to be. She simply did not concern herself with Lebanon or with the idea that she, a woman, was travelling alone to a war zone, to an Arab country which was such a bane to all Westerners.

She sometimes wondered about the stranger, James Smith. Maira was intrigued by the address he had left her which appeared to complement the number six-one-six in portent. But she was not travelling to fulfil some obscure destiny, nor was she acting under Mr Smith's avuncular and much-riddled advice. Maira was going to find Adyt, to learn its secret, and above all its purpose. Everything else was secondary.

When she had decided to leave for Lebanon, she had understood that Adyt held the key to something far more important than extraterrestrial contact, of greater significance than the secret of travelling at speeds faster than light. It had dawned on Maira that whatever had broadcast a dash from Baalbek could also provide the clue to mankind's future.

On the road to the airport in Las Vegas, she spotted an eagle or a buzzard or a vulture hovering effortlessly over Death Valley, and she wondered what manner of a beast Adyt would be.

ZACHIEL

During the sandstorm on this timeless, spaceless world, the dune due west from where we stand had melted into a dome supporting a crescent moon. Judgement – east on the Celtic cross – is affected by its opposite like the tide.

All the doorways are now as black as the sky, except *The Moon*'s, where a window in the crystal dome shines a fierce blue light. For the first time, I am to leave the familiar past and near future to witness a distant advent in a world which has become totally alien to me.

THE MOON

9

ANNO DOMINI, 2010
ANNO HEGIRAE, 1431

The Imam BenKadeemi turned in his sleep and muttered, 'Allah.'

The North African night breezed into the room through the open window, causing the two silk curtains to flutter and dance like courting phantoms. A window shutter creaked rhythmically then slammed against the outer wall; the Imam sat up suddenly.

BenKadeemi swung his legs out of bed and stood unsteadily for a full minute, swaying like a metronome, his eyes hauntingly open, his nightgown clinging to his body with perspiration. Then he turned and rummaged in the room for his prayer-mat.

A servant in an adjacent room heard the noise, ran to the door, knocked and entered. The Imam's bed was placed at an awkward angle in the middle of the room, in order to face Mecca. BenKadeemi tottered with a prayer-mat in his arms and unrolled it parallel to the bed before falling to his knees and prostrating himself.

'Allah,' he murmured again and awoke to find his long grey beard sandwiched between his mouth and the prayer-mat.

He shivered and sneezed.

'Health, Holiness.' The servant approached the crouching figure.

'*Allah akbar, Allah akbar*,' BenKadeemi cried softly.

The servant bowed his head humbly and, reaching for the crumpled cotton blanket on the bed, covered the Imam's shoulders.

BenKadeemi was still shivering. His voice cracked with emotion. 'This night I stared into the eyes of the Angel.'

The servant knelt beside his master. '*Allah akbar.*'

The Imam lowered his head to kiss the mat. 'I see him now like I see my own hands. He spoke to me with the voice of a breeze, a gentle sound among the leaves of a palm tree.'

'*La ilaha illa Allah.*'

'The Angel spoke words of support to me before an ocean of faces, in front of a crowd that was like grains of sand in the desert.'

The servant brought his forehead to the floor.

'The Blessed Jibrayel whispered to me this night,' the Imam BenKadeemi marvelled. 'I am purified by the vision,' he sighed.

Hammad and Naila Ezzedin were in a filthy mood as they entered their penthouse apartment in Beirut. Hammad kicked his shoes off and called for a Scotch.

'Yes, mister,' a Sri Lankan maid replied.

'And Reema,' Naila indicated her husband's discarded shoes, 'peek zat and breeng Mister's *shahata.*'

'Yes, madam. *Shahata*, madam?'

'God deliver us. Slippers,' Hammad growled. Reema was heading off with the shoes in her hand when he called her back. 'First whisky, then slippers.'

'Yes, mister.' The maid dropped the shoes.

Hammad turned to his wife. 'Three-quarters of the world's population are servants and you have to find one who doesn't speak Arabic.'

Naila moved to the mirror in the hall and brushed her sleeves. 'At least she's honest. I trust her.'

'My dick's in honest's sister. Reema, my whisky! And ask whores whether trust exists – they'll tell you.'

Naila's reflection shook its head in resignation. She was getting old. It had taken her forty years of marriage to grow accustomed to his outbursts. 'Instead of shouting obscenities, help me get this necklace off.'

Hammad shuffled past her, collapsed wearily into an armchair, and lifted his feet onto a coffee-table. 'So what's trust in English?'

'What?'

He shouted, 'I said what's trust in English.'

Naila entered the living-room with her hands behind her neck, fiddling with the catch on her pearl necklace. 'No need to raise your voice, Hammad.'

He waved his arm in deprecation. 'There, you don't know what trust is in English.'

'So?'

'So what angelic good is it to have a maid you trust if you can't tell her you trust her.'

'You're talking rubbish.'

'Am I? The shaitan's armpit I'm talking rubbish.'

'I don't have to tell her to trust the dishes for me.' Naila pointed at the shoes by the door as Reema entered. 'Or to trust your shoes in the cupboard.'

The maid, carrying a glass of whisky on a tray, hesitated when she saw madam indicating the shoes.

'Here, Reema, on the table. Not only can't she speak Arabic, there's an ass's brains in her head. She was about to offer my whisky to the shoes.'

The maid placed the glass on the table.

'Reema,' Hammad said.

'Yes, mister.'

'What is trust?'

'Trust, mister?'

'Yes, trust, mister.'

She shook her head. 'I don't know, mister.'

'Reema,' Naila called, and jiggled her necklace, 'elp me tek off zat.'

Hammad loosened his black tie and undid the top buttons of his shirt, releasing the skin of his neck which had grown flabby and wrinkled like a turkey's. 'I take that back,' he said, gulping down his Scotch. 'She's either an ass with no brains at all or a rocket scientist disguised in a maid's outfit.'

'Do shut up, Hammad. I hate Beirut, I hate funerals, and I hate headaches.'

'She's right, of course, your Indian. No-one knows what trust is, not in Delhi, not in Damascus. Every living soul in the world trusts he understands the true meaning, but trust is a bitch on heat. When you least expect it, it turns to bite your dick off. Reema, another whisky.'

'Yes, mister. The shoes?'

'They stay. They have nowhere to run.'

She looked at him, puzzled.

'First whisky, then shoes.'

'Yes, mister.'

Hammad frowned. 'What was I saying before she interrupted me?'

'You were talking to yourself, my heart, being vulgar as usual.'

He appeared astonished. 'I may talk to myself when you're not listening but – ah yes – trust me, I'm never vulgar.'

Naila turned to leave the room. 'I need a bath. It's been a long day.'

'Very long,' he agreed. 'They go on and on and on like dishwashing liquid.'

'Funerals?'

'Our Shiite funerals.' Hammad listed them off his fingers. 'I've been to Sunni, Catholic, Maronite and Greek funerals.' He was left with his thumb. 'And Shiite funerals come out tops for the most tedious, with Greek a close second.'

'Today it was longer because the chief mullah gave the sermon.'

'And why was the chief mullah there?' Hammad answered his own question by mimicking his wife's voice. 'Because you were there, dear.'

'Don't take your anger out on me, Hammad.'

'The mullah shouldn't have been there. Jamil wouldn't have wanted that.'

'You're a cabinet minister, what do you expect?'

'If I'd been the president or prime minister, OK. Maybe. Pimp. Rest in peace, poor bastard.'

'Don't talk of him that way.'

Hammad's eyes were moist. 'Of course I've been to other Shiite funerals. And they're all long, and they're all tedious. And you know why? Shiites, you see, can't wait to get to heaven, but they believe their souls cling to their bodies after death. As you can't use a crowbar to separate the two, you hire a mullah to bore the soul to the garden of eternal springs.'

Naila sat down beside her husband and squeezed his arm. 'He was a good friend.'

'That whoreson will always be my friend, my cousin. I trusted him. See? See what I mean? You trust someone and then he bites you in the dick and, whoosh, explodes into a million pieces.'

Naila hugged her husband. 'He was my friend, too.'

'Would never have happened with a German bomb.'

'No, love.'

'I mean, in war you expect bombs to explode, right? You could be snoring like a constipated camel when a shell explodes in your bedroom. And that's fair enough. It's unlucky but, *ach, c'est la guerre.* End of story. But that poor bastard, digging his garden on a hot summer's day – for what, potatoes? Hashish? – and finding an unexploded shell. That's not fair. Fires of hell! Don't tell me you know what trust means. You trust you won't find a bomb in your garden in peacetime. You trust it won't explode just when you're standing there after it's been asleep with the jinn for decades. That's trust. Trust is a conspiracy.'

'Come on, Hammad, relax.'

'A conspiracy killed my cousin.'

'Yes, my heart.'

'*Ya,* Jamil. Poor Jamil. He believed in a conspiracy. A plot by the fundamentalists to kill all the liberal Shiites. He was right, you know. He knew – that's why they killed him.'

255

Naila held his hand. 'You don't mean that.'

'A conspiracy, I tell you.'

She frowned. 'Jamil wasn't important, I mean politically. Who would conspire to kill him?'

'Everyone. If Kissinger were still alive, I'd blame him.'

'Come on, Hammad, it was an accident. An old Soviet bomb exploded by accident.'

'Everything's an accident. The sun rises by accident, it sets by accident. Allah lives in a laboratory. He does what He knows best: He creates. Lead must turn to gold, but when it does, it's by accident.'

'Don't talk that way.'

'Germans knew how to build bombs. Bombs were bombs. They flew in the air and exploded on the ground, not like the Americans and Russians.' He added in a falsetto, stroking a nipple through his shirt, 'Not today, I've got a headache. Maybe later.' He roared suddenly, 'Thirty fucking years later.'

Naila let go of his hand.

'A conspiracy, I tell you. I've got a pussy if I know how, but it was a Hezbollah conspiracy.'

'He was well liked.'

'The Hezbollah hated him. First they kill his German pilot, steal his sphere, then they kill him because he won't be like them.'

'Everyone had such sad expressions in the mosque.'

'Fuck the extremists. Fuck everyone.'

Naila stood up. 'Time for my bath,' she said curtly.

'I never noticed the sad expressions,' he said as she walked out of the living-room. 'I was too busy staring back at everyone.' He had to shout to be heard. 'I thought people went to funerals to pay their last respects to the departed soul, not to eye the Minister of Culture and Tourism.' He looked at his empty glass. 'Reema, another whisky.'

The videphone in the corner of the room blipped; Hammad made no attempt to answer it. A few seconds later the screen came alive with a message, which he made no effort to read.

Reema entered with a whisky which she placed beside him, picking up the empty glass.

'Staring at me like sheep.'

'Pardon, mister?'

'Like sheep,' he said automatically.

'Yes, mister.'

'What, yes, mister?' Hammad frowned at her.

'I like sheep, mister.'

'Reema.' He pointed. 'The shoes.'

She nodded and left him to his thoughts.

Hammad recognized the stares. The expectant, desperate looks of people seeking reassurance, as if he possessed a wand to dissolve Lebanon's problems, as if he were a leading political head who could steer the nation clear of land-mines, or a seer who sensed the destinies of nations. They stared at him with gaunt expressions, like sheep in a van facing a junction – right to greener pastures; left to the slaughterhouse.

They called him Hammad Bek, Lord Hammad – yet he was neither helmsman nor prophet. The title bestowed on him honoured a grander past in the Ezzedin family, and they were honouring not the man but the blue blood in his veins. They were respecting his eccentric grandfather, the legendary Ali Pasha, feudal lord of Baalbek and the Northern Bekaa in 1910. Exactly a century later, Hammad Bek was nothing but a token Shiite in the Cabinet.

(Hammad had erupted in fury when he had first read that scathing description of his ministerial appointment in a leading newspaper. 'Token? I'll shove my token Shiite dick in those reporters. See if they like being tokened.')

In his present morose mood, he accepted the qualification. His pessimism was allowing him to admit that he had little grass-roots support within the Shiite community. Hammad was the only Shiite politician without direct or indirect links with the Hezbollah, and was the only Shiite minister in the government for

257

precisely his anti-fundamentalist views. Hammad could not forgive the Party of God for having turned his people into hollow shells.

'Everything's for later with them. You must leave everything till after you die: living, loving, thinking. A young Hezbollahi is promised a houri bride in heaven, and the virgin is sent off to be a martyr. Where's the justice? You think Allah wants that?' Hammad was talking to himself in his fury.

'We have been robbed of our free will. We must follow the false prophets like the tides follow the moon. When the Hezbollah commands "heel", we must grovel like amahs of ancient history. The Party orders, "Kill", and Shiite farmers shout in unison, "How many?" as if they were shooting birds for a feast. You think that's part of Allah's plan? You think the Hezbollah is the *Hisb Allah*?'

The fundamentalists described democracy as an amoral Western invention; and many Shiites clamoured for a change in the constitution.

'How can they be such fools? Don't they know that *we* invented democracy? *We* are the Phoenicians who invented democracy and the alphabet. In Jubel, Baalbek, Tyre and Sidon, we had ministers of culture and tourism when the Greeks were still lighting fires with flint. How can they be so ignorant of so glorious a past?'

'Yes, mister?' Reema popped her head around the door.

Hammad held his head in his hands and the maid returned to the kitchen.

In 1946 the French yielded control of Lebanon to the first president of the newly independent republic. On 22 November of that year, a constitution was drafted and signed, whereby the president, chosen from the Maronite community which reflected the then majority, exercised complete legislative power, supported – on second and third tiers respectively – by a Sunni prime minister and a Shiite leader of the house.

From the ashes of war-ravaged Beirut, a new constitution spread its wings in the early 1990s, and
Lebanon's political structure crossed the Atlantic from
the States to Britain, whereby, in the Second Republic,
legislative power was handed down from the Maronite
president to the Sunni prime minister. Two decades
later, in 2010, the Shiites – now outnumbering all the
other sects put together – were attempting to pull the
political system down a further notch, so that power
would rest firmly in the hands of the leader of the house
of deputies.

Were a Third Republic of Lebanon in the Hezbollah's
plans, Hammad, as an ambitious Shiite, might have
been for the proposal, perhaps even a proponent in the
Cabinet. However, the fundamentalists were seeking
power for two reasons, both shaitans to a liberal mind
such as Hammad's.

The first was to replace the Franco-Ottoman law of the
land with the Islamic shariah. The second, and more
radical, was Hezbollah's aim to join the Watan Arabi
(the Arab Nation) – Europe's equivalent in North Africa
and the Middle East: the extremist super-country that
had emerged with the fusion of Algeria, Libya, Sudan
and Iraq.

The day that his cousin, Jamil, was buried in the
eastern half of the city marked the beginning of the
Conference for the Islamic Brotherhood in the southern
outskirts of Beirut. The conference was a forum for all
the fundamentalist organizations in the Muslim world,
both those in power and those underground.
Representatives had arrived from Egypt, Syria, Jordan,
Morocco, Afghanistan and Iran, and, of course, the
Watan Arabi. The Gulf states had imposed visa restric-
tions on its nationals travelling to Beirut; small Saudi
and Kuwaiti contingents were, nevertheless, expected
from Europe.

The Lebanese government had succumbed to the
Shiite lobby to hold the conference in Beirut which

inflamed Christian and Sunni deputies. The ensuing polemics led to a summary walk-out by the fifty-strong Hezbollah block in the chamber, and Lebanon faced its gravest crisis since the war.

To add salt to the injury, the leader of the powerful Watan Arabi was attending the conference in person. His Holiness, the Imam BenKadeemi, had flown in from Algiers and, striking a diplomatic slap in the face, was refusing to meet the prime minister until the end of the conference.

'This is how it started last time. The Algerians have taken the role of the Palestinians. This is like the 1970s all over again.' Hammad smiled grimly. 'Even flares are popular again.'

'Hammad?' Naila walked in, astonished.

'What?'

'Who are you talking to?'

'To Jamil, my love, he just came for a drink before – you know – going uptown.'

'You *are* going mad. The phone's ringing, why don't you answer it?'

'Phones ring. Our videphone blips.' Hammad was smiling. 'I bet the whore-brother would be surprised to find Peter or George manning the gate instead of Ali.'

Naila had moved to the videphone terminal. 'It's from Toufiq Fattoush. The message is: "Crisis. Call me back urgently." And there's a message from Beauty.' Naila looked across at her husband. 'It's Ibtihage.'

'That woman,' Hammad said admiringly. 'She's been in our home for more years than I can remember. Why couldn't you find someone like her for our city house, instead of this Indian ass who can't speak Arabic.'

'She's dead.'

'What did you say?'

Naila repeated slowly. 'Ibtihage is dead.'

'What? Why?'

Naila was punching keys on the videphone. 'I'll find out.'

'Shit. Pimp. Why is death so popular all of a sudden? And whore-shit.'

'No-one's answering. We need to return to Beauty.'

'Phone the chopper pilot. Tell him to expect you. I have the ministers' meeting tonight. If we end early, which I doubt, I'll fly to Baalbek tonight. If not, tomorrow morning.' Death comes in threes, Hammad thought darkly, *ya*, Jamil, what have you started?

The helicopter flight to Baalbek would take half an hour, time enough for Hammad to have a bath and change into clean clothes for the extraordinary meeting called by the prime minister.

The videphone blipped twice before Hammad flicked the console on the receive mode.

'Naila,' he said, expectantly.

The screen lit up with Toufiq Fattoush's face. 'Hammad, where have you been, man? Why didn't you answer my calls?'

'Listen, Toto, I've been to my cousin's funeral and I—'

'Have you heard the news from the conference? It's a mess. A national crisis—'

'Toto, I have to cut you off. I'm expecting an important call.'

He flicked the machine to stand-by and the videphone blipped almost at once.

'Naila,' Hammad said, 'Naila, flick your screen on.'

'I ordered the death of your maid.'

The whisper was devoid of any emotion.

Hammad stared, dumbfounded, at the blank screen.

'She met with an unfortunate accident. A passing car. She was like a member of your family. Please accept my condolences.'

Hammad yelled, 'Who is this? Did you also kill Jamil?'

There was a long silence.

'No.'

'Show your face, cock-sucking whore.'

'My face? My face is the shaitan's compared to your angelic wife's.'

261

'Naila,' he spluttered, 'what do you—'

'Shut up and listen. Your wife is with my friends. If you interrupt me, if you say one word, she dies. Understand?'

Hammad controlled his rage.

'Good. I'll say this once. I'm faxing your letter of resignation from the Cabinet which you will personally present to the prime minister at the meeting tonight. If you do not, your wife dies. If you give any other reason for your resignation than that in the letter, your wife dies. If you try to call Beauty, your wife dies. I trust you understand these points. Hammad Bek, hear me well, I have ears everywhere and I will add your wife's head to my collection if you fail me.'

The videphone was disconnected and the fax extension printed a page of text.

He read his letter of resignation and burst into tears.

Hammad Ezzedin walked out early from the extraordinary ministerial meeting convened to discuss the Hezbollah-sponsored conference. He left the letter of resignation in the prime minister's hands and said sombrely, 'I'll explain it later tonight. I have to leave now.'

There was a stunned silence in the room as the last Shiite minister in the Cabinet made for the door. He took the lift to the roof of the high-rise building, onto the helipad, where his pilot waited to fly Hammad to Baalbek. He spent the next half-hour cursing the fundamentalists and their mothers.

'I'll never resign,' he threatened his silhouetted reflection in the porthole window. 'I'll never resign, you dick-sucking whores, even if I have to hire an army to protect my Naila.'

In the Nineties, with the end of the war, the government had forced the disbandment of all the militias except the Hezbollah. Hammad had been allowed to keep only a few security guards in Beauty. Government or no government, he now resolved to form a new militia for his fiefdom.

Hammad had carried out his part in the minatory

bargain. He planned to fly Naila to safety, to contact the prime minister for his letter of resignation to be burned, and then to curse the fundamentalists to hell in public.

When Hammad landed in Beauty, on the lawn by the living-room house, his three guards ran up to the helicopter to greet him.

'Where's Naila?' Hammad shouted over the din of the rotor blades.

'Inside, Hammad Bek, the Army's here,' one of the men shouted back.

'The Army?'

'The Second Bureau uncovered secret plans to take you hostage.'

Hammad was striding towards the living-room house, his three men keeping up with him.

'The Army's here now?' Hammad demanded.

'Yes, Hammad Bek. They've secured Beauty and posted guardsmen everywhere.'

'Thank Allah. Thank Allah for that.'

'We wanted to phone you, Hammad Bek, but the Army thought it best to let the extremists think we didn't know their plans.'

Naila, escorted by two Lebanese soldiers, emerged from the house.

'Naila, thank Allah.' The two hugged as the soldiers saluted the minister.

'They killed Ibtihage, Hammad.'

'I know, my heart, I know. You're safe now.'

'Why would they kill an old woman? Why, Hammad?'

He held her tightly and then led her to the house. Inside, an officer was talking into a cellphone; Hammad recognized the rank on the uniform. The officer flicked his phone to stand-by and smartly saluted Hammad.

'Thank you, Captain,' Hammad said warmly. 'You've done an excellent job.'

'Doing our duty, sir.'

'I'll see there's a promotion for you – for your speed and professionalism.'

263

'Thank you, sir.'

'What's your name, son?'

'Saleh Shmali, sir,' the man said, grinning.

The first day of the Conference for the Islamic Brotherhood was running late into the night. The Imam BenKadeemi, sitting restlessly in the seat of honour in the front row, stifled a yawn.

Every leader of every fundamentalist organization was being offered the chance to address the assembly. In the morning BenKadeemi had been privileged to deliver the first oration, followed by the Hezbollah. As the day dragged on the speakers became more obscure, the organizations they led more deeply buried. No fixed time had been allotted to the speeches, so that most orators, after the perfunctory '*Allah akbar*', seemed to ramble aimlessly like a camel with a month's supply of water in its hump. Every speaker was introduced by name and function within his organization; and the leader of the Watan Arabi frowned when the next speaker was introduced simply as the Sayyed Khaled Sulman.

The Imam BenKadeemi turned to an aide. 'Who is this man?'

'I don't know, Holiness.'

'If every man in this conference speaks we'll be here till the end of the world.'

The aide turned to ask a Hezbollah leader sitting beside him; then he turned back to the Imam. 'He's the leader of a secret organization in the Hezbollah, Holiness.'

Khaled Sulman stepped onto the podium and turned to face the crowd. The Imam BenKadeemi became pale.

The man whispered into the microphone; his hushed tones amplified to reverberate around the hall like a breeze among palm leaves.

'Allah,' BenKadeemi whispered, and brought his hand up to tug his long grey beard.

'*Allah akbar?*'

264

'*Allah akbar,*' the crowd returned Khaled's call.

'No. *Allah akbar?*'

The amplified whisper silenced every man in the room.

'Answer me. Is Allah almighty?'

'*Allah akbar! Allah akbar! Allah akbar!*'

The man raised his arms and silence returned momentarily to the hall.

'Brothers, Allah is weak.'

There were cries of rage. Khaled brought his hands together over the microphone; the echo resounded around the hall like a clap of thunder.

'Allah is a fly to be squashed in the palms of your hands.'

The delegates stamped their feet, thumped their chests and roared for the man to be removed. Hezbollah attendants waved at the mob to be still and Khaled, staring patiently at the furious crowd from the podium, waited for the calm to return.

'Brothers, I have sat all day among you, listening to the many speeches. At times my stomach could have exploded with disgust. I heard our Egyptian brothers, our Jordanian and Gulf brothers talk bravely today. Yet we all know that their return to their homes will be either as curs, tails between their legs, or as sacrificed halal.'

There were some shouts.

'I can't hear you, brothers. Shout louder. Cry for justice so that Allah may hear you. Because perhaps Allah is mighty. Perhaps He does not help our brothers only because of His deafness. Or perhaps He has taken sides with the governments. Perhaps Allah is a traitor.'

The crowd erupted again; the Egyptian delegation rose to its feet and tried to force an exit through the mob.

The next two whispered words immediately, magically, silenced the crowd.

'*Allllllllaaaaaaaaaaaaaaaaaaah akbaaaaaaaaaaaaar.*'

The delegates were startled; the Egyptians turned their heads.

'*Laaaa ilaaaaaaaha illllla Allllaaaaaaaaaaaaaaaah.*'
Khaled stared at the crowd.

'Brothers, I now greet you. *Allah akbar.*'

'*Allah akbar! Allah akbar! Allah akbar!*'

'Allah is not a traitor. Nor is He deaf nor blind. Nor is
He weak. You, brothers, have told us of your problems
in Egypt. And you, brothers, yours in Jordan, and the
Gulf. With every word you spoke, you weakened Allah
in our minds. How dare you talk of nations in His name
when He is the Creator of the universe. Western impe-
rialists and corrupt men draw lines in the desert to
separate men. Allah creates a planet to unite men. I am
your Muslim brother. And you are my Muslim brother
living in Cairo, and he is my Muslim brother living in
Washington. That is the will and commandment of
Allah as revealed to the Prophet, by Holy Jibrayel.

'There are two true brothers for whom Allah is
unquestionably almighty. Two men with vision. One
man is here with us today. He is the Imam BenKadeemi.'

BenKadeemi tugged his beard and muttered, 'Allah',
as the *déjà vu* focused into clarity.

'Allah is greater in the minds of the citizens of the
Watan Arabi than he was for Iraqis, Algerians, Libyans
or Sudanis. There the brothers are united in the law of
the shariah in their humility towards Allah. There is the
ordered future for us, my friends. It is written that Islam
purifies every man. It is our duty, brothers, to seek
purification and to purify the world with us. The Watan
Arabi, under the wise and far-sighted leadership of the
Imam BenKadeemi, will become the Watan Islami – for
not all men are born Arab, nor can a man's race be
changed. And the Watan Islami will grow to unite the
world in the worship and justice of Allah.

'*Allah akbar*, brothers.'

Men cheered and clapped and thumped their chests;
the Hezbollah attendants again waved for calm.

'The second man with foresight – the true brother for
whom Allah is the Almighty – will come as a surprise

266

to you. For he is a secret brother, a great man of peace, who has been fighting our cause from within the enemy's camp. He has shared our vision secretly, until today, hoping to avoid violence by explaining our ambitions to the oppressive regime. Until today. Until tonight, when the government would no longer listen to the wise man. Earlier tonight, the champion to our cause was forced to resign from the Cabinet. The true brother, my friends, is Hammad Bek Ezzedin.'

It all took place rapidly yet in slow motion, like the abrupt end to a nightmare.

Hammad had noticed the blue sash around the captain's waist with a scimitar attached to it.

'That's not regimental issue, is it?' Hammad asked, pointing at the sword.

'Yes, sir.' Saleh Shmali drew the blade out, appearing to offer Hammad a better look. Five more Lebanese soldiers entered the living-room house as Saleh added, 'It is for me.'

'For you?'

'I'm a Scorpion.'

The scimitar slashed the air in front of Hammad's face.

He turned and looked uncomprehendingly at Naila's head toppling off her shoulders, bouncing once on the ground.

His three guards were stabbed in the back and Naila's body joined her head on the ground.

'Brothers, it is easy to be brave when you are repeating the words of those around you. Hammad Bek is the bravest man of all men. You cursed him when he was your secret friend. You shouted abuse at him as he tried to bring power to his Shiite people. It is because of men like the Imam and Hammad Bek that we know Allah to be almighty.'

*   *   *

267

The curved blade travelled through the air like a ship on an ocean, with blue turbulence foaming behind.

'Brothers, long live the Imam BenKadeemi. Long live Hammad Bek.'
   '*Allah akbar! La ilaha illa Allah!*'
   Every man in the hall was on his feet.
   '*Allah akbar! Allah akbar!*'

The central coffee-table was removed to make room for three crates.
   Saleh pointed. 'Heads in there. Arms in there. And the bodies in there. Come on.'
   'What about the guards, Janizary?' a soldier asked.
   'Leave them where they are.'

'*Allah akbar! Allah akbar!*'
   The Imam BenKadeemi, on his feet, climbed slowly onto the podium. The crowd was settled into silence by the unscheduled appearance of the leader of the Watan Arabi. The Imam approached Khaled in small steps with a pallid mien. He reached for Khaled's hand with his two, and squeezed the skin as if feeling the ripeness of an Ashtini plum. Then, in a gesture that deadened the delegates, he brought Khaled's hand to his mouth and kissed it reverently.
   The Imam's whisper was amplified and resounded around the hall.
   'I have seen you in my dreams. You are the Blessed One. You are Al-Hameed.'

The conference was cut short on its second day by the news of the brutal murders of Hammad Bek and his wife. The Hezbollah claimed that the late Minister of Culture and Tourism, the blue-blooded Ezzedin, had been one of their own, and his mutilated body, discovered in the army barracks outside Baalbek, sparked the riots of Black January, 2010, by Shiite partisans. The

Imam BenKadeemi flew to Algiers on the day a mob seized a Lebanese army outpost in the southern suburbs and lynched the Lebanese soldiers.

The second Lebanese war, the War of Shiite Succession, was declared the following day, lasted a year and ended in 2011, with the peremptory invasion and annexation of Lebanon by the Watan Arabi. This war, coming a mere two decades after the War of Sunni Succession, was comprehensively covered by the Western media and largely ignored by American and European politicians. Memories of the deathly Gordian knot in the Levant were still vivid: hostages, car bombings of US Marines, the trappings of another Lebanon.

In the first months of the war, before BenKadeemi answered the Hezbollah's call for help, history was repeating itself imperfectly. The Lebanese army split its brigades among the opposing factions, militias on both sides were formed and armed, and fighting broke out on the streets of Beirut. Again a green line skeletonized neighbourhoods. But where previously the trace of no man's land had cleaved Beirut vertically, halving the city East versus West, now the line ran horizontally: East/West versus South, pitting the Shiites against all the other sects.

The Hezbollah attack came at night. By early morning the twelve defenders found their building completely surrounded by the enemy. They were besieged for two days, repelling repeated onslaughts on their positions with sheer determination, hoping their side would counter-attack to regain the lost territory, to force the front back to their building. In the event the relief never came, and at the end of the two days the defenders were exhausted of ammunition and strength.

Pierre, the leader of the motley band of haggard defenders, shouted their surrender through an opening in the fortifications.

A group of thirty Hezbollahis climbed over the

obstacles and entered the building warily.

'Drop your weapons,' ordered a Shiite captain, waving his machine-gun, 'and backs against the wall.'

Eleven defenders lined the wall, the twelfth lying fatally wounded on the floor.

'We're your prisoners,' Pierre said. 'Show mercy.'

The captain ordered his men to gather the fallen arms. He turned to the weary defenders. 'Which of you are Muslims?'

Three men raised their arms.

'Any of you Shiites?'

The three shook their heads.

With cool detachment and no further comment, the captain shot the three in the head. Like puppets at a show's abrupt end they collapsed to the ground, leaving three gory trails on the wall.

A defender closed his eyes and began to recite the Credo in a quavering voice. '*No'min bi illahi wahad.*'

'So the rest of you are Christians,' the captain said calmly. 'Any Greek Catholics? No? All Greeks and Maronites then.'

'We surrendered in good faith,' Pierre spoke out.

'When a man steals, his hands must be chopped off. When he sleeps with another's wife, he must be castrated. When a man kills, he must be killed. Which of you are Greek?'

The defenders remained motionless.

'So you're all Maronites,' the captain stated incredulously.

'I'm Greek.'

A youth with blond hair took a step away from the wall.

'Cowards,' the captain reproved the other defenders. 'There must be three or four Greeks among you and you let this boy come forward alone. And I have orders to let only the Greeks live. How old are you, boy?'

'Fifteen.'

Five men stepped away from the wall.

The captain spat. 'Cowards,' he yelled and shot all five.

'*NO'MIN BI ILLAHI WAHAD.*' The man's Credo turned more desperate, higher-pitched.

Pierre, the only other man left standing against the wall, glared at the Hezbollahi and said in a loud and defiant voice, 'I'm a Maronite. I'm more than a Maronite. I'm a Marda'ai! Do you know what a Marda'ai is?'

'I'm not interested, Maronite,' the captain said, levelling his machine-gun. 'Now, say your prayers like your friend.'

'Then listen to my prayer. I believe that the Marda'ai spirit will return to Earth. The same Marda'ai who, for fifteen centuries, gave their blood so that Mount Lebanon would remain a holy Christian island in a sea of filthy infidels. The same Marda'ai will return as angels from heaven. And on that Judgement Day, Allah will fill the pits of hell with you and your brothers and He will return the crescent to the shaitan's temple. *Bism-al-Ab-wal-Ibn-wal-Roh-al-Qadis. Ameen.*'

The blond youth was left standing alone.

'The Blessed One might want him, sir,' a militiaman whispered to his officer. 'He's young enough.'

The Hezbollah captain nodded slowly and took in the bloody carnage in the room. 'The boy was the bravest anyway. Tie him and take him to the Blessed One.'

'Yes, sir.'

The militiaman trussed the boy with rope and drove him to the citadel, the erstwhile conference halls in the southern outskirts of Beirut, where Khaled, the Blessed One, had set up his headquarters.

The youth was brought before two men. The smaller man, seated behind a desk, motioned for the boy to be unshackled and spoke with a whisper.

'What's your name, boy?'

'Gaby.'

Saleh Shmali slapped the boy hard on the cheek. 'Try again.'

271

'Gaby, sir.'

'Who are your parents, Gaby?'

'I don't have any, sir.'

The smaller man sighed and massaged the bridge of his nose. Then he rose from his seat, walked around the desk towards the boy. He ran his fingers through the springy blond hair. Khaled stroked the boy's grimy cheek and cupped his chin.

'An orphan like us, Saleh.'

'He looks European, Khaled.'

The smaller man scrutinized the boy.

'Yes, he does, doesn't he. Gabriel, come with me.'

Khaled Sulman led the boy by the hand to the door.

'We need to go through some plans,' Saleh said.

At the door, Khaled turned, and Saleh recognized a hint of a smile.

'I probably won't be long.'

Saleh understood. Few boys brought to the citadel survived the test.

Khaled led Gabriel to a large bathroom. By the tub, on the bathroom mat, was a birdcage wrapped in blue linen like a turban.

'Strip and get in the tub.'

The boy might have been frightened were he not numb with fatigue. He had been through five days of fighting and shelling, had not slept for two of those days, and had witnessed the massacre of his fellow militiamen. By rights he too should have been dead, and that thought lodged itself in his mind so that he looked with weary unconcern at the bathroom and the man, and asked, dispassionately, 'What are you going to do to me, sir?'

'You will either die or join me. Do as I say and the rest is up to fate. Now, strip naked.'

The boy nodded and started to peel the clothes off his dirty and aching body.

Khaled moved to the bathroom shelf. On it was a bottle of purified alcohol and a black lacquered box which he opened reverently. Inside, padded by a velvet

272

lining, were a richly adorned sixteenth-century Ottoman dagger, curved like a scimitar, and, incongruously, a cheap plastic figure of an angel, painted blue.

Khaled lifted the Ghazi dagger out of its box and held it against the bathroom light. The sapphire and turquoise gems on the scabbard reflected a dim blue light onto Khaled's face. He gripped the handle and gently unsheathed the blade, his hand arcing to respect the blade's curve. He replaced the scabbard in its box and approached the naked youth with the dagger in one hand and the bottle of alcohol in the other.

Gaby, in the bath-tub, trembled.

'I'm not going to kill you. Show no fear and you might live.'

'I'm cold.'

Khaled wiped the blade clean with alcohol and, kneeling by the tub, he spattered the spirit on the boy's chest.

'I'm very cold.' Gaby shivered uncontrollably.

Khaled brought the Ottoman dagger to the boy's bare chest; Gaby closed his eyes. The Blessed One gently slit the boy from sternum to navel and waited for the blood to trickle through the wound before turning to unroll the turban that covered the birdcage.

Gaby had made no sound. He looked at the blood oozing from the straight gash as if someone else's blood was bleeding from someone else's chest. He felt a warm comforting sensation pervade his body. He relaxed; to the extent that he appeared only mildly worried when the man brought his hand over the rim with three scorpions.

Gaby jolted as Khaled placed his scorpion-laden hand on the youth's navel. With his other hand, Khaled stroked Gaby's hair and the scorpions crawled onto his bloody chest.

'You are Jibrayel. That is your new name.'

The scorpions rubbed their claws together and crawled up and down the boy's chest like excited children wading up and downstream.

'My friends like you. How old are you, Jibrayel?'

'Fifteen, sir.'

'We're almost the same age. You're a year older.' Khaled put his hand on the boy's chest and the three scorpions obediently crawled off the boy's skin. 'I was fourteen last year, on Thursday the nineteenth of March.'

He placed the scorpions in their three separate compartments in the birdcage, which he then tightly wrapped with the blue linen into a turban.

He turned and saw the boy's eyes were closed.

'Yes, relax. You'll live. You've passed the test, Jibrayel.'

Khaled leaned over and pressed the front of his face to the bloody chest. He paused, suspended, and drew back.

'I like your smell. I trust you.'

The Blessed One, his nose and mouth bloodied, looked quizzically at Gaby.

The youth snored softly.

Khaled smiled, delighted.

'You'll make a fine Scorpion, Jibrayel.' He leaned over again and brought his lips to the boy's.

10

ANNO HEGIRAE, 1441
ANNO DOMINI, 2020

The three operations were named after oriental sweets. *Camardin* – *kamar-ad-din*, literally, the Moon of the Faith – was jammed apricot dried into a paste; *loukoum* was Turkish delight which, contrary to the Western appellation, was created and perfected in Cairo; *moughlabieh* was sweet semolina offered to pilgrims setting off for the Hajj in a time-honoured tradition spanning almost one and a half millennia.

Camardin, Loukoum and Moughlabieh were three phases of a two-year plan, whose aim was to provide one man with the absolute power of an empire greater than the early Omayyad, stronger than the Roman, more united than the Mogul. For two years, Khaled Sulman marked time as a patient spider on its web, plotting, calculating, then mobilizing his Scorpions to Nevada, Cairo and the Gulf. The timing was key. Camardin and Loukoum were to proceed simultaneously; Moughlabieh would follow the two courses a month later.

The coach was travelling across Death Valley at an average speed of 60 miles an hour. It was noon and far too hot for any eagle, buzzard or vulture to be flying overhead. Most of the passengers were watching a documentary on a large screen above the driver's seat. Cool air wafted down from the deck to refrigerate the tops of their heads, air which was inhaled through masks, which even the driver wore, as if the coach were experiencing a drop in pressure. One passenger,

275

seated towards the back, was curled up uncomfortably and snored softly. Notwithstanding the motion of the bus, the man's head of blond hair brushed against his seat from side to side as if drawing from it a loving caress.

The man groaned in his sleep. A woman sitting across the aisle turned to glance at him before resuming watching the documentary.

The passengers were sightseers on an organized tour of Biosphere III, the model city of the future. Biosphere III was a complex of four titanic domes initiated at the turn of the millennium in the heart of the Nevada Desert, wholly insulated from the earth's environment both below and above ground. Three of the domes were enormous greenhouses and farms, while the fourth housed a town of 2,000 volunteers, complete with school and hospital. The residents had been sequestered in their beehive microcosm for three years, breathing the air which the plants recycled, drinking the water which the soil in the domes filtered. The experiment was a success, proving that models of ecosystems could be controlled, given enough plants, soil and inhabitants. Biosphere II had been a similar experiment in the early 1990s on a far smaller scale, which had failed partly because its seven isolated residents, all scientists, had jarred on each other's nerves.

This would be the first of mankind's new cities. Plans had already been drawn for Biosphere IV – to be called Selena – a hundred times larger than III and the first extraterrestrial human colony; a city to be built on the relatively flat lunar Sea of Tranquillity.

As for Biosphere I, there was only one Jerusalem, one Rome, one sphere, flattened at its poles, in whose thin film all creatures had been crammed.

In 2020 it had become fashionable for documentaries to begin with an allegory taken from mythology. The documentary on the Biosphere projects opened with a scene on the discovery of music by the Greek gods:

276

Apollo was asleep when his young brother, Hermes, stole his lyre. The youthful shepherd god skipped across his fields with a crook in one hand and the stringed instrument in the other. He stopped by an old oak, his attention drawn to two vipers in a territorial dispute. Hermes laid his staff against the trunk and sat on a gnarled jutting root to observe the fighting snakes. Perched on a bough above him, a chaffinch broke into song. Hermes looked up and answered the call with the lyre; the bird listened. When the shepherd stopped, the chaffinch sang; when he struck the lyre, it listened. Hermes played a long cheerful tune and the bird flew down onto his shoulder. The two vipers, charmed by the music, stopped fighting, crept to the tree trunk and coiled up the crook, hugging the staff in a double helix.

The sleeping passenger stopped snoring and his head refrained from brushing against the seat. Gaby groaned.

Apollo was furious when he found his lyre missing. With thoughts of severe retribution, he sought out his young brother. From a distance, when he could barely see the old oak, he heard the soft strains and was moved by the most beautiful music ever played. Apollo had invented the lyre; his thieving brother had mastered it. He ran up to Hermes, picked him up and embraced him. Mercury's punishment would be to teach heavenly music to the sun god. The melody had also lured their sister, Selene. When the brothers moved away, hand in hand, she emerged with an arrow at her bow. She stepped up to the oak, and saw the vipers still coiled lovingly around the crook; she aimed and fired, nailing both serpents to their staff.

Gaby woke up with a stiff neck and the coach's hum in his ears.

> The two snakes coiled around the herald's wand – the caduceus, symbol of the physicians since Hippocrates of the fifth century BC – fell to the ground as a sudden storm raged around the old oak.
>
> This represents the greatest set-back medicine has faced since the Spanish flu, which had caused more deaths than the Great War it trailed.

Many passengers nodded; some adjusted their masks uncomfortably. Everyone on the coach had heard of Miasma Cerebrovirus, the new killer virus which, like the HIV of a generation back, seemed to appear out of nowhere.

> MCV is rodent-borne like the Plague and, more devastatingly, airborne like its common cousin, influenza. This supervirus has the shortest lifespan, with a week's incubation period. It invades its victim, and avoids detection by constantly changing its chemical make-up. Dormant for six days in its cerebrospinal niche, the sufferer experiences only mild headaches and a slight fever upon contracting MCV. On the seventh day, the virus goes to war. First it attacks and reproduces in the pituitary gland, then it invades the entire cortex. The victim endures a series of palsied convulsions and dies of a stroke.
>
> Miasma Cerebrovirus grew to epidemic proportions in a matter of months. It became

pandemic in under a year. Medicine is fighting a losing battle. As many Christian and Muslim extremists claim, the MCV pandemic is a bane from an angry God, a scourge of biblical proportions.

Gaby had a Bible in his hands, a phone clipped to his belt, and some orange Semtex in his pocket, disguised as a bar of *camardin*. He gazed at the Saharan landscape galloping past as he heard Armstrong taking his first small steps on the moon.

'. . . and one giant leap for mankind.' Apollo 11 returned with the first rock samples from the moon's surface. Tested rich in iron, scientists have inferred that the lunar outcrops alone contain enough raw materials to build an entire city. Selena, the first extraterrestrial city, where mankind will never again be plagued by viruses.

Americans were always doing things for mankind. Their superiority complex made Gaby sick. They had perfected all sorts of bombs, gone to the moon, beaten Communism, all for the good of mankind. Now Americans were building MCV-free cities for themselves alone, like first-class passengers on a liner reserving all the lifeboats.

Biosphere III is proving that man now has the technology to create model planets. For the past three years, residents in Nevada, in Biothree, have lived free from the threat of Miasma Cerebrovirus.

They had the gall to claim they were the cream of mankind. Scratch the bravado and one discovered their true weak and cowardly natures. Soft and runny and not at all funny, Gaby thought. Americans were diarrhoea.

> The site for Biosphere III was chosen by NASA. In the past, it had been the centre for the Search for Extraterrestrial Intelligence, the SETI Institute. (The film showed vintage footage of the sixteen radio telescopes, before focusing on the chief of operations whose name appeared in a caption: Bill Walters, Head of SETI 1980–97.)

Gaby gripped the Bible in his hands. Biosphere III – the NASA project that would launch Selena on the moon – was only a phone call away from sinking. One code word from Saleh the janizary and the show would begin; the sorcerer coming alive to fire his magic.

The driver's voice, muffled by his mask, cut off the documentary. 'Ladies and gentlemen, ETA at Biothree in fifteen minutes. If you look out to your left, you can begin to see the domes.'

Four titanic domes which, from a distance, looked like the four largest Greek Orthodox cathedrals mankind had ever built came into view.

The annual meeting of the Watan Islami's leaders was convened on 21 *Muharram* 1441 – 7 October 2020 – in the Cairo suburb of Zamâlik, a few kilometres away from Giza and its Sphinx and Pyramids. Brother Mahdi received the Imam BenKadeemi and the two Mohafez at his modern high-security palace with its incongruous Andalusian courtyard where wind towers, plants and water fountains cooled the Saharan air.

Khaled Sulman embraced BenKadeemi warmly and whispered, 'Seeing you, Holiness, my heart reaches to my lips.'

In an unusual show of respect, the Blessed One kissed the Imam's nose. He then turned to his fellow governors.

'Brothers, I am a deep well filled with admiration for you.'

The Imam BenKadeemi was the Watan's *Ab-ad-Din* –
Father of the Faith, Commander-in-Chief of the
Faithful. Below him in the nation's hierarchy were three
governors: the Mohafez al-Maghreb who governed the
western extent of the Islamic empire, the Mohafez al-
Mashreq in the east, and the Mohafez al-Motawasset,
suzerain of the median territory.

Sandwiched by the giant North African Mohafaza to
the west and the erstwhile states of Iraq–Kuwait–Iran of
the Mashreq, the Motawasset, Syria–Lebanon–Jordan,
was the smallest dominion, a charred tomato, skewered
and wedged by two swollen *kiftas*.

Brother Abbas, the Tehrani Mohafez of the Mashreq,
secretly maintained that the central Motawasset had
been carved out of the empire in order to promote the
Imam's heart's blood, Brother Khaled. When the
Lebanese war ended in victory for the Hezbollah in
2011, the Blessed One was rewarded with the hastily
formed satrapy of the three newest additions to the
Watan. Brother Abbas had been strongly opposed to
the move, insisting that the Levant be incorporated in
his Mashreq.

'A man has two arms, two eyes, two legs,' he had
complained to the Imam. 'Holiness, if you add a third of
each, the man becomes a beast.'

'We are not adding a third, brother, we are gaining a
One. The Blessed One brings strength to the nation.'

Abbas believed that this was a political ploy to check
his power. Brother Khaled was as blessed as wine-
marinated pork consumed on a sunny day in Ramadan,
and as strong as his voice was loud. The Beiruti's acces-
sion had been a standard divide-and-rule tactic by
the Imam. The nation became a *trium viri sub pater*,
where the three sons competed for the Imam's favours.
The Mohafez of the Maghreb, the Alexandrine Brother
Mahdi, was a diffident cipher, partly due to the fact that
the Imam, based in Algiers, was the true decision-maker
for North Africa. The governor in Cairo was nothing but

a sycophant to BenKadeemi, agreeing with every word, seconding the Imam with only slight variations, like cud pretending to be fresh grass.

Brother Khaled, whom Abbas despised from the day they met, was his true rival. He represented a dangerous threat to the Tehrani's ambitions despite the masked reassurances from the Imam that, of the three viziers, Brother Abbas was the most able leader. Abbas trusted no-one; as the legitimate heir to the throne, he could not afford to be duped by flattery.

'I thank your kind words, Brother Khaled,' Abbas said in the reception hall of Maghreb's palace. 'I will always endeavour to fill your well still further.'

Top of the agenda at the Cairo conference was the unremitting spread of the American virus, the name given to MCV within the Watan Islami. Brother Abbas had proposed the topic; he began the discussion in the salon, the Ottoman-style *iwan*.

'Holiness, the shaitan's disease has grown by thirty per cent in the last year in Mashreq. It is time for us to take radical action to stop this growth.'

'What do you suggest, Brother Abbas?' the Imam asked.

'Holiness, our mosques have become accursed with the evil disease. Most of our sick brothers are being infected by fellow worshippers. Many citizens refuse to attend the Friday prayers despite the Mo'aqibeen.'

The Mo'aqibeen, the Punishers, was the religious arm of the police force, whose officers patrolled the streets with rattan sticks to inflict immediate chastisement on women who exposed any part of their bodies in public, on anyone eating, drinking or smoking in the daylight hours of Ramadan, and on men caught avoiding the compulsory Friday prayers in the mosques.

'The people are frightened,' the Tehrani added. 'They have to be dragged screaming into the mosques, forced to remove their shoes and shaken to perform their ablutions. This cannot continue, Holiness; the fear is turning to anger. We must abolish the obligatory attendance and allow worshippers to enter the holy mosques without having to remove their footwear or wash. It is a time of crisis, Holiness.'

The Imam tugged his long grey beard. 'What do you say, Blessed One?'

Khaled nodded slowly. 'It is a time of crisis, Holiness.'

The Mohafez of the Maghreb suggested, 'Perhaps our citizens should be made to wear the Western masks in the mosques. They say they are very efficient against the disease.'

'It is a time of crisis,' Khaled repeated, 'which is why we need greater not less faith. What Brother Abbas proposes is un-Islamic.'

The Mohafez of the Mashreq glared at Khaled. 'The brother completely misunderstands, it seems. I wish to save lives and to save the Watan.'

'As for Brother Mahdi's suggestion. I consider it perfidious that our brothers should protect themselves from the American bane with American masks.'

'We were discussing options,' the Alexandrine complained.

'No matter how great the temptation, selling one soul to the shaitan is not an option, Brother.'

'What do you recommend, Brother Khaled?' the Imam asked.

'Holiness, we are the guardians of the holy words. Our course is clear. We cannot move against the flow of the divine shariah. It is written that man must pray to Allah in His house, that he must respect the Lord by removing his shoes, that he must perform the ablutions to indicate that he is committed to being blessed with the grace of Allah. We become deceitful as infidels if we change a single interpretation.'

'Holiness,' Abbas countered, 'millions are dying. We will provoke a revolution if we do nothing – or else there will be no faithful left in the Watan.'

'Cursed is the man who hides behind a woman's veil to pray to Allah, and blessed is he who faces the dangers fearlessly. Indeed, Holiness, I am surprised Brother Abbas chose to begin our meeting on this less important issue.'

'I have heard reports,' Abbas said deliberately, 'that

Motawasset is not greatly affected by the American virus. Perhaps this would explain our brother's lack of concern for the killer disease.'

'I consider Saudi Arabia's refusal to allow our pilgrims to the Hajj a higher priority for our discussions. But to reply to my brother's statement, he has read, as I have, a Western intelligence report which claims that the Motawasset has the lowest number of new cases of the American virus in the world. Brother Abbas, do not fall for the insidious Western tricks. They fear our faith, our unity, and will speak any lie to cause friction between us. We, in the Levant, are as exposed to the demon killer as anyone,' Khaled paused, 'with the exception, of course, of the sinful cowards in the American desert.'

'If that is the case, Brother, how can you let our people die?'

'Allah is almighty. If a man is to die before old age, neither fabric nor black space will save him from his fate.'

The Imam BenKadeemi nodded. 'I agree with Brother Khaled. We are mortals, ignorant of the divine plan. All that we are expected to do, and all that we are empowered to do, is to bind our people to Allah's commandments. There will never be any changes to the shariah.'

'Holiness,' the Tehrani said passionately, 'what if such a measure leads to our overthrow? To the destruction of the Watan and everything we hold sacred?'

'Then we will be remembered as holy leaders who strictly abided by Gabriel's dictates.'

The Alexandrine nodded enthusiastically. 'We are the preservers of truth.'

This comment caused the Imam to frown disapprovingly, the Mohafez of the Mashreq to shake his head contemptuously, and the Mohafez of the Motawasset to applaud. 'Spoken like a true mujahidin, Brother Mahdi.'

Maghreb gave him a quick but grateful smile.

'Next, brothers,' the Imam directed.

Second on the agenda at the Cairo conference was Saudi Arabia's refusal to grant visas to Muslims outside the Gulf Co-operation Council. On the basis of the health risk involved in accommodating millions of pilgrims, the kingdom had closed its borders, and for the first time since the rise of Islam, Hajj was cancelled to all but Gulf citizens.

'It is every Muslim's duty to undertake the pilgrimage to Mecca at least once in his lifetime. The holy words teach us that a man who has the means and the health to travel must embark on the Hajj if he is to save his soul from eternal damnation. The refusal by the custodian of the holy shrines to allow our brothers' salvations amounts to an act of aggression against true believers.'

'I disapprove of the king's decision,' the Imam said, 'however, I understand his motives. It is impossible to medically check millions of Hajjis.'

The Alexandrine nodded. 'Saudi Arabia has assured the Watan that the borders will be open to our brothers once the virus passes.'

'Brother Mahdi, if by some shaitanic magic it were discovered that alcohol was a remedy to the American virus, would you encourage Maghrebis to drink wine?'

'No, of course not.'

'And you, Brother Abbas?'

The Mohafez shook his head. 'Alcohol is not a cure.'

'That all our people would be saved from death if every man, woman and child were to drink a glass of wine a day. Would you condone it?'

'Alcohol is a *haram*,' Mahdi stated.

'In other words, even though all men could be delivered from the plague, you would persist in refusing them alcohol.'

Mahdi hesitated. 'Yes.'

'Again, spoken like a Ghazi, Brother. I fully agree with you. We would fall for the shaitan's temptation were we to ignore the teachings of our Prophet, peace-and-blessings-be-upon-him. Life begins not from a mother's womb but from the deathbed. Come war, famine or plague, man may not drink alcohol. Equally, before his birth into the kingdom of Allah, man must be purged of sin at the Holy Kaaba in Mecca, in an act of humility taught to us by the father of compassion – Abraheem. The mortal king's treacherous decree against all our Hajjis is a declaration of contempt for the Koran; and we, Holiness and Brothers, must treat it as a declaration of war against the faithful.'

285

'What is the Brother suggesting?' Abbas exclaimed. 'That we invade the Gulf?'

'Without Mecca in the nation we are without a heart. It embarrasses us to turn our heads five times a day, eighteen hundred times a year, to a city that does not fear Allah with our passion. Brothers, we are a powerful lion whose fangs have been removed; a blessed angel trapped in a cage. *We* are the custodians of Islam, not the sheikhs nor the emirs nor the maleks of corruption. Allah would choose us to guard His holy shrines.'

'Has the Brother considered the West's reaction if we were to invade the Gulf?'

'Brother Abbas, we are not invaders but converters. When the Prophet, peace-and-blessings-be-upon-him, returned to Mecca to convert the townsmen to the true faith, he did not think whether it would please or displease the powerful Byzantine and Persian empires at his borders. He was guided by the mighty hand of Allah. The time has come for us to return to Mecca, to grant our faithful eternal salvation, and to rescue our brothers in the Gulf from the hypocrites who lead them.'

There was a short silence, broken by the Tehrani. 'Brother Khaled's proposal is extreme. Holiness, we are in no position to risk confrontation with Europe and America. I wish to remind our brother that when Kuwait joined the Watan of its own free will, we came very close to a war with the West. In Kuwait we were invited as brothers. In the Gulf we would be considered the enemy. It is certain that Americans and Europeans would come to the aid of the Gulf Co-operation Council. We are not prepared for a war – a war we cannot win nor indeed have to wage.'

The Imam adjusted the turban on his head. 'I agree with you, Brother Abbas. Brother Khaled is right, though, about the dangerous precedence set by Saudi Arabia in refusing our pilgrims. We shall exert more diplomatic pressure on the king to rescind the ruling. We may even initiate trade sanctions and an air embargo; the only avenue to the Gulf would then be from the Indian Ocean. However, war is not on this year's agenda.'

Khaled bowed his head humbly.

'You are the Imam.'

Abbas frowned suspiciously as he noticed a twinkle in the eyes of the Beiruti.

Saleh Shmali waited for his friend and master by the central fountain in the courtyard. The opening verse of the Koran was engraved in the pink marble rim of the basin in calligraphic script. Saleh walked around reading about the Creator of the universe and thinking he could have done a more aesthetic job with the chiselled writing. He reached the end and looked up at the Imam's window. Above the courtyard's rectangular portico were the four walls of the palace's inner façade. Central to each wall was a large window with twin arches, supported by three thin columns built into the wall, a cursive M resting on three Is. Behind the four Ottoman windows were the royal chambers, one for each of the Watan's leaders. Saleh faced the eastern wing which had been allocated to the Imam BenKadeemi out of respect for his higher rank: of the four chambers, the Imam's was marginally closer to Mecca.

For greater security, all the rooms in the palace were under constant closed-circuit surveillance from the guardroom, located in a bunker below the courtyard. Saleh's men were in position. All good plans needed few professionals. Excluding Saleh, the janizary, three Scorpions were to take part in Loukoum. One, who had infiltrated the palace guards two years ago, would wait for the signal in the guardroom, a second for the Imam, and a third for Khaled.

Three video films had been prepared months in advance, where computer-generated stand-ins for the Imam, Khaled and Abbas acted on a blue screen before being pasted to the backgrounds of the three chambers. The bedrooms had been photographed. The video editing completed, Loukoum was deliciously prepared and now waited only for the guests to arrive.

In another continent, one Scorpion expected a similar signal from Khaled to set Camardin in motion.

The jet of water landed in the Moresque basin with a regular beat.

> *Plish-plosh plish-plosh plosh-plosh-plosh.*

It reminded Saleh of a secret rhyme from a distant childhood when, in a skeleton of a building, he had first realized he loved the Crier.

> *Plish-plosh plish-plosh plosh-plosh-plosh.*
> *Hatta bya'tal ma bi 'oul.*

The fountain sang:

> *Saleh saleh a'alatoul,*
> *hatta bya'tal ma bi 'oul.*

He had done everything for his friend, and, for ever, Saleh saleh would follow his master. Khaled emerged into the courtyard. Their gazes met and the two boys grinned at one another.

'How was the meeting?'

'I could ask for no better. I have a friend in the west and an enemy in the east.'

Saleh understood the references to the two other rulers, Maghreb and Mashreq. 'And the Imam BenKadeemi, the Father of the Faith?'

'The father's wishes are important only until tonight.'

Saleh nodded. Now, he needed only the green light for the operation in America. 'And Camardin?'

'Yes, Camardin as well. And when you're through, come and have dinner with me, my Saleh.'

Khaled returned to the Imam and the governors as Saleh left the palace to contact Nevada; and the water in the fountain wailed like a blue siren, Saleh saleh for ever.

*   *   *

288

'Brother, I bring you greetings from our father.' Saleh's voice was carried across two continents.

'How is our father?' asked the Scorpion.

'He would like some *camardin*.'

'Understood,' Gaby said simply.

'Salaam, Brother.'

Gaby switched off the phone and returned it to his belt.

The coach had driven past the security gates with a sign that read 'Checkpoint Joey – no unauthorized personnel beyond this point', and had parked in the shadow of the first colossal dome. The tourists had disembarked and had been led into Biosphere 0.3 by a tour operator.

Biosphere III was out of bounds to all but its inhabitants. Besides the risk of contamination, the new city of the future had been designed for a set number of O_2-inhaling, CO_2-exhaling humans and animals. Hence, in the last three years, the hermetically sealed hatchway that provided the sole access to the microcosm had been opened only once, in a medical emergency, when the doctors in Biothree had been unable to treat a patient.

Biosphere 0.3, or Biopoint-three, was designed to attract tourists to the site. At a scale of one to ten, Biopoint-three was faithful to the mother microcosm in every detail – only miniature humans were missing from the model.

The tour operator was explaining the principle behind the Biosphere projects and led the group to a human dummy wearing what appeared to be a spacesuit.

'It's all a matter of precise control,' the operator stated, his voice stifled by his mask. 'Control the atmosphere, the water and the temperature and you can create a miniature world in a bubble.' He indicated the space-suit. 'This, ladies and gentlemen, is a VEIL – Vector-Immune Livery. The residents of Biothree are the only humans on Earth today who can safely breathe the air without risking infection by MCV. But if they have to leave their clean world, this is the armour they must wear outside, both in order to protect them from biological hazard and to maintain the fine oxygen–carbon dioxide balance of their world.'

The group moved on, the shepherd and his flock. Only Gaby remained behind to study the VEIL closely, taking note of the oxygen cylinder strapped to the dummy's back. Alien cowards, he thought. If you can't breathe miasmic air like real humans, then bring me your clean air.

He waited for the tourists to move on before returning to the coach. He unwrapped the bar of Semtex and was oddly amused that it was of a similar hue of orange and as sticky to the touch as the real *camardin*. Kneeling, he pressed the explosive under the driver's seat, patting it into place to remain like a good dog. He unclipped his phone, removed the electronic card with the receiver chip, and carefully inserted it into the orange putty.

Gaby paused briefly as though to pray, then left to return to Biopoint-three.

'Can I help you, sir?'

Gaby betrayed no surprise as he turned to face the driver. *'Pardon?'* Here, he was a French tourist.

The driver had gone to chat to the guard at the gate and returned to spot the blond Frenchman leaving the coach. He spoke deliberately to the foreigner. 'You lose something, sir? I help you?'

'Thank you. *Merci bien.*' Gaby waved the Bible in his right hand. 'I leave my book on ze bus.'

'You can leave it there, sir.'

'Yes,' Gaby agreed, 'better safe in my hand, yes?' He moved away into Biopoint-three without waiting for the man's reply. He walked briskly to catch up with the group.

The driver shook his head and thought no more of the Frenchman as he climbed onto the coach.

*   *   *

The Imam BenKadeemi stirred in his sleep. In an unrealistic flaming moonlight, two angels flew into his chamber.

'Allah,' the Imam muttered sleepily. 'Holy Gabriel, you have returned.'

The first angel landed by his bed and folded his wings; the second angel hovered above the Imam's bed.

'Why is the moon so bright, Holy One?'

'It calls your name, my son,' said the archangel kneeling by the bed.

'My name?'

'Come, Azrael,' Gabriel ordered, and the Angel of Death landed astride the Imam.

BenKadeemi awoke. 'Brother Khaled?' he gasped, looking at the kneeling man on his right. 'What are you doing here?'

Khaled reached for the Imam's long grey beard and stroked it affectionately.

'Father of the Faith, *Abaddin*, you are the father I never had.'

He leaned forward to kiss BenKadeemi's nose, and as he brought his head back, he gently lifted the Imam's beard, curling it in his hand like a divine hand supporting a crescent moon in the sky. With the neck exposed, the Scorpion atop the Imam set to work, squeezing the throat with both hands in a pincer movement.

BenKadeemi tried to scream.

Khaled stroked his chin, kissed his forehead, and whispered, 'Thank you, Baba.'

The last thing the Imam saw was the red signal light of the security camera on the ceiling. It turned to orange, to green, to blue as the night, before snapping into extinction.

Gaby waited till all the tourists had boarded the coach, then he took four steps back and switched on his phone. The driver, in his seat, eyed him with an expression that changed from impatience to puzzlement.

'Now, you American pimp,' Gaby muttered, 'let's see you leap for mankind.'

Gaby dialled his own number. The transmitter in his hand, the receiver under the driver's seat.

A controlled explosion. A small dragon, only strong enough to kill the driver and the first rows of passengers, yet powerful enough to throw Gaby off his feet, kissed once more by the burning spirit of his father.

Shrill alarms went off everywhere like a thousand phantoms crying in the wilderness. The coach was severed in two, a headless cockroach and its flaming head, which glowed redder and redder still, and bellowed a second and final time as the fuel tank exploded.

Gaby was quick on his feet, running to the wreckage like a hero – or, Bible in hand, like a priest. He climbed aboard the rear end of the coach and hurried up the aisle, oblivious to gore and destruction, focusing only on the wounded with a war veteran's eye. He was mentally making a doctor's triage of priorities: those who were already dead, those whose wounds were not fatal, and those who needed immediate treatment in order to survive. Concentrating on the latter, Gaby found three ex-tourists, blood gushing out of them, their faces twisted with terror and pain.

He opened the Bible.

The pages within had been cut in the form of a tranquilliser gun; the gun had been primed with three shots and then wedged into the good book. Calmly, the Scorpion laid the book by the legs of one of his victims, in a pool of blood, in order to use both his hands to liberate the gun from its biblical hold.

One hand on his mask, he held his breath and shot three darts into three dying passengers. He brushed away the tell-tale darts before lifting one of the three – the woman who had sat opposite him – down the aisle as two guards climbed aboard.

'Fucking shit!' screamed one of them.

The other, tight-lipped, helped Gaby carry the woman off the coach.

Outside, more guards were running to the carnage; an officer yelled orders above the screech of sirens. 'Put the fire out!'

'Got Las Vegas, sir,' a young guard told him. 'Choppers are on their way.'

'Get the wounded out!' The officer turned to the young guard. 'Get me Biothree. I need some doctors now – not in an hour. Now, dammit!'

The young guard tapped some keys on a console.

The one door to Biosphere III opened for only the second time in three years. Four VEILed doctors arrived at the scene as Gaby and the guards carried the last of the wounded off the coach. The doctors from Biothree had brought plasma and their own clean oxygen in cylinders. Gaby noted, almost with a sense of pride, that of the four doctors who set to work on the most seriously injured, two chose his first and third victims, strapping breathing masks to their faces, forcing them to inhale pure air and to exhale air that was less salubrious.

Gaby collapsed, feigning shock. Two contaminated cylinders would return to the Biofortress so as to maintain the precise control. Miasma Cerebrovirus, borne by the air, would be seeped to the plants for recycling. But MCV was no gas molecule to be absorbed, it was an animal. And, as with all the fittest animals, it would survive, finding a new home in the microcosm.

Malignant. Cruel. Violent.

MCV was a born killer, a biological scorpion.

In the Alexandrine's palace, the officer in the guard-room saw two strangers enter the Imam's chamber. He reached for the alarm switch and stared in confusion as his hand disobediently fell to the ground. He looked at his bleeding stump, then at a stranger wearing a blue sash, with a scimitar in his hand. The officer closed his eyes to black out the sudden excruciating pain.

Khaled returned to his chamber where a Scorpion stood to attention by his bed. Khaled climbed into bed and the Scorpion, in one swift movement, unsheathed a curved dagger and stabbed his master in the right shoulder.

Khaled, gritting his teeth, did not flinch.

The Scorpion removed the dagger and held it aloft in both hands, blade pointing down, a shaman in a sacrificial rite.

'*Allah akbar*,' he said simply.

'Go, my brother, Allah waits for you.'

Without any further encouragement, the Scorpion brought the dagger down into his chest, twisted the blade, and fell on the bed, the dagger penetrating deeper.

In the guardroom, Saleh watched the monitor. He waited for Khaled to pull the dead Scorpion on top of him before removing three video films from his pocket. Three guards lay dead on the ground; the fourth, the Scorpion who had admitted Saleh, now guarded the entrance.

The janizary erased the recordings of the three royal chambers between midnight and twelve-thirty, and replaced them in the video bank with his computer-generated versions. He checked the three films, pressing the fast-forward button.

The first video. In the chamber of the Mohafez of the Mashreq, Brother Abbas rises from his bed as a man (later the assassin in Motawasset's room) enters his bedroom. After a secret hand gesture, both exit at 00:11 on the video clock. The room is empty until 00:24 when Brother Abbas enters alone and returns to bed.

The second video. At 00:16 Brother Khaled is snoring softly in bed when the assassin enters his room. He awakes as the intruder pounces on him with a dagger. Brother Khaled breaks free from the assassin but receives a stab wound in the shoulder. There is a long struggle in which Brother Khaled succeeds in forcing the blade into the intruder's chest. At 00:30 precisely the intruder is dead on top of Khaled.

The third video. At 00:14 Brother Abbas enters the Imam's chamber. The intruder kneels astride the Imam and, visibly smiling, Brother Abbas strangles the Imam in his sleep. At 00:21 the murderer leaves the room.

It was exactly 00:30 when Saleh untied his blue sash with the empty scabbard and fastened it around the Scorpion's middle. They embraced and kissed one another.

'*Allah akbar*,' said the Scorpion, rolling back his sleeve.

Saleh pulled a mask down over his face, before removing a syringe from a small box in his pocket. 'Allah is with you.' Saleh's voice was muffled by the mask.

Saleh injected the fluid into his man and briskly walked away.

The Scorpion, with three dead guards at his feet, buttoned his sleeve, sheathed the scimitar, counted to thirty, then picked up the severed hand and pressed the alarm switch with the blue index.

'You are the shaitan himself,' the grand mullah accused Brother Abbas.

The courtroom was packed. Voxiscribes had recorded the sensational trial, and the evidence against the ex-Mohafez was broadcast to every home in the Watan Islami. Besides the damning films of the murder of the Imam BenKadeemi and the attempted murder of Khaled, the Blessed One, Abbas's conspirator in the guardroom had confessed live, to millions of viewers, to the reactionary plot aimed at installing the Tehrani as the new shah of the east.

There was no jury, only a chief justice fully versed in the sacred law: a *Qadi al-Qudat* of the shariah. Given the high rank of the accused, the Mohafez of the Maghreb had been called to assist the trial.

Brother Mahdi, sharing the tribune with the mullah, had remained quiet throughout the trial, occasionally shaking his head in disgust, often glaring at Abbas. He was tired and at a loss. The Imam was dead; Brother Khaled was recovering from his stab wound in hospital; Abbas was a deceiving traitor. There had been so many violent changes in the last few days that Mahdi's world would never recover. He had to show his people that he was firm and resolute, a confident leader. But the truth was that he missed the reassuring presence of the Imam, the paternal shadow overseeing his work. Mahdi wished Khaled were by his side now.

'Before I sentence you in the all-seeing eyes of Allah,' the mullah spoke clearly, 'is there anything you will confess to this court?'

The two prisoners were on their feet.

Abbas raised his handcuffed hands towards the Alexandrine. 'Brother Mahdi,' he pleaded.

Mahdi looked coldly at the man. 'When you killed our father you stopped being my brother.'

'I am innocent.'

'And I am guilty', responded Mahdi, 'of having trusted you.'

'I did not kill the holy Imam, but I know who did.'

'We are not interested in your lies, mother-of-demons,' said the mullah angrily. 'We have all witnessed your cursed hands on the holy throat, the malicious joy on your face as you strangled the saint. If you have nothing to confess, be quiet.'

Abbas shouted, 'Khaled Sulman killed the Imam.'

'You add sacrilege to your list of crimes. The Blessed Brother was almost dead when he was taken to hospital. Nearly killed by the murdering hand of your conspirator.'

'It's a lie.'

'Quiet, serpent.'

'Watch out for yourself, Brother Mahdi, he'll come after you.'

296

'Be still or I'll have you whipped like a petty thief before I pass the sentence.'

'*Allah akbar! Allah akbar!*' shouted the second prisoner. 'Wise one,' he addressed the grand mullah, 'allow me to confess.'

'You have already confessed.'

'There is more, Wise one.'

The grand mullah nodded his approval.

The man pointed at Mahdi with both manacled hands. 'I may only tell the Mohafez al-Maghreb.'

'Tell the court', the mullah commanded, 'or tell no-one.'

'Please, lord Mohafez, it is a great secret,' the man pleaded, 'I know I will soon die. If I confess to you, maybe Allah will have pity on my miserable soul.'

The mullah was about to refuse; Mahdi put a restraining hand on the judge's arm and motioned the prisoner forward.

The man shuffled towards the Mohafez with shackles at his ankles, escorted by two policemen.

'Thank you, lord Mohafez.' The man bowed humbly.

'Well, what is it?'

The prisoner leaned forward to whisper into Mahdi's ear, then, with the speed of a scorpion's tail, he moved his head sharply around and kissed the Alexandrine on the mouth. The prisoner was immediately pulled back, but he succeeded, in front of millions, in spitting in the face of the Mohafez for good measure.

Mahdi wiped his face. The man shouted victoriously, '*Allah akbar!* Long live Shah Abbas! *Allah akbar!*'

The grand mullah spoke solemnly to the two accused. '*Bismillah-ar-Rahman-ar-Raheem,* you are guilty of the murder of his Holiness, the Imam BenKadeemi, and of the attempted murder of the Blessed One, Mohafez al-Motawasset. By the power of the Divine Law, I sentence you to death. You are to be taken away and beheaded before the end of the next prayer at dawn.'

Abbas brought his hands to his face.

The ex-guard looked stonily into the void.

Despite the Watan Islami and the Islamization of the region, St George had remained the patron saint of Beirut. In the past, when gold coins could be found in every exchange office, only British sovereigns were ever displayed, reverse side, to the potential customer. Gold being equal, nothing could beat the mercantile nature laced with a certain pride, and generations of Beirutis had bought the coins, ignored the succession of British monarchs on the obverse, and fingered the embossed features of their George slaying the dragon.

Gaby landed in Beirut on the day the dragon rose from the dead to prowl the streets of the city. He alone saw it. But it was real, scaly in the flesh, green with blotches of brown.

Gaby was driving on the Beirut–Damascus highway on the way to the caliph's palace to report to the janizary. It was a hot, Indian summer's day, and Gaby's left arm was hanging limply out of the window to cool off in the apparent wind. He was speeding, overtaking a taxi on the inside lane when a bright light – a shooting star – plunged from the sky and stopped some hundred metres in front, hovering above the road.

Others had seen the star. Ahead, a car was veering sharply, preparing to crash into a truck. Behind him, two cars were set to collide with the kerb and then with each other.

Gaby frowned. His car had stopped. He looked at the speedometer: the needle was glued to 110 kilometres per hour. He shouted to the taxi-driver on the outside lane; the man did not flinch but remained transfixed, his eyes hauntingly open, staring ahead. Gaby looked at both sides of the highway, at the city streets.

Life had come to an abrupt end. Men, women and children became petrified statues. Covered by an invisible lava, their last gestures were frozen in time.

The only thing that moved, other than himself, was the ball of light which grew like an inflating balloon.

'I'm going mad,' Gaby said, frightened. 'The jinn are stealing my mind.'

On the road to Damascus, the ball of light grew and steadily took the form of a dragon which only his damned eyes could blink and see.

Normal daylight returned as the bright light extinguished itself, but the monstrous beast remained. Standing on its four legs, like four columns, it turned its gargantuan head left, its tail right, as if to scan the city, to observe the changes since the last time, before George's arrival on his white horse.

The dragon then turned and stared straight at Gaby. Not cold reptilian eyes, nor the ghoulish look of an accuser; the dragon stared at him with blue eyes full of mirthful cheer and vitality, as if preparing for a joyous banquet.

Gaby was mesmerized by the eyes. The two eyes became six; the dragon had grown two heads. Behind it was a black hole, like the entrance to a cave. The cave itself was the bottomless pit – Hades – and the beast guarding the entrance was now a three-headed hound. In the transformation, only the creature's eyes had remained unchanged; deep as the Zurruk, blue as Azazel himself.

Cerberus, the guard dog at the gates of hell, moved among a hundred billion corpses lying scattered and heaped like layers upon layers of grains of sand. The hound reached down and closed its three jaws around three corpses and carried them to the cave. It returned for three more, and three more. Time had stopped; the beast had all infinity to clear the ground of bodies.

'Stop,' shouted Gaby.

He felt a sudden pain in his chest and his back and found himself being lifted into the air. He was wedged, gun in a Bible, between the canines of the beast's middle jaw. Paralysed, he was unable to offer the least resistance as Miasma Cerberus carried him to the black cave.

'No!' screamed Gaby as his car crashed with the taxi in the outside lane. The car in front collided with the truck, and the two behind bounced off the kerb to spin out of control.

The ball of light had hovered over the Damascus road for less than a tick before ascending to the blue sky.

Gaby's left arm had remained limp outside the window. Streams of blood now flowed from several lacerations. Gaby did not bother to look at it.

'Our Father,' he breathed softly and tried to remember the Christian prayer before losing consciousness.

The Izhan al-Mashreq, the prayer to greet every dawn, woke Khaled. He sat up in the hospital bed as the first rays of daylight swept across Cairo and listened to a crier in a nearby mosque.

'*Allah akbar! Allah akbar!*'

'*Ash-hado ana la ilaha illa Allah!   Ash-hado ana la ilaha illa Allah!*'

'*Ash-hado ana Muhammadan rassoul Allah!*'

'*Ash-hado ana Muhammadan rassoul Allah!*'

Whoooooooosh!

'*Hayya a'ala s-salla!   Hayya a'ala s-salla!*'

'*Hayya a'ala al-falah!   Hayya a'ala al-falah!*'

Whoooooooosh!

'*Allah akbar!   Allah akbar!*'

'*La ilaha illa Allah!*'

Khaled relaxed and closed his eyes.

Loukoum was over. In exactly a week's time, as the sun entered Scorpio, Brother Mahdi would die suddenly, another hapless victim of the shaitan virus. The new Father of the Faith would be the sole ruler of the Islamic empire. His first edict would be to abrogate the compulsory attendance of the Friday prayers and the removal of shoes and ablutions at the entrances to the mosques. The people would understand that the new leader had a vision to save his brothers and sisters, unlike his blinkered senile predecessor and the late evil vizier of the east.

Camardin, the operation in America, had also been a

success, except for the odd behaviour of his favourite Scorpion. Gaby had returned to Beirut, but he had still not reported in to Saleh the janizary. But the mission itself had been accomplished. Biosphere III now shared Earth's misery. Three weeks later, as the West's attention was still focused on the tragedy in Nevada, Saudi Arabia would be converted: Moughlabieh, the operation to recover Mecca, set in motion.

Khaled fell asleep with a smile on his face.

ZACHIEL

The gabriel indicates the white doorway that leads to *The Star*, to a time when even I was still alive.

He beats his wings and flies into the black night before gliding down to carry me to the third and last point of the equilateral triangle, to complete the past on the Celtic cross.

Azazel's victory is thorough. St John has lost to Nostradamus. The Messiah of the Revelations is Malus of the quatrains.

Damn Patéras Michel's prophecies, I think as I remember: *Un qui des dieux d'Annibal infernaux, fera renaistre, effrayer des humains: oncq' plus d'horreur ne plus dire journaulx, qu'avint viendra Babel aux Romains.*

Damn the quatrains to hell.

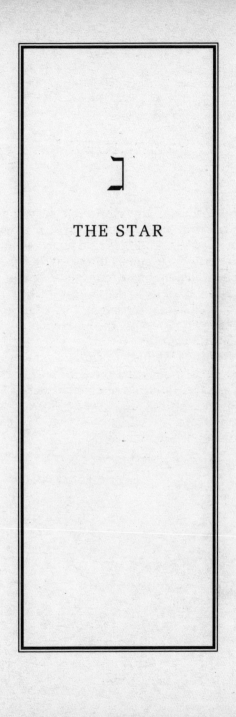

THE STAR

11

A THIMBLEFUL OF GABRIELS

1982 AD

The second thing Maira noticed was the atrocious driving.

She had landed at Beirut on the previous morning, on a sunny day in May 1982, and had come to the unwavering conclusion that the Lebanese were probably the worst drivers in the world. This she decided when her yellow airport cab had, with three miracles, avoided three major accidents on the short trip to the Bristol Hotel in West Beirut. Initially it had crossed her mind that her taxi-driver was mad, and she accursed to have chosen him. But she soon realized that everyone drove in the same satanic way, veering abruptly right and left, bullying other cars off roundabouts, and managing breakneck acceleration from first to third in crawling traffic. And then there were the stupid left arms.

Now, in her second taxi in Beirut, Maira saw that most drivers had their left arms hanging out of the windows like jousting knights. Maira would have been amused had she first observed this outside a car. However, she was now in a cab with an even worse driver than the airport cabbie. This man not only had his left arm outside and spoke in a very broken English, but had hand gestures to boot. In true Mediterranean style, the driver felt impelled to emphasize his speech with at least one hand. What Maira could not understand was why the left hand – which was outside and doing nothing but drying in the apparent wind – remained outside, while it was up to the right hand – the hand which simultaneously controlled both the car and her life – to lend emphasis to the spoken words.

'This I do only, see?'

The driver waved expansively at a Beirut street and then moved his hand back rapidly to honk loudly at a car which had appeared, without warning, from a side-road. He braked, shook his head, and with his hand reproachfully indicating the car ahead, added, 'See?'

All Maira saw was that Lebanese men were essentially overgrown boys, so that driving with one arm out amounted to riding a bicycle with no hands. At any rate, it partly explained the deplorable driving.

The first thing Maira noticed when she landed in Beirut was everyone's nervous disposition. Perhaps that too partly explained the driving. The coach with the airline insignia painted on the side drove the passengers the short distance from the airplane to the arrivals terminal. As soon as it stopped, Maira panicked. She panicked because everyone else seemed to, and all the passengers became agitated and crowded the exit as if a bomb had just been discovered on board the bus.

Inside the ill-lit building, the passengers' angst only increased in the presence of the many heavily armed guards, who lounged and chatted in distinctly unmilitary fashion. It struck Maira as absurd to see the passengers so much more alert than the soldiers. Maira did like the Romans: she looked only glancingly at the guards before joining a queue and fidgeting with her passport. She shuffled her feet and kicked her hand luggage ahead of her on the floor till it was her turn to bend uncomfortably and hand her passport over the counter to the officer. Then she was off again, rushing to join another long and disorderly queue for the *bribes* – as she later dubbed customs control.

She was indicated towards two men standing behind a short table. One was uniformed, middle aged and decidedly mournful; and the other young, revolver strapped to his jeans and furtive-looking. As Maira approached the table, the older man smiled sadly. 'Do you have anything to declare?'

Maira smiled back and said no.

The young man grinned unkindly and said, 'Do you bring anything for me?'

'I'm sorry?'

'Airport tax.'

'Tax?' She waved at the table and at the sign 'Customs' and added incredulously, 'Here?'

'You American?'

'No, British.'

He looked puzzled. 'English?'

'Yes, English.'

'OK. English like tax and for English, ten-dollar airport tax.'

Maira crossed her arms. 'May I have a receipt?'

The man frowned as the older official translated her request.

'OK,' he said at length, 'five dollar. If no dollar, your bag for me.'

'And I still want a receipt.'

'Your bag for me,' the man said with such vehemence that Maira took a step back.

The young officer picked her hand luggage off the short table and she said, exasperated, 'I don't believe this.' Then she smiled, and in her sweetest voice said, 'Five dollars? Fine, I give you five dollars which one day you will choke on. Inshallah. OK?' Her first Arabic word, she thought proudly.

The man grinned, surprised by the Arabic, and nodded. 'OK. Inshallah.'

The older official looked less sad and said in English, 'God willing.' He winked at Maira and added warmly, with engaging sincerity, 'Welcome to Beirut.'

'He, Lebanese government,' the airport cabbie explained later. 'The other, he militia. How much you pay militia? Five dollar? Good, he like you too much.' He was evidently pleased by his joke and began to laugh loudly, and only just missed slamming sideways into a car. The other driver sounded his horn warningly, and the taxi-man honked even louder with obvious irritation.

He turned to Maira and said in a complaining tone, 'See? You see how he drive? He *khara*.' And he laughed some more.

This second taxi-driver seemed just as excitable and worse behind the wheel. 'Eat and sleep and work.' He showed Maira his right thumb, then the index, then the middle finger. 'This I do only. See?'

'Yes. Yes, I see. Could you keep your hand on the wheel?'

'Much war, no money.' He wagged his right index at her. 'No money, no hope. No hope, no peace. No peace, no money.'

Maira could not recall a longer and more hair-raising journey in her life. She was heading for Baalbek from where Adyt had broadcast the last message. An official at the British Embassy in Beirut had tried to dissuade her from travelling to the Bekaa, astonished that she was in Lebanon at all.

'Lebanon isn't a cup of tea.' The official was Lebanese; almost all the embassy's British staff had been transferred from Beirut. 'You must hit and run from here.'

'I see.' Maira did not see at all. 'However, I need to go to Baalbek.' She was resolute.

'OK.' The man shrugged. 'But you need a pass. No,' he added when she naïvely pointed at the Lebanese visa in her passport, 'you want a visa for Baalbek. OK? It's a matter of life and death, sure? So you got bread? So I'll get you the pass from the Baalbek militia.'

The following morning, the official had appeared at the Bristol Hotel with her pass. 'I spoke to the militia boss in Baalbek. He invites you to stay with his family.'

'Actually, isn't there a hotel I can go to in Baalbek?'

'It's safer with him. Don't worry, Lebanese are hospitable as apple pie.' He grinned childishly and added, 'I hope you'll dig Baalbek.'

Maira had posed as an archaeologist whose thesis depended on visiting the Roman temples.

'Lebanon, no hope,' the cabbie insisted now.

The sea was behind them, and they were finally clear of Beirut and the bedevilling traffic jams. However, because there were fewer cars on the roads, enabling higher speeds, there were still enough cars for devastating pile-ups, and driving became far more dangerous. This applied particularly to drivers – like Maira's taximan – who were unconcerned by the extra hazards and who continued to emphasize their speech with their right hands.

'Children?' Maira prompted, impatiently.

'Yes. Childrens.' The man had signed three small people with his steering hand.

'My childrens,' he continued. 'How they eat? I am good. I no steal and I no politics. So how they eat? No money, see? How they go to *madrasah*?'

'Keep your hand on the wheel, please. Your hand.'

'How they go for teach? No money. No hope in Lebanon. No.' The man ended emphatically.

There was a long pause and Maira realized he was waiting for her reaction; she nodded sympathetically. It occurred to her then that he might be mistaking her for a journalist who would report to the Western media on this man's trials and tribulations. This thought was interrupted by the car in front, which braked suddenly.

'Today, money,' the driver was saying, and pointed ahead without bothering to look. 'Today I go to Baalbek. But tomorrow?'

Maira saw the car in front approaching in slow motion, like in a sports replay.

'Or tomorrow's tomorrow? No hope.'

'Watch out!' Maira cried out.

The driver braked in time with little more than an inch to spare. 'Fuck the sister of the one who gave you a driving licence,' he yelled out of the window in Arabic and resumed calmly in English, 'Lebanon no hope. Tomorrow I drive you back to Bristol Hotel, yes?'

'Does that pimp say where he buried the treasure?'

'No,' lied Samir.

Before returning to Baalbek, Samir had already decided not to tell Hammad about Tanit's Jewel. He wanted to find Carthage's greatest treasure more than ever, but not to sell it in some auction house in Erab. Rather to cherish and admire it himself, to pretend he was a new *rab-shomam,* safeguarding the gem from Carthage's enemies. This was hardly likely to happen. Hezbollah, the new Party of God, had, it seemed, already discovered the sphere that was small as a maiden's eye yet equal to her weight. The black ping-pong ball had been sent *esh* to Iran, to the militia's paymasters.

Hammad shrugged. 'We have the tablets though. We'll sell them, eh?'

'Right.'

Hammad spotted a taxi coming up his drive. 'You got decent clothes with you?' he said, rising to his feet.

'What's wrong with what I'm wearing?'

Hammad brushed some imaginary dust off Samir's legs. 'You can't impress a girl with dirty jeans.' He held Samir's jaw. 'And look at your face. You look like a dustman – either shave or grow a proper beard.'

'What girl?'

'I invited someone here for you tonight.' He smacked his fingertips like an Italian. 'A beauty with a brain. An English archaeologist, so you can talk ancient Greek to her.'

Samir shook his head, but was smiling.

'What? You got a girl?'

'No,' Samir admitted.

'Hah.' Hammad rested his case by waving expansively.

'So what's her name?'

310

He hesitated; he had approved the pass over the phone. 'Miriam.'

'You don't even know her.'

'So?'

'So how do you know she's Miss World?'

Hammad headed for the French windows. 'You've a lot to learn, my young friend.' He slid the window open and waited for Samir to pass through onto the lawn. 'All English women are beautiful. It's one of the laws of nature.'

Maira reached Beauty in the late afternoon as the light outside dimmed rapidly from twilight to dusk. Her host, the leader of the small Baalbek militia, emerged from one of the many houses to greet her enthusiastically.

'Welcome to Beauty,' he said in English, grinning broadly.

'Thank you,' Maira said as she was hugged and kissed.

Hammad was his friend, but Samir was slightly irritated by the obvious hypocrisy. Hugging and kissing the foreigner three times would have been considered not only a *faux pas* but definitely a *faut pas* had she been a Muslim.

'Hello,' Samir said, offering his hand.

'Samir Khoury, Miriam,' Hammad introduced.

Her hand was as sweaty as his.

'Maira,' she corrected.

'I prefer Miriam,' said Hammad with a wide grin. 'It's more Lebanese, yes?'

'Yes, of course, Harry.'

'Hammad not Harry. Mmm,' he stressed. 'Hammad. Not Hamad, not Ahmad, not Muhammad. Hammad, Miriam, Hammad.'

'But Harry is so much nicer.' She gave him her sweetest smile.

He wagged his forefinger at her in mock reproof and, turning to Samir, he said in Arabic, 'Thank me, you lucky dog.' He shouted, 'Ali, Ali.'

Ali appeared. 'Yes, Hammad Bek.'

'Take the lady's bag to the pink guest-house.' He asked Maira in English, 'How's London?'

'Er, fine.'

'I have a friend in London. Andrew Cook – do you know him?'

Maira shook her head.

'But London's so much smaller than Beirut,' Samir said sarcastically.

Maira looked at him quizzically.

'Come see Naila my wife.' Hammad led her by the arm. 'Are you coming?' he asked Samir over his shoulder.

'Yes, sure.'

'Jamil will be over later,' Hammad told Maira. 'Jamil is my cousin.'

'For another light snack?' Samir teased.

'Oh no.' Hammad patted Maira's arm. 'We have a special friend tonight. And tonight it is food for kings and queens.'

In Lebanese etiquette, an esteemed guest is presented with the highest honour by choosing the lamb to be slaughtered. It is a solemn occasion with echoes of ancient sacrificial rites when priests sanctified the land with the blood of a gutted animal. In modern-day Lebanon, wealthy landowners, beks, and even poorer farmers celebrate this old tradition when they show their respect to important visitors by delegating to them the role of priests in choosing the animal which will die to grace the banquet table.

All four were in a barn with about two dozen frightened lambs. Hammad and Naila smiled indulgently like proud parents, Samir was trying hard not to laugh, and Maira thought she was going to be sick.

'A difficult choice,' Samir said.

'Can I help you, Miriam?' Hammad offered.

'Oh, please. If you could,' she said quickly.

'They're all good. But you need one with most, ah—'

'Baby fat?' Samir suggested.

'Yes, baby fat. Baby fat on young sheep is, aaah, soft like warm butter, and juicy like the milk she drinks. Now, if you want, touch all of them. Here, look. Feel here.'

Hammad held on to a lamb which bleated, stricken, and squeezed and rubbed the sides and belly of the poor animal like a potter teasing clay.

'Come, Miriam. Feel here and here. This is good meat.'

The lamb looked up at Maira with big mournful eyes and bleated again.

Maira, disgusted, swore she would become a vegetarian. She pointed at a lamb at the far end of the barn which was lying on its belly and appeared dead anyway. She said simply, 'That one.'

'He small, no?' Naila said, disappointed.

'No,' Hammad replied, letting the other lamb leave his grip. 'Miriam wants that sheep. Miriam has that sheep. Good, OK. Ali, Ali.'

'Yes, Hammad Bek.'

Hammad continued in Arabic, 'Ali, take that lamb over there. Let Ibtihage prepare it all. Just sharpen the knives for her and hold it down.'

Ali nodded. 'Yes, Hammad Bek.'

Samir looked at the foreigner and wondered if she knew anything about how halal meat was prepared. For her sake, he hoped not.

'Now we wash,' Hammad said, 'and then we go to the bar house for a drink. You drink, yes?'

'I could murder a gin and tonic,' Maira said.

'Ach. The English and their gin and tonics.'

As they left the barn, Maira asked if she could make a long-distance call to the States.

'To Kissinger?' asked Hammad.

Maira was bemused. 'No, of course not.'

'Then, OK.'

'I'll pay for it, naturally.'

'Miriam, please, here you are a princess in her castle.'

'But—' she began.

313

Samir whispered in her ear. 'You're breaking the rules of conduct. Just accept gratefully.' Her red hair smelt of nothing; neither shampoo nor spray, just of hair. He liked that.

'That's right,' Maira shouted into the phone, 'Baalbek. What? I can hardly hear you, Bill. Can you talk louder. Where's Baalbek? You know, that's where Adyt transmitted the last message. Oh, where am I staying in Baalbek. Just outside the town – someone's place with many houses. Listen, Bill, has Adyt been broadcasting? No? OK, good. Because Ric's tracker isn't showing anything – I'm not sure that it works yet. So Adyt's been quiet. OK, better sign off, this line is – I said, we'll say goodbye now. My love to you and Ric. Ric. I said Ric. I said – Goodbye, Bill.'

The barman brought a gin and tonic, a Lebanese rosé for Naila, and two Scotches for the men. Jamil and his wife entered the private tavern as the barman went to the bar for bowls of pistachio nuts, fresh almonds in a side dish of ice, sliced cucumbers and carrots, and a bowl of unripe Ashtini plums.

Jamil's wife was characteristically quiet and sipped her lemonade while Naila asked Maira in a broken English if she was married, and if she was planning to get married, and why not.

The men held their own conversation about Carthalo and Erab and Esh.

'Samir and I believed that the damned treasure existed,' Hammad told his cousin bitterly. 'All we found were marble tablets. Words.'

'That must be worth something,' Jamil said reasonably.

'Sure, but it's not a treasure. That treacherous pimp.'

'Hammad,' Naila exclaimed reprovingly.

'What? What?' he said impatiently to his wife. 'She doesn't understand Arabic.'

'Oh, by the way,' Samir said, turning to Jamil, 'you

314

remember that story about Johann? Johann Strauss. You never told me how he—'

'Miriam,' Hammad interrupted Samir. 'You will like this story. It's true, like an American bestseller on TV.' Hammad turned to Jamil and added, 'Can you tell it in English?'

'Yes.'

'OK,' Hammad continued. 'Miriam, do you believe in—' He hesitated and asked in Arabic, 'How do you say Martians?'

'Extraterrestrials,' Samir said.

'Aliens,' Jamil added.

Maira frowned. 'I beg your pardon?'

Samir shook his head. 'You don't want to hear the story.'

'On the contrary.' Maira turned to Hammad and added sweetly, 'Do tell me this story – it's true, is it?'

'Oh, yes. Very true,' Jamil began.

As he finished the tale of Johann Strauss, Maira turned to Samir. She noticed he had a strange withdrawn expression, a forlorn look, and she had a sudden and irrational desire to run her fingers through his hair and to comfort him. Perhaps it was the effect of the alcohol, but as he smiled sadly at her, she pictured herself touching that smile. Maira blinked and reached for some sliced carrots.

'It's ready, Hammad Bek,' Ali said.

'Good, good. Let's go to the dining-house.'

'Do you believe in this sphere?' she asked Samir.

'The thirty-six kilogramme black ping-pong ball and ball of light?' he said with as much scepticism as his voice would carry.

'Yes.'

He shook his head. Something in the eyes, Maira thought, but he's not telling the truth.

'When will you believe, Samir?' Hammad said jocularly.

'So tell me, Jamil, how did Johann die?'

There was the sound of breaking glass, and in the tense silence that followed everyone turned to look at Jamil's wife. She had dropped her lemonade and now covered her mouth with both hands.

'Are you all right, dear?' Naila said, concerned.

Jamil's wife nodded but looked upset.

'Don't worry, it's only a glass. You're sure you didn't hurt yourself?'

Jamil said unsympathetically, 'Be careful next time.' His wife smiled apologetically at Naila and followed her husband out of the bar-house.

The large teak table was regally set with about forty dishes, placed in a line on the table like a spine running down a wooden monster's back. The largest dishes were the most centrally located, sealing the comparison with a flattened stegosaurus and its vertebrae of ascending and descending steps.

Hammad led Maira into the dining house while Naila held on to Samir's arm like a royal couple changing partners in an official ceremony.

'You tell me if there is something you don't know, yes?'

'What is that?' Maira said, pointing at the largest and most central dish.

'*Kebbé nayé*. Meat with burghul, seasoned, with olive oil and surrounded by mint leaves. Very good. You will try?'

'It looks raw.'

Hammad laughed. 'Of course it is raw. *Nayé* means raw. There, the little balls in the other plate, that's cooked *kebbé*.'

It was as Hammad pointed out the plate of *kebbé* that Samir recognized first the dish and then all the dinner service with the distinctive Cyrillic cursive Н for Nicholas. Hammad certainly knew how to regale both with charm and style.

'Is that the lamb?' Maira asked, nodding towards the central *kebbé nayé*, which resembled a light-coloured grainy pâté.

Hammad laughed good-humouredly. 'Miriam, you will recognize the lamb when you see it.'

The first part of the meal lasted two hours, which was fortunate as Maira considered that it was just enough time to sample a mouthful from every dish in the lavish display. She tried everything that was cooked and drank arak with the men.

'You drink like a man,' Hammad said, beaming.

'Yes,' agreed Naila, with a hint of disapproval.

'Cheers.' Samir clinked glasses with her.

'It's good,' she said, feeling light-headed. 'It's tastier than Pernod.'

'Pernod? Hah,' Jamil said dismissively.

'This is real arak.' Hammad added, 'The Greeks and the French, they make what is now passing through our bodies.'

'Hammad.' His wife gave him a stern look.

He raised both hands, questioningly. 'What? You want me to lie?'

'How did Johann Strauss die?' Samir asked abruptly.

'What's wrong with you?' Hammad said in Arabic. 'We're talking arak, keep up with conversation, will you.'

Samir turned to Jamil and repeated, 'How did he die?'

'Shot himself,' Jamil answered simply and dispassionately.

'Why?'

'Because it's made from my grapes,' Hammad said, turning to Maira. 'That's why the arak is good, yes?'

'It is very good,' she agreed.

'So he just shot himself?' Samir insisted in Arabic.

'In the head,' Jamil said.

'No headache,' Hammad continued, 'no throwing up. This is good arak, and good for health.'

'So long as it doesn't put hairs on your chest.' Maira smiled.

'With his old Luger.'

'Ach, German machines,' Hammad interjected in

317

Arabic. 'I wouldn't buy anything but a German car if you gave me all the money in the world.'

'You have all the money in the world,' Jamil said.

'He just killed himself? Was there no reason?'

Both Hammad and Jamil looked irritated.

'Right, no reason,' Jamil replied.

'You know, talking of German machines,' Hammad persisted, 'take that old Luger, for example. That gun spent fifty years in a closet; it must have weighed as much in dust when the man used it, and it still worked perfectly. I tell you, Germans may have lost all the wars in history, but they're a great people. If I had to choose between—'

Hammad was interrupted by Jamil's wife, who thumped the teak table violently.

'Behave yourself, woman,' Jamil shouted.

There was a short uneasy silence, and Hammad resumed, 'They'll always be way ahead of the Americans and English—' He turned to Maira. 'Excuse me.'

'What for?'

'And do you know why?' Jamil said, almost angrily.

Hammad's laugh was strained. 'Of course. Because Americans and English will never know how to manufacture Mercedes cars. German cars are the best, right, Miriam?'

'If you insist.'

Jamil was staring straight at Samir when he said, 'Because they got rid of all the parasites in their society. It was worth it. The Germans suffered for a few years, but they managed to guarantee a millennium of prosperity. Before the war, German society was like a man suffering from an abscess in a tooth. It needed a dentist to extract the tooth in order to save the gum and the other teeth.'

'Are you talking about the Jews?' Samir said.

'The Jews, the niggers, the homosexuals. All the parasites who suck the very morality from society.'

'Sounds like a heated discussion,' Maira told Naila.

318

'Men,' she replied.

Jamil's wife thumped the table and cried loudly.

'See, Samir?' Hammad said accusingly. 'See what you've done?'

'I was asking about Johann's death, I wasn't expecting a lecture on the merits of Fascism. All I want to know is how and why Johann Strauss died, that's all.'

'He shot himself up the left nostril for no reason with his Second World War Luger, OK?'

'Fine. That's all you had to say.'

'Murdered,' Jamil's wife shouted so loudly and unexpectedly that everyone jumped.

'Woman,' Jamil said in a warning tone.

'Murdered, murdered, murdered,' she shouted. 'Murdered, murdered.'

Maira frowned at everyone and asked, 'What did she say?'

'He was murdered.'

'He was murdered,' explained Samir in English.

'Who was? The German pilot?'

'We don't know that,' Hammad said calmly.

'He was so happy, so alive. So, so, so very happy and alive. He was murdered. You know; we all know he was killed—'

It seemed inappropriate timing that at that very instant Ali and Ibtihage entered carrying an entire cooked lamb on a large platter.

Maira looked at the animal and felt first guilty, then sick. It looked as it had in the barn, on its belly with its eyes closed, except that now it lay naked and quite dead.

'Like that,' Jamil's wife shouted. 'Sacrificed like a lamb.'

'I'm warning you, woman, shut up.'

'Who killed him?' Samir asked.

'He killed himself,' Jamil said.

'He was murdered,' she shouted and then fell silent again.

'Don't talk back, do you hear?' Jamil shouted furiously. Then turning to Samir, he added hotly, 'Fine,

319

you want to know about Johann's death? OK.'

He downed his arak, signalled Hammad for another and spoke in Arabic: 'After Johann's experience with the sphere, he became strange. I've already told you that he stopped flying my hashmay to Rhodes. But that was understandable; he was getting old, and the thing had scared the piss out of him. But what happened to him next was really strange. He still worked for me – helped out around the house, that sort of thing, nothing strenuous. A bit of gardening; he was good with electrical appliances. Anyway, I first realized that something was seriously wrong with Johann when I noticed that he had stitched small Stars of David on all his shirts over the left breast pocket.'

Samir frowned. 'The star he'd seen as he was flying to Rhodes?'

'No,' Jamil replied, 'that star, the ball of light, turned him insane. But the stars he stitched on his clothes were without doubt Jewish Stars of David.'

'Why?' Samir was trying to make the link.

'He was obviously going a bit mad. Johann, the young and brilliant officer in the *Luftwaffe*, stitching Stars of David.'

'The nightmare he had in the plane. The visions.' Jamil shrugged as Samir added, 'The sphere made him feel guilty, don't you see? First he dreams of the addicts using hashmay, then that he is a young Jew being persecuted by the Nazis, and his last and worst nightmare is of young Germans playing football with his head.'

'So?'

'So,' Samir paused, 'he saw the light and felt naked in his sin. Everyone has his own act of contrition, maybe for Johann it was stitching Stars of David.'

Jamil shook his head. 'Anyway, those were small, later he painted a large Star of David on his door with yellow glossy paint, as if he was opening a fucking synagogue. You must know I liked the man, so at first I joked with him, asked him if he'd become a Jew. I even said it in German, with the few words I know, "*Bist-du ein Jude?*" He said he wasn't, but that he wanted to keep all the stars. Hammad, you remember how much he loathed everything Jewish, don't you? In fact, he was always a bit strange because, while hating the Jews, he had a deep – and secret – admiration for everything Israeli. He was attracted by the short twentieth-century history of a nation which had survived a surrounding sea of enemies, which had succeeded because of Israeli efficiency, hierarchical order, and the sense of tragic heroism where everyone acted selflessly for the good of all. Of course, that was standard Wagnerian stuff, and we knew and liked Johann for what he was.

'But then he changed. He started to like Jews and dislike Israelis. He preached, for God's sake, about how we all needed to love our neighbours. Can you believe the rubbish—'

'That doesn't sound like rubbish,' Naila said.

'It is,' Jamil retorted. 'This isn't paradise, it's the Bekaa. And here, it's all right to love your neighbour if your neighbour is Syrian or Iranian, but you must draw the neighbourly line at the southern border with the enemy.'

'So he started to like Jews,' Samir said.

Jamil stressed. 'He *became* a Jew. I mean, he may as well have become one, he liked them so much. It just wasn't him any more. Samir, I'd known this man for decades and believe me he just changed completely.'

'The sphere changed him,' Samir said, more to himself as he thought, Tanit had found herself another *rab-shomam*.

'Changed him into a Jew-loving mad jinnee, that's what the sphere did to him. My wife is right, rude but half right at least. He did become happy. He became an imbecile, he looked so at ease with himself. And he did become "so alive", if you call running to the ruins in Baalbek every day being "alive". Personally, I call all of it madness. And one day it was simply too

321

much for him, he just couldn't live with his insanity any longer. So he found his old Luger from his *Luftwaffe* days, and shot a bullet right through his jumbled brain.'

'But you mentioned murder,' Samir insisted.

Hammad said bitterly, 'Why are you so interested in Johann all of a sudden?'

Samir shrugged.

'Hezbollah,' Jamil said simply.

'What's that?' Maira asked, finally understanding a word. That was the militia the West feared the most.

'Hezbollah?' Samir repeated. 'Why?'

'Maybe the Hezbollah killed him one night because of his new and outspoken views on the fraternity with the enemy. Maybe. I still believe he killed himself, ultimately proving his return to sanity in choosing an honourable, heroic end, Prussian style.'

'Right,' Hammad said resolutely, 'your morbid talks can wait, but this poor lamb will catch its death of cold if we don't eat it soon.'

It dawned on Samir. He finally understood. 'They killed him for the sphere, didn't they?'

Jamil was silent.

History had repeated itself. The Eshite Hezbollah, like the Erabite Romans of the Punic Wars, had wanted Tanit's Jewel. 'He wouldn't give it to them. He died protecting the black ping-pong ball.'

'I hope he's in Valhalla,' Jamil said softly, 'laughing with that loud voice of his, with all the other heroes at Odin's feast.'

'And then you had it. And they threatened you until you handed it over. That's it, isn't it?'

'My dick, Samir,' Hammad said angrily. 'You don't even believe in the sphere.'

'Maybe I do now.'

Jamil almost whispered, 'But it never changed me.'

Hammad said, 'Miriam, you are first to choose. Where do you want to start?'

Maira had been in a stupor brought on by the sound

322

of Arabic, the arak and the heavy meal. She blinked, 'I'm sorry?'

'The sheep, which part do you want?'

She looked horrified. 'Oh, no. I couldn't, I simply couldn't. I've eaten so much already.'

It was Hammad's turn to look aghast. 'What? See what you've done, Samir?'

Samir reached for her plate and, leaning over towards Hammad, he said, 'A fillet please, Hammad. She told me earlier she'd want a fillet.'

'Good choice,' Hammad said, his broad smile returning. 'Very good choice, Miriam.' Hammad sharpened a carving knife with zest and then picked up a large fork.

Maira was about to complain when Samir said, under his breath, 'You were highly honoured when you chose his lamb. If you don't finish all your meat and smile, you may as well spit in his face now – that would be more polite.' He was a fine one to talk, he thought; he had ruined his host's evening. He had, at any rate, prompted Jamil's wife to ruin the *pièce de résistance*: the big entry of the cooked lamb. Looking at Hammad, who was clearly enjoying slicing the fillet, he said, 'Hammad, that looks so good, could you add a shoulder for Maira too?' He smiled at her. '*Bon appétit.*'

She narrowed her eyes at him and sighed deeply.

In the pink bedroom, Maira, lying on her back, snored loudly and irregularly. Her face was turned towards the bedside table, on which a small digital alarm clock flashed the seconds in a faint green light. It was 3:10.

Maira had just fallen asleep. The evening ended after one in the morning, and for roughly two hours she had lain awake, feeling sick from both the lamb and the arak. When she turned off the lights, the room spun like a shuttle, wildly out of control.

It was now 3:13, and Maira breathed more agitatedly. Another small green light lit up suddenly, adding to the clock's own glow. This new light came from a black box which looked like a hybrid between a walkie-talkie and a boy scout's compass. Below the green light, a red light came alive, flashing slightly off sync with the clock's green colon, so that at times they blinked at Maira together and, seconds later, followed and lagged one another like two buoys alerting ships to shallow seas in the dark night.

The compass was now 'it' in a game of tag among the electronic circuits, as the needle came alive, spinning to the north-west, then to the east, then south-west, north-east, faster, faster and faster still, overtaking the clock itself.

It was still 3:13 and the clock was now recording its longest minute since its manufacture. A blinding white light came and went suddenly.

Maira, still asleep, turned on her side and stopped snoring. She was no longer facing the clock and, instead, breathed softly on a small matt-black ball which now shared her pillow, depressing it considerably for its small size. As she exhaled, her moist breath was completely absorbed by the sphere, whose surface remained coldly pristine.

The light in the blue bathroom was always kept on at night when Samir visited Beauty. The bathroom door was slightly ajar, and part of the light shone into the blue guest-room, on to a bed where Samir had just woken up. He looked at his wrist-watch, then crossed his hands under his head and pillow, and stared up at the light.

It was just after three, and given the regularity of his body's cycles, he would be asleep by about three-fifteen. This meant that he had a quarter of an hour to think of the sphere and of Johann. Jamil's story did not particularly help him understand the sphere's purpose. He wished Jacob had been present, perhaps he would have understood the significance of the German's conversion

324

and death. Had the ex-Nazi been divinely inspired? Or did the sphere simply induce nightmares?

The image of Maira appeared suddenly and he smiled. He felt attracted to her. She was so completely different from other women he had known. Naturally she would be different from Lebanese women, but even the women Samir had met in Europe could not compare to her. He liked her confident manner, her unhennaed red hair, the way she used only eye-liner to make up her plain face, and how, consequently, her pallor verged on anaemia. Tiny breasts, disproportionately long legs; she was more attractive than any Miss World. He kicked himself for having spent the evening talking about a pilot he had never known rather than showing an interest in her.

He jumped out of bed and headed for the bathroom. Pausing by the window, he looked wistfully at the pink guest-house. He froze.

At first he did not understand where all the light was coming from. He could see the house clearly lit, as if by several full moons. He gazed at the sky and saw a large shooting star – bright as a small sun – plummeting, at great speed, straight towards Maira's house. The ball of fire stopped abruptly, barely inches above the roof, and just hovered in full view of Samir.

Then, as he stood mesmerized, the ball of light passed effortlessly through the roof into the house, like water trickling through a fine sieve. He saw a bright light coming from Maira's room and then sudden darkness.

He stormed out of his house, sprinted the short distance to the pink guest-house, pushed the door open and flicked on the lights.

'Maira,' he shouted.

Maira woke with a jump and sat up. Picking up her pillow, she hugged it and looked sleepily at Samir.

'Are you OK?'

She nodded, dazed.

'Are you really OK?' he repeated.

She nodded again and said sleepily, 'What are you doing here?'

Samir opened the bathroom door and moved cautiously inside.

'What is it?' Maira asked, now awake.

'I don't know,' Samir replied from inside the bathroom.

'What?'

'Johann's sphere,' Samir said, returning to the bedroom. 'The ball of light, I saw it. It's here.'

He moved to the cupboard and swung it open dramatically.

'Samir, I'm sure this is very gallant of you – but please leave.'

'You don't believe me.'

'The ball of light.'

'It came from the sky.'

'Like a UFO?'

'Nothing like a UFO. I don't even know what a UFO is. But this was a ball of light that entered through the roof.'

Maira hugged the pillow tighter. 'Please leave.'

Samir was next to the bedside table and opened the drawer to check inside. 'Now,' he answered. 'Not more than five minutes ago.' He glanced at his wrist-watch, then, pointing at the alarm clock on the bedside table, he added, 'Your watch is slow. It's almost twenty past three.'

The clock registered 3:14 and, as Maira turned to look at it, she discovered Ric's tracker with its red light still flashing insistently. She leaned across the bed and looked down at the compass. The needle was spinning wildly clockwise. She was wearing only a nightie and knickers and, as she bent over, her nightie moved up revealing her thighs and offering Samir a view of the barely concealed crack between her buttocks.

'Adyt,' she said excitedly. 'It works.' She turned abruptly and caught his stare.

They were silent and Maira looked into his eyes. She

326

cleared her throat. 'It was here, you're sure?' She sprang out of bed and reached for Ric's tracker. 'I'll help you look.'

Samir glanced at the electronic instrument in her hands. He frowned. 'You're not an archaeologist,' he said suspiciously.

'Let's find Adyt and then we'll talk.'

He gripped her arm. 'That's why you're here. You came for Tanit's Jewel.'

'Let go of me.'

'Not before you tell me the truth.'

The sphere had rolled off the bed onto the carpeted floor when Maira had picked up her pillow. It burst into white light and drifted upwards, through the bed, through Samir and Maira, then heavenwards through the roof, before turning south.

3:30 . . . 3:45 . . . 4:00 . . . 4:15 . . . 4:30 . . . 4:45 . . .

The digital clock registered 4:49. Samir released her arm to read the time on his wrist-watch; it was just after twenty past three. Wordlessly, he showed her his watch and then pointed at the clock on the bedside table.

Maira moved with Ric's tracker in the palm of her hand. The compass needle had settled on a south by south-west direction. 'It's gone,' she said softly.

'What was it?' asked Samir, sitting, tired, on the bed.

'I don't know.' Maira sat beside him.

'What happened to us?'

Maira shook her head.

'Did you see the clock?'

She nodded. She too had stood frozen as the minutes flew by. 'So who's Tanit?'

'Who's Addit?' He brought his face close to hers.

She looked into his eyes. Again she felt a sudden urge to run her fingers through his hair, and before she knew it she had done just that. He moved closer and their mouths met in a passionate kiss.

'Maybe I should stay tonight,' breathed Samir, 'in case it returns.'

'Yes,' she said, hugging him tightly.

By late morning, before they finally climbed out of bed, Maira reached for the tracker to find that the needle was still pointing south. Samir was asleep in a foetal position. She sat up to collect her thoughts. They had spent hours talking about Adyt, Tanit's Jewel, Carthalo the Historian, alien messages from deep space, Queen Elissa of Carthage. This was definitely far more bizarre than anything she might have dreamed of in her ivory tower in Cambridge.

Remembering the bald man in Nevada, Maira had asked Samir if he'd been to a mosque in Jubel, whose name she had forgotten.

'Al-Aala Mosque,' he had exclaimed.

'Yes, why?'

'A coincidence. I was there just before coming to Baalbek.'

'Is there anything special about it?'

'It's very old. You might have liked it if you had been an archaeologist.' He pinched her. 'It was once a church. There's a verse from the Revelations still engraved in the dome.'

'What's the verse?'

'I can't remember. Something about Chronos. It's written in ancient Greek.'

Chronos, thought Maira, the old master of time. If Samir was right about the times on his wrist-watch and on the digital clock, then Adyt had the power to slow time, like the freezer in her experiment with her father's watch so many years ago. She wondered whether physical laws were actually reversible, whether CTT was wrong and Adyt could halt or even reverse time.

She leaned over and woke Samir with a kiss. 'Do you want to come south with me?'

12

ASHTIN

1982 AD

Compared with Mount Lebanon, the land in the south was drier and the air wetter. This was no man's land in a dual sense: a strip that separated the Lebanese from the Israelis, and the fertile land from the desert. Here, the hills were considerably lower and the pinnacles more rotund than the northern summits. In the villages above Beirut, daybreaks were near white, as the sun rose several degrees of arc to surmount the opposite peaks before shining into houses. There were no such obstructions in the south of Lebanon and, consequently, dawns were bloodier.

A small group of ten men hurried northwards from northern Galilee. Like counting tree rings, one could gauge their ages according to the amount of facial hair, and, clearly, some of the men were not much more than saplings. The youngest in the group was perhaps fourteen, with long single strands of hair drooping, goatlike, from his otherwise smooth chin. The oldest, in his mid-thirties, had a fully grown ungroomed black beard to complement his equally bushy head of hair, now turning grey in places. Indeed, were it not for the red headband strapped tightly around his forehead like a tennis player, he would resemble a ball of fur; an animal's head – a bear's or a gorilla's – on human shoulders. If everyone in the group sported unequal and distinctive beards, they all wore the same headbands which, with the rising sun, now shone defiantly redder.

329

Prompted by these first rays of daylight, the militiamen quickened their pace and walked on in silence as they prepared to skirt the final hill which would lead them back to base in the western Bekaa. They carried Katyushas and Kalashnikovs which had recently fired on northern Galilee and at pro-Israeli militiamen respectively. This attack, like innumerable ones before it, was just a token of the ongoing resistance against Israel. To be sure, a rocket aimed at an outlying Israeli farm hardly constituted a military or strategic success, nor would the death of three patrolmen herald the collapse of the South Lebanon Army. But this was considered a major symbolic victory. To succeed in firing the smallest calibre even a yard past the Israeli border fence was proof that the resistance was as resolved as ever to move the battleground to the enemy's home turf.

The Israeli riposte was always swift and calculated. The proportion was approximately ten to one, so that an attack on an Israeli farm was promptly followed by the decimation of a Lebanese village; the destruction of one in every ten houses chosen almost at random. This algebraic policy was not foreign to the land. It had been introduced millennia ago by the Romans – past occupiers – who had dealt with mutinies and revolts in a similar fashion. But in those distant days, seventy generations away, Jews had been on the receiving end of Roman justice, losing ten Semitic eyes and teeth for a Roman eye and tooth, and sharing this chastisement with the Canaanites, their brothers in arms, speech and religion.

Those early Jews would have understood these militiamen. They, too, had been motivated by the heady mixture of oppression and religious fervour. God was on their side, and this alone was the most potent drug, which no earthly missile could shoot down. A martyr was fearless as he drove his explosive-laden car towards his enemies because, in the moments before impact, those he had been sent to kill became blurred in the hero's vision, grew indistinct, amorphous, only to be remoulded, like putty, into God's arms, outspread in welcome; and the hero drove on, blindly blissful till the end.

The algebraic reprisal inflicted tenfold on the hero's village did not concern the faithful. The enemy was always motivated by the shaitan – and besides, martyrs had no need for logic.

The older fighter signalled to the others and all ten hid in the scrub as three Israeli helicopter gunships flew overhead, northwards to the western Bekaa, not registering the small group of men. A few moments later the man with the thickest beard signalled again and the company silently moved on, back to their homes where the helicopters would precede them. Only the fourteen-year-old with the goatlike beard looked vaguely worried.

Ric's tracker was still pointing south. Maira held the black box and allowed her gaze to move down to the boy-scout compass which now indicated the altar. Behind the altar was a quarter-sized emaciated Jesus on a wooden cross, who forlornly watched the people who had stormed his house earlier that morning. Overshadowing the Christ, at the far end of the church, was a gigantic painting of a man with a flowing white beard and a bloodstained scimitar in his hand, who looked down at another man lying dead at his feet. Behind the painting was the church wall, and beyond the wall, further south somewhere, Adyt was still calling.

But Maira returned her attention to the painting, which a few moments ago had drawn her from Samir and their pew. Conversely to what one might have expected, the man doing the slaying was the saint, judging by the oversized golden halo, while the man with a white turban was the fatally struck infidel. The saint fixed his fallen enemy with a mixture of contempt and smug satisfaction, like one who had just killed vermin or picked weeds. This body language which the artist had succeeded in conveying could not be misinterpreted, and so, perhaps, it was also no coincidence that the slain had collapsed in an implausible curled position, crescent-shaped. Maira almost imagined that the Christian's next move would be to wipe his blade clean as callously as one wiped a mosquito and its last meal cleanly off the palm.

'A Maronite saint,' Samir said, moving closer. 'Saint Elie.'

Maira nodded, though this explained nothing.

Samir now examined the painting. The childlike portrayal of the saint was only marginally truer to life than Egyptian attempts at drawing pharaohs. In the Maronite's elongated face, Samir recognized the Byzantine influence from the icons of his own church. 'Mar Elias,' he said abstractedly in Arabic, and thought no more of the painting.

'Is it safe now, do you think?' Maira asked.

'Safer.'

'I mean, is it safe to move on?'

Samir looked momentarily surprised. 'It's safer to go back.'

'We haven't come all this way to go back.'

'You are very brave, Dr Maira Brisden.'

'Oh, I don't agree.'

She wasn't brave, just mad, Maira thought, as Ric or his Anglophobic cousin would have been quick to concur. They had reached this village from Hammad's Beauty without much of a hitch. Maira had attracted considerable interest and suspicion at the single road-block, but their passes were accepted, if grudgingly and after much delay and more stares. It was in this village, twenty miles from the Israeli border, that their progress had been brought to an abrupt halt.

At first Maira had been frightened by the violent

explosion, believing it came from the car: the grey Peugeot was dying with a bang and taking them with it. She was therefore puzzled when Samir stepped on the accelerator instead of the brake, and completely dazed as the next shell met its mark and poured a tall plume of black smoke into the sky like an untapped oil well. Maira looked up and believed she saw a vulture hovering over the village.

Samir finally braked the car to a screeching halt in front of a church and dragged Maira inside. He had to pull her because she would have been content to sit and stare, mesmerized, from the car. Inside the church they discovered a family – Mr and Mrs Trabulsi and their two young children – under a pew. The next shell crashed close to the church and, irrationally, Samir and Maira dived under another pew and held one another tightly while the proverbial hell broke loose all around them.

In one brief episode Maira caught the Lebanese disease. This village would remain nameless to her, yet she would always remember its demographics: half Shiite and half Maronite. The Trabulsi couple across the cold stone floor were shaking more than their children. They, too, were visitors, as Maira would later learn and, feverishly, she knew she could never forget that an Anglican, a Greek Orthodox and a Sunnite family had been caught in a Maronite church while the Shiites were getting the shit bombed out of them by the Jews.

After the last shell had exploded, Maira opened her eyes, her vision drawn to the painting at the far end of the church, and to the brightest colour in that painting: the infidel's blood burning defiantly on the saint's scimitar.

Mr Trabulsi, sitting on a pew with a radio on his lap, shook his head and told Samir, 'It's bad.'

'Tell him he shouldn't have brought her here,' said Mrs Trabulsi to her husband.

'An Israeli family was killed. Some kids died.' Mr

333

Trabulsi added bitterly, 'The whole world cries when there are dead little Jews.'

Mrs Trabulsi, avoiding all eye contact with Samir, said to her husband, 'Beirut is safe for Westerners. Tell him that. Especially with her hair.'

'What's a dead little Jew?' asked one of the children.

'He should know it's not safe for her kind here,' the woman said, and licked her thumb to smooth out her son's eyebrows.

'The attack is over, right?' Samir asked.

'What's a dead little Jew?'

The man shook his radio. 'There's something happening at the border. It's not over.'

'Great,' said Samir. 'That's just great.'

'Did you come from Beirut?'

Samir nodded.

'We came from Saïda.'

'And we're going back there,' Mrs Trabulsi added. 'Tell him to go back to Beirut.'

'I'm a dead little Jew,' said the young Trabulsi at the top of his voice.

'You're going to be dead all right,' his father shouted and shook the radio violently. 'Woman, make your son shut up.'

Samir moved away as Mrs Trabulsi pulled her son towards her and tucked his shirt in his trousers. He heard the boy speak softly, '*Immy*, what's a dead little Jew?'

'A little boy like you who kills Arabs like you.'

The child looked unimpressed for a while, and then asked, 'What's a border?'

Maira was waiting impatiently and said, 'Well?'

'The attack's over.'

'Good,' she said, and led the way to the exit.

'You're sure you want to carry on?'

Maira glanced down at Ric's tracker. 'Absolutely.'

It was late afternoon and the sky was turning progressively darker from the east. The *fidei* manning the roadblock to Ashtin looked above his head at the ball of light suspended high in the air.

'Ass whore-brothers,' Hassan shouted at the unfamiliar light. 'Stupid pimp-fuckers.' What a waste of a flare, he thought. A bright one, too, shining like a star. Soon, bored with looking at the sky, the Palestinian scanned the empty road and cursed the curfew that was making his watch duty more tedious than usual. Manning a roadblock when there was a steady stream of traffic – of drivers to harass – was dreary enough, but manning a roadblock on a day when everyone observed the curfew was particularly unbearable. He swung his hammer and dented an oil barrel that served to barricade the road, listening to the deep resonant sound. He had whiled away many an hour of boredom by making holes and craters in oil drums, iron sheets and anything else he could find on the side of the road. A fly landed on the barrel; Hassan swung again, missed, and made another dent. The fly buzzed briefly around Hassan then landed once more on the barrel; he ignored it.

A car had rounded the bend in the road and drew nearer to the roadblock. All the car bombers used Mercedes, usually the 180 models. How unimaginative, Hassan thought. How boring. If he were a car bomber, he would use a Peugeot. Any Peugeot – he hated them all.

Hassan twirled his hammer and waited for the car.

'*As-salaam a'aleikom*,' said the driver through the open window.

Hassan narrowed his eyes at the man. He had seen him before, but where . . . ? Where? 'Papers,' he ordered gruffly.

The driver handed him a Lebanese passport. Hassan kicked the door. 'I said papers.'

'They were burned when a bomb exploded in my house.'

Only IDs mentioned the holder's religion, not passports. 'Where are you from?' demanded Hassan, flicking the passport open.

'Beirut.'

'Where in Beirut?'

'Sodeco.'

Ah, Greek, thought Hassan. He had grown up in the Palestinian camp near the Greek neighbourhood; had played Indian to the Greek Orthodox cowboy, George Khoury, who had lived in Sodeco. Hassan scrutinized the picture of a younger man who looked even more familiar. He must have seen him in the Greek neighbourhood as a child. This must have been before the war when Palestinians could still go to East Beirut.

It was when the *fidei* read the name, Ya'acoub Haddad, that it all came back to him. George's brother's bum-friend.

Hassan thought, that's why the bastard wouldn't show me his ID. He grinned at the driver and said conversationally, 'What happened to your Peugeot?'

'My Peugeot?' repeated the driver, astonished.

Hassan picked up his hammer and used it to scrape some grime off the windscreen. 'This is a nicer car, but you should clean it.'

The driver nodded.

'Thinking of blowing it up?'

'No, sir.'

'Then you wouldn't need to clean it, right?' Hassan grinned at his wit.

'I know nothing about politics. I'm going to Ashtin to congratulate a friend on the birth of his son.'

'Road's closed.' The jollity had left the militiaman's voice. 'Out of the car,' he ordered. 'Open the boot.'

As the driver complied, the hammer swapped hands, so it was now gripped in the left hand; the Kalashnikov was held in the right hand, finger poised on the trigger.

'I've got nothing,' the driver said, showing an empty boot.

'You've got eyes,' growled Hassan. In a flash it had become clear to him. Israel suspected the PLO was building secret bunkers. That explained the flare above

Ashtin. But the enemy needed the exact co-ordinates. 'You're old,' said Hassan with a sneer.

The driver nodded slowly, and tried to appear older still.

'So Mossad uses old men now.'

'No, sir.' The man shook his head emphatically. 'I'm a civilian.'

'Liar,' he yelled and swung the hammer down on the man's right leg.

The driver screamed with pain and fell to the ground. 'You're making a mistake,' he uttered in a strained voice. 'Allah keep you, I swear you're making a mistake.'

Hassan slung his Kalashnikov over his shoulder and, kneeling over the man, he put the hammer against the man's chin. He was now holding it in his right hand.

'Your God is the shaitan,' he spat. 'Tell me you're not a Jew. Go on, lying whore.'

'I'm not a spy.'

'You're the Israeli enemy,' Hassan screamed into the man's face.

'Please. I can pay. I'm not a spy.'

'All Israelis are cunt-spies.' He brought his hammer down hard on the man's chest. 'I fuck you and all your Jewish whore-mothers.'

The man groaned and tried to move. Hassan swung his hammer on the bald head.

Thud.

Nothing like an oil barrel. He tried again, this time harder.

Thud. Thud.

Strangely hollow; a satisfying sound, so Hassan went on hammering at the forehead. Blood trickled from the man's nose, mouth and ears, but what was really fascinating was the dent in the skull. Not bumpy and uneven like an oil drum, but smooth to the touch like a perfect crater on the moon.

After a while, Hassan wiped his hammer clean on the

dead spy's shirt and looked up at the reddening sky. The hammer-wielder grunted with satisfaction; the flare had vanished.

Samir and Maira were only 4 kilometres away from Ashtin when the red and green diode lights on Ric's tracker went dead.

'Adyt's stopped,' said Maira frowning.

Samir pulled over on the side of the road and looked at the tracker in her hands.

'Damn thing's stopped,' she repeated and turned to him. 'What do we do now?'

'We wait,' Samir said, switched off the engine, and lit a cigarette.

They waited two hours until the dark night had totally surrounded them. Then they turned the car around and drove wordlessly and uneventfully back to Baalbek.

As Samir parked the Peugeot in Hammad's Beauty, he broke the long silence. 'Maybe Tanit's Jewel will guide us tomorrow, or the day after.'

Maira nodded. 'But it stopped so abruptly.'

He stroked her hair. 'I mean, I'm the *rab-shomam* and you're my Queen Elissa, right?' He tried to be cheerful. 'Tanit just has to guide us.'

'Oh well.' She opened the car door.

'Maira?' He leaned over to kiss her. 'Thanks.'

'What on earth for?'

'For being such a great archaeologist.'

'You fibber,' she said with a sad smile. 'You're just as frustrated.'

'Hammad will be suspicious if you don't go to the Roman temples. May I accompany you tomorrow to the houses of Jupiter, Venus and Bacchus?'

'Sure. I'd like that. I've got a feeling Adyt will be quiet tomorrow.'

As they walked hand in hand, Samir told her, 'Heliopolis – Sun City – the Roman name for Baalbek. You'll see the greatest Roman temples ever built

338

anywhere. Honestly, they're more spectacular than the ones in Athens or Rome itself. I've always wondered why Rome had such magnificent temples built in far-flung Heliopolis. You see, there was a never-ending war between the Semitic and Hellenistic cultures, and it just didn't make sense for the Romans to build such temples in Phoenicia for Semitic gods. I've got a theory, are you interested?'

'Yes.' She squeezed his hand, but she was thinking about Adyt, about phoning Bill to see if there were new messages.

'Jupiter Heliopolitan was the Roman name for Baal. Baal and Jupiter were one and the same, with differences which arose only over the centuries. You see, I think Baalbek represented the birthplace of Rome's own pagan religion. And therefore, Romans would have paid homage to Baalbek in much the same way as Christians honour Jerusalem. But the fact that the temples in Baalbek were named Jupiter, Venus and Bacchus instead of Baal, Astargatis and Adon implies that the Romans, who were therefore aware that their religion had a Semitic root, were ashamed of that fact. These deities were hence rebaptized and Romanized. The envy of the Semite's achievements, and the shame of finding them worthwhile – that's the true curse of Erab and Esh.' Samir realized that he had been thinking aloud. 'My best friend taught me this.' He grinned suddenly. 'I'm even starting to sound like him.'

'Let's have a drink,' Maira suggested.

'I got carried away,' he apologized.

'Maybe I ought to see the temples first.'

The grin had left his face. 'I wish I could see Jacob now.'

She phoned Bill after her third gin and tonic.

'Maira,' Bill's voice crackled, 'are you OK?'

'No, I'm pissed off. Look, Bill, I'm not paying for this call, so we'll have to be quick. Was Adyt broadcasting earlier today?'

339

'Yes, but Adyt's stopped.'

'Right, I—'

'But the Sombrero started again as soon as the last message left Adyt. We received one signal from the M104 Galaxy as instantaneously as Adyt's reply had been. A short signal and nothing from either since.'

'End of transmision?' Maira wondered.

'You think?'

'What was the last message from the Sombrero?'

'Dash-dot-dash-dot-dash-dot-dash-dot-dash-dot.'

'Let me write that down.'

'Six-eight-two in binary,' Bill gave a nervous laugh, 'which Ric guesses is the real number of the *bestia* because if you subtract six-one-six, you're left with sixty-six.'

'OK. I got that.'

'So how long are you staying?'

'Until I'm sure Adyt's not going to reappear.'

'Did you say reappear?'

'I've got to go, Bill. Speak to you soon. Bye.'

She hung up and looked at the binary number. She wrote a 'B' where she saw a dash, and an 'A' for the dots. The Sombrero Galaxy had started it all off, and the Sombrero had now ended it. It was the master; Adyt the slave. And on her sheet was the scribbled command for 'stop' in an alien tongue of dots and dashes.

Maira, hunched over the sheet, muttered, 'BA BA BA BA BA.'

ZACHIEL

'LA LA LA LA LA.' I repeat the death-toll that resonates from the desert itself.

I am empty of all emotions. Painlessly, I have witnessed my murder through the callous eyes of my murderer. My assassin has bludgeoned all emotion.

'LA,' I tell Zachiel. The angel indicates north, a blue doorway under the crystal sculpture of a sun. No, I won't go. No, I don't want to see the future. Five times no, angel of misery. I despise my torturer. If I had limbs, I'd fight and run rather than allow him to carry me to the blue doorway.

Emotions are slowly returning: hatred, anger, and – pity.

> *Malus puis tost alors mourra, viendra,*
> *De gens et bestes une horrible defaite:*
> *Puis tout à coup la vengeance on vera,*
> *Cent, main, soif, faim quand courra la comet.*
> Centurie II: Quatrain 62

Malus will then soon die and there will come a terrible destruction of people and animals. Suddenly vengeance will be revealed, a hundred hands, thirst and hunger when the comet will pass.

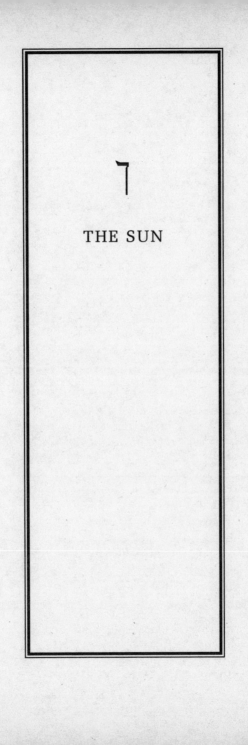

ז

THE SUN

13

KHALEEF OF JINN AND MEN
2020 AD

Adonai – my Lord, in extinct Phoenician – was known to the Greeks as Adonis. He was a man who was so legendarily handsome that the goddess Anat fell in love with him and attempted to seduce him. The fertility god, Tammuz, was angered by his sister's infatuation with a mortal, and vented his ire on the humans by drying the rivers and turning the land barren.

Adonai left his people on the coast and climbed Mount Lebanon to a rocky cave. There he prayed to Tammuz and offered his life to save his people from starvation. He stabbed himself in the heart, and from his dead body the blood trickled, then poured, then mingled with Anat's tears to gush like a torrent out of the cave, cascading down the precipitous slope to the arid lowlands. The soil absorbed the rich blood and yielded its bountiful nutrients to the crops, and the Phoenicians of Byblos gave thanks to Adonai who had lifted the curse. Tammuz, mellowed by the sacrifice, decreed that every spring, Adonai's blood would flow from the mountain to irrigate the fields and orchards, so that men would forever remember his selfless act. Adonai died periodically to be reborn in wheat and fruit: the twin concepts of self-sacrifice and resurrection were innate in every Edenite soul.

The river is called Nahr el-Kalb, Dog River. Mount Lebanon, running parallel to the Mediterranean coastline, has a single outcrop by the Dog River where mountain abruptly collides with sea. The mountain range is a giant resting on his right side, with the top of his head inclined towards Asia Minor, his feet lying on the burning sand of the south-western extremity of the Syrian desert; his left arm reposes on the hip, adding altitude to his considerable width; his right arm is outstretched with fingers idle in the Mediterranean pond. He looks like a fallen martyr.

The Dog River, turning red with alluvium from every melting of snow, cascades across the arm from a wound in the giant's neck.

The first recorded large-scale invasion of the Levant was by Asserhaddoun, King of Assyria, Prefect of Babel, King of Sumer and Akkad. The Assyrian conqueror had contoured Mount Lebanon in order to capture the Phoenician cities, crossing not from east to west but from north in Cilicia to Byblos in the south. Even on this more accessible geological route, the Assyrian had to ford the Dog River at the treacherous pass, his lightning progress halted by the giant's arm. When the Assyrian army crossed the river, it represented such a remarkable feat that Asserhaddoun had a stela erected to mark the event. Unwittingly, he started a trend.

The conquering road from north to south or south to north involved marching across the narrow pass, and every invader felt the irresistible urge to leave his mark on the imposing rock-face by the Dog River. From Alexander the Macedonian, on his way to Tyre and Egypt, to the Romans, to the Omayyads, to the knights of the Crusades, to the Ottomans, to Napoleon's army on its journey from Alexandria to Alexandretta, to the Australians sent halfway across the world to fight the Turks, to the Free French invading the French Vichyists. Historical interest aside, the rock-face by Dog River resembles a wall in a public lavatory: 'I was here' conjugated in a host of scripts and languages, both living and dead.

Another aspect which all the invaders had in common was the unwillingness to venture deep into the hinterland of the Lebanon. The rugged terrain, sheer ravines, harsh winters and porcupine covering of pine forests dissuaded the most fervent empire builder.

In the 630s AD, a mere decade after Muhammad's flight from Mecca, Caliph Omar I added Syria, Palestine and Egypt to the growing Muslim empire. The indigenous Christians were given the choice to embrace the new faith or become an underclass of oppressed serfs. In Egypt and Palestine there were mass conversions, leaving a minority of downtrodden Copts and Greek Orthodox Christians (emulating the Roman Empire, Christendom had recently been fissured into the western patriarchate of Rome and the eastern patriarchate of Constantinople).

In Syria the Christians, under the leadership of Maro, opted for a third course of action: they fled. They left their homes and lands in the towns and plains and migrated to the impregnable shelter of Mount Lebanon. The first Maronites lived as a Stone Age tribe. They hid from the Islamic hordes in the caves of the virgin mountains, prior to finding unassailable sites for the new Christian villages. Future generations of Maronites would sanctify these caves with the name Qadisha – blessed with the Holy Spirit.

If the mountain range had, in the past, proved unconquerable, in the following six centuries the giant was manifestly indomitable. Islam galloped across North Africa into Spain, pushing the doorstep to southern France while, in its living-room, by the hearth, an independent Christian state flourished, with its capital, Baskinta, a safe 2,500 metres above flood level. Maro's supporters were an embarrassing thorn in Islam's side which successive caliphs were unable to extract.

Besides the rough terrain, the invaders had to contend with the Marda'ai, the fierce military wing of the Maronites who were organized into an effective guerrilla army, and whose renowned bravery and sheer resilience against greater odds were reputedly enhanced by their predilection for the wild hemp of their mountains –

smoked or chewed before battle as a magic potion.

Isolated from the rest of Christendom for four centuries, the first contact with the West occurred with the start of the Crusades when Frankish knights crossed the sea to the Levant. There, near the Holy Land, the Franks were surprised to discover Arabs who believed in the same Christian God, and Arabs whose mother tongue was not Arabic – the Aramaic script and language was closer to Hebrew than it was to Arabic, and was the tongue that Jesus himself had used.

The knights returned to Europe and reported their discovery of the secluded Christians to the pope. This resulted in the Vatican's recognition of the Maronites as a bona fide Christian sect within the Catholic Church, and in the canonization of their first leader, Maro. The Maronite romance with the French began many centuries before the mandate of the 1920s.

Gaby's climb up the ravine was arduous. There was a fresh bloodstain on the tight bandage around his left forearm. He ignored the bleeding arm and continued his slow progress towards a wide ledge on the rock-face, his progress further hampered by a length of rope coiled around his left shoulder.

Gaby had seen the cedar tree from the opposite and more accessible side of the ravine, on a sister mountain. It was the only tree in the precipice, growing unexpectedly on a ledge midway between the valley floor and a monastery at the summit. He had chosen that particular tree because its stark solitude appealed to him. The final act of the soul-sick required a cedar; he needed the most venerable yet saddest of all trees, whose flattened boughs spread with the centuries like wrinkles of sorrow. This tree was even more triste than its cousins; remorseful and frightened. Gripping the ledge for dear life, half its branches curved downwards, peering at the valley below, saying '*Ya Mama*' with every strong gust of wind.

As for the route; he could have driven to the monastery and descended to the ledge by the thousand-odd steps grooved into the rock-face which Gaby had noticed from the opposite slope. Instead, he chose to drive to the bottom of the precipice to reach his destination the punishing way.

Gaby believed that one should not commit suicide in a leisurely fashion, snugly in bed asleep with poison, or hugging a grenade. One had to sweat to die, to risk death by accident climbing a hazardous cliff with neither harness nor proper boots and with a wounded and bleeding arm.

He looked up and saw the cedar's branches weeping over him. He was sweating profusely despite the cool breeze of early morning – the sun still shone on the other western side of the mountain. The tired ache in his right arm now equalled the pain in his left. His body was on fire, crying out for restful peace. A trained warrior, Gaby found the inner strength to be insensitive to the pain and fatigue, and he climbed on with a hero's determination.

He reached the ledge panting and exuding perspiration. He lay spread-eagled by the cedar's protruding roots; his arms and legs twitched, not yet informed that the climb was over. He closed his eyes for a brief moment to listen to the pulse in his ears, roaring in the deadly stillness, a galley at ramming speed. Gaby was tired. He had not slept in the three days and nights since the accident. In the day visions of his victims hounded him, appearing wordlessly before him; the wispy blue wraiths materialized simply to stare at their assassin. The nights were reserved for Cerberus – even the dead did not dare enter Gaby's nightmares.

The dragon had taken his mind and there was only one sure way of killing it. He opened his eyes and chose a branch from which he planned to hang, lifeless, forsaken and forgotten but for the grateful vultures. He rose unsteadily to his feet.

Shielded from view on the opposite slope by the

mature cedar, which was raised like a polite hand before a mouth, the rock-face behind Gaby yawned. He jumped around; the sun crossed the ridge of Mount Lebanon to cast a slanted light on the ledge. All around the entrance to the cave, shadows began to flit and dance like jinn at an impromptu fête. By the mouth, the shadow of a large hand was extended in welcome, pointing and shaking insistently as the cedar's uppermost branches caught the breeze.

Somsom, Sesame, had opened. The jinn beckoned. Gaby hesitated only for a second, then dropped the rope and entered the cave of the bottomless pit. Down some roughly hewn steps by the opening, the cave was as cold as a grave, dank and dark but for a lit candle shining feebly from an end wall.

He moved cautiously towards the weak light, to a small table against the wall. The candle, nearing its end, was in a brass candlestick. It threw a dim light on to a tablecloth which draped to the ground, on to a plain vase filled with wilting flowers, and on to a rosary hanging from the corner of a painting propped against the wall. Gaby brought the candle closer to the picture. To judge by the halo crowning the central figure, a saint held a scimitar dripping with blood, and fought alone against an army of warriors in turbans. At the saint's feet was a dead fighter, while all around him men with snarling faces prepared to pounce on him – their faces further tormented by the dim light into demonic expressions of abject hatred. Their dark Arabian features contrasted sharply with the saint's white Maronite skin.

Gaby picked up the painting, causing the rosary to fall on the table. He turned it against the light to strain at the two words by the scimitar: Mar Elias – Saint Elie.

To be a saint and not a sinner Gaby would sacrifice his left bleeding arm, would sell his soul.

He was about to replace the painting when the shadows again pointed – the corner of the frame blotting out the candlelight on the end wall. The arrow indicated an engraved cross, over which the tableau had rested. Gaby placed the painting on the ground, fingered the cross in the wall curiously, then dragged the table away, disrupting St Elie's shrine.

Below the cross, hidden by the draped table, was a single slab of pink marble in the limestone wall. Candlestick in hand, Gaby squatted and read in bold Roman letters, from left to right, three obscure phrases:

**DAMVS TE
ORAMVS TE
RIFICAMVS TE**

Below each phrase were sentences – seven in all – in a script he had never come across. He felt the icy smoothness of the marble. It felt like rest, secure and comfortable; like a recollection that was deeper and purer than his recent memories.

Gaby had opened his penknife and was grooving into the brittle clay that held the marble slab in place. He worked all around the rectangular pink rock, loosening the wall's hugging grip. The slab moved. Gaby inserted the blade into the deepest crack and leaned against the handle until the blade snapped and a section of the slab rotated towards him. With an opening wide enough for his fingers, he held the wide edge and tugged in a deter-mined battle against the wall. Deliberately, grudgingly, the wall yielded its pink prize to expose its secret black orifice to the intruder.

A forbidding rank smell wafted from within; centuries of rot and humidity escaped into the greater atmosphere as demons were liberated from their hellish cell. Gaby, struggling with the heavy slab, dropped it face up on the ground before reaching for the candle-stick and squeezing through the opening head first like a newborn.

The secret cavity in the cave was just as much a hidden annexe as a tomb. The faint light was now weaker as it recoiled from both the sheer blackness of the room and the putrid stench. The room was full of grey shadows in a jet-black background, shadows which the intruder only recognized by looking slightly to one side, like gazing at dim stars. Thus he recognized a writing desk, a stool – which he almost tripped over – a wardrobe, a small bed and a skeleton.

The skeleton, resting on the bed, had an iron helmet beside its skull, a scimitar and a small round shield on either side of its crossed arms.

It was at this moment, before the ghoulish remains of an ancient warrior, that the candle, with a brief flicker, chose to die. The grey shadows, unquiet phantoms in the sorcerer's light, returned to their black graves. And it was then that the nightmare returned.

Slowly, very slowly, the skeleton moved its head to fix Gaby through its twin cavities.

He felt for the stool and sat on it. Pock-marked with age, the stool cracked, and Gaby fell on the floor.

The skull slowly appeared to stare down at the intruder from the bed.

'Who are you?'

The skeleton grinned at him.

'What do you want with me?'

Creakily it raised its left arm, the hand dropping, to point with its humerus at the wardrobe behind the intruder.

The wardrobe flew open as he turned. Steps.

He heard steps.

The coach driver appeared, his eyes like the dragon's. 'We're all waiting for you, monsieur.'

On the coach, all the passengers looked at him with disdain. He found his old seat opposite the woman who, glancing at him, asked, 'Why do you persecute us?'

The coach set off on a tour to Hades. 'Leave me alone!' Gaby shouted.

The tourists arrived at the citadel, guarded outside by scorpions as large as demons. Inside the dragon sat on its throne, the three-headed hound by its master.

'Come, Jibrayel,' whispered the dragon, and Gaby sat on the beast's lap.

The creature stroked Gaby's cheek with its scaly palm and brought the man's head to its jaws.

'No,' screamed Gaby.

Its tongue flitting into his mouth, the dragon kissed him. The kiss took his breath away. He gasped and spluttered. 'Help – me.'

Tight in the beast's embrace, Gaby was paralysed.

Abruptly, a gust of wind entered the cave, pushing some precious air into the secret annexe. The dragon lost its grip; the man spluttered then inhaled deeply.

Gaby sobbed, wept like a small boy. 'It hasn't stopped.'

The skull looked on.

'The nightmare hasn't stopped. It just gets worse.'

The skull returned to its restful pose.

'I'm so tired.' Gaby moved to the bed. 'Our Father, help me kill the dragon. *Aidez-moi, mon Père.*'

Wordlessly, Gaby crawled onto the bed, brushed his head from side to side against the ribcage, drawing from the skeleton a loving caress.

Curled in a foetal position, Gaby soon fell asleep, despite the dry bones on his right cheek. It was not the usual wakeful slumber of an alert Scorpion; nor was it the profound sleep of innocent children – but rather the in between, grateful rest of a troubled man.

Saleh Shmali knocked on the door and entered.

'The generals are here, Khaled,' he said.

Khaled was sitting at his desk with a small blue object in his hands. He gave a brief nod without looking up.

'I told them to wait in the salon.'

'Good.'

The janizary turned to leave the study.

Khaled's whispered speech was slower than usual: 'Has Gaby contacted you?'

Saleh faced his friend. 'No, Khaled.'

The caliph fingered the lacquered box on the desk which housed the Ghazi dagger. 'He has turned against Ahhal.'

Saleh was quiet.

Khaled resumed, now contemplating the blue object. 'Do you remember the Islamic Foundation for Boys?'

'Of course. I remember the citadel. The Sayyed.'

'Did you keep anything from those days?'

Saleh grinned. 'Only you, Khaled.'

The Crier gripped the blue object and brought it to his lips to kiss it. He smiled sadly and said, 'When I was six, an angel flew into my hands.'

The janizary approached his master and friend.

'I was alone when, from the sky, Jibrayel dropped into my open hand. Without warning. Do you believe me?'

Saleh stared. 'I believe in you, Khaled.'

'For four years, until you and I became friends, Jibrayel spoke to me, slept with me, bathed with me.' He paused. 'He called me Lakhed, and whispered when he spoke so that no-one else would hear him. He was my eyes and ears when mine were shut with sleep, my teacher who told me of Ahhal and of Mumahhad. He was my friend, so very blue that only I could see him.'

Saleh realized with astonishment that the Crier was nervous for seemingly the first time in his life.

'When you and I became friends, Jibrayel flew away. But he told me he would return one day to dictate the words of Ahhal.'

Saleh frowned.

Khaled nodded and fidgeted with the black box. 'Holy Jibrayel, father of angels.'

The frown had not left Saleh's face. 'I don't understand.'

'The time has come for new revelations, a new sacred text in the name of Ahhal.' The Crier smiled suddenly at his friend. 'You, too, have been chosen. You are the caliph's rightful successor.' Khaled rose decisively to his feet and dropped the blue object on the desk. 'It's time to meet the generals.' He strode to the door and then stopped to whisper, 'Kill Gaby on sight.'

Khaled exited the room, leaving Saleh alone by the desk. The janizary picked up and examined the blue object curiously.

It was a plastic figure of an angel in a flowing robe, with wings outspread in mid-flight. The blue paint was flaking off on the underside by the feet to reveal an original cream colour. Saleh recognized it as a decoration which Christians used on their Christmas trees. This was confirmed by a phrase on an open scroll, curved like a scimitar, in the angel's two hands. The Christian message was printed in Arabic: 'Glory to God in the highest.'

Examining the text closely, Saleh noticed that a letter had been added to God and that the last had been effaced so that the phrase now read: '*Al-majdo khaled fil-'ola.*' 'Glory to Khaled in the highest.'

Saleh shook his head, bewildered. Then, opening the lacquered box on the desk, he placed the angel beside the Ghazi dagger and turned to leave the room.

'Your Holiness,' said one of the generals, 'our ambassador to the United Nations has stated that the North African army is currently only on a military exercise in East Egypt.'

'Good.'

'When will the North African troops cross into Saudi territory?'

'The conversion of the imperialist kingdom will begin tomorrow.' Khaled closed his eyes. 'There are no countries before Allah, only men in cities and towns. You have my order to liberate our Muslim brothers from their infidel gaols in Mecca and Medina.'

The generals bowed.

'Mecca is the soul of our nation. A man is but an animal without his soul.'

One of the generals spoke out, 'Holiness, what if the West attacks us?'

When Khaled opened his eyes again, there was a look of glory on the caliph's face, of inner quietism. He looked up, imagined the cloudless blue sky through the ceiling, and whispered, 'Saved is he who believes in me.'

*   *   *

As was his daily routine for twenty-odd years, Brother Nadeem set off down the 467 steps from the monastery to the holy cave of Mar Elias. There were exactly 467 roughly hewn steps because one step always remained after a double recital of the Credo. Brother Nadeem left the monastery in the late afternoon, once the blustery winds of the day had died down. He pocketed a new candle in his brown habit, held a bunch of wild flowers in his left hand, and descended the steps in the rock-face a syllable at a time.

'*No'-min bi Il-la-hi wa-had—*'

He paused by the last step, bowed his head, then moved to the cedar to cross himself. A millennium ago, the old tree had been a sapling plucked from its forest of cedars and planted here, reputedly by St Elie himself, in front of his cave.

Brother Nadeem bowed his head again and spotted a length of rope by the trunk. He picked it up, puzzled, then dropping it, he ran into the holy cave.

The saint's retreat was pitch-black.

'Is anyone here?'

'Here Here Here,' echoed his voice.

Brother Nadeem lit the new candle and moved warily inside. He reached the shrine against the end wall where he found the candlestick. Someone had been here, the monk knew, the vase was now to the left of the painting, the rosary now hung from the right corner.

A faithful had come to the cave to pray, he decided with relief, fixed the candle to its holder and rearranged the shrine.

He knelt before the altar, intoned a brief prayer and, out of a habit that was two decades old, he lifted the altar cloth to stroke the marble gravestone reverentially.

When he was confronted first by the marble slab on the ground, then by a gaping hole in the wall, the monk screamed, 'God deliver us!'

'*Jeena Jeena Jeena.*'

He screamed again. '*Allah yinajeena!*'

'*Jeena Jeena Jeena.*'

The monk jumped to his feet, dragged the altar away from the wall, ignoring the painting and rosary that crashed onto the pink marble. He reached for the candlestick and moved, trembling, to the opening. It was so dark within the secret chamber that the monk strained to see nothing.

He dared not enter.

Mar Elias was a prophet in that he had foreseen one event, only one omen, but so portentously cataclysmic that his gravestone had been engraved with the warning in the saint's Aramaic. The saint had foreseen that the Day of Judgement would dawn on the day his tomb was opened.

The Maronite monk looked down at the slab and read the seven sentences he knew by heart – text from St John's Revelations, engraved between the incomplete Latin laudations from the Gloria:

lau**DAMVS TE**
And I saw heaven opened, and behold a white horse;
and he that sat upon him was called Faithful and
True,
ad**ORAMVS TE**
and in righteousness he doth judge and make war.
His eyes were as a flame of fire, and on his head were
many crowns;
glo**RIFICAMVS TE**
and he had a name written, that no man knew but
he himself.
And he was clothed in a vesture dipped in blood:
and his name is called *The Word of God.*

'God deliver us,' Brother Nadeem muttered.

He rushed out of the holy cave, turned to climb the 467 steps to the monastery, when he stopped, suddenly aware of a new phenomenon.

The sky in the west was red with the dying day. The

357

sun had set, yet in the southern sky, a new, smaller sun had risen. Not a star shimmering in the distance, but a small sun growing brighter with every minute.

'*Allah yinajeena!*'

For the first time in twenty years, Brother Nadeem climbed the steps to the monastery without reciting the Credo. The only thing the monk could think about was of the descending angel of judgement called *The Word of God*.

The old man lived on his own in Toronto. He went to bed early, so he first learned of the extraordinary news only the following morning.

Bill Walters climbed wearily out of bed, went downstairs to the kitchen, turned first the kettle on, then the radio. He was irritated by an interference that was affecting his receiver, a regular crackling, and was about to retune the set when the commentary stopped him dead in his tracks.

'Unconfirmed reports are emerging that the Watan Islami has invaded Saudi Arabia. This unverified news would appear to coincide with the breakdown of all communications to and from the Middle East. A powerful electromagnetic pulse which is believed to have caused the malfunction of all satellites in geostationary orbit above the Middle East is equally blamed for the blackout in the Watan Islami and certain southern areas of Europe. Experts suspect that the energy of this pulse, increasing since 22:00 hours GMT, has induced disturbances in the electricity supply in the whole of Europe and most of Asia. Greece has – '

Bill switched the kitchen light on and gauged that the current was oscillating at regular bursts between 200 and 260 volts.

' – joined Cyprus, Turkey and Bulgaria as non-Watan areas that have suffered a complete blackout from this powerful radiation. Canada and the rest of America is beginning to feel this pulse—'

Bill moved to the living-room and turned the screen on to see a US news channel. The two images of an anchorman and a Pentagon spokesman flickered rhythmically.

'Colonel,' the anchorman was asking, 'do you agree with this new weapon theory?'

'The shoe fits. The facts confirm that the Islamists have created a lethal weapon. We recorded troop movements to the Suez Canal facing Saudi Arabia. Almost the entire North African army was mobilized to eastern Egypt. Then this powerful electromagnetic beam was switched on, and all our surveillance went dead. A particularly smart tactical move by the Islamists. In one go you disable not only the satellites tracking your movements and the foreign reporters on the ground, but all the radar stations for several hundred miles. It's a classic case of a surprise attack in an age when instant information should have rendered such attacks impossible.'

'Surely, Colonel, the loss of radar affects both sides.'

'Of course, but the Watan's strength lies in the number of its infantry. Saudi Arabia had the technological edge. Now, however, smart bombs are as dull as Second World War shells. Technologically, the playing field has been evened. The Gulf states don't stand a hope in hell of withstanding a concerted attack by the Islamists.'

'But Colonel,' argued the anchorman, 'is it possible that the Watan Islami, which is, as you pointed out, technologically inferior, could have constructed such a device? I understand that all the continents are now affected by the pulse. This is very advanced science, wouldn't you agree, Colonel?'

'Well, we didn't build this weapon, and nor did Europe, Russia, ASEAN or China.'

'But does America possess the technology to construct such a powerful emitter to affect the entire world, and to cause power stations to break down?'

'I'm not at liberty to answer that question. However, I believe we have grossly underestimated the calibre of the scientists working for the Islamists.'

'You're absolutely convinced, Colonel, that this is the work of the Watan Islami?'

'There's irrefutable evidence. I would like to draw your attention to an image of Earth recently taken from Selena.'

An image of the blue planet came on screen, centred on the Levant.

'We believe', resumed the officer, 'that the unidentified white dot you see above the Motawasset region of the Islamic empire is the source of the powerful electromagnetic radiation and that this—'

Bill was no longer listening.

His mouth dropped open. He turned to the oscillating light in the kitchen.

'Fuck shit,' the old man exclaimed and scrambled for a pen and paper.

The current was oscillating at two different frequencies – a short and a longer period. Bill, below the kitchen bulb, counted the pulse and scribbled on the paper:

$$\cdot - \quad - \cdot \cdot \quad - \cdot - - \quad -$$

He looked down at the sheet. 'A–D–Y–T. Oh my God.' Closing his eyes, Bill was transported back thirty-eight years to the Nevada Desert, to the SETI compound where he, Maira Brisden and Ric Garcia had tracked the extraterrestrial broadcast from the M104 Galaxy, and the reply signal from the Middle East.

'Antichrist Do Your Thing,' Bill remembered. 'And Die You Terrestrials.' Adyt had never been this strong. Something was happening, something far greater than anyone else alive could imagine. He turned to the flashing screen and the anchorman and the colonel.

'Assholes,' he shouted at them. 'This thing's not human.'

14

THE DEATH OF MALUS

Yessou' al-Massih, Jesus the Christ, was the prophet Muslims recognized by the name, 'Issa bin-Youssef. Before the Islamists came to power, many Muslims of the Levant, especially in the middle class, celebrated 'Issa's birthday as befitted a lesser prophet's: less solemnly than Muhammad's, thus secretly with more enthusiasm. Respecting the Massihi calendar, Sunnis and Shiites alike offered small gifts to their children on the eve of 24 *Kanoon al-Awal*, the date of birth of Joseph's son in Bayt-Laham.

In Lebanon the first region to cancel Christmas was the poor Hezbollah stronghold of Beirut's southern suburbs, where it was ruled that the joyous occasion trivialized 'Issa's birthday. In 1988, a late afternoon of Christmas Eve, another bin-Youssef, a six-year-old boy, stood in an empty backstreet, staring at a giant mural of a cleric.

The imam, painted across a building's entire back wall, towered threateningly over the small boy; the eyes glaring down at him below a giant blue turban; the tangled grey beard as long as the boy's height; the colossal arms reaching out, commanding reverence.

Young Khaled Sulman, transfixed by the Great Man, emulated the gesture and extended his thin arms, palms up. He remained motionless in the deserted street.

'Have you gone mad, woman?' the man shouted at his wife.

He had just returned home to discover a miniature Christmas tree on top of the television set.

'Of all the crazy places, what's it doing by the window?'

'It's just for tonight,' his wife said in a subdued voice, 'just for the children.'

'We're not Massihi,' the man growled. 'You want people to think we are?' The man opened the window by the television and hurled the tree out of the window.

The cream-coloured angel was the only decoration on the tree. It slipped off its plastic branch and flew through the air to land in the open palm of the small child whose fingers closed around the object like a newborn baby's reflex.

Young Khaled looked at the angel in his hand, then up at the sky-high imam. The Great Man's glare had changed to an expression of paternal benevolence.

A week later, on New Year's Eve, the small boy was in a foetal position, asleep on a bath mat, punished for mispronouncing the holiest names. The ugly fat woman checked on the child.

His cousin, the Hezbollah fighter, Abdullah Shawqi, had told her the boy's village in southern Lebanon. 'The shaitan from Ashtin,' Hameeda Ashraf muttered to herself over the sleeping boy and smiled at her wit. In Arabic, Ashtin was an anagram of Satan.

The boy breathed regularly. The fat woman turned to the sink to brush her teeth and to apply some perfume to her skin.

Then, the night being the last in 1988, she toasted her reflection, 'Kol a'am wa inti b'kheir' – may you be well every year – and swallowed a larger sip of perfume than usual. She left the bathroom and turned the light off.

Hameeda Ashraf had failed to notice the little angel in the boy's hand, recently painted blue, which had turned to face her every movement.

*   *   *

362

'My eyes and ears when mine were shut with sleep.' Khaled told Saleh his janizary, 'I must go to Ashtin. There, Jibrayel will reveal Ahhal's new commandments to man.'

Saleh Shmali gazed at the break of dawn over the unlit city. The new star had grown brighter overnight, so that the sky in the east, usually fiery and sanguine at this time, was a pastel shade of red – flesh pink, Mars peach.

'We must cancel Moughlabieh, Khaled.' Saleh was tired. They had been up all night and no decision had been reached.

'He is calling me. He waits for me where I was born.'

'We're defenceless against this technology. No communications, no electricity – we can't fight this war.'

'I have waited for this sign all my life.'

Saleh spun around to look at his friend. Ever since Loukoum, Khaled had not been the same. Al-Hameed, who stared at a candle's flame, was no longer thinking clearly.

'Khaled, this is a sign from the American devils, not from your angels.'

'The most faithful will doubt you.'

Saleh said angrily, 'They have sabotaged all our power stations; we can't even run a generator without it shorting. They're probably bombing our North African army this very minute and all you can think of is Jibrayel.' He added desperately, 'Don't you see we must call off Moughlabieh?'

'He will fill the pits of hell with jinn and men.'

'If your angel's so strong, ask him to help us. Tell your Jibrayel to destroy the ball of light in our skies, to bomb Europe and America.'

Khaled peered at his janizary and whispered dispassionately, 'Do you not hear him singing in our skies? Do you not see him when he dances before you like a flame? Can you not feel his power that turns mountains into cotton scattered by wind? You of all brothers, are you blind and deaf like the weakest insect?' He waved his hand dismissively. 'Go, Saleh. Crawl away from here if you doubt me. Fly with a moth's insensitive wings to Egypt. Call off Moughlabieh to prove

363

how much you really despise me. Go. I don't want you here by my side if you no longer trust me. I will suffer your hate but never your contempt.'

'I don't hate you,' Saleh said, hurt. 'You know I love you, Khaled.'

'Love is not enough. Believe in me.'

'I do. With all my heart and with all my soul.'

'Then believe with me. We have been graced with the star of Jibrayel. Do not question its divinity. You blaspheme like a shaitan when you call it American.'

Saleh frowned. 'But why is Jibrayel here and now, my Crier?'

The sun, rising from the east, chose that moment to shine its first rays into the janizary's eyes. Khaled became indistinct, a wraith, a mirage in the blinding desert, and for the first time, Saleh heard his master's voice.

'I am to be the last prophet.'

The light leaped about the silhouette; the sound rang in his ears in the ensuing silence like beguiling jinnee music.

'You spoke,' Saleh said at length, awed.

'Come, my brother. Come put your tired head on my lap.'

The janizary approached, fell to his knees, and rested his head on Al-Hameed's lap. Khaled caressed his hair.

'A baby must be taught to speak. No man is born a prophet. Only a few, apostles, are chosen by Ahhal. These must be prepared before He blesses them with His Revelations.'

Saleh moved his head to the Crier's groin and felt his erection through the jellaba; he pressed his cheek against it.

'Jibrayel is Ahhal's mullah who prepares the young apprentice in the shariah.'

The janizary turned his head to kiss the penis.

'I have whispered like an angel all my life. But the third time Jibrayel comes to me, he will carry Ahhal's holy words on his back in a heavy sack. The words will be shouted in my ears that I may shout the same to my people.' He held Saleh's head firmly to him. 'The light you see in our skies is mightier than any mortal flame. Not a weapon but a trumpet. The blessed angel's, Ahhal's Crier. If you listen you will hear Jibrayel whisper, Lakhed come to me – come, my friend.'

He reached for Saleh's hand, pushed his head away, and rose to his feet. 'We mustn't keep the angel waiting for long.'

He led the janizary by the hand to his chamber. Saleh undressed as Khaled entered the bathroom to return with two scorpions in one hand from the birdcage that was covered in an oversized blue turban. In the other hand he held the Ghazi dagger.

Saleh lay on his back; Khaled gently placed one scorpion on his navel and the other on the engorged member. Saleh froze. The two scorpions frolicked; one in his pubic hair, the second moving down to step then dance on his testicles.

Khaled slipped out of his jellaba, straddled Saleh, and slowly lowered his body until he could feel both scorpions. Hemmed in by the two groins, the creatures moved frantically in the forests and on the dunes. Five seconds and a scorpion's panic would turn to aggression. Khaled counted to four and moved off to lie on his front.

Saleh placed the two scorpions on his master's back and, drawing the Ghazi dagger from its scabbard, he slit the skin between the shoulder-blades before returning the dagger to his friend.

Khaled held the sheath in the right hand and the curved dagger in the left. The scorpions scuttled up his back to skip on the blood. Khaled slowly put the dagger in its sheath, all the way in, then slowly drew it out again, then back again as the scorpions on his back went wild with excitement.

Bill listened to the news of the West's ultimatum to the Watan Islami. The electromagnetic oscillations had grown more powerful. Italy, the Iberian peninsula and southern France were the latest European regions to be cut off from electric power.

The UN Security council issued its ultimatum to the Watan's ambassador. The Islamic nation was to turn off the electromagnetic source above Motawasset or face the military consequences. The European and American fleets in the Mediterranean and Indian Ocean had already been mobilized, on red alert and set to attack the ball of light in six hours. The Watan's ambassador had been denied more time, despite his argument that Beirut was incommunicable.

Who would bother to listen to a senile man, that an evil alien entity was responsible for all the deaths.

Humanity would be sucked into Lebanon, the old man thought.

AND DIE YOU TERRESTRIALS

Bill Walters did something he hadn't done in over sixty years: he closed his eyes and prayed.

'Ahhal akbar! Ahhal akbar!'

Khaled and Saleh stood to attention, facing Mecca to pray.

'Ash-hadou ana la ilaha illa Ahhal.'

Khaled had reproved Saleh when the janizary prostrated himself.

'A new way to pray for a new beginning. Ahhal does not want animals for men. Do not cower like a cur before its master. Stand firm on the two legs Ahhal has blessed you with when you pray to him. And do not bow your head unless you hide a secret from the All-Powerful. You are a Scorpion before me and before Ahhal.'

'La ilaha illa Allah,' they ended the prayer.

Saleh fastened a scimitar to his blue sash, and the two emerged from the palace to meet the archangel in Ashtin.

Outside, there was pandemonium on the streets. Women wailed through their black veils, beseeching the gods in their sorrow, as if grieving for dead relatives. Groups of men quarrelled; boys milled around their elders, listening to the heated disputes. Beirut, under the lurid and portentous light of the stationary comet, was shaking at its foundations.

'Allah akbar!' people cried.

'Allah yinajeena!'

'La ilaha illa Allah!'

His hand firmly on the car's horn, Saleh drove through the agitated crowds on the streets, forging a way through the impromptu anti-carnival of black mourners, past mosques filled to capacity, from where clerics sermonized in virulent tones. Khaled was crouched down on the back seat.

Gaby could not remember the Our Father or the Hail Mary. He sat in his car outside the caliph's palace and muttered, *'Notre Père, Salut Marie, Notre Père, Salut Marie, Notre Père, Salut Marie . . .'* He tapped a slow beat on the steering-wheel, the rhythm of a tolling bell.

He stopped when the palace gates opened. The crowd surged forward only to be pushed back by yelling guards. An ordinary car drove through the mob with an ordinary man in the front seat. The sea of faces glanced at him curiously then returned to focus on the palace.

'Notre Père, Salut Marie, Notre Père, Salut Marie, Notre Père, Salut Marie . . .'

Gaby resumed his prayer, his tone becoming more desperate. He put the car into gear and followed the janizary.

Down the sandy path was a group of squat, bombed-out shells of houses. Beyond, in the deep distance, north, east and west, Beirut's skyline was discernible. This isolated land had defied urbanization, a country-side besieged by the hungry city, looking haggard after the long years of war. Past the invisible lines of defence, the land was slowly dying of thirst. Sewage now filled its artesian wells, overflowing through rusted pipes to run, thickly, across the overgrown orchards of fruit trees. The depressed trees had forsaken even their natural rhythms; rotting plums and peaches still clung to the branches, seemingly oblivious of the shorter November days. The black plums were especially grotesque, not seductive city whores but dry spinsters with wrinkled buttocks, forced to accept the unloving

367

attention of half-starved black ants.

The car reached the cluster of fallen houses where the jagged walls prepared to carve the blue sky, and where the black holes of doorways and windows haunted from their skulls of brick and mortar. It stopped in front of a larger ruin where a skew sign, creaking as it swung in the breeze, read, diagonally, in French and Arabic, Casino Ashtin.

Khaled stood by the car and took in the remains of his natal village. He looked up at the ball of light, vertically above the dead village, and smiled at the bright sky.

'Jibrayel, I have come for you.'

Saleh had moved to the dilapidated café to scout the terrain. When he turned to look back at the *khaleef*, he froze for a split instant before drawing his sword.

On the other side of the dust track, standing on a rock behind Al-Hameed, was Gaby, naked but for an iron helmet on his head, a small round shield on his left arm, and a dull scimitar in his right hand.

The Spartan warrior, his sword curved high in the air, stood boldly; the tableau of a Mardaite hero.

Khaled turned, his smile slowly fading. Saleh sprinted back.

Gaby snarled, 'Die dragon, mother of evil.' He leaped and, in one smooth stroke, smote the *khaleef*'s chest.

'Jibrayel.'

Khaled reeled back and fell to the ground. Saleh jumped on the car, his scimitar arcing towards the intruder's neck. The Mardaite blocked the attack with his shield and riposted, aiming for the janizary's legs. Saleh jumped off the car.

Khaled slowly rose to his feet, felt his chest, surprised that even his jellaba had not been cut. Bruised, he moved deliberately towards the café, away from the duelling Scorpions.

Saleh spotted his master and friend. 'Whore-brother-traitor,' he grunted at Gaby with contempt. 'Your sword is as sharp as your loyalty.'

'Hell-hound,' Gaby shouted back. The swords clanged rhythmically.

A small ball of light left the stationary comet above Ashtin and flew down to the fighters, hovering around them.

Gaby looked at it with fright, expecting another dragon. His guard was down.

A second was all the time Saleh needed. His keen blade found its mark on the Mardaite's left elbow joint. With an executioner's experience in aim and speed, the janizary sliced through the skin and cartilage.

Gaby cried with the sudden excruciating pain; his left arm, still strapped to the small round shield, fell limply to the ground.

Gaby dropped Saint Elie's scimitar and fell on his back. The janizary's sword at his neck, blood flowing from his stump like a gushing stream from a cave, he looked at the ball of light which slowly drifted up to the heavens, lit by the twin suns. As it returned to the growing star, Gaby remembered and said the Our Father.

'Come back, Jibrayel, I am the prophet—'

Gaby was blinded by his tears and by the white light of the stationary comet. 'Lord, my murderous arm has offended you. *Merci, mon Dieu.*'

Khaled looked up at the star of Ashtin. 'I am the Messenger of Ahhal. *Ana Rassoul Ahhal.* Why do you leave? How can the straight line of fate branch left or right, swinging like a door that is neither open nor closed. I am he. Lakhed Sumlan, open to you, my friend. Come, my house is yours as ever. I am your favourite, your brother. Jibrayel, come to me. Come with your sack that I may drink like an angel. I order you. I have done everything you have asked of me and more. Why do you make me doubt now that you are so close to me. Come, my brother, come to your lover.

'Look at my arms, stretched out to you, my hands open for you to fly to me. I am a hollow ruin, like Ashtin, without your guiding whisper. Cold without your affection. Live through me, Holy Angel, and the hearts and souls of all men will be yours. I shall succeed where Mumahhad failed. Show me your blessed face that I may worship

369

like none has worshipped before. Come Jibrayel. I call your name: Jibrayel, Angel of Ahhal. Jibrayel.'

'*There's your blue angel. He never left your side.*'

Zachiel has given me a powerful voice. He has brought me down and left me to witness the end on my own.

Malus's mouth opens with wonder; his janizary has also heard me.

'Jibrayel. Jibrayel,' exclaims Malus, staring straight at me.

I shake my head and point at Saleh.

The janizary's ears have become pointed; his skin has turned blue, and his hands grip not a scimitar but a curving scroll with the bold words: 'Glory to Khaled in the highest.'

'Khaled?' Saleh frowns.

Khalil bin Youssef jumps to his angel, hugs him and kisses his mouth.

'Friend, friend for ever,' says the shorter man and weeps.

Saleh grins and replies, '*Hatta bya'tal ma bi 'oul.*'

The light from the star grows suddenly intense, pulses briefly, and then is extinguished for ever.

Gaby can no longer see.

Khaled and Saleh are in a passionate embrace.

Only I, the stranger to this time, look up to where the comet had been before passing away. In the weaker light, I see 500 thin cloudy trails criss-crossing the skies above the Lebanon, like the fingers of a hundred hands seeking vengeance.

I move to Gaby, kneel beside him, and stroke his hair.

'*Mon Père,*' he says to the surrounding blackness. 'Forgive me my sins, Father. *Pardonnez-moi.*'

'Forgive us all,' I whisper, and look up again at the American bombers circling Motawasset and see the sun growing in the sky – the real sun, not the dead comet.

I brush the blond hair off Gaby's forehead and he

smiles. It is the first time I see him smile. I recognize the smile as that of another Greek, of my student Samir Khoury. The flickering light from the sun plays on the man's teeth, and I imagine they are dancing the *dabké* in this final moment.

The last thing to cross my mind is, unexpectedly, a scientific discovery: light from the sun takes eight minutes to reach the third planet, ergo the sun knew of the death of its twin eight minutes ago, ergo the sun is not just a fireball of hydrogen and helium but a living and sentient entity.

In a searing second, Earth perished on Tuesday, 24 November, Anno Domini MMXX, 10 *Rabiul Awal Anno Hegirae* 1441, two days before Malus would celebrate the beginning of a new era.

Apollo, god of the sun, music and prophecy, sent his light cavalry and his chariots of fire to burst all the bubbles of life. They galloped past his brother, Mercury, who had taught him to play the lyre; his sister, Venus of love; past the blue planet and the red of war, conquering all the space before his father.

From Jupiter-Baal, the sky burned crimson with shame.

ZACHIEL

I am an inanimate rock on a dead world, where there is no sun to shine on life. But for the angel of God standing beside me, this is hell – a land of eternal drought. Were he to leave, even for an instant, I would go insane with only the sculptures of Azazel's cross for company.

The past: *The Magician & The High Priestess*; *The Tower*; *The Star*.

The future: *The Devil*; *The Moon*; *The Sun*.

The distant future: *Judgement*.

The distant future is affected by the present. But Satan has won the war. There cannot be a distant future for mankind. Zachiel points due east but the doorway remains black; so black, in fact, that it seems to radiate a black light. I have always known that Armageddon was a possibility. However, never in my worst nightmares could I imagine AL losing to the forces of evil.

Earth is destroyed. I came briefly to life, as a phantom, to witness the end. The patriarchs had spoken of this moment, when all the dead souls that ever lived would be granted two insufferable minutes to visit home one last time. One minute followed by another – and then no more.

Zachiel sings: 'LALA AL AALA.'

Poor misguided creature. Doesn't he know all is lost? Why should anyone glorify God?

'AAL AALAL LAL.'

And peace on Earth – that's rich. So that's what AL understands by peace. Creation was a sublime mistake.

'LA.'

The gabriel reads my mind.

What then, angel?

He points at the black doorway, east on Azazel's cross.

I see. Now I'm to be judged for my past and how my actions affected the future.

'LA.' The voice has come from neither Zachiel nor the desert, but from the black sky above.

A second angel has appeared and lands softly by us. Zachiel bows reverently. This second angel is older and has larger wings. But other than his age and wing-span, he looks like my angel: clad in a simple white tunic with sandals on his feet.

Gabriel?

The archangel smiles kindly. 'LA,' he denies, 'LLALA AL.'

It is Raphael's turn to point at the doorway with the black light. But he explains, to my amazement, where the doorway will lead, and I understand what must be done.

There is hope yet.

'It was always meant to be,' Raphael says in the Divine Language.

Yes, I think. Only God has the mercy and compassion to forgive mankind. 'LALA AL AALA,' I rejoice. 'LA ALL ALAA AL.'

A new Earth will rise from the ashes by the grace of God.

My exultation vanishes abruptly when I see the blank expressions on the gabriels.

Am I mistaken, angels?

'A son of God must be human before he can become divine.' The archangel points to the glass sculpture of the Devil. 'A messiah must live with Satan before finding life with God.'

I am confused. Why?

'What is colour to a blind man? A man can only know true goodness if he has tasted evil. And a saviour can

373

only redeem his fellow man if he has first learned to despise mankind.'

The forty days of temptation were forty long years. It had been God's plan all along. A blueprint for a prophet. A soul that was divinely inspired remained aware of a parallel existence, and only the unique combination of Christ–Antichrist could understand true evil in order to fight it.

As both Mind-of-God and God-has-healed take off to carry me together to Judgement, I finally understand that the prophecies of Nostradamus and St John the Divine are one and the same.

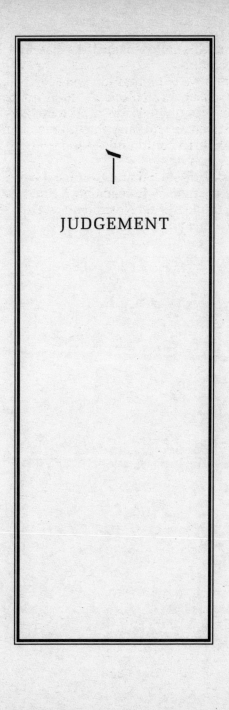

JUDGEMENT

LALA AL AALA

'Your God is the shaitan,' the militiaman spits at me. 'Tell me you're not a Jew. Go on, lying whore.'

I feel intense pain. Bliss. I have a right leg that is in agony. I smile and then laugh ecstatically.

The *fidei* is momentarily taken aback. 'You think this is funny, cunt-spy? Laugh then.' He is about to strike my chest with the hammer, but I have anticipated his move and catch his right arm in mid-swing. He tries to break free from my grip, but for an old man I am suddenly strong.

'Jew-shit,' the Palestinian yells at me.

'Why do you blame my God, when the shaitan is all around you?' I hold his arm easily with one hand, and with the other I point to our left.

Hassan looks and screams. There is nothing and no-one, but memories have become apparitions. The ghost of Hassan's mother appears to stare at him with reproach. All around him, phantoms rise from the ground. Familiar spirits from his childhood; wraiths of strangers he has killed. All are blue jinn.

'And who but a demon would hold a snake in his hand?'

The militiaman looks down and screams again. The hammer is dropped and, in his eyes, writhes on my chest.

I release the man; he jumps back and fumbles with the Kalashnikov.

'Az-Zurruk,' I shout from the ground.

My voice is like a punch in the face; the *fidei* reels back.

'Leave this man in the name of AL.'

He doubles over.

I sing: 'LA ALL ALAA AL.'

He drops his machine-gun in order to block his ears. 'No! Stop!'

Above Ashtin, the ball of gabriels picks up a different tune: 'LALA AL AALA. AAL AALAL LAL.'

Hassan wretches violently and glances at me with sheer terror before running off the road pursued by the song and the blue sprites.

I rise to my feet and limp to the oil barrel that barricades the road. I feel alive. With renewed strength, I have removed the barrel by the time the Peugeot rounds the bend in the road.

Both emerge from the car.

'Jacob?'

'James Smith?'

And they look at one another in surprise.

'Salaam-shalom.' I grin at Samir and Maira. 'Come, my friends.'

'What are you doing here?' Maira nods at Samir's question.

I indicate the instrument in Maira's hands and then wave at the sky above the village. 'You won't need Ric's tracker any longer.'

The sun bleeds over the western horizon and the evening star in the south glints at an unfamiliar twin. The newcomer courts Venus, unlike any star that has ever danced before human eyes. It maps the most convoluted orbit in the heavens; arcing slowly across the sky, it swings low then high, and pauses to hover around the planet as if in two minds about falling for Aphrodite's attraction. With dusk, a crescent moon becomes visible, and the star of Ashtin turns to dance around Selene before settling, like a tired bird on a branch, vertically above a small house.

378

The three stop by the Maronite church for some incense. Maira has remained in the car and ignores the small black box, discarded by her feet, whose red and green lights flash unremittingly. She is marvelling at the ball of light which grows steadily brighter and reverses time by turning dusk back into twilight.

By the altar, Samir says, 'Jacob, back in Cyprus, I was wrong.'

I shake my head. 'No words, Samir.' I cup his chin in my palm. 'My Greek student. I'm proud of you.'

We return to the Peugeot and drive on to the Sulman residence. Zoozoo and his friend Farid are outside, about to enter to carry Maya to the car. They have paused to gaze at the stationary ball of light and now turn their attention to us, three strangers approaching them.

'Joseph Sulman,' I say, 'peace and blessings to you and your family.'

'Who are you?' Zoozoo asks, frowning.

'We have come to congratulate you on the birth of your son. Mabrouk Abou Khalil.'

Zoozoo turns in astonishment to Farid who demands, 'How do you know his name? Who brings you here?'

'Salaam to you, too, Farid, and to your wife, Salwa.' I reach for Zoozoo's hand and hold it firmly. 'Return to your wife, Zoozoo, her fever has broken.'

I release my grip and, for a while, he remains on the spot, unsure. Then he hurries inside, followed by Farid, who gives me a brief questioning look.

'He knew their names,' Samir is explaining to Maira, 'and that the man's wife had a fever.'

'What's all this about Mr Smith?'

'You've become very dear to me, Maira. Please call me Jacob or James.' I hold the door open to the two. 'Come, I'll show you.'

We move into the house uninvited, through the dining-room, where trays of *kol-oo-shkor* and baklawa remain untouched on the table, and on to the bedroom. Samir and Maira wait outside as I enter.

379

'She wanted her son.' Salwa, complaining to Zoozoo, squirts a mixture of holy water and *eau de toilette* in the air. 'The boy shouldn't be with her. Maya's ill.'

I hand her the incense. 'Burn this instead; it's stronger.'

Salwa looks at the incense and then suspiciously at me. 'Are you a priest?'

'Yes.'

She nods, satisfied, and leaves for the kitchen to prepare the smoke.

The midwife stands between the men. 'What your wife needs, Mr Sulman, is a doctor not a priest.'

The star casts a cleansing beam of light on the mother and child on the bed. Maya, sweat streaming down her face, ignores everyone in the room except the baby cradled in her arms. 'My lovely boy. My perfect baby.'

The love in her voice overwhelms me. My own voice cracks with emotion. 'Your wife needs neither priest nor doctor.'

I approach the bed and kneel. Maya turns, smiles, and proudly shows off her son. Baby Khalil blinks at the light from the star as I lean over to kiss the two soles of his feet.

I utter softly, like a lullaby: '*Al-majdo lillah fil 'ola, wa a'alal-ard as-salaam.*'

Again I hear the echo from the sphere of gabriels: 'LALA AL AALA, AAL AALAL LAL.'

Maya nods reassuringly at her husband; the blue nightmares have passed.

I rise slowly, creakingly to my feet, suddenly feeling very old. I shuffle past Zoozoo and his friend, and Samir and Maira, who have entered to see the baby, and sit exhausted at the dining-room table. I reach for a puff pastry, pop a *kol-oo-shkor* in my mouth, push the tray away to give me some room, and bring out the tarot cards from my pocket.

I find *The Magician* and *The High Priestess* and place

them one on top of the other, face up on the table. Then, shuffling and cutting the pack, I deal a Celtic cross with the cards face up.

The equilateral triangle of the past has remained unchanged: ⊐ *The Tower*; ⊒ *The Star*.

But now the future:

South, the legs: ⊓ *Justice*.

West, the right arm: ⊓ *The Chariot*.

North, the head: ⊤ *The World*.

And the distant future, the most important card in the new cross: ⊤ *The Lovers*.

I hold the card of the east in a shaking hand and sigh deeply. There remains only one thing for me to do. I reach for a pen and write Glafkos Mikhaelides's address on the back of *The Lovers*.

Samir comes up to me. 'Are you OK, Jacob?' he asks with concern.

'Oh, yes.' I want to tell him about the end that almost was, but the world now has a different future. I also want to tell him of his life with Maira, of a son they would name Gabriel. 'Oh, yes.' I offer him a puff pastry. 'Eat-and-say-thank-you.'

I rise shakily to my feet as Maira, Zoozoo and Farid enter the dining-room.

'I am grateful to you,' Joseph Sulman tells me. 'I believed my wife was very ill.'

I give him *The Lovers*. 'You are not safe here.' I am thinking of the Divine Society and especially the impending Israeli invasion of Lebanon. 'You will go to Cyprus where the man on the card will care for you.'

Zoozoo falls on his knees. The other three look at me wide-eyed.

I am bewildered. 'Rise, Abou Khalil.'

Zoozoo shakes his head. 'Oh Lord, *ya rabbi*.' And now Farid, crossing himself, kneels as well.

I turn my head.

Adyt, Tanit's Jewel, has passed through the roof of the

house. The ball of light comes to rest behind me and changes into a doorway of brilliant white light.

But the four are not looking at the doorway – the light is too strong for their eyes. They are marvelling at the wings behind me that began to glow with the supernatural light.

Zachiel has followed me here, I think. But through the blinding frame of light, I alone can see Zachiel smiling at me, standing next to the archangel Raphael. Behind them, in the background, are many angels. But then, the wings?

Where is that angel who has crept up behind me?

'Come, Brother Kilmatel,' says Zachiel in the Divine Language.

'Come, Word-of-God,' smiles Raphael.

Oh Eli, Eli, I have become your instrument, a gabriel myself.

I take a step towards the doorway and my physical body collapses like shed skin. I turn one last time to face my friends.

Samir is weeping uncontrollably, but his mouth curves slowly to smile me his divine smile.

Maira crosses her forefingers, then shows me her right index erect, and then her left index curved like a hook.

Oh, yes, sweet Maira, not an antichrist. Quite the contrary.

I can fly. I can beat my wings; but no, I shall walk into the thimbleful of angels.

The ball of light waited a short while before shooting northwards, streaking across the heavens like a comet. It reached the Pillars of Truth and dropped out of the sky, landing as a black ball in the gap through which nothing wider than a watermelon could pass. There was the briefest flicker and, like a hot knife falling through butter, Tanit's Jewel was swallowed by the narrow ground between the obelisks, coming to rest in the middle of the garden where AL had first spoken to man.

It was home.

THE END

A SELECTED LIST OF FINE WRITING
AVAILABLE FROM BLACK SWAN